jt
ELLISON

MIRA

First published in Great Britain 2011
MIRA Books, an imprint of Harlequin (UK) Limited,
Eton House, 18-24 Paradise Road,
Richmond, Surrey, TW9 1SR

ISBN 978 0 7783 0432 6

60-1211

Printed and bound by
CPI Group (UK) Ltd, Croydon, CR0 4YY

J.T. Ellison is a thriller writer based in Nashville, Tennessee. She writes the Taylor Jackson series, and her short stories have been widely published. She is a weekly columnist at Murderati. com and is a founding member of Killer Year. Visit her website, JTEllison.com for more information.

For Jay and Jeff: my ribs
And as always, for my Randy

And now Snow White lay a long, long time in the coffin, and she did not change, but looked as if she were asleep, for she was as white as snow, as red as blood, and her hair was as black as ebony.

—The Brothers Grimm
Snow White

Prologue

Would the bastard ever call?

Smoke drifted from the ashtray where a fine Cohiba lay unattended. Several burned-out butts crowded the glass, competing for space. The man looked at his watch. Had it been done?

He smashed the lit cigar into the thick-cut crystal. It smoldered with the rest as he moved through his office. He went to the window, grimy panes lightly frosted with a thin layer of freezing condensation. It was cold early this year. With one gloved finger, he traced an X in the frost. He stared out into the night. Though nearly midnight, the skyline was bright and raucous. Some festival on the grounds of Cheekwood, good cheer, grand times. If he squinted, he could make out headlights flashing by as overpaid valets squired the vehicles around the curves of the Boulevard.

He tapped his fingers against the glass, wiping his drawing away with a swipe of leather. Turning, he surveyed the room. So empty. So dark. Ghosts lurked in the murky recesses. The shadows were growing, threatening. Breath coming short, he snapped on the desk lamp. He gasped, drawing air into his lungs as deeply as he could, the panic stripped away by a fluorescent bulb. The light was feeble in the cavernous space, but it was illumination. Some things never change. After all these years, still afraid of the dark.

The bare desk was smeared with ashes, empty except for the fine rosewood box, the ashtray and the now-silent telephone. The room, too, was spartan, the monotony broken only by the simple desk, a high-back leather chair on wheels and three folding chairs. He opened the humidor and extracted another of the fortieth anniversary Cohibas. He followed the ritual—snipping off the tip, holding the lighter to the end, slowly twirling the cigar in the flame until the tobacco caught. He drew deeply, soothing smoke pouring into his lungs. There. That was better.

The isolation was necessary. He didn't like people seeing him this way. It was better if they perceived him as the strong, capable man he'd always been, not this crippled creature, this dark entity with gnarled hands and a bent back. How would that image strike fear?

Not long now. Fear would be his pale horse, ridden from the backs of red-lipped girls. His duplicates. His surrogates. His replacements.

The ringing of the phone made him jump. Finally. He answered with a brusque "Yes?" He listened, then ended the call.

An unhurried smile spread across his face, the first of the night. It was time. Time to start again, to resurface. A new face, a new body, a new soul. With a last glance out the window, he snubbed out the cigar, closed up the humidor and braved the shadows. Moving resolutely toward the door, he disappeared into the gloom.

The phone was ringing. Somewhere in the recesses of her brain, she recognized the sound, knew she'd have to answer. But damn it, she was having a really nice dream. Without opening her eyes, Taylor Jackson reached across the warm body next to her, positioned the receiver next to her ear and grunted, "Hello?"

"Taylor, this is your mother."

Taylor cracked an eyelid, tried to focus one eye on the glowing clock face—2:48 a.m.

"Who's dead?"

"Goodness, Taylor, you don't have to be so gruff."

"Mother, it's the middle of the night. Why are you calling me in the middle of the night? Because you have some kind of bad news. So if you could just spit it out so I can go back to sleep, I'd appreciate it."

"Fine. It's your father. He's gone missing. From *THE SHIVER*."

A rush of emotion filled her, and she sat up, swinging her legs over the side of the bed. Win Jackson. Winthrop Thomas Stewart Jackson IV, to be exact. Her illustrious father, gone missing? Taylor let the lump settle in her throat, blinked back the uncharacteristic tears that came to the surface.

Her father. Her chest tightened. Oh, man, she didn't even want to think what this might mean. Missing. That equals dead when you're gone from a boat in the high seas, doesn't it?

Father. Amazing how that one word could trigger an

avalanche of bitterness. She heard the rumors fly through her head like migrating birds. *Daddy got his little girl a place in the academy. Daddy bought his little girl a transfer out of uniform into Homicide. Daddy gave the mayor a major campaign contribution and bought his little girl the lieutenant's title.* Good ole Win Jackson. Corporate raider, investment banker, lawyer, politician. An all-around crook, wrapped up with a hearty laugh into a deceptively handsome package. Win was a Nashville legend. A legend Taylor tried to stay as far away from as possible.

Sitting on the edge of her bed in the darkened bedroom, the thought of him evoked a rich scent, some expensive cologne he'd gotten in London and insisted on importing every year for Christmas.

She heard her mother shouting in her ear.

"Taylor? Taylor, are you there?"

"Yes, Mother, I'm here. What was he doing out on *THE SHIVER* anyway? I didn't think he was sailing anymore."

"Well, you know your father."

No, I don't.

"He decided to take the yacht to St. Bart's. St. Kitts. Saint, oh, who knows. One of those Caribbean islands. I'm sure he had some little slut with him, sailed off into the sunset. And now it seems he may have gone overboard."

There was no emotion in Kitty Jackson's voice. Devoid of emotion, of love, of feelings. Taylor wondered sometimes if her mother's heart had ceased to beat.

"Have the Coast Guard been called in?"

"Taylor, you're the law enforcement…person. I certainly don't know the answer to that. Besides, I'm leaving the country. I'm wintering in Gstaad."

"Huh?"

"Skiing. October through January. Don't you remember? I sent you the itinerary. I won't have time to deal with this and get packed."

The petulant tone made razor cuts up Taylor's spine. Kitty's first concern had always been Kitty. For Christ's sake, her husband was missing. It was possible he had gone overboard, was dead…but that was Kitty for you. Always ready with a self-absorbed tale of woe.

"Thank you for letting me know, Mother. I'll look into it. Have a lovely vacation, won't you? Goodbye."

Taylor clicked off the phone before her mother could respond.

Jesus, Win. What kind of trouble have you gotten yourself into now?

Taylor started to roll back into place, determined to get at least another hour of sleep, when the phone rang again. Now what? She looked at the caller ID, recognized the number. Answered in a more professional tone than she'd used with her mother.

"Taylor Jackson."

"Got a dead girl you need to come see."

"I'll be right there."

One

Two months later
Nashville, Tennessee
Sunday, December 14
7:00 p.m.

A vermilion puddle reflected off the halogen lamps. It was frosting over, lightening as it inched toward the freezing point. Little bits of black hair floated under the hardening surface, veining the blood. As it froze, it pulsed once, twice, like the death of a heart. Life's blood, indeed.

The woman was naked, purple with bruises. She was sprawled on her right side, facing back toward the hill leading up to the Capitol. Long, jet-black hair flowed around her like a muddy stream. Her face was white, paler than a ghost; her lips were painted crimson. She looked like a fairy-tale princess locked in a glass coffin. But a poisoned apple hadn't propelled this girl to her final resting place, surrounded by love and remorse. Instead, she had been thrown away on the marble pedestal, discarded like so much trash. Her naked body arched around the center pole. The smaller flags circled her protectively, snapping with every gust of wind. Her left leg sprawled wildly, blocking one of the recessed lights tastefully highlighting the scene.

On closer inspection, a gaping knife wound was clearly visible, slashing merrily across the woman's neck. In the darkness, it smirked and shone deep burgundy, nearly black in places, with bright hunks of cartilage and bone showing through the wound.

Taylor arched an eyebrow at the mess. Oh, the joys of being the homicide lieutenant. She shivered in the gloaming, pulled her arms tight to her sides and rocked slightly. She was dressed for the weather—a thigh-length shearling jacket over a cream cable-knit sweater and jeans, mittens and a scarf, but the cold seeped in through minuscule cracks, making her own blood sluggish. The air smelled of snow, sharp and bitter. The temperature had been hovering well below the freezing mark for several days, and the atmosphere was dense, portending a storm for Nashville. Winter's coming this week, people said. Taylor scuffed a cowboy boot in the frozen grass.

Waiting. She was tired of waiting. It seemed she spent her whole life in some form of suspension, glancing at her watch, knowing it would only take a few minutes, a few hours, a few days for something or another, for someone.

The M.E. would be on the scene soon. All she had to do was wait.

It was too chilly to stand still any longer. Taylor stretched her arms to the sky, felt a kink release below her right shoulder blade. Too tense, and the freezing temperature didn't help. She wandered into the night, happy to let the stench of death leave her sinuses, only to draw back in pain as the reek was replaced by mind-searing cold. Her eyes teared. Giving a brief glance back over her shoulder, she paced the granite wall bordering the amphitheater. Distanced a bit, she turned, taking in the entire scene.

She had to admit, Nashville's Bicentennial Mall was a lovely setting for murder. Opened in 1996 to celebrate the 200th anniversary of Tennessee's statehood, it had never reached the pinnacle of success the city leaders had hoped for. It was still a charming walking mall, a favorite for outdoor lunches and the odd midday jogger. A very quiet area at night, too. The only crowd that had gathered to mark this murder was a multitude of blue-and-white patrol cars, still flashing at attention. That would change as soon as the media got wind of the scene. And the condition of the victim. Most likely, this was victim number four.

"Damn."

The national news vans would continue to line the streets of downtown Nashville, waiting for any police misstep that would give them another day in the news cycle. Two months of constant media attention had everyone's nerves frayed. Three families were torn apart—make that four, once they had an ID on this new girl. More sleepless nights than Taylor could count. *Keep moving. It's going to break soon.*

The south edge of the mall, where the dead girl lay prostrate, was a tribute to the Tennessee State Flag. Eighteen flags, eight encircling one taller, delimited each side of a granite walkway. They waved gaily, buffeted by the chilled breezes, unaffected by the gory scene in front of them. Perhaps that was fitting. Tennessee had earned its nickname—The Volunteer State—for the multitudes of men who joined in the fight during the Civil War. LeRoy Reeves of the Third Regiment, Tennessee Infantry, had designed the flag. The crimson fabric, overlaid with three white stars, highlighted the blood and bone inert at the base of the flagpole.

It was a beautiful scene, if you liked postcards from hell. The fourth such tableau since the Snow White Killer had materialized from under his goddamned rock and started killing again.

Taylor looked past the flagpoles, past the body. Bordered by an ornate concrete railroad trestle, the view rose directly up a well-manicured, lighted hill, atop which perched the state Capitol, its neoclassic lines glowing majestically in the darkness. The heart of downtown stretched beyond the building. Her town. Her responsibility. Taylor turned away, continued her walk.

Their killer wasn't being subtle, the setting was designed to capture their attention. Two blocks from Channel 5 and four from police headquarters. There were traffic circles on either side of the mall, an easy way to slip in, throw out a body and continue right on out to James Robertson Parkway. Taylor was shocked the local CBS affiliate wasn't already on the scene.

A flake of snow drifted in front of her eyes, its fragile crystalline beauty entrancing. How something so beautiful could wreak such havoc—the weather was turning for the worse. The forecast called for at least a foot in the low-lying areas around Metro, up to fifteen inches on the plateau. Midstate gridlock.

To top it all off, in a little less than one hundred twenty hours, five short days, Taylor was due at St. George's. For her wedding.

Taylor took a deep breath and walked back to the body. She pulled up a sleeve and glanced at her watch. The M.E. should have been here by now. She was good and ready to have this body moved. To get out of the cold. To get some rest before the big day. To do whatever needed to be done to assure that the event would go on as planned. A little voice niggled in the back of her mind. *It wouldn't be the end of the world if we needed to push it back. How the hell are we supposed to get married and go on a honeymoon in the middle of a major murder case?*

A media satellite truck slipped by on the main street, silent as a shark. Taylor figured they were angling for a full shot of the scene, coming around the back of the mall on James Robertson Parkway, slinking up to Charlotte and Sixth. Shit. Time to move.

Shivering in the cold, she reached into her coat pocket for her cell phone. As she flipped it open, a white van with discreet lettering pulled into the klieg lights. The M.E. Finally.

Taylor snapped the phone closed and strode across the grass, heedless of the groomed path she was supposed to follow. She fairly leapt to the side of the van, motioning for the driver to put the window down. The medical examiner, Dr. Samantha Loughley, complied, and Taylor shoved her face into the warm interior. Bliss.

"Taylor, get out of the way." Sam put her hand under Taylor's chin and nudged her face back out the window. She slammed the gearshift into Park and stepped from the van. Clothed for the weather in a black North Face fleece jacket, Thinsulate-lined duck boots and pink fur earmuffs, she nodded brusquely.

"Okay, where is she?"

"On the flagpole pedestal. You really should take a minute before you start, walk down the mall and look back up here. It's quite pretty." Taylor smiled.

"You're a ghoul. Any idea who she might be?"

"No. She's naked, no sign of any purse or clothing. Do you think it's going to snow as much as they said?"

"I heard we might get twelve inches. Or more." Sam winked at Taylor and started for the body. Taylor followed her, questioning. Visions of airport closures, snowplows running into ditches, caterers with no electricity ran through her mind like drunken mice. She shouldn't be so happy at the thought of her wedding being postponed. *Good luck with that, Taylor. Even if it snowed ten feet, in five days people would manage to get it in gear.*

"They're never accurate, though. Seriously, weathermen are notorious for getting the forecast wrong. Right? Sam?" *Maybe the snow would hold off until Thursday....*

The M.E. wasn't listening anymore. She'd just caught her first glimpse of the body. She went rigid, stopped in her tracks.

Taylor put a hand on her best friend's shoulder, all personal worries pushed away for the time being.

"I know," she murmured, squeezing Sam's shoulder. "It looks that way to me, too. Meet Janesicle Doe."

"Wow. Certainly appears to be his work." Sam knelt by the body, staring intently at the dead girl's face.

"He's changing it up. This isn't a separate dump site—judging by the amount of blood, I'd bet my badge she was killed right here."

"And not that long ago, either." Sam reached for her bag. Taylor knew what came next and stepped away to let Sam do her work.

The lights of the sneaky satellite truck snapped on with an audible hum, catching Taylor in the gleam. She excused herself, went to block the cameras. The media was getting bolder with each killing, Taylor had no intention of letting them ruin her case with suppositions.

Behind her, she heard Sam whisper, "Bingo."

Two

Taylor fidgeted under the hot studio lights of the Fox affiliate in Nashville. Their parent network, Fox News, wanted to get the lowdown on the Snow White case from the inside, and Taylor had been ponied up for the slaughter. As soon as she'd been set and miked, the remote anchor had been drawn into a breaking-news story: a suicide bomber had taken out a group of diners at a restaurant in Jerusalem, claiming the lives of fifteen and injuring two Americans. The news alert had been going on for a while, giving her plenty of time to second-guess agreeing to be interviewed.

She was grateful for the opportunity to get the word out, though she would have preferred the newspeople talk with Dan Franklin, Metro's official spokesman. She wasn't fond of doing on-air interviews. Understandably, the reemergence of the Snow White Killer had the entire country up in arms, not to mention her own city and her homicide division. That meant everyone was pulling cross duties.

She wiped her fingers across her forehead, gathering little beads of sweat. It would be nice if they turned off the lights while she waited. She stared blindly into the bowels of the studio, her mind in overdrive. The network had specifically requested Taylor's presence. She suspected it had more to do with her notorious background than the fact that she was the lead investigator on a sensational series of crimes. The anchor had been warned to steer clear of the Win Jackson story, and Taylor hoped they would listen for once.

Oh, Win. Where in the world are you?

There was a commotion. The tech was signaling they were going live. He counted down, then went silent, showing his fingers. Three, two, one. She took a deep breath, blew it out slowly and smiled for the camera.

"We're back now with Homicide Detective Lieutenant Taylor Jackson from the Metro Nashville Police Department. We're talking about the horrific string of murders plaguing Music City, a town more accustomed to the shenanigans of country music stars than murderers. Just last night, a new victim of this dreadful killer was found.

"Lieutenant Jackson, have you identified the body of this latest victim?"

"No, we haven't. We—"

"And this is victim number four, correct?"

"It's too soon to—"

"Two months ago, police found the battered body of young kidnap victim Elizabeth Shaw. The girl had been raped and her throat cut with a sharp object presumed to be a military-style knife. Three weeks later, the body of Candace Brooks was discovered, the cause of death identical. Last week, a young woman named Glenna Wells was found near Percy Priest Lake, raped, beaten and showing signs of exsanguination due to a knife slash across her throat. The crime scenes showed eerie symmetry, and the Nashville police are investigating what seems to be a serial murderer."

Oh, God. Great. An editorializer.

A voice sounded in her ear, making her jump. She could never get used to producers popping into her brain unannounced.

"Sorry 'bout that. Feel free to step on her next lead-in."

Taylor checked her smile; she didn't want to go back live grinning like a fool. *I'll do that.*

The monologue continued. "These serial killings are dreadful enough in their own right, but they have been traced to a man known to all of America as the Snow White Killer, the fanatical murderer who killed ten women in the 1980s and has never been caught."

The screen went blank, then female faces and names floated into the space. The anchor's voice filled Taylor's ears as the prerecorded voice-over began. They were recapping the 1980s murders, drawing the parallels to her current cases. Taylor watched the montage, only half listening.

She'd been in middle school at Father Ryan when the Snow White Killer was picking and choosing his way through beautiful girls, and was only a few years younger than the youngest victims. When she made the force, she checked out the files and memorized them, hoping to someday find the killer. It seemed now she might have her chance. The irony that she was now the lead investigator into the new slayings wasn't lost on her.

Taylor realized the anchor was still talking, and dragged her attention back.

"The media christened the killer with a suitable moniker, the Snow White Killer, because all of these beautiful young ladies bore a strong resemblance to the Disney character, with black hair, pale skin and painted-on red lips."

Of course they'd latch on to the more commercially viable and recognizable version of Snow White. Taylor felt the victims were much more the Grimm brothers' fairy tale, but who was she to argue? She looked closer at the anchor's overdrawn features. *Hmm, Kimberley, if we slipped some bright red lipstick on you, you'd be an excellent candidate.*

The voice sounded in her left ear again. "Okay, Lieutenant, we're back to you in three, two…"

"And then he stopped. People never forgot, but they went on with their lives. Until now." The montage ended and Taylor's face filled the screen.

"So, Lieutenant Jackson, it seems the Snow White Killer has resurfaced. Do you have any additional proof to confirm this theory? Where has he been all this time?"

Time to get this back under control. Taylor cleared her throat and smiled warmly.

"First off, let me thank you for having me tonight, Kimberley. As you know, the Snow White Killer was active in the mid 1980s here in Nashville. In 1988, he went off our radar, and we just aren't sure what happened to him. He could have gone to jail, he could have died. He could have moved, changed his MO and started killing in a whole different city, but that isn't very likely. It's rare for a serial killer to change his stripes, as you're well aware."

As the whole world is well aware, thanks to programming like this that features profilers and forensic scientists giving their opinions on any murder case that happens along.

"Isn't it true, Lieutenant, that the police believed he was a man of means and that he may have skipped the country?"

"Yes, Kimberley, that's one scenario we looked into. Though the homicide team is confident that he was still in the state of Tennessee for at least another year."

Because they got a polite letter from the fucker saying he was still in town, but didn't plan to kill any more girls. But you don't need to know that.

"Lieutenant, what makes you think that the Snow White Killer has resurfaced?"

"Well, Kimberley, that's something the media has seized upon and run with. We have no corroborating evidence at this time that indicates that the same person is committing these new crimes. The staging is familiar, the MO similar, but there isn't anything substantive that proves that the Snow White is culpable here."

Except the notes and the knots, and I ain't sharing that little tidbit with you, either.

"He's been dormant for more than twenty years, Lieutenant. Just like Dennis Radar, better known as BTK, the Bind, Torture and Kill murderer in Wichita. Could the Snow White Killer be living among your fine citizens, be a part of society, paying his taxes and coaching Little League?"

"Anything is possible, but that's not a realistic scenario. Killers like this rarely stop. There is often an escalation in violence over time, and most will kill until they're caught or incapacitated in some way. It's more likely that the man responsible for the Snow White murders is dead or in jail for another crime. We don't want to cause a panic here."

"Isn't it true, Lieutenant, that all of these new murders have something in common? Weren't all of the victims found to have high blood-alcohol levels indicating that they may have been drinking heavily just prior to their abduction and murder?"

"Yes, the victims had elevated BALs. That's as much information as I'm able to divulge for you at this point."

We'll leave the roofies out of it.

"Okay, Lieutenant. Do you have any warnings for the women of Nashville tonight?"

"Just the usual commonsense precautions, Kimberley. Women in the Nashville area should always be alert and not put themselves in compromising situations. Don't accept drinks from people you don't know, always watch the bartender make your drink and don't leave your drink unattended. Don't leave with a stranger. Always keep your doors and windows locked, your car doors locked. Be aware of your surroundings at all times, and if you see or hear anything suspicious, call 911. We'd much rather come check things out and see that all is well than get to a scene too late."

"That's great advice, Lieutenant. Let me ask you one more question. How does this make you feel, personally, that a serial killer is on the prowl in your city, picking beautiful young women as prey? What do you do to sleep well at night, knowing a monster like that is out there?"

I don't.

"Kimberley, we are all very concerned about the emergence of this killer. Nashville Metro has many very talented and dedicated officers who are on this case, working diligently to capture this murderer before he strikes again. We want to calm the fears of the people of Nashville, not raise hysteria. Again, if you have a concern, please, call 911 or the hotline. Do you have that number up on the screen?"

"Yes, Lieutenant, we do. I do have one more question. Your father, Winthrop Jackson IV, went missing from his yacht nearly two months ago. We understand that the federal government has been involved in the manhunt. Have you had any new information on his case?"

Taylor felt her blood pressure rise. Just couldn't help herself, could she?

"No, Kimberley." She clamped her lips together and crossed her arms. There was a brief moment of dead air, then the anchor spoke quickly.

"Thank you for your time, Lieutenant, and good luck catching this horrendous monster. Next, we'll talk with a forensic scientist about the clues found in the case and what it means to the old investigation of the Snow White Killer."

The disembodied voice came again. "Sorry. I told her to stay away from your dad. Nice job. You have a good night."

There was a snap in her ear and the blinding lights were extinguished.

"And, we're out. That was a great job, Lieutenant Jackson." The tech from Channel 17 was smiling at her in admiration. He couldn't have been more than eighteen, and he made Taylor feel old. The interview had gone as well as could be expected. The producer was decent, at least. Too bad they'd ignored her wishes and asked about Win, but thankfully they took no for an answer. A serial killer was much more fun than a two-month-old missing-persons report.

She nodded at the boy. "Thank you."

"Do you want a tape? I can get you a tape."

"Sure, that would be great." The boy scampered off and Taylor stood, shaking the feeling back into her left leg. Like seeing the interview again would help.

Four vicious murders in two months, all black-haired, pale-faced girls wearing bright red Chanel lipstick. Snow Whites.

They needed to catch this guy, and fast.

John Baldwin stood with his arms crossed and one long leg propped against the wall behind him. He'd been avidly ignoring the receptionist for a good fifteen minutes; she'd been staring at him like he was a tasty dessert since he'd entered the building. He'd become entirely oblivious to all but the most blatant attempts to get his attention since Taylor had entered his life. He had eyes only for her, much to the chagrin of most of the females he came into contact with. Six foot four and sleekly muscled, his wavy black hair and Lucite-green eyes drew many admiring glances. Enough that women like the receptionist made him uncomfortable.

He saw the door to the studio open, watched as a kid

rigged up with what looked like electrical wire escorted Taylor to the lobby. Sound tech, Baldwin thought to himself. As a profiler for the FBI, and as a well-regarded forensic psychiatrist, he was a veteran of television interviews. Media coverage like this was inevitable. This case was eating all of them alive.

Word had even come down from Quantico that he was to follow the Snow White case, intervening when necessary. He didn't want to step on Taylor's toes. He let her work through her theories, guiding only when necessary. That happened less often these days. His expertise was rubbing off on her. She didn't need his help just yet. She would, but he'd rather she come to that conclusion herself.

Taylor elbowed her way through the glass door. She absently gathered her long hair into a fist, slipped a stolen rubber band off her wrist and captured the blond mass in a ponytail. The young technician stepped aside to let her through the door, gazing adoringly at her like a puppy, telling her his name was Sean and if she ever needed anything, anytime, he was the guy to call. He was fawning and the tips of Taylor's ears were pink.

When she saw Baldwin, the blush extended down into her cheeks, flushing her with a healthy glow. Utterly charming. Beauty, brains and guts. He'd hit the trifecta when he met and fell in love with this stunning woman.

Sean the tech spied Baldwin. A furrow creased his young brow. Not quite a man, yet he still understood the implication. He gave a half grin to Baldwin, a "Hey, you can't blame me for trying" and professionally shook Taylor's hand, winking as he left her in Baldwin's company. He greeted her with a smile.

"Went well, I thought."

"As good as could be expected, I suppose."

"You okay? About your dad, I mean."

"Of course. Why wouldn't I be?" She gave him a look that plainly said no, she wasn't okay about it, but wasn't willing to make a big deal. He put an arm around her shoulders and squeezed, then held the door for her.

They exited the building, walking toward the parking lot. Baldwin sensed the shiver that ran up Taylor's spine, knew it wasn't from the snowy night. The Channel 17 studios were nestled in behind the Ted Rhodes Municipal Golf Course, the northwest corner of downtown Nashville. It was dark and remote; a feeling of dread washed over them both. He knew what she was thinking.

Four girls dead on her watch. The nation paying close attention. And a ruthless killer who was having too good a time toying with her detectives. This wasn't a happy Christmas.

They reached his BMW, and he dropped his arm to her waist. Punched the automatic unlock on his key chain. Opened her door. Leaned in as she sat down on the smooth gray leather, ran his hand along her cheek.

"We're gonna get him. I swear, we're gonna get him."

"I know," she replied. "I know."

Three

Baldwin dropped her off at the office so she could gather her truck and tie up the day's loose ends. She yawned as she snapped on the lights. The murder book was on her desk, all the files neatly arrayed with tabs for crime-scene photos, evidence, logs and reports from the various officers who'd participated in the scene. It had taken three hours in the freezing cold, with snow falling and hampering their efforts, to clear the scene at the Bicentennial Mall last night. They weren't taking any chances. Every ounce of physical evidence had been collected, tagged and bagged.

A quick check of her e-mail and in-box showed nothing that couldn't wait until the morning. She debated for a moment. Read through the case files now, or go home and get some sleep. The thought of a warm bed, a warm body lying next to her, was too compelling. Taylor grabbed the murder book and headed out.

The drive home was eerie. The night air crackled with an icy breeze. Snow billowed from the sky; she felt like she was driving through clouds. There were few cars out and about, and the lack of traffic made Taylor lonely. She hadn't had time to clear her head since the Snow White case had popped. Two months of dead girls, anticipation, setbacks, false leads. The thrill of the hunt.

The thought sobered her. The girl they'd placed in a body bag last night and carted away to be cut open didn't enjoy the thrill of being hunted.

The gash in the girl's neck flooded Taylor's mind and she nearly missed her exit off the highway. Without thinking, she hit her brakes hard, and the wet, sloppy snow declined to help. She had to manhandle the truck until the wheels caught again. She regained control and took the exit, her heart beating hard. The near miss woke her up. Adrenaline coursed through her body. Her mind refused to cooperate, to calm itself. The murder scene popped back into her head, and she went down the exact path she was trying to avoid—thinking about the case. She was so lost in thought that when she stopped, she realized she'd driven to her old house. The cabin.

Shaking her head, she laughed at her distraction. It was only natural—they'd moved just a few weeks ago, still had boxes in the cabin to be transferred to the new house. She groaned at the thought of dealing with more boxes, put the car into Reverse without getting out. The cabin didn't look large enough to hold very much, but when push came to shove and Taylor had finally started packing, the accumulations of her life seemed to explode exponentially.

As she pulled away from her old life, the phone rang. She clicked the speakerphone on. Sam's ebullient voice spilled from the speaker.

"It's the same stuff."

"Jesus, you're there late. Why do you sound so happy? That means he's definitely killed a fourth."

"I've got enough to run it through LCMS. I'll get an idea of what this is, finally." Liquid chromatography mass spectrometry had failed them in the earlier cases. At least now they'd have an idea of what they were dealing with.

"That's great, Sam. Don't stay up too late."

As she got back on the right road, the gaping wound in Janesicle's neck wormed its way to the surface.

John Baldwin was relatively content. He'd closed his last case, his field office was under the control of a surrogate acting director. No orders to take over the Snow White case had come. He had nothing official to do but get married. His most pressing concern at the moment was Taylor.

A fire was roaring in the fireplace, and Taylor stood five feet from him, a cup of hot chocolate held tightly, trying to force the numbness away. She'd come home with her hands practically blue. He considered her profile as she looked out the window, a study in concentration. She was miles away. A rare southern blizzard surrounded them. Snow continued to plummet from the sky, piling onto the Japanese maple bushes in the front yard so rapidly that they bent like old men.

Despite the late hour, a disembodied male voice spoke, deep and languorous.

"Listen to the following statements. How would you respond? *Buon giorno, signora. Lei parla l'inglese? Dove siamo? Come si dice 'Piazza San Marco is here' en italiano?*"

"Whoa, whoa, whoa. It's going too fast. Jeez, this is the easy stuff, too." Taylor snapped the off button on the CD player remote, shaking her head and smiling.

"What's wrong, *cara?*" he crooned, egging her on.

Taylor focused on her fiancé with narrowed eyes. *"Vaffanculo,"* she spat, then grinned at him. Baldwin guffawed in surprise.

"Where'd you learn that one?"

"You like? I've got more."

She had that crazy sexy smile going, the one that held great promise. The mismatched gray eyes flashed. He played with her. "Now, Taylor, there's no need for that kind of language. You'll get yourself in trouble if you say that over there, anyway. How is it you have trouble with the most simple commands, yet you can curse like a sailor in perfect gutter Italian? No, don't answer that," he said, holding up a hand. Taylor's lips had pursed, ready to spew out what he assumed was another charming epithet.

"Relax, sweetheart. You know more than you think you do. I've watched you go through these tapes for weeks. Trust me, we get over there, you'll be fluent in days. I promise. You're just distracted."

He went to the stereo, turning the power off. He glanced around their living room—a spacious compilation of curved arches and exposed beams. Their new home was more like what he and Taylor had each grown up in, elegant and airy, whitewashed walls with simple accents. They both loved it the moment they saw it. The exterior was brick and stone, a Georgian colonial that bordered on federalist, a style so popular in this section of the South. They had much more room than furniture. The plan was to buy the accompanying furnishings and art on their trip. And stock their burgeoning wine cellar.

Over there. Italy. *Italia*. They had scheduled three weeks for a romantic honeymoon, and Taylor had been bound and determined to teach herself the language before they left. He loved to watch her learn, to see the phrases tumble from her lips.

"Distracted. Why would you think that?" She turned back to the window and stared at the winter wonderland that comprised their new front yard, the cul-de-sac and the other houses in the neighborhood. The problem was, there were no defining characteristics between them all. Everything was white. Fifteen inches of white.

And a killer was out there, plotting his next murder. Damn. He watched her mood shift, playful to alert and serious.

"Four new murders, Baldwin. Sam's call all but confirms it. Snow White is really back. Or is this a copycat? If he is, he's a damn good mimic. And we look like a bunch of monkeys fucking a football."

Baldwin slipped behind Taylor, putting his arms around her waist. He started whispering in her ear. *"Siete il mio amore. Non posso attendere per spendere il resto della mia vita con voi. Avete la faccia di un angelo.* Need me to translate?"

She spun in his arms, her breath hot on his cheek. Obviously she caught the gist of what he'd said. He gave her a wink. It never failed.

"You're an easy woman, Taylor. Mutter a few words in a foreign language and here you are, rubbing up against me like a cat." He brushed a kiss against her generous mouth, smiling as she bit his lip.

"I may be easy, Dr. Baldwin, but at least I'm not cheap." She pulled away and punched him playfully on the shoulder. "Do you think they'll have the street plowed by morning?"

Baldwin looked out the window. "We can hope."

Taylor cracked her neck. Snow. Murder. The look in her gray eyes was blatant—if the roads weren't clear by tomorrow, she would murder someone herself.

Baldwin slipped an arm around her waist, drawing her back to him. "We could…"

"No, we couldn't. That was the deal. I want our wedding night to be special. You can hold out a little longer. All I asked is that we try to abstain for a week. A week wasn't that much to ask."

He smiled and pulled her close. "But we already…" He kissed her softly, tasting chocolate, but she fought to leave the circle of his arms. Breath ragged, she pushed him away, gave him a weak smile.

"Stop. Four more days. Okay? Let's just make it through this week, and we'll be horizontal before you know it. I just can't think about anything but that poor girl right now."

Baldwin adjusted his fly and gave her his most wicked smile. "Let me help you forget."

Taylor lay in the bed, realizing she was sleeping with her eyes wide shut. It was an old trick she used, keeping her eyes closed as if asleep, but seeing everything behind the lids. Usually, it worked to allow her mind to process whatever kept her awake, yet she felt rested when she finally succumbed and got out of the bed. It wasn't working.

She opened her eyes, taking in the dim light of the room. Baldwin was asleep on his left side, back to her, and she knew he was out by the soft whispery snores emanating from his pillow. Lucky bastard. Since they'd moved to the new house, he'd been sleeping like a baby. It might have been the bed—a king-size sleigh that afforded them much more room than they actually needed. They could each stretch out and not worry about banging into the other. She missed the old bed, but only briefly. Who was she kidding? She loved to luxuriate in the crisp sheets, to stretch her extremely long legs all the way to the end of the bed and still have several inches to spare.

She did just that, easing the tension in her shoulders with a bit of stretching, tensing and releasing. Maybe a game would take her mind off the case. No sense lying here staring at the ceiling.

The pool table was housed in the bonus room over their three-car garage. Taylor walked out of the master, slipping the door closed with a gentle click. A night-light showed her the path. She walked down the long, wide hallway past empty rooms. Rooms that should hold promise but mocked her with their very empti-ness. Marriage. Babies. Yawning mouths of black-haired, red-lipped girls, all in a row.

Fuck it all. She jogged the last few steps down the hall until she reached the open space that housed the vast majority of her old life.

She flicked the lamp and the room filled with soft yellow light. Closing the door carefully behind her, she went to the pool table, whipped the cover off and bunched it into a ball. Tossing it on the couch, she went back to the table, racked the balls and took a moment to stretch again, two vertebrae in her neck unkinking with a pop. Better. Loosened up, she took the break, cracking ball after ball into their respective pockets.

She ignored the faces hanging on the wall. She'd turned the poolroom into a makeshift office, someplace she could spend her nights thinking about the murders while she tried to relax. Elizabeth Shaw, Candace Brooks and Glenna Wells all smiled down on her. At least they'd been identified quickly. This new victim was nameless.

Smack—Snow White.

Smack—Janesicle.

Smack, smack, smack—wedding, copycat, four dead girls.

The tension drained and she found her rhythm. She'd find this guy. She always did.

She was four games of nine ball in when the door opened.

Baldwin stood in the frame, hair mussed, sleep marks creasing his left cheek. He whistled a low tune and she melted. He looked so damn unbearably cute that Taylor couldn't help herself. All the bad thoughts left her. The worries, the frustrations, disappeared. She put the cue stick back in its holder, went to him. Took him by the hand and wordlessly led him back to the bedroom.

Four

Taylor rose early, gritty-eyed from the lack of sleep. She left Baldwin in the bed, tucked a pillow in his arms, and felt her heart break when he smiled and murmured into it. Seeing him like that, remembering what he'd done to finally get her to sleep, made all her worries about the wedding seem silly.

Long legs ensconced in a pair of jeans, she slipped into her favorite old Uggs and pulled on a creamy cable sweater. She stopped in the kitchen briefly, grabbed a banana and a granola bar, then got in the 4Runner. She backed into a drift of snow in the driveway, but the powerful truck slid through it easily.

The neighborhood was beautiful, sheer and pure, a white only produced by snow fallen from a crisp wintry sky. She felt like she was in the mountains; the deciduous trees masquerading as heavy evergreens with black trunks and feathery limbs coated in ice, the sky cerulean, a shade rarely seen during a Southern winter. The beauty cheered her, and she left the quiet subdivision in a good mood. Moved by the weather. Sheesh. She was getting soft.

Out in the suburbs, the side roads were unplowed and impassable to all but four-wheel drives, but the main roads were relatively cleared and not yet icy. She was careful, made her way to the Starbucks drive-through, got her now standard nonfat, sugar-free vanilla latte and headed toward work.

The autopsy of Janesicle was scheduled for seven, and Taylor intended to witness. Maybe Sam would have the results back from the LCMS tests. If this was definitely victim number four, it would be a hard secret to keep.

She flipped on the XM, used the remote to scroll through the stations until she found some music she liked. No talk radio for her this morning, and she'd given up on the holiday channels after the third murder. It just didn't feel right to be listening to such joyful exuberance when girls' bodies were stacking up like cordwood in the morgue. She needed mindless noise, distraction. She settled on a U2 tune and mouthed the words as she made her way down the highway. The roads were virtually empty and she felt freer than she had in months.

Little by little, as she closed the distance to Forensic Medical, her heart grew heavier. When she entered Gass Street, she turned off the radio.

Sam's offices were housed in a corporate-looking building up the road from the Tennessee Bureau of Investigation. Taylor had been here so often that Sam had issued her a badge that allowed her access after hours. Or before hours, when necessary. They'd have a skeleton staff on a day like today, but Taylor knew Sam would be there.

And she was, already prepped. Taylor could see her, distorted through the crisscross wire embedded in the glass of the industrial door. The air was cool and clean in the compartmented vestibule where she slipped out of her clothes and boots, sliding blue plastic clogs and doctor's scrubs on. She put her street clothes in a locker. No sense making her clothes reek for the rest of the day. With the new gear in place, she went through the door into the autopsy suite. The chemical scent of death greeted her like an old friend. She hardly noticed it anymore.

Sam nodded as she entered the room, already dictating into a hands-free mike clipped to her headgear.

The body of Janesicle Doe lay on the cream-colored plastic slab that encased the stainless-steel table underneath. She was so white; cold, clammy flesh, with that big, black grin across her throat. Taylor felt the gorge rise in the back of her own throat and swallowed hard. Inappropriate reaction. She hoped Sam hadn't noticed. Taylor was as detached as the rest of them, but something about this girl was breaking all her protocols.

The individual murders hadn't bothered her in the beginning. Well, not that much. Not like this.

"Taylor, did you notice? She's got that same stuff on her temples."

Taylor stepped closer, bent over the body. On either side of the girl's face, two smears of a whitish substance glistened under Sam's light. They looked like streaks of moonlight.

"Appears to be identical material. Any chance the labs are back on it?"

"We should have an answer by the time I finish her up. We didn't get anything usable from the earlier samples, they were too degraded." Sam started working her way systematically through the Jane Doe's hair.

"You said it wasn't biological."

"Right. No DNA to obtain. There was plenty of it on this body, though, nice and fresh. I put it into the LCMS."

"That's your special little machine that spits out the chemical compositions, right?"

"Special little machine? How about liquid chromatography mass spectrometer? I'd like to spend more time, do some sophisticated testing to see its composition, but I need a comparison sample with the actual material that's leaving the marks to be sure. In the meantime, we have enough to at least get an idea of what we're working with."

Sam continued her examination, and Taylor stood beside the body, lost in thought.

Two months ago, Taylor had been called on the murder of Elizabeth Shaw, a senior at Belmont University. Elizabeth had disappeared walking home to her apartment from class. The city buzzed, searches were initiated, but it was all too late. Her body was found in the tall grass in a gulch off of Interstate 24. Thrown out of a car door like litter, she'd lain in the gulch for at least two days. The postmortem damage to her body had been animal related. The biological evidence was copious; her arms and legs were hog-tied. They hadn't determined where she was actually killed.

Elizabeth Shaw's murder scene didn't look precisely

like the original work of Snow White, but during her autopsy, flakes of red Chanel lipstick were recovered from her mouth. They reexamined the knots on the ropes, found them to be much more complex than they originally appeared. And in a touch that alarmed even the most seasoned law enforcement officials, a two-decades-old newspaper clipping about the first murder in the original Snow White case had been pulled from her vagina. All thoughts of this being a simple murder flew out the window, and the homicide team found themselves quietly reopening a twenty-year-old case.

In quick succession, two more girls were taken and murdered. Candace Brooks was killed three weeks later, left by the side of Interstate 65 this time. The press started attributing the killings to "The Highwayman"—the interstates being the one common denominator between the two crimes. Candace's autopsy was eerily similar to Elizabeth Shaw's, right down to the newspaper clipping—though this one detailed the twenty-year-old report about the Snow White's second murder.

When victim number three, Glenna Wells, showed up on a boat ramp on Percy Priest Lake, the media beat the medical examiner to the scene. A sharp-eyed young reporter had managed a glimpse of the body, saw the glowing crimson lips, the presentation of the body, and ran back to her producer with video footage. The producer was an old-timer, recognized the tableau from his early days on the crime beat. The Highwayman was relabeled the "Reemergence of the Snow White Killer." Taylor and the rest of Metro were lambasted for not warning the area that a serial killer long dormant was back in their midst, and the media frenzy began.

Glenna's body gave them a third newspaper clipping and no more clues.

And now there was a fourth.

The girls were linked in death by gaping neck wounds, the newspaper clippings, the knots and that damnable Chanel lipstick. Blood tests indicated they were over the legal limit for intoxication, with BAL's in the 1.5-2.0 range. Rohypnol showed on the tox screens. It was obvious they'd all been killed by the same man. Whether it was the original Snow White or a copycat was still up for debate. A marked difference in the new murders versus the 1980's slayings was the slick, creamy residue on the girls' faces. Hindered by the fact that they couldn't do their own DNA testing, Sam was still waiting on DNA results. The DNA would tell the truth—a copycat or the original killer. Taylor leaned toward the former. The differences were subtle, but there.

"Yo, earth to Taylor? Can I get some help here?"

"Oh, gosh, Sam, sorry. I was thinking about something else."

Sam gave her a sharp glance, then pointed at the girl's lower body.

"Can you pull up her right leg for me? I should put her in stirrups, but since you're here…"

"Sure, of course. Yeah, no problem."

Taylor reached for the dead girl's leg, ignoring the bizarre sensation of dead flesh against her thin latex gloves. It felt a bit like the skin on a store-bought chicken breast, rubbery, loose. Her hand almost slipped, and she chided herself. Jeez, girl, get a frickin' grip already. She took a better hold and pulled the leg back, exposing the girl's genitals. Sam was already at work, swabbing, following the necessary indignities. Taylor tried to watch the back of her friend's head, but saw something glint, a reflection of the light. She looked closer.

"A clit ring?"

"Yeah," Sam replied, a bit of disgust in her voice. "You'd be amazed at how many I see. Not someplace I'd particularly enjoy having a needle shoved through, but hey, that's just me."

Taylor shuddered at the thought. Ouch.

"Here it is."

Taylor's heart sank as she watched Sam ease a small package out of the girl's vagina. Wrapped in cellophane, it was coated in junk—blood, sperm and whatever else—Taylor really didn't want to know. Sam eased the package, no bigger than a business card, onto a stainless-steel tray. She gestured to Taylor.

"It's all yours, if you want."

"No, I think I'll let you dissect it for me, but thanks."

"You're never going to get the hang of this, are you?"

"Sweetie, that's the reason I didn't go to med school and you did. Open it up, let's see what we have."

Sam picked the packet open gingerly, putting aside the cellophane for later testing. "Trace is going to have a field day with that," she murmured.

Taylor gazed at the body. What was it about this one that felt different?

"How long had she been dead, Sam?"

"By the time I got there? No more than an hour."

"So we just missed him. Why did he change his MO?"

"Beats me, T. You're the detective. Detect."

Taylor gave her a brief smile, then grew serious again.

"How is no one missing this girl? All three of the other victims had missing-person reports on file. She looks maintained—fresh manicure, eyebrows shaped, hair's healthy and well cut. She got drunk somewhere, with someone. She's not lost. We should have a report on her."

"You're right, we should. She's younger than the earlier victims. Look at her X-rays over there. The dental series shows that her third molars are still developing. If I had to wager, I'd say she was between fifteen and seventeen. I don't know, sweets. Maybe the system just hasn't been updated, or her parents are out of town and don't know she's missing."

Sam finished tweezing out the contents of the little cellophane package. It was a piece of paper, newsprint. They both knew what it would say once they got it open.

They were right.

Murder in Nashville
Snow White Killer Strikes Again

The date on the article was December 14, 1986.

Sam was staring at the body, a troubled expression clouding her face. Taylor watched as she bent over the girl's neck, then stood abruptly and walked out of the suite. She disappeared for a moment, came back bearing a large magnifying sheet. She held it over the spot she'd been staring at before, her lips white.

"Sam, what is it?" Taylor bent over the girl's neck wound and looked through the magnifier. Her finger shook as she pointed toward the lower edge of the slice, horrified.

"Is that what I think it is?"

Sam's face was pinched. "I'll have to do a swab, but it looks like it."

That was enough for Taylor. She held up a hand in apology, scooted to the nearest sink and lost the latte.

Twenty minutes later, once she was feeling better, Sam handed her the details of the LCMS findings. The amount of slick material on the earlier bodies had been minute, but their newest victim had plenty to test thoroughly. The base compound was an arnica emulsion. There were traces of other ingredients; more tests would be needed to confirm all the components of the matter. But two listings from the LCMS stood out from the rest.

Frankincense oil and myrrh oil.

Taylor sipped a pygmy-size ginger ale and reread the LCMS findings. "What in the world do you think this is about, Sam? Should we be looking for three wise men?"

"You're hysterical, you know that? Feeling better?"

Taylor swallowed hard and nodded. She despised throwing up.

"If I had to guess, there's something sacred about the oils. But its base is arnica cream, which is a common homeopathic remedy for bruises and sprains and such. Those are the initial findings, they could be off the mark. Without a control sample and more tests, I can't be absolutely positive. They could be separate items or they could all be from one place."

"Frankincense and myrrh, though? Surely there's something more important there. And the fact that's it's on their faces, like he's anointing them…"

She trailed off. Sam met her eyes and nodded. "That makes the most sense. He's done so much to their bodies. Maybe he feels guilty and is trying to redeem himself. Maybe he's just a sicko and likes the way it smells on them while he's raping them. I don't know, Taylor. Go catch him and you can tell me. No matter what, this latest girl was treated differently. Could be her age, could be she said or did something while he held her, but she was marked."

Taylor nodded. "And by marking her, he deviated from the pattern."

Five

Taylor was on overdrive, the new information spinning in her head. She called Baldwin the minute she hit the truck.

"Baldwin, I need you. The basic elements of this murder are different from the first three. And wait until you hear this. This one was special. She meant something to him. He rimmed her neck wound in lipstick. Like he did her lips. I couldn't believe it when I saw it. I mean, it's already such a gory wound, I would never have noticed, but Sam did, and she swabbed it and looked under the microscope and there was lipstick mixed in with the blood. It was, it was…really. It's like he dressed her up. And there was a lot of the creamy stuff on her face.

"Sam's going to send out the full tox screen and finish the autopsy now. She's already confirmed the high BAL and the Roofies. She said she'd get back to me if anything major popped up. I can't imagine what would be more major than this, I mean, it was—"

"Fascinating."

"Not exactly the word I was going for. Sick, is more like it."

"But 'sick' is fascinating, Taylor. Talk to me about the neck wound. This is definitely the first time he's done it?"

"As far as Sam can tell. She's going back through all the wound swabs now, but she didn't see anything like it before. Why would he do that?"

"Why, I can't answer. It means something to him, I'm sure. We just have to figure out what that is. Are you headed to the office?"

"I am. I've got more for you."

"More? What?"

"Sam ID'd the substance we found on their faces. Get this. Frankincense and myrrh. There's more components in the matter, but she'll have to do more testing to gather that. We're assuming that they were being prepared, I guess."

"Jesus. Listen, Taylor. I'm going to be at your office when you get there. I'll call Stuart Evanson, the new head of the BSU. He requested that I take over the case last week. I told him I'd wait, see if it solved or you asked me in. We'll officially offer every power we have to your chief, make it legit. That work for you?"

At the moment, Taylor could think of nothing better. She'd worked cases with Baldwin before. He respected her boundaries, treated her team with respect, won over her captain, Mitchell Price, with his "It's your case" attitude. She wanted him on the Snow White case full-time. They needed the FBI resources, anyway.

"I'm cool. I'll see you there."

"Taylor?"

"Yeah, hon?"

"Thanks for last night." His voice rumbled in her ear, and he hung up before the blush could spread to her capillaries. Damn the man already. She wasn't in love; she was in heat. That's what all this was about.

Taylor navigated in four-wheel drive, forced to take her time to get downtown. The plows were working the streets again, the salt trucks followed dutifully. Abandoned cars littered the roadways; the tow trucks couldn't get to them, so the plows were pushing large drifts against the driver's-side doors that reached to the side mirrors. If the temperature didn't rise soon, it would take days to get them unburied.

She tried to drive carefully but was impatient with the roads. Aside from the plows, four-wheel drives were the only things moving. The hospitals had put out emergency calls for people who had trucks and SUVs to help staff get to work. It was surreal, an all-white landscape with little movement—the vehicles like desultory ants after an outsized picnic.

Swerving around a public works truck, she whipped off the highway past the Tennessee Titans stadium, LP Field, and crossed the bridge over to Third, where her offices within the Criminal Justice Center waited.

She pulled into the parking lot too fast, skidding on the ice and nearly taking out a lamppost. Her pulse took a few beats to get back to normal. She hadn't been paying attention. Again. That was all they needed, for her to wind up wrapped around a pole. She recognized a few other vehicles—Metro police didn't get the day off when the city was snowed under.

Calmed, she got out of the truck, made her way carefully across the street and up the stairs that led to the back door of the CJC. She passed the ubiquitous ashtray and felt virtuous—she'd finally managed to quit. It had been three months since her last puff. She fumbled in her pocket for a minute, trying to get a hand on the plastic pass card that would allow her into the building. Her gloved hand was too bulky to feel anything. Swearing under her breath, she took it off and delved deep into her pocket. Her bare fingers hit hard plastic. Triumphant, she swept the key card and stamped her way into the building.

Some cruel individual was subjecting the third floor to a bastardized version of their child's Christmas recital; strains of children's wavering voices streamed from the fingerprint room, mixed with a heavy rap beat. The resulting discordance made a headache take root behind Taylor's right eye. Muddy puddles of water trailed four feet into the hallway where people hadn't knocked the snow off their boots. Clumps had collected, melting on the cream-colored linoleum. After the fact, someone had used his head and spread a copy of the morning's *Tennessean* on the floor. Glancing at the headline regaling the Snow White Killer's latest victim, Taylor tapped her boots against the wall, dropping the excess snow on a picture of the Bicentennial Mall, then stepped around the puddles and followed the hallway toward the homicide office, leaving the wailing music behind her.

Lincoln Ross rounded the corner from the opposite direction. Tall, handsome, with three-inch dreadlocks, he gave her a gap-toothed smile that hit her deep.

"Yo, LT, what up?" He gave her five, up high, down low, and she laughed at him, cheered instantly by his enthusiasm.

"And what's up with you this morning? You're awfully chipper."

"Hey, you know, it's a thang."

"Am I to infer that the 'thang' is of the female persuasion?"

Lincoln grinned like a schoolboy. "Why, yes, I believe you could *in-ferrr* that if you'd like. Oh, sorry. I wasn't supposed to dangle the sex carrot in front of your nose."

She raised both hands and laughed. "Well, I'm not doing so good abstaining on my end, so don't worry about it. What's with the ghetto speak?"

Lincoln rolled his eyes, went back to his usual elucidated drawl. "I've been with my new C.I., the kid who's ratting out Terrence Norton."

"Oh, great. What's Tu'shae up to now?"

"He's hopping, actually. He scored a DJ gig in South Nashville. A lot of Terrence's gang hang out there. We've got a good stakeout going with the TBI; they're being very cooperative. But Tu'shae won't talk to them, he'll only talk to me. So I'm stuck ferrying all the information through to the TBI boys and girls."

Damn the Tennessee Bureau of Investigation. Why couldn't they do their own work? Cooperative or not, she needed Lincoln for these new murder cases exclusively.

"Do you have anything we can use? I'd really like to get Terrence Norton out of our hair if we can."

"Not yet. Tu'shae hinted that Terrence is controlling the drugs running through the club, but he's got nothing to back that up."

Administrative bullshit, that's how Taylor saw the ongoing situation with the local gangster, Terrence

Norton. He'd been plaguing her for three years, starting as a kid with a bad attitude and a minor rap sheet. As time passed, he got stronger, more jaded and in more trouble. They'd almost nailed him for jury tampering a few months back, and the TBI had to take over the case. Lincoln was doing a great job running backup from Metro's side, and she told him so.

Terrence was an annoyance. Taylor dismissed him from her mind; today just wasn't the day to deal with minor miscreants.

"Let's move on to bigger and better thugs. Are Fitz and Marcus here?"

Lincoln made a vague gesture toward the door to the homicide office. "Yeah, they're in there. You want some coffee or something?"

"No. You might want to wait, too. Tossed my cookies already this morning, wouldn't want to put you in the same situation. Let's go."

Chastened and intrigued, he followed her into their warren office and went to his desk.

Taylor's team was a force to be reckoned with. Lincoln Ross was her computer guru, an insightful and intriguing man. His jocular seriousness was a perfect counterbalance to her ferocity, and he'd been the voice of reason too many times for her to count. He was one of the few people that she trusted implicitly.

Lincoln was partnered with Marcus Wade, the youngest detective on the force. Marcus was forced to confront his demons publicly; his lanky frame, floppy brown hair and Roman nose had garnered more than one confession from the opposite sex. He had grown as a detective, and Taylor knew how much he admired

Baldwin's profiling work. She was always worried that she might lose him to the FBI; his instinctive skills could be honed into a sharp point with the right training. He walked the line, happy to take on assignments, soaking up investigative methods like a sponge.

Sergeant Peter Malachai Fitzgerald, known only as Fitz to the troops, was her second in command. Half father figure, half mentor, he'd been the one cheering the loudest when she'd been bumped to lieutenant, and was thrilled to be working for her. Fitz had been a rookie homicide detective when Taylor joined the force, and they'd gotten on like a house on fire from day one. She still remembered their first crime scene together, seeing him lumber up to her, wondering whether he was going to make some crack about how cute she looked with that utility belt around her waist, and wouldn't she like a new tool for her belt. Instead, he'd considered her gravely for a moment, then asked what her impressions were.

She always felt he should have gotten the lieutenant's position before she did, but knew he didn't want it. Bureaucracy and making nice with the brass wasn't his idea of a good time. He was happy to let her draw the heat.

The homicide offices were overly warm; an appropriated space heater propped against the far wall was stuck on high. The television that hung from the corner ceiling was on, blaring *Stormtracker* weather updates from Channel 5. The combination made the room loud and toasty to the point of stifling. Taylor crossed the few feet to her office and opened the door to a draft of relatively cool air. She set her gloves on her desk. The little room was cramped, a television tuned to a different channel blared from the filing cabinet. One of the boys had been watching *Oprah*. She flipped back to the weather alert.

A sorry-looking fern sat next to the television. Taylor glanced around, spied a bottle of water that had a few sips left. Tipping it into the plant, she watched the soil absorb the water in a frantic attempt at sustaining life. She wasn't much with plants, felt sorry for the fern. There was another bottle of water on the desk, unopened, so Taylor took it and emptied it into the plant. It was gone as quickly as she could pour it. Terrible. She'd be an awful mother; she couldn't even keep a plant watered.

Where the hell did that thought come from? She threw the empty bottle in the trash, the plastic-on-plastic thud appeasing her sudden penchant for violence. She shook her head, muttered sorry to the fern.

A cough made her jump. Fitz was standing in the door, staring at his boss with a baleful eye.

"Let me guess. You're sad for the plant." His voice was thickened by years of former cigarette smoke. The deep grumble was comforting.

"Well, it is alive. Sort of."

"And you think it has feelings? Or that it understands English?"

She raised an eyebrow and looked Fitz over. His face was weathered and lined, tan even in the early days of winter. Blue eyes dark as blueberries usually held a twinkle, an unspoken joke or gibe. He was twenty years her senior and starting to look his age. Taylor attributed that to the weight loss—he'd dropped at least thirty pounds in the past few months—a concerted effort to slim down paying off in wrinkles. Still barrel-chested and stubborn, Fitz glared at her, obviously irritated.

"My, you're in a mood this morning. Who peed in your cornflakes?"

"You did. Why didn't you call me about the lipstick and the damn oil?"

Taylor spied the cause of Fitz's sudden consternation over his shoulder. Baldwin tried to look innocent but failed miserably.

"Oh, I see. Fitz, I wasn't holding out on you. I was more, trying to keep my stomach in control, okay? I just wanted to get here first. Since you've heard all about it, tell me what you think."

Baldwin joined Fitz in the doorway and blocked her in. Fitz shifted, trying to look intimidating.

"I think this is one sick fuck and you'd be better off leaving him to us and going off to get married without this on your conscience."

She didn't smile. "Oh, Fitz, that's sweet of you to say, but it's not going to happen. Now, Baldwin, why don't you stop sending emissaries, and let's try to catch this guy *before* the wedding. How's that for a plan?"

"Taylor—"

She held up one hand. The look on her face brooked no more arguments, and the men stepped aside, allowing her to step out of the cramped space.

Marcus Wade was waiting for her, a soft suede jacket thrown over his arms. He'd excelled during their last case and had been promoted to detective second grade; the new jacket was a reward to himself for the pay raise. He looked eager as a puppy this morning, a nice counterpoint to the now-rancorous environment. The air of excitement around him was palpable. Taylor knew he had something for her.

"Whatcha got?"

A broad smile crossed his features. "An ID on the latest Snow White. Her name's Giselle St. Claire."

Six

Taylor put both thumbs up and punched her hands skyward, a victory sign. "Yes! Good job, Marcus. Let's go to the war room, get it all plugged in. Giselle St. Claire. Why does that sound familiar?"

As she said it, it hit her. She groaned, long and loud.

"Oh, shit. Marcus, you better get Price on the phone. He's gonna want to know this."

"Who is she? Why don't I recognize the name?"

"Just go get Price for me. I'll tell you in a minute."

He stepped away, and she turned to Baldwin. "Do you know who this is?"

"Isn't she the kid of someone big?"

"You could say that. Remy St. Claire. It's her daughter. That's what's been bugging me, the girl looks an awful lot like a dark Remy. Damn it, she can't be more than, what…" Taylor calculated. Man, she was getting old. "I think Giselle was about fifteen. She looks older. Oh, fuck. This is not good. Remy and the press are going to be on us like white on rice. Damn, damn, damn, damn!"

Remy St. Claire. Taylor didn't know what to make of
her. She was an actress, but didn't find much lead work
anymore. Instead, she did the rounds relentlessly, reveling
in her roles as a "character actor." She was a constant on
the talk-show circuit. Her gadfly antics made her a perfect
target for the gossip instigators. She'd left Nashville years
before, made it in Hollywood for a while, then fluttered
away. Married three times to two different men, she'd had
a child by one of them. Taylor couldn't remember which.
A little girl named Giselle, with dark, flowing hair.

When little Giselle grew up a bit, the paparazzi constantly buzzing around her caused her mother endless
headaches. Remy wasn't happy with that overattention,
and sent her only child to live with her parents, away
from the glare of Hollywood. Giselle's grandparents
immediately enrolled her in her mother's alma mater in
Nashville, Father Ryan. They assumed the first-class
Catholic school would be good for their beloved granddaughter, used the abundant love to compensate for her
mother's recurring absences.

At Father Ryan, Remy and Taylor had been friends,
albeit briefly. They weren't enemies, just didn't hang in
the same crowds. The woman was a drama queen, a
scene stealer, an attention getter. When she found out
her only child had been murdered on her old classmate's
watch, there would be hell to pay.

Taylor leaned against the wall and damned herself for
not listening to the advice of her old buddy Fitz, walking
out of this place and spending the next three days fretting
over Chinese gobans and monogrammed bath towels.
Despite a declaration that they didn't want gifts, wedding
presents were piling up. And all those unwritten thank-

you notes just made her think of her mother. Kitty wasn't available for the wedding, thank God. Though if she knew Remy St. Claire's daughter had been murdered, she'd be back from Gstaad in a heartbeat. A brush with a minor celebrity would stoke Kitty for a few weeks, though she'd look down her nose and pretend it meant nothing. God, her mother was such a bitch.

Baldwin leaned against the wall next to her, toying with the curled-up end of her ponytail.

"Evanson called. The official requests have been approved. My team at the field office is available to you at any time. How do you want to handle this, Taylor?"

She appreciated his show of respect. Baldwin could have asked to step in at any time but had held off, allowing the locals to work the case with his peripheral involvement until now. The FBI's active support would shift the dynamics, but they could use the help. "Let's see what Price has to say."

Marcus was signaling from the conference room. Taylor took a deep breath, then went in and sat at the long table. The speakerphone was on.

"Hey, Cap. How's Florida?"

Captain Mitchell Price was on a long-overdue vacation. Or trying to be. Calling him in Florida was a sure sign that the shit was hitting the fan back in Nashville. He didn't bother to play along.

"What's wrong?"

"Other than our happy little Snow White murderer decided to off Remy St. Claire's daughter, nothing much. How's the fishing?"

Taylor almost laughed when the groan came through the phone loud and clear.

"Do I need to come back?"

"Well, I think we can handle it, but if Remy blows into town and there are cameras at the ready, the chief's gonna get involved."

"I got a call from Quantico. Baldwin there?"

"He's right here. I asked him in this morning—the official request just came through. Two items came up from yesterday's murder. The substance we've been trying to identify is a compound that has frankincense and myrrh in it. We're about to discuss that right now. The second thing is he's escalating. He killed that girl at the scene, and rimmed the neck wound in lipstick."

The curse words were clear and loud, and Taylor envisioned the man's mustache jerking up and down in response to the utterances. It almost made the conversation bearable.

When he finished cursing, he sighed.

"I'll make a reservation."

Baldwin tapped Taylor on the shoulder, then spoke. "Hey, Price, no need. I'll send the plane for you."

"Thanks, Baldwin, that's mighty nice of you. I love having the Bureau on my cases. I'll see y'all tonight. Let's get St. Claire notified and get this ball rolling. Jeez, what a way to ruin a vacation."

He clicked off, and Taylor looked at Baldwin, the question apparent on her face. He didn't respond, so she asked.

"Should we…?"

Baldwin shook his head. "No, no, no, we are not canceling the wedding."

"Could cause some bad press. Lead investigator heads off on honeymoon…."

"Screw them. No. We are not canceling."

She patted him on the forearm. "Okay, sweetie, okay. Just throwing out options. I'm going to go get the Santa Barbara police on the phone, see if they can't get a chaplain roused to go notify Remy. And see if Father Ross is available to go talk to her grandparents, since they were primary caregivers. We'll need to interview them, anyway, find out what they know about Giselle's last steps. You're in it now. Get ready for the shit to hit the fan."

Taylor, Fitz, Marcus and Lincoln sat around the conference table, reviewing the facts of the Snow White cases. Taylor's stomach had settled, they had sandwiches from Panera, a froufrou delicatessen, and a round of fruit tea, that bizarre Southern concoction. Baldwin had demurred on the lunch offer, instead leaving to procure the FBI plane for Price. They were shoveling in the food, needing fuel for the long day ahead. The room fairly hummed with their intensity.

Four dead girls, each murdered more horrifically than the last. A serial killer who'd been dormant for years. Among the paper lunch boxes, the murder files were spread before them, white elephants in their midst.

Nashville hadn't seen much in the way of serial killers, per se. They had plenty of serial rapists, and many high-profile murders. But the vast scope of the Snow White Killer hadn't ever been repeated. The terror, the manipulation, the horrific crime scenes—Snow White held the title for the worst their town had ever seen. Ten girls. Now there were four more. Most likely not by the hand of the original Snow White, but by someone with close ties to him.

The evidence from the earlier murders alone was staggering. Ten murder books, ten evidence files and conclusion files drawn after each case. The paperwork was overwhelming, but Taylor had gone through it all. More than one hundred boxes were stacked along the back wall of the conference room, ready for battle when called upon. Each previous victim had a stack. On the wall above the boxes, the photographs of the victims were hung, a head shot side-by-side with a blown-up picture from their individual crime scenes. The similarities were mesmerizing. Taylor caught herself staring at the pictures, thinking, man, twenty years. That's a long time to be dormant. Where did you go?

Taylor's gaze went around the room, stopping in turn on each victim, a silent tribute. She'd done this every day for two months.

The first murder occurred in January 1986. A young woman went missing from an evening out with friends. Her body was found a week later, her lips painted in a wide red grin, brutally assaulted, raped and her throat cut. Her name was Tiffani Crowden. The brand of lipstick was identified as Chanel Coco Red. She was the first confirmed kill for the Snow White Killer. Each subsequent murder scene was identical, though he never left the bodies in the same place twice.

The next victims were Ava D'Angelo, an eighteen-year-old waitress, and Kristina Ratay, who attended the prestigious all-girls' school called Harpeth Hall. In late October 1986, Colette Burich was killed; she worked as a nanny for a wealthy family.

In early 1987, Evelyn Santana, a Belmont coed whose parents were well-respected doctors in town, showed up dead. In late summer, Danielle Seraphin and Vivienne White, both French exchange students, were found together in Centennial Park, slain in a double homicide.

In 1988 there were three more murders, Allison Gutierrez, Abigail McManus and Ellie Walpole. Each girl was found with her throat cut in various parks around the Nashville area.

And then he stopped. She wished she knew why. And why it had started again.

Ritual complete, Taylor brought her attention back to the table. There was a separate pile of information in front of them. On the top was the key piece of evidence from the killings—the letter written by the Snow White Killer back in 1988. A polite fuck you, you'll-never-catch-me type of communication to the police. Every bite Taylor took, her eyes were drawn to the letter. She just knew, in the way of all good detectives, that there was something in the killer's words that would help solve the cases. There must have been something in the old files that the detectives who handled the cases back in the eighties had missed.

That was next on Taylor's agenda, speaking to the homicide detective from the case. His name was Martin Kimball, and he'd retired the year before Taylor joined the homicide team. She needed to interview him, glean all she could from his memory. She hoped it was solid and intact.

Taylor swallowed her chicken salad and mused. She also needed to talk to the reporter who'd handled these cases from the beginning. She'd been trying to reach the man but had been stymied; he was in Europe. He was due back tomorrow, and he was aware that she needed to talk to him. Those were her next steps, talking to Martin Kimball and Frank Richardson, the *Tennessean* reporter.

She put down her sandwich and started in on her Kettle chips.

"So," she crunched, "the crime scene was clean. No new evidence. Talk to me. Why are we so sure that this isn't the Snow White Killer?"

"We've gone over this a million times," Fitz grumped at her.

"I just want to have all the information in front of me to think on. Start talking, old man."

"Naw, I'll go. He still has half a sandwich left." Marcus threw the older man one of his trademark puppy-dog grins, and Fitz nodded his thanks.

"Yeah, let the little man speak," Lincoln teased.

Marcus responded with a halfhearted "Shut up, Lincoln." Taylor was reminded of two wildly diverse brothers, two boys who loved to razz each other. They all interacted in a family dynamic. The closeness of their unit simply escalated their success rate. Taylor oversaw all of Homicide, Fitz was her sergeant—the troops reported to him. But this core group of four was responsible for an eighty-six percent close rate on their individual cases, a record unheard of in the rest of Metro.

Marcus was running the case down. "Okay, here's what we know for certain. Snow White was left-handed. He attacked from behind, pulling on the hair of the victim to expose the throat. The knife moved across the girls' necks from the right side, severing the exterior carotid artery and moving across, through to the internal carotid, to the left. The knife impressions were deeper at the end of the slash. This was consistent on all of the victims.

"Our new killer is right-handed, though he's trying to make it look like he's left-handed. He's cutting their throats from the front. The knife enters the right side of the victims' necks, moves across, severing both carotid arteries. But the knife slash is deeper at the point of origin, instead of at the end. So it's safe to conclude that this new killer is right-handed."

"That's a biggie, too. Good. What else?" Taylor finished her last chip, pushed her plate away.

"The DNA hasn't come back yet, but the blood types match. The rope fibers lifted from the victims' wrists and ankles are inconsistent with the fibers from the earlier cases, though the knots are nearly identical. Obviously the original Snow White killer didn't leave presents in his victims' hoohahs, either."

Taylor suppressed the urge to laugh. "Hoohahs? Something wrong with the technical term?"

Lincoln and Fitz cracked up when Marcus blushed.

"No, I just hate that word. It sounds so, I don't know. Fine, never mind. He didn't leave news articles in the victims' vaginas. Happy now?"

"Very, puppy, very. What else?"

"Tox screens on the first three new victims show high levels of Rohypnol, and elevated BALs. So they all drank doctored drinks. That wasn't something the original killer did, either."

Taylor fished a piece of paper out of her pile. "Make that four. Giselle's lab work was identical. He's getting them wasted to lower their inhibitions."

Fitz chimed in. "You're right. I was in uniform when these cases were ongoing. The word from Homicide was Snow White was a charmer, he sweet-talked the victims instead of drugging them. All the reports say he'd approach them in a safe environment, was someone they could trust. Girls nowadays aren't as trusting, they'll need a little extra incentive to go with a stranger willingly."

Taylor nodded in agreement. "Well, now we have the makeup of this cream found on their temples. Arnica, frankincense and myrrh? What's up with that?"

"I think we're dealing with a religious nut. Look at the biblical aspects—the gifts of the Three Wise Men were gold, frankincense and myrrh. They also used myrrh oil in Roman times to cover up the smell of dead bodies. I looked up the modern uses—perfume, anti-inflammatory, homeopathic cholesterol-lowering agents…there's tons of uses and tons of availability. But the most common use is in churches and synagogues. It just makes more sense that this has some sort of significance to the killer. And the placement on their temples makes it seem like he's anointing them."

"Lincoln's right, there might be a religious component to all of this. Toss that into the mix."

Marcus played with one of his chips. "Maybe he stopped killing back then because he got called to God. You know, took the opposite road, tried to repent. Hell, he might have become a priest or something. And then he just couldn't stand it, broke free and started killing again."

They were all silent for a moment, thinking about those implications.

"I wish we had the DNA comparison. That would at least tell us definitively if we are dealing with the same man or a copycat," Fitz said.

"You're right, Fitz." Taylor absently twirled a piece

of her ponytail around her forefinger. "Without the DNA, we can't go too much further."

"Have you heard what the holdup is? I know TBI is backed up and they passed it up the chain to Quantico, but still. This should be a priority case for them."

"I know, Fitz, I know. Now that Baldwin's assigned to the case, I'll ask him to tag a priority to the lab work. Remind me, okay?"

"When's Price back?" Lincoln asked.

"He should be here tonight. Baldwin sent the plane for him. Let's get back to the rundown, boys. Now, the lipstick. Giselle St. Claire's neck wound was rimmed in red lipstick. Tests aren't back yet, but I'll throw out the assumption that it's the same lipstick that was found on all of the previous victims' lips, that Chanel Coco Red. As far as we know, this is a new step, one he hasn't done to any of the other victims. Coupled with the fact that there wasn't a separate dump site. Why? Any ideas?"

Marcus nodded. "There has to be a pathology behind the lipstick in the first place. Something from Snow White's past that drove him to defile the girls, to paint them. To alter the way they looked naturally. Something his mother did, perhaps? But the new killer, he's just copying his predecessor. So the lipstick on Giselle's throat could just be his way of saying this is my kill. I did this one. It screams 'Mine.'"

"That's a good start, puppy. Why wouldn't he do it to the first three?"

"Because he knew by this kill we would have figured out that he was a copycat. He knew we'd have DNA to match, and would know he was right-handed instead of left. He's ready to be acknowledged."

Lincoln pointed a finger at Marcus. "But we don't have the DNA results, so we can't be absolutely sure that this isn't the work of the original killer. They've been known to lie dormant for years, have lives, make a name in the community. That could be the case here. If it is the original killer, what would drive him to the tipping point? What would make him start killing again?"

Taylor nodded. "The usual stuff. Loss of some kind. We have to find out what the trigger was. I'm open to ideas."

No one answered, all four heads shaking slowly. Fitz started crumpling the paper insert his sandwich had been wrapped in, and Taylor decided to call it quits.

"All right, that's it for now. Go focus on Giselle St. Claire. I want to know what she was doing, where she was headed, and why she was targeted. Did he know she was the daughter of a celebrity or was it chance? All that stuff. Let's talk again later this afternoon. I'm going to go bug Baldwin for the DNA." She started to turn, then stopped.

"Fitz? You know what? Let's go talk to Martin Kimball right now instead of waiting. Can you be ready in half an hour?"

"Yep. I'll meet you out back."

They scattered, teasing one another. A solid team confident in their ability to break another major case, to right the wrongs of this egregious killer. Taylor watched them go, filled with a sense of pride and a small nugget of hope. They were hers, and she loved them.

Fitz drove to Martin Kimball's house. He wanted to check out Taylor's new ride and had the 4Runner in four-wheel drive, powering the truck through the icy streets.

They talked casually of the case, the impending wedding. Taylor was always open with Fitz. He was more like a father to her than her own ever was. She never had to worry about her image, never was concerned that he had a problem being the older man, the second in command to the younger woman. Fitz was edging closer and closer to retirement; he'd been making noises about leaving sooner rather than later. Taylor hoped this visit to Martin Kimball would change his mind; maybe Kimball would be bored and depressed, and that would be enough to convince Fitz to stay on board for a while longer.

They arrived in front of the bungalow on Granny White Pike. The land itself was worth at least $500,000, the cottage another $200,000. The houses on the left and the right of the Kimballs' had been razed and rebuilt into monstrosities, a stone-and-timber Tudor on the left, a red-brick, columned colonial on the right. Each would easily sell for well over $800,000. Both had elaborate landscaping that belied their small lawns, wrought-iron gates across their tiny driveway entrances. This area was booming, and the Kimballs' cottage, though the original plan for the area, looked out of place among the finery.

That news had not reached the Kimballs. Christmas lights decorated every square inch of the front their home. A festive evergreen wreath hung on the door, festooned with curling red ribbons. The walk had been meticulously shoveled. A fine spray of cat litter was scattered along the bricks in polite readiness for any guests who might arrive. Taylor and Fitz took this path, Taylor's boots squeaking on the remaining snow. She knocked on the freshly painted bright red door. It may not have the biggest house on the block, but it was clean and cared for.

The door opened, a small face peeked out at their knees. "Merry Christmas. Welcome to the Kimball home. May I help you?"

Taylor bit back a laugh. The urchin couldn't have been more than seven or eight, but what a presence.

"Yes, miss. May we speak with your grandfather?"

"Do you have an appointment?"

"He knows we're coming." Taylor bent at the knee, got face-to-face with the little one. "I'm Taylor. This is Fitz. What's your name?"

"Sabrina." The little girl stuck out her hand to shake. Taylor took it, all seriousness now. Sabrina gave her a nod, as if she'd been judged and found worthy, then opened the door fully.

The rooms within were filled with gaiety and love. A warm fire crackled in the hearth, the house was decorated to within an inch of its life with red and green—popcorn and cranberry strings, garlands, paper rings. Sabrina led the way to the kitchen, where the aroma of pumpkin pie and gingerbread wafted. She announced their visitors to the two people in the room.

"Gran, Grampy, this is Taylor and her friend Fitz. Grampy, they say they have an appointment with you. Are you ready to see them?"

Martin Kimball turned to his granddaughter with a glint of amusement in his eye. He reached out and grabbed her by the waist, swinging her into his arms as he stood. The waif reined in, he smiled at his old friend Fitz, nodded politely to Taylor.

"Well, well, well, look what the cat dragged in. Pete Fitzgerald and his lovely lieutenant. What can I do for you fine folks today? We've got a lot of pie, and we're building a gingerbread house for Sabrina. Plenty of gumdrops hanging around. Care to help?"

Fitz looked wistful for a moment; Taylor knew his love of sweets was undermining his willpower. He gathered himself, a pillar of strength and resistance. If retirement meant a warm, loving home and a happy family, it didn't look all bad. But Fitz had never married, didn't have this built-in infrastructure to keep him satisfied.

"Wish we could, Marty. We need to talk. You got someplace private where we can chat?"

"Sure, we can go in the den. Here you go, sugar." He handed off the child to his wife, a cheery-looking woman with red cheeks and a plump chin.

"Don't be too long, Marty. The gingerbread is about ready."

He kissed her on the forehead, patted the child's hair, then signaled to Taylor and Fitz to follow. He went the length of the kitchen, through a swinging door and into a short hallway. The first room on the right was a small, cozy office/den, the blue-and-white choo-choo-train border along the ceiling giving away the space's previous employment as a child's bedroom. There was a plush, soft chocolate chenille couch and a cherry desk with two ladder-backed chairs on either side. Three weathered brown corrugated boxes sat on the desk. They bore the mark of private evidence files. All investigative cops had one or two stashed away.

They got settled, Taylor and Fitz on the couch, Kimball leaning against the desk. Taylor took the chance to size the man up.

Kimball's hair was gray, cut in a military-style bristle top. His face had a permanently mournful expression, his eyes hangdog. His clothes were old-fashioned, from a previous generation. He wasn't old, but he was certainly not doing anything to make himself seem any younger than his sixty-four years.

He was soft-spoken, and Taylor imagined he'd been a shy man once, with jug ears and a slow, sad smile. Retirement had eased some of the pressures on his mind, but the years were etched on his face. He'd seen too much, witnessed too many vicious crimes, to have a smooth, carefree aspect. He stooped slightly, and Taylor wondered if it was the weight of all he had seen in his years on the force.

Fitz had told Taylor that Kimball was the detail man of the old homicide unit, the one attuned to every nuance and ripple in a case. He was the homely one, the man any victim would confide in, the man every criminal confessed to.

He rested against the desk and waited for them to speak. Just like the old days, she assumed. No sense pushing an issue if it was going to come to you, anyway.

Satisfied they were in good hands, Taylor started. "We wanted to talk to you about the Snow White murders. The early ones. We're pretty sure these new ones are a copycat, but you'd be the best person to confirm that with. The DNA isn't back yet, but you know this guy. You can tell us if it's him doing these crimes or if it's someone else."

"Okay." Kimball walked behind them and shut the door. No sense in scaring his granddaughter if he could help it. Fitz got up and examined his friend's bookshelf, whistling softly.

Kimball reperched himself on the edge of the desk.

"What do you want to know?" He held up a hand. "No, let me ask you something first. Why do you think this is a copycat?"

"To start with, the wound tracks are inconsistent. Snow White was left-handed, you confirmed that with all the original autopsy findings. This guy looks like a righty trying to make himself look like a southpaw. He's cutting them from the front instead of from behind. There are two other major discrepancies—the news articles placed in the vaginas, and there's a cream on each girl's temples. It looks like it's arnica cream, and we've found the composition includes frankincense and myrrh. We can't be sure that the substances are combined or separate just yet, but regardless, it's a big deviation from the original murders. We're tossing around the idea that this might be some sort of religious ritual."

"So there's no hair evidence?"

"You mean at the scenes? Not that we've found."

"No, I mean the new victims' hair wasn't pulled out at the roots like the first girls'?"

Taylor and Fitz exchanged a glance, and Fitz answered, "Not that we've come across, no."

Kimball went to the boxes on his desk, flipped the lid off the center box, slipped on a pair of gold-rimmed reading glasses. He thumbed through the center of the files and pulled out a manila folder marked Photos. He paged through until he reached one he liked. He held it out for Taylor to look at.

"That picture is of the back of Vivienne White's head. See that little bald patch? We always figured he was yanking their heads back so hard that he pulled the hair out at the roots. It was the same for all ten girls. A bald patch, right at the nape of their necks. I don't know about any cream being found on the bodies, but the missing hair was a big deal for us."

Taylor's lips were pursed. "That wasn't in the files." She looked at Kimball then, a mean thought niggling her mind. She hated to think the worst, but it had happened before.

"Kimball, is there something we're missing? Are our files incomplete?"

He raised an eyebrow. "I can't answer that for you. That's why I pulled these from the garage, just in case. You know how it is. Files get lost over time. The case is twenty years old. You're welcome to these, if you want. Compare and contrast."

"I appreciate that."

Kimball circled the desk, sat in his leather chair. He pulled out a pipe and loaded it up. The scent reminded Taylor of her grandfather, a man she hadn't known very well. When she looked in a mirror there was a likeness, and when she felt her temper rise, she knew it was his anger.

"Anything else top your list?"

Taylor smiled. The man was still as sharp as ever.

"Tell me. Why did they name him Snow White?"

Kimball smiled, then turned and went to the bookcase. He ran his fingers along the spines on the third shelf from the bottom, the wood just high enough that he didn't need to bend over to read the titles. He made his selection, a tattered, beaten book that looked quite old.

He turned back to them. "That was my fault, I'm afraid. My daughter, Stacy, Sabrina's mother, was a little girl when the first murder happened. I was reading to her before I tucked her in, a ritual I tried to maintain even when I was working the B-shift on Homicide. I'd read, get her to sleep, then go to work."

He fingered the cover of the book. Taylor could see that the edges of the pages were gold.

"Well, this was the story I'd read to her that night. It was snowing hard, and I got to work thinking we'd have a slow night. Instead, we got called to the lot behind the old Chute Complex, those gay bars out in Melrose. You know where I'm talking about, off Franklin Road? It's all built up now."

Taylor nodded.

"That was Tiffani Crowden's final resting place. I got on the scene and saw her, lying there in the snow. The story popped right into my head."

He cracked open the book. No bookmark was necessary; it opened to the page he wanted. The words he read made a chill spread through Taylor's body.

"*Once upon a time, when the flakes of snow were falling like feathers from the sky, a queen sat at a window sewing, and the frame of the window was made of black ebony. And whilst she was sewing and looking out of the window at the snow, she pricked her finger with the needle, and three drops of blood fell upon the snow. And the red looked pretty upon the white snow, and she thought to herself, would that I had a child as white as snow, as red as blood, and as black as the wood of the window frame. Soon after that she had a little daughter, who was as white as snow, and as red as blood, and her hair was as black as ebony, and she was therefore called little Snow White. And when the child was born, the queen died.*'"

Kimball closed the book, cleared his throat. "Fitting, really."

They were silent for a few beats. Taylor was the first to venture in. "Wow. I had no idea."

Kimball offered her the book. She took it and glanced at the cover. *Fairy Tales of the Brothers Grimm.*

"That was my copy from when I was a boy."

Taylor met Kimball's eye, gave the book back. "Thank you. This helps. Did you ever think that he'd read the story and was trying to re-create the scenes?"

"Sure. Made perfect sense. Too perfect. I always thought there was more. Hate. Lust. Power. All excellent motives. But why does any killer develop his MO? Maybe Snow White's mother read to him before she went to work. Maybe he had someone who he read to, and lost her? Attaining the unattainable, always a rich source for motivation. We won't know unless we catch him, ask him."

"Can I ask you about the note he sent you? I'm curious about that."

"Smart girl. I bet you are." Taylor took the praise and realized she would have enjoyed working with this man, had she ever gotten the chance.

He puffed, sucking the fire into the tobacco, ruminating. "That damn note. I swear, we went over it and over it. Didn't have all the fancy tests y'all have nowadays, but we could do a fair amount of work back then. The computers were young, and the printers weren't as plentiful. Just the fact that it came off a computer told us something. He was well-off. It came from an IBM 8580, PS/2 Model 80 386, one of those early desktops, and the printer was a Hewlett-Packard Deskjet Inkjet."

Fitz shook his head. "You remember that offhand?"

"Yeah."

Taylor was beginning to understand the reputation Kimball had acquired as the detail man. He continued his recitation.

"Top-of-the-line printer, too. Those things were a thousand bucks a pop when they first came out. At the time, not too many people here in town had one. We traced the ownership, came back to a fellow in Green Hills, man by the name of Mars. Wasn't him doing the killing, but it was his computer that the note got written on, his printer that spit it out."

Burt Mars. Taylor knew that name. He was a friend of her parents. An accountant, if she remembered correctly.

"But it wasn't Mars who wrote the note, right?"

"We never could prove it was him. Never thought so, either. He just didn't seem capable of pulling off something so elaborate as ten murders. Now, he could bilk Uncle Sam out of a pretty penny, I'll give him that. No, we always thought it was one of his clients. Someone who had access to his office."

"Why a client? Why not an employee?"

Kimball gave her a look, then smiled at Fitz, who had rejoined Taylor on the couch. "Because whoever this guy was, he had money. Now, Mars was a generous guy, but not that generous. His employees didn't have the cash flow that Snow White did. No, it was one of Mars's clients, all right. Someone who paid other people to do his work for him. I've always been confident about that."

"Why? What was so special about him that you think he came from money?"

"The signet."

Taylor shook her head. "What?"

"The signet ring. Jesus, that wasn't in the files, either?"

"I know nothing about it. Fitz, what about you?"

"Don't remember anything in there about a ring."

"Found it at one of the last scenes, let's see, I believe it was Ellie Walpole. When they rolled the body, the ring was caught in her hair. It was a gold ring, scroll work on the sides, big sucker, with a monogrammed *F* in the crest. That's all. Just an *F.* We went through Mars's files with a fine-toothed comb, interviewed every single person whose name started or ended with an *F.* Didn't get anywhere, but that didn't mean too much. It could have belonged to the killer's parent, grandparent—hell, cousin or friend, for all I know. It looked old, like it might have been passed down, you know what I mean?"

"Now, that isn't in the files, I know that for sure. I went through all of the evidence by hand three weeks ago when we pulled some of the boxes for our investigation. There's nothing about a signet ring. And nothing in the interviews about a ring, either."

"Don't know what to tell you, LT. It was there. Saw it with my own eyes. I wrote a lot of those reports myself— that's why I know they were there. I'm getting the feeling you aren't working with a full deck on this one."

Taylor looked at Fitz. This was a problem.

Kimball took a last puff on his pipe, emptied it out in a clay ashtray that looked homemade, and stood.

"You can take these files, just be sure you get them back to me in one piece, okay? I want to go be with Sabrina now. We don't get to see her as much as I'd like, and she's growing up too fast. Pretty soon she won't have any desire to make gingerbread houses with Gramps, you know?"

Fitz carried two boxes, Taylor one. Kimball escorted

them out through the kitchen, where Mrs. Kimball and Sabrina stopped them and put cookies wrapped in foil on the tops of the boxes, a treat for later. Kimball saw them to the door, a sad smile on his face as they drove away.

Taylor was three feet tall and fit perfectly into the space between the banister and top step, slightly shrouded by a Doric column that abutted the crown stair. She could see the ball going on below her. There seemed to be hundreds of people, all dressed in the most elaborate of costumes. It was New Year's Eve, her parents' traditional masquerade ball, though the house and environs were new. This was Taylor's second home, but the only one she ever remembered.

The music was loud, and the people twirled around like marionettes, flutes of champagne disappearing at an alarming rate—tuxedo-clad waiters circling the foyer and ballroom, keeping the guests well supplied.

A woman in a large Marie Antoinette wig, powdered face, a black triangle patch meant to be stuck to the corner of her mouth askew and half-unglued, sat down hard on the bottom step—a full forty-seven steps away from Taylor in her little hiding place. Her mother was dressed as Marie Antoinette, but this wasn't her mother. Taylor felt the concussion of the woman's sudden not-quite fall, smelled the alcohol waft up the stairs mixed with another scent, a powdery musky smell.

Three people rushed over to make sure she was okay, but she giggled and shooed them, assuring them she'd purposely taken a seat to rest her weary feet. After three waiters had helped her up, she waddled away, dress swinging precariously.

Then there was quiet for a few moments before her father and mother came into view, several people at their heels.

The women were simpering back and forth to one another, but the men talked loudly, expansive with drink.

"Win Jackson, you've obviously made a deal with the devil," a dark-haired man brayed.

"Yeah, Win, your own little Manderley, is it? What did you do in a past life to get so goddamned lucky in this one? The judge should have thrown you in jail, not dismissed the charges." A sandy-haired man with thick black glasses smacked her father on the shoulder. Win laughed.

"Manderley? Shit, let's just hope the place doesn't burn to the ground. Kitty would have my head."

And so they went, on and on, poking and gibing at one another, until Taylor's governess found her and snatched her from under the curved balustrade, shuttled her back to the nursery.

Taylor squeezed her eyes shut, trying hard to place the moment, the spot where one of the men turned....

"Jesus, Taylor watch out!" Fitz shouted.

She opened her eyes, disoriented to see the road in front of her, her hands on the steering wheel of the truck, and a small car swerving through a slide on the ice right into her path. The ballroom was gone. She swung the wheel lightly to the right, steered into the slide and scooted around the Camry, which righted itself and slowed, creeping away in her rearview mirror.

Something there, she thought to herself. Something there. But the memory was lost in the glare of the snow.

Seven

Charlotte Douglas knew how to enter a room.

She preferred to do it late in the evening, wearing Valentino or Cavalli, delicate feet strapped in some fanciful creation by Louboutin or Blahnik, on the arm of whatever delicious flavor of eye candy she'd chosen for the evening. To stop just inside the doorway for a priceless moment, giving every head the chance to turn and take in her glory. Once all eyes were upon her, she'd glide in, smiling, touching an arm here or a buttock there, depending on the level of intimacy she had with the player involved. The sea of men would proverbially part to allow her access, champagne would magically appear and the evening was instantly considered a success.

She generally reserved those shenanigans for the high rollers: senators, congressmen, people who had funding levels under their watchful command. She had an image to project—glamour, posh and publicly unattainable. It drove the power-hungry men in Washington wild, assured her of a place at most every event of significance.

But she couldn't be on the A-plus list all of the time; she needed to finesse the peons, as well. She'd never waste her couture on them, designer fare from Nordstrom was entirely appropriate. So for the dates with the underlings, the chiefs of staff and deputy secretaries, she made sure she was dressed as elegantly as possible, was perfectly coiffed and made up, and reached or exceeded their height. Charlotte had been handmade for stilettos.

The previous evening, she'd spent half the time talking to a minor Saudi prince, a full half hour with the head of the Ways and Means Committee, and shared a snippet of conversation with an NBC affiliate reporter being groomed for the network before calling it a night. Working D.C. could be awfully tiresome.

She'd pulled into the gates of Quantico at 7:00 a.m. sharp, clear-eyed and ready for the day.

She smiled to her coworkers, flirted with the maintenance man fixing the service elevator, and happily went about her morning routine. She grabbed a coffee from the break room, stepped into the bathroom to fluff her hair, then made her way down the hall, unlocked her office and turned on a gentle lamp. The glow from the environmentally friendly bulb cast a shadow on her nameplate; she moved it an inch to the right so it wasn't obscured. There was no sense of pride when she looked at the engraving—Dr. Charlotte Douglas, Deputy Chief, Behavioral Science Unit. The "deputy" part wasn't to her liking.

Logging on to her computer, she leaned back in her

chair and picked a piece of imaginary fluff off her shoulder. The machine would only take a second to boot up; it was password-protected so she generally left it in sleep mode when she left the office for any appreciable length of time. The display flashed at her a few moments later, the FBI seal centered on the screen. She typed in her password, a carefully chosen combination of letters and numbers. L96in69gu0S. A personal joke between her and the webmaster. Who was quite talented, she'd come to find out.

Setting down her coffee mug, she'd gone trolling. Looking for unusual murders, repeat offenses, unsolved cases was time-consuming, but it had to be done. She could have reports compiled and left on her desk like the rest of the D.C. automatons—the junior staff of every department was responsible for the morning reports, pages of media items of interest to their bosses. The other profilers in her unit did just that, allowed the FBI interns to aggregate the news reports, police filings and anything else that might be relevant to keep the unit up to speed on the goings-on of their law enforcement brethren. But Charlotte preferred to look for her own information. Regardless, no one else could really gather the tidbits she was looking for correctly.

There was nothing unusual to be seen—the usual amalgamation of crazies, unsolved cases she was already familiar with, and Web sites catering to serial killers. She made a note of a new site that advertised for killers. "Contact us, tell us your most gruesome kills, here's how to do it anonymously. WE'RE NOT COPS!" Just what they needed. The gilded information age, perfect for computer-literate sociopaths.

She continued through her prescribed protocols.

The new ViCAP updates were in. The Violent Criminal Apprehension Program's purpose was straightforward—detect patterns within criminal activities. Charlotte used it to compile missing-person cases, unidentified bodies and sexual assaults, coordinate multijurisdictional reviews, and help to share information between often competitive law enforcement agencies. ViCAP was one of her darlings.

She opened the icon, logged in to the database and looked around. She didn't see anything new that needed her immediate attention. Nothing out of the ordinary.

She went on to check CODIS. The Combined DNA Index System was a beauty of a tool; once they got the DNA uploaded for all the bad guys in the system it would be a lifesaver. She plugged in her pass code.

The Snow White case was her number-one priority right now, for a variety of reasons. The DNA profiles from the Nashville serial murders had been uploaded the previous evening. She'd configured the DNA submissions from the latest cases personally.

Once she was logged in, a small icon in the lower-left corner of her desktop started blinking. She opened the link and smiled. The DNA test results from the Nashville murders were back. Wonderful. It wouldn't do to leave any stone unturned, or turned in the wrong direction.

She read through the results, combing the reports. She could turn this in to the Nashville field office immediately. Or at her leisure. Whichever fit the mood she was in ten minutes from now.

She closed the elaborate analyses and moved to a separate part of the CODIS database, where DNA profiles from unsolved cases across the country were inputted to be compared against one another. The theory was excellent, but the practical applications hadn't caught up with the backlog of DNA analysis. Slowly but surely, the files were being uploaded into the system, but it would take years to get reality matched to the theoretical.

Two backlit icons were flashing. On the left icon, a code number that matched her uploaded Nashville DNA blinked slowly. On the right icon, the same numbered sequence glowed red. A match. A cold-hit DNA match between the Nashville suspect and… She sucked in her breath. What she was seeing couldn't be right. There must be a glitch in the system. Having a cold hit on CODIS wasn't a regular occurrence. More files popped onto the screen. Charlotte tapped her fingers on the desk while the rest of the icons lit up like Christmas trees. Match. Match. Match. Match. CODIS was showing four separate cold hits, from four states, not including Tennessee. All the DNA pointed to a single contributor.

Charlotte cursed.

She called the webmaster, told him there was a problem. He called her back five minutes later and assured her there wasn't. Not on his end.

A tingle had started then. Just at the base of her spine. The databases were programmed to spit out patterns, and that was what Charlotte was seeing before her. She'd designed this section of the database herself, and now here it was. Her anomaly. Despite all her best efforts, her hand would be forced now.

Mind buzzing, she forced herself to close CODIS. She opened a buried file within her system, typed in a new pass code. A private personnel file Charlotte had misappropriated a few months back opened on the screen.

There she was. Taylor Jackson. Charlotte stared at the picture, the JPEG file sharp and clear. Tawny-blond hair past her shoulders, gray eyes, a full mouth, a slightly crooked yet elegant nose—stunning, but Charlotte knew she could compete.

She gave a mental review of her own attributes. Her hair had often been described as the color of a young pinot noir. Porcelain skin, amber eyes, striking cheekbones, and if she wasn't mistaken, her bottom lip was just a touch fuller than Jackson's. She had to admit, the girl was attractive. Good to know Baldwin continued to have excellent taste.

The flashing green eyes of her former boss flooded her memory. She forced all thoughts of him away reluctantly. She could get bogged down for hours in the memories of their brief time together. And they would only lead back to this little bitch, the woman who'd stolen him right out of Charlotte's hands.

She lingered for a moment longer, touching a forefinger to the screen, tracing the outline of Jackson's heart-shaped face. She touched the finger to her lips, then forced herself to close the window and brought up the previous screen.

Jackson was forgotten. The new DNA profiles were enough to make her lick her lips in anticipation. She loved a challenge. What to do? What to do? The match in CODIS was highly unexpected, and unfortunately, couldn't be held back. She'd have to share this information, others would see it soon enough.

She opened the latest crime-scene photos submitted

by the Nashville Police Department overnight. The fresh kill. The photo named the victim as Giselle St. Claire. What a delicate name, she thought. Poor girl. Giselle was naked, blue from the cold. She showed signs of exsanguination; the gaping wound in her neck gave that away easily. A second smile. The blood was pooled below her head, framing the scene in a macabre ruby border.

Charlotte clicked on another file. Naked bodies tumbled across her computer screen.

The media had christened the killer well. Every time she saw these photos, the first thing that popped into Charlotte's mind was Snow White. Delicate beauty, alabaster skin, red lips, jet-black hair. All that was missing was a red cape and a grouping of dwarves.

If she were rushing, at first glance all the photos could have been of the same dead girl. Only a detailed examination showed the subtle differences: height, weight, hair length. The similarities between the victims were downright eerie. She opened two more windows and speculated for a moment. The physical victimology was so similar from girl to girl—it took time and effort to pick out women who looked so alike. She'd had a case a few years back where the killer had bought identical wigs to place on his victims prior to their death. But in these cases, the hair was real, ebony as a raven's wing, long and thick. Definitely not a wig.

With a sigh, she went back to the CODIS cold hits, printed out the cover sheet from each murder, started a new file, marked it Snow White DNA/CODIS, then walked the long hallway to her boss's office. She was the lead profiler on the murders; she needed to present her findings. This case was hers. Her future. Her success.

Stuart Evanson had taken over the BSU when Baldwin left. He reported to Garrett Woods, the top dog in the Critical Incidence Response Group. Evanson had power and clout, but not as much as he'd like. Woods was the real star, mentor to the great profiler John Baldwin. Woods was reputed to be a smart, seasoned agent who might be running the whole Bureau if he wasn't careful. Charlotte disliked him immensely; he'd passed her over in favor of Evanson after Baldwin split. Made it about the relationship she and Baldwin had engaged in, though Charlotte knew Baldwin had made it clear to Woods that she shouldn't be running the show. She didn't know which burned her worse, their breakup, or the fact that he'd shanghaied her career in the process.

Evanson had replaced Baldwin only a few months before. She remembered that storied morning vividly. Baldwin had announced he was quitting the BSU, the FBI and all that he knew to play house in Nashville with a homicide detective he'd met on a case. Charlotte had been shocked to hear that. Of course, Baldwin hadn't been in the game for a while before that had happened; he'd been on extended leave after a shooting incident with a suspect that got three agents killed.

She'd been with him then. But he hadn't turned to her for solace. He'd hightailed it out of town, gone home to Nashville and tried to drink himself to death. Then he'd met Taylor Jackson, pulled out of his funk, solved a huge case and returned to the BSU triumphant, the golden boy yet again. Charlotte had been forgotten in the mix.

Baldwin's plans to retire had been usurped. The Bureau wasn't willing to let a talent like him leave for good. He was given a special dispensation—his own shop, free from the prying eyes of Quantico. But still a division of the FBI. Doing the work of the BSU without the constraints shoveled upon them by the government. He worked out of the Tennessee field office now.

Stuart Evanson had been placed in charge, and instead of gracefully appointing Charlotte second in command, he'd moved her to Training, making her conduct the symposiums that the BSU often gave to law enforcement. Like he didn't care that she had a Ph.D. from Georgetown and had worked tirelessly in the BSU for five years, moving up every review period. He wanted her to be the "spokeswoman" for their unit. Fuck that. She wanted to work cases, not train wannabe profilers from Sheboygan.

Evanson was a power-hungry prick, and like most pricks she'd known, was desperate for a piece of Charlotte pie. Charlotte made it very clear what she'd be willing to do if he gave her the deputy posting, her rightful spot. Trying to engender good will from her, he'd "promoted" her within weeks, making her the number two in the BSU. Deputy chief. Head profiler, that's what she was. She should have been the chief, but she would take this for now. Dangling the slightest whiff of opportunity in Evanson's face from time to time was an easy price to pay.

Hearing her boss's voice raised in anger and frustration on the other side of the door didn't bother her in the least. She had a knack, a touch, for defusing even the most egregiously charged situation. Glancing at her watch, she gave him thirty more seconds to scream, touched a hand to her deep auburn hair and knocked once, hard. She opened the door and stepped into the director's personal space.

"I don't give a damn what the President says. This is the way it's going to be." He hung up the phone with a bang and took in Charlotte, standing calmly in his doorway. He'd fire any other agent for simply daring to knock on his door while he was talking to the White House. He was a blustery soul, prone to fits of pique. But Charlotte was a different story, and she knew it.

Stepping into the room, she handed him the file folder, coded with a red sticker that read Priority—High.

"We have an anomaly."

"Charlotte, could you say hello first? Maybe ask me how my day is going?"

Stuart Evanson leaned back in his chair, crumpling the corners of his pin-striped suit. Why he never took the jacket off was a mystery to her. Perhaps he thought it made him look more professional being fully dressed at all times, but she suspected that he was hiding sweat stains, and was thankful that he chose to. Nothing disgusted her more.

"Sir, from what I can tell, your day isn't going very well."

"Impertinence will get you nowhere, my dear."

"Thank you, sir. I'm not trying to get anywhere right now. I'm just bringing a significant anomaly to your attention."

"Which is?"

"If you'd look at the file, sir, I believe it will make itself quite apparent."

Evanson gave her an unfathomable look and flipped open the file. Charlotte watched as his bushy eyebrows grew crampons and hiked into his hairline. Told you, she thought.

"Is this certain?" Evanson asked.

"Yes. The Nashville police don't have this information."

Evanson was obviously in a seriously bad mood. He dismissed Charlotte without pretense, already had his hand on the phone. "Get on it, then. Report back to me as soon as you have more. Fill in the field teams immediately."

"Yes, sir. Will Dr....?" She stopped, certain of the answer. It wouldn't do to look too anxious. Word had already come down that John Baldwin was helping the Nashville police work the Snow White killings, his field office running behind the scenes. In a peripheral way, he'd always had this case. She'd be required to work with him directly, exactly as she wanted.

"Never mind, sir. I'll get back to you on this." Evanson grunted, he had already tuned her out. Charlotte turned and left the inner sanctum. Damn it all to hell, what was she thinking? It was that kind of carelessness that would get her hurt. Again.

Back at her desk, she brought up the Nashville file.

As Charlotte started to work, she had a deep, satisfying knowledge that she was about to be a very happy woman. Call it instinct, premonition, whatever. She hadn't planned for things to go this way, but maybe it was for the best. This was big enough for her to capture the undivided attention of Dr. John Baldwin, all right. Pull him away from that little lioness he'd attached himself to.

If she played her cards right, he would come back to her. She debated with herself for a few moments. Decided she would have to get there sooner or later. She dialed the 615 area code, tapped out the rest of the numbers and chewed lightly on her pen. Her moment had arrived.

Eight

Taylor nestled Martin Kimball's boxes in back of the 4Runner and closed the door with a slam. She'd gone through the files briefly after she and Fitz returned to the office, but quickly realized that a physical search through the evidence still in storage was necessary. The paperwork and the murder books had been moved into their conference room, but the actual material evidence had to be kept in the warehouse—checking out the individual pieces was too much of a hassle. Fitz had volunteered to go, and she'd accepted his offer. He promised to call and she decided to head home.

She turned the heat on and tried to ignore the strains of Christmas carols spilling out of her speakers. As soon as her hands warmed up, she turned off the radio, but "Silent Night" had wormed its way into her mind, and she repeated the words absently in a nonreligious mantra as she drove out of downtown.

"Silent night. Holy night. All is calm, all is bright." Yeah, she wished.

The fact that they might be missing information gnawed at her. That information could be nothing or everything.

Knowing Baldwin would be hungry, she stopped at City Limits, a great New York-style deli close to home, and bought chicken Caesar salads and warm, freshly baked baguettes.

Once she got home, she opened a nice sangiovese, a simple inexpensive bottle they drank all the time, wondered briefly where Baldwin was, stashed the salads in the fridge and took the files and her wine to the living room. She opened the first box, set the lid on the floor and breathed in the scent she'd been nostalgic about earlier. Pipe smoke and dust. Why the aroma made her smile, she wasn't quite sure.

She riffed through each file. Nothing new there. It was filled with the typical cold-case material—the murder book, which was really multiple binders, ten of them, one for each murder; folders of photos; copies of the evidence sheets. She went through those with care, searching for a mention of the signet ring. She found it, on murder number ten, Ellie Walpole. It was just as Kimball had said. In his neat handwriting, a detailed description of a gold signet ring.

She cross-referenced it with her file. The page was not there. It didn't mean anything—something like that could go missing easily. One piece of paper among five thousand. It had happened before.

After an exceptionally close reading of the autopsy reports, she found references to the bald patches on the back of the women's heads. It hadn't been deemed very important.

Taylor knew it was probably Snow White's souvenir. Many killers take a token with them—a license, panties, something symbolic to treasure, to remind them of their kills. To help them relive the actual crime.

There hadn't been anything reported missing from Snow White's victims. But a lock of hair from each kill would make a grand prize indeed.

Taylor stood, impatient, circling the couch with the wineglass in her hand, pacing, thinking. She glanced at her watch, wondering when Fitz would call. The evidence warehouse could be a time/space vortex if one wasn't careful. Looking for something as small as a signet ring might be completely unfeasible. If the ring was actually gone, not simply misplaced, then they had a problem.

She looked out the front window, took a lap around the downstairs, poured another glass of wine, then sat back on the couch. She continued going through the files, matching hers to the originals. There were a few other pieces missing, but for the most part, it was all there. The one thing that was in Kimball's files that wasn't in the main files was his notes. Sheet after sheet filled with his neat hand, speculation, ideas, drawings and doodles. Every ounce of paper that he'd generated over the course of eight years was included. Taylor read through them. She admired his thoroughness but found nothing else of note. All the rest was consistent with the files she had.

The phone rang, and she jumped up to answer it.

Fitz grumbled in her ear. "I'm covered in dust. There's no ring."

"Are you sure?"

"Absolutely positive. There's no ring in any of these boxes. Trust me, I went through one hundred and forty-three of them."

"That's what I was worried about. The page that would show it isn't in the official files, either. Damn it, Fitz, why?"

"Little girl, it may be something as simple as one of the evidence jockeys took a shine to it, and figured after all these years, why let such a pretty thing go to waste. It's happened before, you know that."

"Why do I get the feeling that isn't the case? This ring has something that can lead us back to the killer, I can just feel it."

She heard the garage door go up. "Hey, Baldwin's home. Let's talk about this in the morning, okay? Fitz, thank you for doing that. I appreciate you spending your evening in dust."

"Yeah, you owe me a beer. Tell the fed I said hi."

"See you." She hung up the phone, went to meet Baldwin in the kitchen. He was shrugging out of his shoulder holster, balancing a Starbucks cup and his briefcase in one hand and a bundle of roses in the other. He jumped when she entered the room.

"Hey, turn your back. I've got something you aren't supposed to see yet."

"I already saw them. You got me flowers? Aren't you the sweetest man alive?"

"Oh, trust me, I'm sweeter." He handed her the roses, white and red, intertwined with brick-colored gerbera daisies. She took them with her left, used her right to help him unhook from the leather harness.

"Special occasion?"

"Do I need a special occasion to bring flowers to my almost wife?"

"No, of course not." She dropped the holster on the counter and buried her nose in the flowers. "Mmm, they smell great. I better get them in some water. Where'd you find gerberas this time of year?"

"A man must protect his secrets."

She rolled her eyes at him, eliciting a laugh. It was all so comfortable, it didn't feel right. She got the flowers into water, set them thoughtfully on the kitchen table. Baldwin watched her; she felt his eyes on the back of her neck. Jesus, what was wrong with her?

"How was your day?"

"Other than the fact that we're missing a piece of evidence from the Snow White case? The old cases, I should say."

"What kind of evidence?" He opened the refrigerator. "Oh, good, you got dinner."

"Like I'd let you starve."

They bustled around the kitchen, getting their salads on plates, buttering bread, pouring wine, and Taylor told Baldwin about her afternoon. He listened with sympathy until she asked about his day. They sat on the floor in the living room, their plates on the coffee table, their backs propped with pillows, and talked while they ate.

When they were settled and Taylor was a few bites into her salad, Baldwin answered her question.

"Well, it was interesting, I'll say that. Tomorrow might be a little crazy."

She just raised an eyebrow. As if anything could be crazier in this case, in their lives.

"Charlotte Douglas is coming to town."

"And she would be…?"

"FBI Special Agent Charlotte Douglas. She's a profiler. Deputy chief of the unit."

"Well, that's not unexpected. Are you going to be able to run interference?"

"She's coming to see you, actually. And bringing one of her forensics team. They have the DNA results."

Taylor let her fork rest in the romaine, shaking her head at that statement.

"Why the hell haven't they called and given us the information? Or faxed the report over, at the very least. What's the big deal? It's either Snow White or it's someone else."

"Yeah. Well, that's the problem with Charlotte. She's a bit of a…how do I put this nicely? She's a drama queen. She wants to swoop in and break the case. She wouldn't give me the information, either. I told her how unprofessional she was being, but she told me to go to hell."

"Why am I getting the feeling that there's more to this?"

"Because you're a very astute, brilliant, beautiful woman who's made the incredibly intelligent choice to marry me on Saturday."

"Did you sleep with her?"

Baldwin shifted. Taylor leaned away from him, plunged her fork into a piece of chicken and fed it into her mouth, watching him struggle with an answer as she chewed.

"So you slept with her. When?"

Baldwin tried for a chagrined smile. "Long before you, I'll tell you that. Taylor, you have to understand, she means nothing to me. It was a thing, a heat-of-the-moment kind of situation. She's a viper. A true bitch. I hate her, if that makes you feel better."

"Why do I get the sense that Miss Charlotte doesn't hate you?"

"Fair enough. There may be some tension with this. I'm sorry. She's a piece of work, and the minute you meet her, you'll understand why I'm with you and not with her. Will you trust me on that?"

"Of course. It's not like I expected you to come to our marriage bed a virgin."

She got up, picked up her plate and went into the kitchen. Baldwin followed.

"Hey, are you okay?"

Taylor set her dish down on the counter, carefully considering that question. Of course she was okay. My God, they were adults. It wasn't like Baldwin was her first. But leaning against the counter, watching him watch her, it struck her how little she really knew about him. He was a complicated man, layer upon layer of self-containment. They'd just never delved too deeply into "Who have you fucked?"

She pushed away from the granite, gave him a half smile. "I'm fine. It's funny, actually. I never saw myself as the jealous type."

"I like it. Makes me feel wanted." Baldwin put a hand lightly on her chest and pushed her back to the ledge. He nuzzled in close, insinuating his legs between hers. She reacted, slipping back onto the counter, wrapping her legs around his lean hips and accepting his kiss.

"It's late," she murmured when they came up for air.

"So it is." He picked her up, walked her backward

into the living room, set her on the couch and followed her body down. "So it is."

It was nearly midnight when the phone rang, jarring them out of a cramped sleep on the couch. Taylor fumbled the phone to her ear.

"Taylor Jackson? This is Frank Richardson. Late of the *Tennessean*."

"I don't have any comment.... Oh, wait. You're the reporter from the old Snow White cases. Sorry. I didn't think you were back until tomorrow."

"I'm not, really. I had a layover scheduled in New York so I could visit a friend, but he's come down with the flu and I'm stuck at JFK. It's 7:00 a.m. my body time—I've been in France for the past few weeks. Am I calling too late?"

It's never too late for murder, she thought.

"No, no. Just give me a moment, okay?"

She set the phone down, disentangled herself from Baldwin, who sleepily opened his eyes and happily closed them when she shook her head, telling him he wasn't needed immediately. More and more, the late-night phone calls were strictly for Taylor's benefit.

She slipped her sweater on, dragged the afghan off the back of the couch. It trailed behind her like a security blanket as she moved into the kitchen with the phone. She sat at the table, pulled the afghan around her legs. It had grown chilly; the fire in the hearth was nearly out.

"Sorry, Mr. Richardson. Caught me off guard."

"No, no, I'm the one who's sorry. I didn't mean to wake you. Didn't know you cop types ever slept."

"Yeah, we're regular vampires."

He laughed. "Seriously, I figured you'd want to talk to me as soon as you could. I can't believe this has come up again. And call me Frank."

"You and me both, Frank." She reached over the back of her chair and pulled a yellow notepad from the phone desk, set it on the table in front of her. She stifled a yawn with the back of her hand.

"I'm ready. Shoot."

She racked the balls, taking shot after shot, trying to sort through the hour's worth of information Frank Richardson had given her.

He'd known about the signet ring.

He'd known about the hunks of hair ripped from the victims' heads.

He had theories about the killer, about why he'd stopped, that were incredibly sound, very credible.

He had his own speculations about who the killer might be. Most were similar in scope to the theories postulated by the homicide team. They ranged from a teacher at one of the girls' schools to a sexual predator who'd been killed in jail. All had been explored and ruled out.

But it was a word he'd used, an offhand remark, that kept coming back to Taylor. The moment she heard the term, she knew she wouldn't sleep again that night. Frank wasn't even talking about the case, he was recounting a moment in Caprese, the hometown of the painter and sculptor Michelangelo Buonarroti. Frank and his wife were touring the tightly winding streets and their guide spoke of a Florentine painter named Domenico Ghirlandaio, who worked with the young

Michelangelo before he turned to sculpture and the
eventual patronage of Lorenzo de' Medici. Michelangelo went on to greatness, but, for a time, he was a
novice, learning the ropes, his natural talent shaped by
the great men around him.

He was an apprentice.

Nine

"Can I get you another Corona, Jane?"

Jane Macias looked at the clear bottle, the lime shoved through the neck. Maybe another sip left. "Yes, please, Jerry."

"Sure thing, kid."

The bartender moved toward the cooler situated to his right, plunged his hand into the ice and pulled another beer free. He snapped the lid off and placed the bottle in front of Jane, then slipped a thinly cut lime wedge into the neck for her.

"Voilà."

"Who knew you were so worldly, Jerry? Thanks." She smiled warmly at the older man. He'd been nice to her, not prying, not hitting on her, just serving her beer and leaving her alone, which was what she wanted.

Jane went back to her book. There was something

horrifying about sitting alone in a bar reading, but she needed the break and the beer was half price tonight. Her roommate's gargantuan linebacker boyfriend had come over—a benchwarmer for the Tennessee Titans, and Jane knew there would be no rest in their cramped apartment tonight. So she'd grabbed a novel off the bookshelf and headed down here, two blocks and a lifetime away from her normal haunts.

She'd been slipping into the bar next door to the VIBE strip club more and more often lately. Called Control, it was quiet, usually empty, and there was something homey in the atmosphere. Granted, next door the music throbbed and the lights flashed while not-so-beautiful women slid up and down the stage in five-inch Lucite platforms, but hey, it could be worse. She could be the one up on the stage. Instead, Jane sat in the semi-darkness of the anonymous R-rated bar next door, feeling warm and fuzzy as she sipped cool beer and forced the noise from her mind. The clientele was good for the mental novel she was writing, anyway—she needed a fictional population and she certainly was exposed to it here.

Control gave her the added advantage of anonymity. People from work and from her apartment building wouldn't be likely to frequent this place. It was nice to know she could be alone. Though Jerry knew her first name, the place turned over so many times during the course of an evening that there were rarely faces present for an entire night. People peeked in after leaving VIBE next door to see if anything was hopping, but not a lot decided it was worth their time to stay. She should have found a nice coffee shop to hang out in; there was a Starbucks right around the corner, but Skip would find her there. He'd never in a million years venture anywhere near this bar, housed in the same building as the sin factory.

Skip Barber. Poor sap. A struggling songwriter, he followed Jane around Nashville thinking she was going to make it big time. When she professed the desire to just go to work, not land a recording contract, Skip thought she was kidding.

He'd seen her in a weak moment, down at Tootsie's, tipsy and singing karaoke like her life depended on it. Jane's voice was sweet and true, built for the microphone. She'd been told several times since she made her way to Nashville that she should pay her dues and become the next Julie Roberts or Faith Hill. Jane just smiled and nodded. She didn't want to be a singer, she wanted to be a writer. She had no desire to be on the stage, was more than content to have her words on the page, read by others. A singer? Hell, no. She was a writer. She aspired to a Pulitzer. She wanted to win a George Polk. She wanted to turn the world upside down with her insights.

She didn't care that the printed word was supposed to be dead. That the Internet had blown traditional journalism, that people went to their computers for news instead of the paper. That didn't matter. She could always find a way to present a story.

That's why she'd taken the job at the *Tennessean*. It used to be one of the last bastions of pure investigative journalism. *Tennessean* reporters Nat Caldwell and Gene Graham had won a Pulitzer, taking on the United Mine Workers. David Halberstram and Tom Wicker had worked there. John Seigenthaler had been the publisher for many years. They were great men to emulate.

But Skip, well, he wanted her to go for it, become a recording artist. Like hell she would. She kept telling him to go home, to leave her and his dreams for her alone, but Skip was still convinced he could change her mind. He'd write the words and she'd sing them. They'd go on to glory and fame. As if.

Her cell phone rang and she glanced at the LED display. God, it was him. Would he never take the hint? She ignored the call, not in the mood to deal with the man. She just wanted to read quietly, just for a couple more hours.

She'd just gotten lost in her book when a group of women blew into the joint, all smiles and flash. Bachelorette party from next door, Jane thought. On a Tuesday night, too. When did it become au courant for women to go to a strip club for a bachelorette party? Eyeing the room, the leader of the group, a tall, well-shaped brunette, spied three chairs free near Jane's hideout. Well, crap.

The three tipsy celebrants made their way over, weaving a bit. Obviously not their first stop of the evening. They fumbled to the stools and clambered in, shouting and whooping like they'd never been allowed out of doors before. The leader called for Jerry.

"'Scuse me, bartender? We need some drinks down here."

She turned and eyed Jane, her dark eyes cool. Jane could see the thought process. Competition? Nope. Jane was dismissed after a moment without a second glance. Good.

But they were loud and drunk, and Jane couldn't help but hear the conversation going on.

The middle woman, the bride, it looked like, was drunker than her friends. When Jerry attended the group, she leaned over the bar, fake tiara sliding off her strawberry-blond curls, and brayed, "Hey. Din't you used to be on *Gilligan's Island?*"

Her cadre cracked up, and Jerry, who *was* a bit of a ringer for Bob Denver, rolled his eyes good-naturedly.

"What can I get you ladies?"

The bridesmaid on the left, an anorexic bottle-blonde with roots showing, announced they would be having cosmopolitans.

They then broadcasted their presence to the nearly empty bar, the dark-haired bridesmaid doing the introductions.

"Yoo-hoo, y'all. I'm Coco, the redhead down there is Barbie, and this bee-utiful gorgeous creature in the middle here is Sierra. Sierra's getting married, y'all. Buy us a drink!" Separately, the names were all fun and unique. Coupled with this group, they seemed more like naughty burlesque pseudonyms, a compilation from the game "Get Your Porn Star Name"—matching your first pet's name to the first street you lived on. Jane wondered if they had normal last names, or something bizarrely exotic to match.

Jerry went to do their bidding and the women turned away from the bar, sighting on any available man in the premises. Jane looked over her shoulder; there were only two other patrons in the bar, one a lonely-looking older man who'd been staring into a glass of beer for the better part of an hour and a handsome, military type with a wedding band. Jane smiled. He seemed like a sweet kid. She figured his friends were all next door, and he was just being true to his bride.

An anemic surplus for the bridezillas to choose from. Maybe that would assure that they'd leave sooner rather than later.

But no. Unaffected by the lack of male companionship, the women were getting louder by the second. Jerry brought their drinks, which they slurped back, and immediately demanded seconds. Coco, Barbie and Sierra didn't seem to care that there weren't any real targets for their affections; they turned to each other, closer than regular girlfriends should be. The brunette brought out a pack of cigarettes shaped like penises, which bowled over the other two women. Bellowing laughs like water buffalo, soon all three were sucking down the smelly cigarettes. Noisy, smoky drunks. Not what Jane had signed up for tonight.

Jane got tired of sitting near them and moved, closer to the jarhead. He seemed to be minding his own business, maybe he'd leave her alone.

But the jarhead leaned in when she sat, a conspiratorial smile playing across his handsome features.

"Didn't know that when you built up enough seniority at the strip club, you get Tuesdays off, did you?"

"Ouch," Jane replied. "That's kind of harsh."

The man blushed and Jane felt bad. "Harsh, but funny. They're a trip. I hope I'm never so ridiculous in public when I decide to get married."

The man lit up. "You're not married?"

"No, hon, but you are." Jane looked pointedly at his gold band.

"Yeah, I am. Well, sort of. She left me. I just got home and found out."

"Home? From?"

"Oh, you know, I can't really talk about it." He colored slightly. "Sorry, it's just one of those things."

"Of course. I understand."

Jane dismissed him by sticking her nose back in her book. Maybe he'd leave. He was cute, but she didn't need another male situation. She already had Skip panting after her, though he didn't seem to get it. No career singing, no girlfriend to Skip. He just never truly believed.

"Troy."

Annoyed, Jane mentally marked her spot, again, and met his eyes. "Excuse me?"

"My name. It's Troy." The soldier was giving it one more go.

"Nice to meet you, Troy. Now, if you don't mind, I need to…"

"Sure, yeah, totally, I understand. Tell you what. Let me buy you a beer."

Jane frowned at her bottle. Gosh, it was almost gone. She must have been sipping while she watched the bachelorette train wreck. She looked back at the bar. Barbie, no, it was the bride-to-be Sierra, had started to loosen the ties to her halter top. She was trying to climb out of it and into warmer climes: Jerry the bartender's lap, as if she just realized that it was clearly an inappropriate outfit for the cold weather. Jane giggled out loud at the sheer ridiculousness of the situation.

"Sure, Troy, you can buy me a beer. But after that I need to get to get back to my studies." Studies. She nearly blushed. She was reading a bodice-ripper she'd snatched as she walked out the door; it was hardly keeping her attention.

"Great. I'll be back in a flash."

Jane watched as Troy went to Jerry, held up two fingers and turned back, leaning against the bar in a casual "I don't notice the three drunk and half-naked women crawling around on the bar next to me." He smiled at her, but the three women glommed onto him immediately, and Jane shook her head. It might take a few minutes for Troy to get her beer back to her.

Jane tried to smile back, but her head was getting foggy. Man, how many beers did she have? She remembered the two, but her head felt like she was bombed. Wow, her equilibrium was gone. A little voice inside her said get up and walk it off, but her body wasn't cooperating. She felt something clawlike and hard, a hand under her arm, saw a vague outline of a face, and realized the older guy had come to her rescue.

"Thanks, I've got it," she tried to say, but the words came out garbled, nonsensical.

There was a brief moment when she realized that this was no good, that she needed to yell out to Troy. He was big and strong and could fight off this creepy man with the wispy hair, help her break free, but the moment was lost and she swam away into the ether, feeling nothing.

Ten

Quantico, Virginia
Wednesday, December 17
8:00 a.m.

Charlotte Douglas stretched, arms over her head, her breasts pulling against the thin silk of her blouse. Three interns walking by her office lingered in the hallway, watching the show. She knew it, arched her back a little more and tossed out a high-pitched sigh. One of the interns groaned aloud, and his friends hustled him away. Charlotte relaxed and giggled. Boys. So easy to manipulate. They'd be hanging around for days, willing to do anything she might need. It helped to have gophers, especially handsome dark-haired runners from Ivy League schools. Mmm…

She'd called Baldwin's office, had a brief, nasty tête-à-tête with him. He dumped her into the lap of his acting director, who in turn touched base with the Nashville homicide office and set up an appointment with the head of Metro's Criminal Investigative Division,

Captain Mitchell Price. Everything was in place. She knew the Snow White Killer inside and out. And she knew she could catch him. It was just a matter of timing.

Charlotte had hung up the phone with a smile on her face and made another brief call. Within five minutes, Pietra Dunmore was standing in her doorway.

There was nothing about forensics that Pietra didn't know. She'd written or coauthored at least six books on the subject, lending her expertise to universities and training seminars all over the country. She was the preeminent forensic scientist on the BSU staff, and didn't care who knew it. The diminutive Pietra stood only five feet tall, but was a giant in all other respects. Charlotte had a level of admiration for the woman, and knew that because Pietra was black, they would rarely be competing for the same pool of men. Pietra didn't do white guys, and Charlotte didn't go black. Simple.

"What can I do for you, Charlotte?"

"We're heading down South."

"For what?"

"I need you to present some findings on the Snow White Killer case. I've e-mailed you the details."

Despite Charlotte's dramatic presentation, Pietra wasn't rattled. "Old or new?"

Charlotte had given the woman a broad smile. "Both. We have some fascinating new information to share."

Now Pietra stood in her doorway, her briefcase in her hand. It was time to go. Time to make her mark. Time.

Eleven

Taylor pulled off Highway 70 into the parking lot of the Belle Meade Galleria, a strip of high-end stores in the heart of Belle Meade. Luck was with her—she found a spot near the door of the restaurant. Le Peep was a neighborhood favorite, an eclectic breakfast and lunch place that attracted many of the denizens of the local community. Even on a freezing Wednesday morning, the place was nearly full. Taylor spotted Frank Richardson sitting at a table in the rear of the restaurant, happily munching on eggs and toast and plowing through a liter of hot coffee.

She joined him, shrugging out of her shearling jacket. The waitress came by and she asked for a Diet Coke, toast and fruit. The late night, coupled with no sleep and a gnawing in her stomach, meant she'd be better off without the jarring caffeine rush of coffee and a full breakfast. No more iron-clad stomach for her. As she'd gotten into her thirties, she'd been keeping all her stress in her gut. It was just easier to avoid the causes that made things worse.

Frank Richardson hadn't missed a beat, continuing his forceful eating frenzy as she got settled. He dipped his toast into a sunny-side-up egg, practically groaning with pleasure.

Taylor watched him chew and swallow with gusto, entranced by the shine of grease on his lower lip. The sight made her already unsettled stomach turn, and she looked away briefly. He wiped his mouth and gave a tiny, delicate belch.

"The Europeans just don't know how to do eggs, you know? They try their damnedest to make 'em like you want, but there's just something missing. Maybe American chickens lay better eggs than the French. I don't know."

"Well, my fiancé and I are supposed to go to Europe soon, so I'll keep that in mind, do some testing myself. See if the Italians are better at eggs than the French."

Richardson looked at her left hand wryly. "You're getting married and heading to Italy for your honeymoon?"

Taylor nodded, and he gave her a genuine smile. "Lucky girl. When?"

"Supposed to go on Sunday. At this rate, I don't think we're going to be able to pull it off."

"Yeah, I know what you mean. Missed my eldest daughter's birth when Martin Luther King got hit. Had to leave right from the hospital, my wife having contractions every two minutes but breathing fire down my neck to go, to get the story. She's a mighty fine woman, to send me off for my career when I should've been there, helpin' her."

"She sounds amazing. You got the story, of course." Taylor knew he had, of course he had. He'd won numerous journalism awards for his coverage of the civil rights leader's assassination.

"I did at that." His blue eyes twinkled, and Taylor couldn't help but smile. Robust and full of life, that's how she would describe Frank Richardson.

Her food arrived and she nibbled at the toast, followed it up with some grapes and cantaloupe. Even in winter, there were summer's touches all around, and she longed for a warm breeze.

Richardson finished mopping up one last bit of egg with his toast, shoveled two bites of biscuit in his mouth, then pushed his plate away.

"Okay," he mumbled, a few bits of dough spraying onto the table. "You ready to do this?"

Taylor pushed her plate back, as well. "Yes."

She followed him, silently offering a ten to cover her part of the meal, but he shooed it away, paid at the counter in the front of the restaurant. They walked into the milky sunlight, not needing to shade their eyes.

"I'll see you there," Taylor said, and Richardson nodded. Good humor was gone. They were preparing to delve into the Snow White murders, feel the slippery, viscous blood, bear witness to the knife wounds, taste the scent of carnage on the backs of their tongues.

Frank Richardson had masterfully documented the reign of terror the Snow White Killer induced, and going through his old files would bring those ten murders to life in a way the dry tomes of the police reports and murder books couldn't, wouldn't. Richardson was the writer, not the homicide team. His words were stronger than pictures.

Taylor started up the 4Runner, suddenly weary. She could have done this herself, or assigned one of the homicide team to do it. But something in her wanted the company, the close quarters of another soul who understood. Journalists and cops, the best of friends, the worst of enemies.

Plus, Baldwin was bringing the illustrious Charlotte Douglas to the homicide offices at some point this morning, and Taylor really wasn't in the mood for it, not right now. She'd never met Charlotte, but knew plenty of women who fit the bill. A viper, that's what Baldwin had called her. If it were the truth, there'd be plenty of fireworks to deal with at lunchtime, thank you very much.

On the phone with Richardson the previous evening, Taylor had suggested they just go to the library, pull the information up on LexisNexis. That's what she would have done, that or hit the microfiche machine. But Richardson had offered to take her directly to the source. To use the paper's morgue would assure them a thorough look through all of the files, all the stories that had gone into print. Richardson had slyly pointed out that the newspaper also had copies of his complete stories, the prepublication drafts that had been edited down for space and public consumption.

Richardson had retired a few years back, an illustrious career behind him. Taylor figured he wanted to visit his old home away from home. All hail the conquering hero. She couldn't deny the man that small joy.

Actually, she understood. If she ever left Metro, she knew she'd no longer be complete.

The trip down West End wasn't long enough, and before she realized it, they were pulling in to 1100 Broadway, home of the *Tennessean.*

They took two spaces in the tiny parking lot in front of the building. They entered through the glass doors, Richardson all smiles, slapping the security guard on the back. Outside those doors, out on the street, Richardson was just another slightly overweight graybeard, finishing out his retired years in relative peace and quiet. Here, he was a rock star.

A brief call was made and three minutes later, the newly appointed managing editor of the newspaper rushed down from the third floor to say hello to his old friend. Introductions were made, the editor looking Taylor up and down before carefully nodding and welcoming her to the paper. He knew there was friction between Taylor's group and some of the crime reporters on the beat. When she didn't raise the issue, he smiled. Time and place, and all that.

As they made their way to the newsroom, Taylor's hand was shaken no less than forty times by people who'd heard Frank Richardson was in the building and wanted to say hello. It was only polite that they acknowledge their homicide lieutenant, as well, the woman who'd told the former lead crime reporter Lee Mayfield to go fuck herself on more than one occasion. The *Tennessean* staff hadn't liked Lee any more than Taylor and the rest of Metro.

Taylor's cell phone rang and she hung back for a moment to answer it. Seeing the number, her heart filled with dread, goose bumps prickled along her arms. She flipped the phone open, held it to her ear.

"Morning, Lincoln. Everything okay?"

"Morning, LT. How'd you know?"

"Who is it?"

"No body or anything like that. There's a missing-persons report. Girl named Jane Macias." Taylor cringed, thought about her earlier Janesicle Doe. Oh, the flippant moniker was coming to bite her in the ass.

"Fits the profile of these girls?"

"Yeah. Her boyfriend called it in, said she left her apartment last night and she's been MIA ever since. He's totally freaking out, says she's got long black hair. I figured there's no sense taking any chances, went ahead and started some of the paperwork."

"Maybe, just maybe, it's not him. And if it is, maybe we can beat him to the punch this time. I'll be over there shortly. Thanks."

She hung up, leaned back against the wall for a minute, caught her breath. Fast moves, this guy. She opened her phone again, made a quick call to Baldwin. His voice mail clicked on. She left a message for him to call her ASAP, or meet her at the homicide office as quickly as he could. No time to worry about lost or past loves. Lincoln wasn't prone to hysterical fits; if he thought the description of the missing girl matched that of their profile victim, she did. So they needed to move quickly.

She strode through the newsroom, made her way to the back of the offices. Richardson was there, chatting it up with one of the archival interns. She caught his eyes, signaled for him to step away. He did and turned to her, concern filling his eyes.

"What's wrong?"

Taylor pitched her voice low; the intern was craning her neck, trying to hear what was up. "One of my detectives just called. There's been a missing-persons report, a girl who matches the victim description. I need to go, follow it up. Can we get together later, talk about all this?"

Richardson had the audacity to look crestfallen for a brief moment, then brightened as if he realized how ludicrous that was. "Of course, of course. I understand completely. Is there anything I can do? Do you need someone from here to help?"

"No, I'm sure we can get it covered. But I need to head back to the homicide offices, see what I can find out. With any luck, it's just some girl with black hair who didn't come home last night."

"Eooop!"

Taylor jumped at the sound, a cross between a hiccup and a deep breath. She looked over Richardson's shoulder to see the archivist, standing with her hand over her mouth. The girl wore a starched white shirt, long black skirt, thick black wool stockings and loafers. Her hair was pulled back with a headband, and her glasses, a nifty modern frame, were askew on her nose. She was white as a sheet.

They rushed to the girl's side, ready to perform any services needed.

"What's the matter? Are you choking? Is everything okay?"

Her eyes started to tear, and she dropped her hand to her side, looking alone in the world. She crumpled, leaned back heavily against her desk. "My roommate has black hair, and she didn't come home last night. I mean, I never saw her after she left."

Taylor stood straighter. "What's your roommate's name?"

"Jane. Jane Macias. She's a reporter here, works right out there in the newsroom. Oh my God, is she dead? Oh my *God!*" She started to fling her arms about, and Taylor grabbed her, held her still.

"Whoa, whoa, whoa, whoa, calm down." Taylor talked to her softly, almost under her breath. "Calm down. It's okay. You're going to be fine."

She caught Frank Richardson's eye, and saw he was thinking the same thing she was.

But your friend might not.

Twelve

He took a long drag on the cigar, blowing the smoke in a blue puff directly at the ceiling. His doctors would heartily disapprove if they knew he was smoking again. He didn't care. Life was too short. He spun the cigar in the cut-crystal ashtray, grateful for the hard edge, which made it easier to knock the burning ash off the tightly rolled tobacco leaf.

He flipped the paper open, overcome with emotion when he saw the headline.

Snow White Killer Resurfaces, Kills 4th
No Leads in Bicentennial Mall Murder

Oh, the beauty of it, the pure, exquisite joy. To see that name again, to know the fear that beat just below the surface of every heart that read those words. *Snow White Killer*. Oh, the boy was doing well, so very well.

The article captured the frisson of fear that was sweeping through Nashville. The previous generation was talking of nothing else. The younger were fed by rumor and innuendo, the vivid fear of their parents making them lock their doors and keep their own youngsters under a watchful eye. The whisper campaign was out in full force. The Snow White Killer had truly reappeared after a twenty-year hiatus; the entire city was in a panic.

And he was the cause of it. Just as he was in the past.

Granted, his hands were gnarled with arthritis; he may never have the strength again to wield the knife at the throats of innocents, but his protégé was so good at sharing the most intimate moments of the kill that he almost didn't have to be there. Of course, watching, holding, painfully touching their tender flesh made it so much the better.

The old feelings rumbled through his belly, taking root in his aching loins. He was too crippled to pleasure himself anymore. He licked his lips and rang the bell.

The door to his study opened, and a man in his midthirties stuck his head through the door.

"Yesh, Father?"

He looked at his spawn, the watery blue eyes, the weak chin. That boy was going to be the death of him.

"Come in here, and stop that lisping!" he roared.

Obediently, the son made his way into the room, coming to stand at the foot of his father's chair. Snow White gazed upon his progeny, his stomach curdling. The boy was a freak—wide, pouting lips, the bottom thick as a finger, so loose as to look like red rubber. His chin tucked neatly into his neck, sloped from bottom lip to clavicle with almost no indentation or marking indicating there was a jawline to prop up his face. His eyes were slanted down and the irises cloudy. He'd been sightless since the age of three, couldn't see the wreck his own father had become.

"Yess, Father," he said again, calmly. A long sibilance replaced the lisp, the boy's best attempt to work within the confines of his deformity. He stood tall, his shoulders back, ready to accept whatever his father could give—be it love or hate.

Snow White was both sickened and proud. It had taken years of work for the child to lose that lisp, though if he hurried his speech it came back with a vengeance. His mood softened when he saw the boy try. He noticed a silver object in his hand and the emotions mixed again.

"You've been practicing again, I see." That fucking flute. Fit so perfectly under that fleshy lip, replacing the chin that wasn't there with silver.

"Yess, ssir. I wass hoping to try out thiss year."

"You know you can't do that. You'll have to content yourself to playing for the cardinals in the backyard. The symphony doesn't take blind musicians."

"Beethoven wass deaf. They let him work."

"Now, now, don't sulk. Take your flute and go. Send along Marcia, tell her I'm ready." He dismissed him with a wave of the hand, something the boy couldn't see but could sense. He left the room, leaving Snow White alone with his thoughts.

Thirteen

Taylor headed to the Criminal Justice Center and brought the *Tennessean* archivist with her. She'd succumbed to shock, and sat woodenly in the truck next to Taylor, unspeaking. A faint shiver ran through her body on a continuous loop, starting at her head, making its way to her toes and starting over again. Taylor knew it wasn't from the cold.

"Daphne," she said softly, not wanting to startle the girl.

Luminous brown eyes turned to Taylor, full of emptiness. As her head turned, the nonglare-treated lenses of her glasses briefly purpled as the light from the snow glanced off them.

"Daphne," Taylor repeated. "It's going to be okay. Just stay with me, all right?"

"It's my fault," the girl muttered.

"What do you mean, it's your fault?"

"Jane was mad. My boyfriend was over on a 'school night.'" She made little quote signs with her fingers.

"So she left?"

They were getting close to the CJC, but Taylor

wanted a few more minutes alone with Daphne. She continued straight on Broadway, taking the long way through the strip, turning on Second Avenue to worm their way up through the clubs and nightspots. Despite the detour, they'd nearly reached the CJC when Daphne spoke again.

"She left. Grabbed one of my books off the shelf and took off in a huff. I didn't mean for this to happen. I'm so sorry. I should have called the police when she didn't come home. I just figured she was pissed off, decided to stay over at Skip's or something."

Taylor's radar went off. "Skip?"

Daphne rolled her eyes and waved her hand in the air simultaneously. "He's this guy who's been mooning around after her since she moved to town. She went on a couple of dates with him back in the summer, but they're just friends. He bugs her."

"Do you know how to get a hold of him, Daphne?"

She turned sharply, staring at Taylor. "You think Skip did this?"

"I want to talk to him, that's all. Hopefully, there's nothing wrong. Your roommate just spent the night elsewhere. But if you have a way I can contact him, that would be very helpful."

Daphne bent her head, tears dripping off her sharp chin. "Jane has his number in her cell phone. I don't know it."

"Okay. That's okay. Don't cry. We'll figure it out." Taylor pulled into a parking spot in the lot behind headquarters. They got out of the truck. Taylor marched the girl around the side of the building, up the back stairwell and through the door. It was stiflingly warm in the hallway, and barely better in the homicide offices.

Taylor got the weepy Daphne seated in her office, then made a quick run to the Ladies'. After splashing her face with water and brushing out her hair, she felt a little more human. She realized she hadn't thought of the wedding for hours, and smiled.

Her boots made a clopping noise on the linoleum, a singsong beat that got stuck in her head, ca-chun, ca-chun. Snapping her fingers in time, she stepped into the homicide office and ran into a wall.

A female wall, to be exact. Taylor stumbled back in surprise. The doorway was blocked by a tall redheaded woman balanced with an arm slung across the opening, as if she knew whoever wanted into the room would have to get through her first.

The blow moved the redhead forward three or four inches. She whipped around with a sneer, then saw who was trying to get in the room. The sneer morphed into a semblance of a smile.

"You must be Taylor Jackson. I'm Dr. Charlotte Douglas, FBI." Charlotte stuck out a hand and Taylor accepted it. They eyed each other coolly. Charlotte made no move to get out of Taylor's way. Taylor dropped her hand and cleared her throat; Charlotte continued to appraise her frankly.

"Excuse me," she said finally.

"Oh, sorry, silly me. Whatever was I thinking? I didn't mean to be in your way, Lieutenant." She didn't move.

There was the slightest bit of mockery in Charlotte's tone, and Taylor narrowed her eyes in response.

A deep voice grumbled past Charlotte's body check. "Knock it off, Charlotte."

Charlotte's eyes flashed and she stepped out of the

doorway just far enough for Taylor to stride through, shooting daggers at Baldwin, who was sitting at the desk just outside her office. He jumped to his feet, reached to stop Taylor, but she was past him in an instant. At the threshold to her office, she stopped and turned.

"Miss Douglas, it's—"

"Doctor." The cold, imperious tone was meant to intimidate, but all it did was annoy Taylor further.

"Fine. Dr. Douglas. I'll be with you shortly. I've had a development that I need to tend to immediately. Please, make yourself at home."

She turned to Baldwin. "Could I see you for a moment?"

She heard Charlotte giggle as Baldwin stepped into the office and shut the door behind them.

Baldwin started to talk, but Taylor cut him off.

"I don't have time for foreplay right now. I assume you just got here?"

"Two minutes ago, and it's already been a long half hour since I picked her up. The sooner we can get her presentation, the sooner we can get her out of town." He ran a hand wearily through his hair, making the ends stand up like porcupine quills.

"Okay. We have a development." There was a quiet whimper from Taylor's chair, and she waved a hand at the girl. "This is Daphne Beauchamp. Her roommate, Jane Macias, has gone missing, and she fits our profile."

Daphne had become a small, unkempt girl in the few moments that Taylor had known her. Sitting at Taylor's desk, she exuded none of the edgy savoir faire she'd given off at the paper.

"Daphne, this is Dr. John Baldwin. He's a profiler

with the FBI. He's working with us on the Snow White cases. I'd like him to hear a little about Jane. Could you share some of what you've already told me?"

Daphne sat up a little straighter, visibly pulling herself together. "Sure, of course. I mean, I don't know how much to tell. Jane's a great girl. Really smart, going places, you know? She wants to be an investigative journalist, the old-school, hard-nose type. Wants to bring down administrations and change the course of humanity."

Taylor watched the girl speak. "Those are pretty tall orders. Does she have what it takes?"

"Yes, she does. She's brilliant, can write like the wind. I'd...well, I admire her. She's got what it takes to make something in this industry. Went to the J School at Columbia, that's as good as it gets. Wrote for the paper there, had some freelance jobs for the *Times*... she's a sharp cookie." Daphne fiddled with a pencil she found on Taylor's desk, *tappity, tappity, tap.*

"So why is she working here? If she was that talented, couldn't she get hired onto one of the big papers?"

"No, no, that was her choice. She decided to take a year and get out of New York, see if it didn't broaden her horizons. She chose Nashville because she's got some god-awful crush on John Siegenthaler." *Tappity, tappity, tap.*

"Siegenthaler Senior? Isn't he a little old for her tastes?" Taylor reached over the desk and took the pencil.

Daphne stared at her for a moment, then broke into the first smile Taylor had seen from the girl.

"No, no, not in a sexual way. His mind. She finds him intellectually stimulating, wanted to walk in his footsteps for a bit. Of course, the *Tennessean* isn't the investigative powerhouse it used to be, we all know that."

Taylor shot Baldwin a look, put the pencil back in its holder. He took the hint, continued with the questions.

"Jane is from New York?"

"Yes. She's such a city girl, too. Really kind of funny, the way she reacts to all the Southernisms around here. She's got this nasally accent, not a hard, brassy one, just definitely uptown. When she orders food she gets all kinds of looks."

Ah, good, Taylor thought. Something like that would make her stand out, and someone might remember when they saw her last.

"Where would she have gone last night, Daphne? You said she wanted to get out of the house because your boyfriend was over. Did she usually leave when he stopped by?"

"Yeah. She thinks Zac is some kind of idiot because he plays football. He isn't, but she just turns up her nose. She's like that—has the literati attitude. Like just because she can manipulate words, she's smarter than everyone. She was actually having kind of a difficult time here. She pissed off a few people at the paper with her attitude. I mean, yeah, she's brilliant, but sometimes you don't need everyone in the room to know just how brilliant you are."

Taylor leaned back against the door and crossed her arms. "Who did she piss off?"

Daphne laughed softly.

"Who didn't she piss off? She just grates some people the wrong way—it's the Yankee in her. She doesn't see the need for subtlety that often, and you know how it is here. People bristle when you put on airs. Not that she was so bad, but any time you get a young, pretty little thing mouthing off, it's going to cause problems."

"Any idea where she might have headed when she left the house last night?"

"No. I mean, she'd go to Starbucks sometimes, hang out there with her laptop. But she left it at home last night, just took some book and jammed, obviously pissed at me. I wasn't really worried about it, that's just how she gets sometimes. Likes to have a quiet environment, and Zac's a little rowdy sometimes. Especially during the season, he can get temperamental. But since the Titans put him on injured reserve, he's been kinda down. We were planning on having a couple of drinks and hanging out, watch a movie or something. Nothing terribly loud. She didn't really have to go. I think she was just in a mood."

"She a big drinker?"

"Naw, not too bad. She'll have a few beers at a bar, or some wine, but she's not into the hard stuff. She's a little goody-goody like that. Total lightweight."

"Does she talk to home often?"

Daphne shook her head. "Not that I know of. She isn't close to her family, she did tell me that. I think her dad is dead. Jane has only ever talked about him in the past tense. She had a picture of him in her room a while ago, but I haven't seen it lately. Her mom must have remarried—she left a message for Jane once and her last name was different. It's not a topic she's ever been open about, you know? I don't think we've ever gone in-depth about her background."

"That's a little strange for roommates, isn't it?"

"Naw. We met through Craig's List. I needed a room-mate fast, so we didn't know each other at all when she moved in. We've only been in that apartment since September, and we can go days without seeing each other. We don't hang out or anything. Just aren't all that close."

"Okay, Daphne. I'm going to have a uniform take you back to your apartment. After you gather some things for me, he can take you back to work if you'd like. I'd like you to give the officer her date book, if you can find it, and any pictures you might have. You said her laptop was still there? Give that to him, too."

"It's password protected. You'll never get in."

Taylor smiled at her. "We're actually pretty good with that kind of stuff, Daphne."

"Jane wouldn't like that, though. She's really proprietary about her stuff."

"You let us deal with that, okay? We'll take full responsibility. If you hear anything from her, I want you to call me, okay? I'm sure this is all going to work out."

"No, it won't. This creep, he does bad things to women. He doesn't let them go once he has them." She teared up, and Taylor laid a hand on her shoulder.

"You're making assumptions. You spend all day with journalists, you know better. Let us look into this. Everything is going to be fine."

I hope, Taylor thought. *I hope.*

Taylor arranged for the girl to be taken home, watching Baldwin stalk her office. Two steps, turn, two steps, turn. There wasn't enough room to pace; he looked more like a caged circus lion in a too-small pen.

"What's wrong?"

He looked over his shoulder at her, a lopsided smile on his face. "What isn't wrong?"

"Getting a bit melodramatic, aren't you?"

"Oh, come on, Taylor. This is supposed to be a great week, and here we are, chasing another madman. We've got the queen bitch out there waiting to drop some sort of bombshell, a possible missing person, and I just want to get on a plane Sunday morning and spend three weeks drinking wine, eating carbonara and fucking you silly."

"Hmm. That doesn't sound so bad when you put it that way."

He stopped and turned to her. "You ready to face the ice princess?"

"Baldwin, Charlotte Douglas doesn't scare me, 'doctor' or not. I can handle myself, thank you very much. Let's get it over with."

As she walked to the door and opened it, she heard Baldwin mutter, "Nothing scares you."

Man, she wished that were the truth.

Charlotte Douglas was right where Taylor had left her fifteen minutes earlier, batting her eyelashes at Marcus and Fitz. Lincoln had retreated to his desk, and Taylor gave him mental brownie points for not falling for the act. She hated women like Charlotte, women who thought the only power they had resided between their legs. Taylor knew where her power was—between her ears and strapped to her hip. She'd never felt simpering a necessity to elicit a response from the opposite sex.

Taylor cleared her throat, and Charlotte stopped mid-sentence and turned. Taylor looked her up and down—an expensive woman. Finely tailored tweed jacket, a pencil skirt, brown calfskin boots—the outfit probably cost more than Taylor's truck payment. Her auburn hair was swept into a chignon, her makeup artfully applied. Yep, this was one high-maintenance chick. Beautiful, if you liked the cold, pale look. Taylor didn't.

"Dr. Douglas, we can go into the conference room for your presentation now."

Charlotte's eyes were bright. "He took another one?"

"We have nothing to indicate that, Dr. Douglas. Now, if we could just get to your presentation, I'd like to know what's so exciting that you felt the need to fly down here to share it with us. After you."

I'll be damned if I'm going to discuss my case with you, you bitch, Taylor told her with her eyes.

Fuck you, too, Charlotte's empty gaze said back.

Ah, detente.

Left with no choice, Charlotte tossed her head and walked out of the room. Taylor, Baldwin and the rest of the team followed her, a pied piper line of cops. They went the short distance to the conference room. A young woman was already there, cocoa-brown skin glowing in the glare from a PowerPoint slide. The presentation was ready to go.

Charlotte took a seat at the head of the table. "This is Dr. Pietra Dunmore. She's the lead forensic investigator for this case and will be presenting her findings on the DNA samples you sent. Pietra, we're ready for you now."

Dismissive bitch, Taylor thought. She'd rather die than use that tone with a subordinate. But the woman didn't seem to notice. Either that, or she didn't care.

The rest of the team took their seats. Taylor saw the tech slide her honey-brown eyes over Lincoln as he sat down, and Taylor could have sworn he blushed. Good grief, she'd have to pass out keys to the locker room for cold showers after these two women left.

"Excuse me, Charlotte." Taylor went to the young tech, extended a hand. "I'm Taylor Jackson. Thank you for coming all this way to present your findings. We're grateful for your time."

Taylor couldn't read the thoughts behind those spectacular chocolate eyes, but Pietra nodded as she shook Taylor's hand. Okay, good. Maybe there was something to be gained from this dog-and-pony show after all.

"Have you met our team?"

Pietra opened her mouth to speak, but Charlotte cut her off. "This isn't a sorority meeting, Lieutenant. We don't need to play the key game. Let's get on with it."

Pietra's face closed again, and she went to the head of the room, retrieving a remote control from her bag and stopping by the screen.

I'll be damned, Taylor thought. "Pietra, this is Lincoln Ross, Marcus Wade and Pete Fitzgerald. You know Dr. Baldwin?"

Pietra smiled and nodded all around.

"Good. Now, if you would please present your findings?" Taylor looked to the screen, ignoring the eyes that bored a hole in her head.

The FBI seal glared at them in all its golden glory. Pietra clicked a button, and Taylor felt like she was in a time warp. The montage of faces floated from the screen just like when she was being interviewed last Monday night. She wondered briefly if the FBI had prepared the slides for the news show, too. She'd been asked to appear again this evening, a request she'd refused. There was no sense going on the news when she had nothing new to say except another girl had died. She had no new information on Giselle St. Claire that could be released. By nine o'clock tonight, word would have spread about Jane Macias, if she hadn't been found. What was she supposed to do, get waylaid and speculate that a new victim had been taken? No, thanks.

After ten minutes of rehash, they finally got into the meat of the presentation. Charlotte stood up, walked to the front of the room and took the remote from Pietra. "That's fine, Pietra. Thank you. I'll take it from here."

Taylor caught Baldwin's eye and raised her eyebrows. He rolled his eyes in agreement. Charlotte Douglas was living up to her reputation as a real piece of work.

She clicked the button and a white slide appeared, broken into two screens. Taylor recognized the blue-and-white levels as a DNA profile.

"The DNA of your current perpetrator does not match the DNA profile of the Snow White Killer."

Well, big shock there, Taylor thought. *We knew it was a copycat.*

"After extensive testing, there is nothing to indicate that the current killer is even remotely related to the Snow White Killer. Speculations that this might be the work of a son or a brother, can be put to rest."

Who the hell was speculating that they were related? Taylor wondered. No one on her team had been pursuing that line of thinking.

A new slide came up on the screen. It was a map of the United States, with red dots in four areas—Los Angeles, Denver, Minneapolis and New York City. Taylor leaned in. What the hell?

"As you see here, we have several clusters identified.

Within each cluster, there was a series of murders. At each scene, DNA evidence was collected."

Taylor felt her heart beat just a touch faster. This time, when she caught Baldwin's eye, she saw only concern.

"The DNA profiles from each of these crime scenes are a positive match. The same man committed the murders in each of these regional areas. The killer has not been caught, the cases remain unsolved."

As she talked, Charlotte moved the slides forward, each one detailing the murders in each location. There were a total of four in Los Angeles, six in Denver, five in Minneapolis and three in New York City. Eighteen confirmed kills over the past eighteen months. Taylor realized what was coming next and cringed. Holy shit.

A slide with a map of Nashville came up, with four red points glaring at her like eyes from hell.

"These four murders in Nashville have been directly connected to the other eighteen. You don't just have a copycat on your hands, you have an obscenely prolific serial killer with victims in five states. The CODIS results are definitive. His pattern is undeniable. It is quite likely that he will move on to another state and kill more young women if you don't stop him here in Nashville."

A hush had fallen over the room. Charlotte met each eye in turn, stopping with Taylor. *I win,* her look said. Taylor wondered just how cavalier the woman could be, and why she'd held back the information for so long. There was no reason to hold out over this; they needed to work together. There was another agenda here— Taylor was sure of it.

Marcus Wade was the first to speak. "Are there any

indications from the earlier murders that he's copying previous killers' MOs?"

The PowerPoint screen went dark.

"Very good, Detective," Charlotte purred. "Gold star for you."

Fourteen

Taylor pulled down her ponytail, ran her hands roughly through her hair and pulled it back up, winding the rubber band around the ponytail three times. It was nearly midnight, she was starving, thirsty and tired. She picked up her Diet Coke can and shook it, willing the empty metal to fill of its own accord and save her yet another trip to the soda machine.

Once the power play was over in the conference room, Charlotte Douglas had proved herself a decent profiler. Her bombshell had floored them all. Five cities, five copycat murder scenarios. But only one copycat. An imitator extraordinaire.

In Los Angeles, he'd copied the Santa Ana Killer from the midfifties, an egregious maniac who dismembered the bodies of the women he killed and left them in the desert. In Denver, it was the LoDo, the Lower Denver Killer, who took prostitutes' lives by strangulation and left them, posed, on street corners. Minneapolis was a dead ringer for the Classifieds Killer of the 1970s, a twisted older man who picked his victims by placing ads in the *Star Tribune* for temporary secre-tarial work. New York City was a variation on the Prospect Lake Killer, who strangled his victims and dumped their bodies into Prospect Lake Park on Long Island. Killer, Killer, Killer, Killer, Killer. By five o'clock, Taylor was contemplating buying the media a thesaurus. The press was terrible at coming up with creative names, and she had to admit, the FBI wasn't much better.

There was one big difference between the previous copycat murders and the Snow White case. All of the other original killers had been caught and jailed. Two had been put to death.

That term popped into Taylor's head again, though she knew it wasn't entirely applicable to all of the cases. An apprentice. A student of murder. And he'd saved his greatest imitation for a murderer who'd never been caught. A thought niggled at the back of her mind. If he was so intimately familiar with the Nashville murders, did he know the identity of Snow White? She made a note of the thought, wrote one more thing next to it. Signet ring.

The ring had disappeared from the evidence files. If it showed up at a murder scene, that would be interesting.

They'd spent the afternoon going through the files, trying to put the pieces together. The DNA matched all the scenes but didn't match anything else in the system, which meant he hadn't been arrested anytime in the past three years. His DNA would have been entered into the system automatically if he'd been taken into custody. It didn't mean he hadn't been picked up somewhere else, just that the technology was behind the game. He could have something sitting in the files waiting to be inputted in any number of states, Tennessee included, and he would be right there for the taking. Instead, they had precious little to go on.

Taylor's head was starting to swim. There was no sign of Jane Macias. If she had been taken, she would be victim number five. If the copycat followed the original Snow White's pattern, there'd be five more to go.

The additional eighteen murders being attributed to Nashville's killer was too big to keep contained; the leaks began immediately. Mitchell Price and Dan Franklin were trying to handle the media, but sticking solely to the Snow White's Nashville murders. They deflected question after question to the FBI, letting them answer just how this massive killing spree had gone unnoticed. Granted, some of the original murders had happened in the fifties, sixties and seventies, and while each city knew they'd been dealing with a kook, for some reason everyone, including the FBI, had missed it until Charlotte Douglas's eyes got on the files. It was one of those proud days for law enforcement.

Taylor started when the door to the conference room opened. She realized that she had drifted off to sleep, only for a moment, but still… She sat up, wiped a hand across her mouth and saw Baldwin staring at her.

"You're beautiful," he said.

"You need some sleep," she replied. "How's Charlotte?" She held up a hand. "Excuse me. *Dr.* Douglas." Taylor drew out the syllables, mimicking Charlotte's haughty lockjaw accent perfectly.

Baldwin half smiled. "At the hotel, drinking cosmopolitans in the bar with a bevy of songwriters at her feet. Some band is staying there. She's completely in her element."

Taylor thought for a moment. Who was playing this week? She knew it was someone big…. "Please tell me it's not Aerosmith."

"Skinny guy, big mouth, funky scarf. That's all I saw."

"Jesus. How in the name of God did you get hooked up with that woman?"

Baldwin took a seat at the conference table, scratched at his forehead like he could erase the memory. "We were working a case. Late night, too much to drink— hell, you don't want to hear this. It was over before it started. She scares me. Not a decent bone in her body."

"Well, she wasn't shy about the fact that she'd enjoy your bone in her body anytime you'd see fit. Stay away from her."

Baldwin smiled. "Is that an order, Lieutenant?"

Taylor got up and went to him, plopped down in his lap and put her arms around his neck. "Yeah. 'Cause you and I have a date in a couple of days, and I don't want her fucking it up. Got it?"

He nuzzled her hair. "Got it, sugar. Besides, you know you're the only woman for me. I was lost that first day I saw you, sitting at your desk, up to your ears in reports and Diet Coke."

She had the image from that moment seared into her brain. "Well, I didn't think you were too bad yourself." She kissed him lightly, then sighed. "I don't know how much more we can do here tonight. I'm tired and hungry and cranky. Want to cut out and grab something to eat?"

"Absolutely."

They gathered their coats and shut the lights off to

her office. Baldwin held her hand as they walked out to the parking lot, the bitter cold making her nose run.

"What are you in the mood for?" he asked. "Barbecue? We could swing into Rippy's."

The thought of fighting the crowds didn't appeal to her. Rippy's was legendary, on the corner of Broadway and Fifth, a regular honky-tonk with a view of Nashville's touristy party life and the best pulled pork in the city. It was a happy, crowded bar with live music and a devil-may-care attitude.

"No, I want something more quiet. How about Radius 10?"

"Oh, good choice. They changed the wine list last month. Let's go see what they did with it."

Baldwin drove, and Taylor watched life pass her by outside the window. Even at this late hour, people jammed the streets. Second Avenue was populated with gangbangers and reckless high schoolers trying to get into the bars with fake IDs. The old staples were gone from the strip now. Her favorite late-night haunt, Mere Bulles, had pulled up stakes and moved to a much more serene location in Brentwood, twenty minutes south of town. Instead, pop and techno music blared into the night; all-hours clubs had forced Metro to maintain a presence. She was sad to see it so lost, so different from what she'd grown up with.

Baldwin turned onto Broadway and they passed through Lower Broad, the country joints and honky-tonks packed with strange faces striving to see one they recognized. The songwriters hung out here—people who couldn't make their own records but wrote for the more famous musicians, the session players who did the

music on spec for submissions, all crowded the bars of
Lower Broad, plying their wares.

They turned at Union Station, swung by the Flying
Saucer taproom, then turned left onto McGavock,
stopping in front of the valet at Radius 10. Baldwin
tossed him the keys and they retreated from the noise
and craziness of the city into a cool, modern space with
exposed beams and an L.A. aesthetic. A very nouveau-
Nashville restaurant.

Nashville had gotten schizophrenic over the past de-
cades. The reputation as Little Atlanta was well de-
served—while the country music scene still ran the
show, there were many more avenues for pleasure. The
stunning Schermerhorn Symphony Hall and the First
Art Center drew a more refined crowd downtown, and
esoteric restaurants and sophisticated bars had opened
to provide succor to the cultivated set. Taylor liked these
places; they were a retreat, a way to get away from her
sometimes mundane world.

They ate well—pan-seared grouper for Taylor, osso
buco for Baldwin—and shared a bottle of Shiraz. Sated,
they leaned back in the chairs and talked in low voices
about the case.

"I'm worried sick for Jane Macias." Taylor toyed
with her wineglass, the ruby liquid swirling gently in the
bowl as she twisted the stem between her fingers. "I hate
this, Baldwin. I don't want to find her like we did the
others. Did I tell you Giselle St. Claire's grandparents
called me today? They were so…sweet. Complimented
Marcus's interview of them, how we're working the
case. Here they are, overwhelmed with grief because
their granddaughter is dead, and they are calling to

provide support and let us know they're praying for us. Don't get that too often."

"Were you able to track Giselle's last moves?"

"It's turning into a nightmare. Marcus has hit a dead end. Giselle and her grandparents were skiing in Gatlinburg. They had dinner, drove back to Nashville. They'd done a full day, were tired and went to bed as soon as they got home. Last time they saw Giselle, she was in their living room, reading a book. It wasn't until they got up the next morning and went to get her for breakfast that they realized she was gone. We found her before they knew she was missing. Pattern is just the same as with the other girls. They disappear out of completely normal settings, no one misses them until it's too late. At least maybe with Jane we've got a chance. If we just knew where to look."

"That's always the issue, Taylor. Have you heard from Giselle's mother yet?"

"She's doing a movie in Poland, can't get back until tomorrow. With the media swarm, she's going to make our lives difficult. God forbid someone get between a camera and Remy St. Claire. But we can handle her. There's something else that's bugging me. This damn signet ring. Why would that piece in particular be missing from the evidence room?"

"It could just be lost. It's been known to happen," Baldwin said. He reached for the decanter, poured them each a splash more wine.

"I know. But something about it is itching at me. You're gonna think I'm crazy when I tell you this."

"Tell me what? Let me guess. Your dad had a signet ring."

She eyed him, unnerved. "How do you do that?"

"Your dad had a signet ring? I was just guessing."

"No, it wasn't him. I think he wore some sort of ring when I was little, but it was a class ring. He lost it, I remember that. He was furious. No, let me explain. Bear with me, okay?"

"Okay." Baldwin sat back in his chair.

"I keep having this…vision, I guess you could call it. From when I was really little. We'd just moved into the big house—"

"Taylor, that wasn't a big house. That was a fucking palace."

"Oh, don't exaggerate."

"Honey, you had a staff that lived in the house."

"They weren't my staff."

"And I suppose you did a lot of your own chores, did your own laundry, washed dishes, that kind of stuff?"

"You're hardly being fair. It wasn't like I asked for my parents' lifestyle. You know that."

"I know, sweetie. I just like to tease. Face it, you were a regular princess."

"Yeah, the princess and the pea. Only the pea was Daddy, getting thrown in jail for bribing a judge or forgetting my birthday because he and Mom were off in Europe."

"At least you had parents." Baldwin looked into his wineglass, and Taylor reached over and touched his hand.

"I know. You're right. Though sometimes I wonder if it would have been better to have been loved, then lose them, than be ignored."

"I wouldn't wish that on anyone, Taylor. When I lost my folks, well, it's not something I would want to go through again. It's impossible to understand when you're young and you don't have that structure anymore. One minute they're there, the next they're gone, and you'll never see them again. It was rough." He gave her a lopsided smile. "Anyway, we were talking about Versailles."

"Oh, shut up. It was a big house, okay? Happy now?"

"Yes, dear. Tell me your vision."

She shut her eyes and tried to conjure up the scene. "It's not really a vision as much as a memory. Every year my parents had a huge party for New Year's. Themed, catered, the whole works. The year we moved into the house it was a costume ball. Kitty dressed as Marie Antoinette, I remember that perfectly, down to the wide-hipped dress and the towering crown of hair. It took four people to get her into the clothes. Just crazy. So anyway, I was spying on them from the top of the stairs. There was this little space that I could fit into, and I'd sit up there sometimes and watch the parties."

"Sound of Music." Baldwin laughed.

"What?" She opened her eyes; he was practically fizzing with mirth.

"You know, the movie? *Sound of Music?* The von Trapp children were presented, did their little song…'So long, farewell—'"

"*Auf wiedersehen,* good night. Yeah, I get it. Considering I was an only child, not so much." She shook her head at his antics. "If you keep interrupting me, we'll never get to it." Her eyes fluttered closed, the memory taking her again.

"I'd watch from the balcony. That night, I remember seeing my parents in the foyer with a group of people. The men were giving my father a hard time about the new place, and there's something about one of them. I can't quite put my finger on it, but every time I think about that signet ring, I see this image, the men talking and laughing, one of them coughing and putting up his hand, but that's it. I can't remember anything else."

"You think one of the men was wearing a signet ring?"

She opened her eyes. "Well, maybe. That combined with what Martin Kimball said, that he always thought the killer was a client of Burt Mars's because the note came off of Mars's printer. Mars was my dad's accountant."

"Was he crooked?"

"Ouch." What a legacy to have, a father who every time his name was mentioned, or a name was associated with his, the first thought was corruption.

"Sorry. I didn't mean it like that."

Taylor let it slide. "I don't know if he was crooked or not. But if he did work with my father, and the killer knew Mars well enough to get on his computer and write a note to the police, I can't help but wonder if maybe, just maybe, there's a connection."

"Let me get this straight. You think your father might have known Snow White while he was active?" Baldwin had leaned forward, wine and joking forgotten.

"See, I told you it was crazy. My dad was a lot of things, but I can't imagine he'd stand by and let something like that happen. No, if he knew him, it was tangentially, not someone he was friends with on a daily basis."

"You sure of that?"

"I'm not sure of anything in this case. I'd really like to find out what happened to that signet ring, though. It might answer a few questions. Whether or not it will help solve the case, I don't know."

"Too bad your dad's not around to ask."

Yes, too bad. Taylor gave Baldwin a weak grin and finished off her wine.

"Excuse me."

It was the valet, with her keys. He handed them to Baldwin. "I'm leaving for the night. I pulled the car up—it's right outside the door."

Taylor looked at her watch. It was nearly 2:00 a.m.

"Oh, I am so sorry. We didn't realize how late it had gotten."

Baldwin pulled out his wallet and handed the young man a ten. He nodded his thanks and took off toward the kitchen, probably to snag some leftovers as additional payment for the evening.

"We should go." Baldwin stood and stretched.

"Yeah. Let's see if we can get some sleep, start fresh in the morning."

They bundled up, got in the truck and headed out of downtown, both lost in their thoughts.

Fifteen

The lights were driving her mad. After a productive evening in the bar, and a not-so-productive tryst back in a stranger's hotel room, Charlotte had retired to her suite. Men. She was always amazed at their selfishness. How hard was it to make a woman come, for God's sake? She'd picked poorly tonight; the fool was too drunk to care about getting her off. He'd passed out after his own release, and she'd stolen from the room like some kind of whore. If he'd left money on the dresser, it might have been a more redeemable situation.

After treating herself to a moment in a warm tub, she crawled between the stiffly starched sheets and tried to get some rest. But the lights from downtown Nashville spilled in through the too-sheer curtains, keeping her awake.

She got up and raided the minibar, sloshing some Scotch on the floor as she dumped three airplane-size bottles of Johnny Walker Red into a cut-crystal glass. Sipping the whiskey, she settled in the chair by the window. Might as well watch the world if she couldn't sleep.

Amazing, at two in the morning there was still life on the streets. The Nashville she remembered from her youth was a quiet, somnolent place after dark. At least in the areas she'd been allowed to traverse. Church, maybe a restaurant or two. In her Peter Pan collar and pressed skirt, Mary Janes and velvet headbands, always on the arm of the latest in a series of nannies, she didn't get a good sense of the town on those few weekends. Granted, she'd been sent away when she was still quite young.

It wasn't until she was older, had gotten junked out of boarding school and was back home on the prowl that she found the raucous city life, the after-hours clubs, the raves, the ecstasy-driven techno punk music throbbing through her veins. Hmm. A hit of X wasn't such a bad idea. She got up and rummaged through her bag until she found a prescription bottle with Klonopin on the label. The little pills of X fit so well with the legal medication—same color and shape. Someone without a practiced eye would have to look closely to see the difference. She shook out a tab and swallowed it with the whiskey, enjoying the burn and near-immediate effects of the combination. That was better.

The joys of traveling in a private jet meant she could bring her pharmaceutical stash with her and not worry about security. It was always such a pain to travel commercial; she had to be much more discreet than hiding a few pills in with her medication.

She lay back on the bed, thinking about Baldwin. And that bitch, Taylor Jackson. How that country frump had captured the eye of a man like John Baldwin was beyond her. Baldwin's strong arms, the thick, unruly black hair, those green eyes… Charlotte started regretting the hit of X. She should have known better; it always made her horny as hell.

Well, tomorrow was another day. She finished the whiskey and lay down on her right side, facing away from the windows. Just as she began to drift off, her cell phone blared to life.

She reached across to the night table and picked up the phone.

A gruff voice greeted her. "Hi."

"How's the old man?" she asked.

"Just that. Old. Bent and crabby and missing his former glory. Just like you said."

"I wouldn't steer you wrong. I told you to trust me. Aren't you glad I did? You've been having some fun, haven't you?"

"Mmm," he said. "I miss you."

Charlotte rolled onto her back and slipped her free hand into her panties. "How much?"

"You can't even imagine."

"Why don't you tell me about it, baby. Tell me *all* about it."

Sixteen

"I gotta make." The little boy was muttering, plucking at the front of his ski pants. "Mama, I gotta make."

"Jeffie, where in the world did you hear that phrase?" Tami Gaylord looked in amusement at her three-year-old son. He was at that stage, picking up every word that floated past his tender ears.

"Don no. Gotta go, Mama, gotta make."

A sledding outing had been the perfect respite for Jeffie's boundless energies. But the reality of nature would strike at the most inopportune moments. The young mother looked around the park. They were on the opposite end from the bathrooms, and a three-year-old with a full bladder wasn't going to survive a five-hundred-yard walk in the snow back to the restrooms. She looked around—no one was close. He was a boy, after all. They could step into the short brush, strip off his snowsuit, point and shoot. She knew his father had been teaching him to write his name in the snow the other night. She'd caught them at it, on the far side of the garage, and scolded while she laughed. Men. She was blessed.

"Come here, sweetie. We'll go right here behind these bushes. Remember what Daddy taught you the other night?"

"I write my name?" Jeffie started stripping out of the snowsuit, and Tami laughed, reaching over to help her precocious son. When he was unbundled, they stepped into the screen of bushes, shielded from the rest of the park. Tami played with the branch of a pine tree while Jeffie started peeing, singing a happy, tuneless song, spelling his name in the snow just like his daddy taught him.

"Big *J.* Little *E.* Little *F*—Aaaah! Mooommmyyy!"

Startled by her son's scream, Tami flew to his side. "What, baby, what's wrong?" Jesus, did he get bitten? Was there an animal lurking in these woods?

Jeffie was pointing, a look of horror contorting his rounded features. Tami followed the boy's finger, straining to see into the gap where her son was pointing and shouting.

"What the hell?" There was a lump in the bushes. It twitched and moved, and both Tami and Jeffie jumped and screamed.

A tired voice rose from the snow-covered surface. "*Por favor.* Please. Help. Me."

The ambulance lights made kaleidoscopes on the crystalline snow blanketing Edwin Warner Park. The icy surface refracted the spinning light, blinding Taylor every third second. She watched the flash spill over the back of the ambulance, watched the dark-haired girl wince every time the light struck her eyes.

She approached the EMS team, who were hovering over the girl. She knew one of the men, a strawberry-blonde named Mike Bunch. He was bandaging the girl's scraped knee tenderly.

She tapped him on the shoulder. "Mike."

He jumped, then smiled at her. "LT," he said. "What can I do you for?"

"Mind if I turn off your rack? They're bugging me."

"Girl, you can do anything you want to my rack." Bunch's mustache twitched. She rolled her eyes at him, went to the driver's side and cut the switch.

She came back to the open ambulance doors, heard a whispered, *"Gracias."*

"De nada," Taylor said. Bunch looked at her in surprise; she just shrugged and looked away.

Twenty minutes ago, Taylor thought she had another victim of the Snow White Killer. The call was nonspecific, a young woman with black hair had been found in the park. She'd rushed to Edwin Warner, lights and sirens blaring, electric nerves tingling in her spine. She just knew they'd found Jane Macias. All things being equal, it was a logical assumption. No one had bothered to inform her that this body was talking. With a Spanish accent.

Taylor stood with her arms crossed, waiting for Bunch to clear out. He aimed a few more questions at the girl in piss-poor Spanish—"Are you hurt anywhere else? Can I bring you some water?"—then he shoved off the ground with a nod at Taylor, his blue eyes clouded with concern for his patient. The girl was all hers, for the time being. Taylor held up a hand—give me five minutes—and he walked away to join a group of officers smoking cigarettes. The odor was especially pungent against the cool air; Taylor didn't know if the smell made her crave a smoke or feel nauseous.

She turned to her victim. Victim of what, she didn't know. The girl's raven hair was dirty, her ribs poked through the skin like a malnourished greyhound's. Her black eyes were clouded, dirty with pain, sorrow and knowledge. She jumped at every sound—the ice creaking against the tree branches, the chattering of a squirrel, the low rumble of men's voices in the background, cars passing slowly on the street forty yards away, their drivers desperate for a chance sighting to explain the commotion. Taylor approached her as she'd done when she was a child and her parents had bought her a skittish colt, hand out in supplication. The girl finally looked up and met Taylor's eyes for the briefest moment, then looked away as if she'd been struck. Damaged, this one. Deeply.

The story the girl told, bundled in the blankets of strangers, broke Taylor's heart to the core. This girl was a victim—not of the Snow White Killer, but of base, despicable men. She was a victim of lust, and greed, and the bad things that make good men go astray. A slave.

Perched warily on a stretcher in the back of the ambulance, her face lowered, her voice soft, the poor thing told a horror story so quietly Taylor strained to hear her speak. Her English was broken but passable. The words left her mouth like vapor heat rising in the cold—soft and timorous.

"I come from Guatemala. My name is Saraya

Gonzalez. I work in kitchen at hotel with my sister. One day, man comes to kitchen, says you look very good, take my sister away. I run after her, but he knock me to the ground. I cry for very long time.

"A year pass. I no hear from my sister. No one hear from her. Then the man came back. He see me in kitchen, says you grow up, you perfect now. I was twelve. He take me from kitchen. At first, he kind, nice to me. He feed me, give me drink and nice soft bed to sleep. I don't need to do work, no more working in kitchen.

"I guess is only natural he want me. Many men want me, but my sister keep them away from me. Once she gone, I have men like bees, swarming me for my honey. I have no choice. When man decide to have sex with me, he takes me to the back bedroom. There is a camera. He does what he likes, doesn't care if it hurts. After, he give money.

"I feel great shame. But what am I to do? I cannot go police, they deport me. I have no man to watch out for me, no sister anymore. I at their mercy.

"He starts by bringing other men, older men who like little girl. They ask for 'massage.' They do all the things that he do to me, force me to spread my legs, my ass, my mouth for their pleasure. I do it, not because I want to, but because I know the sooner they finish, the sooner they go.

"There are cameras in the room. I find the video camera in the closet. They make video, too, sell video of me having sex with strange men."

Taylor had snapped to attention at that.

"Are you sure? There are videotapes and still pictures?"

The girl nodded. *"Yes, I sure. I see them making*

video, then mailing envelopes. There is computer in spare bedroom, that is the man's office."

"What is his name?"

"Oh, no. I no tell. I no want to get dead."

"Saraya, how'd you end up in the park?"

At that, panic had replaced fear in the girl's eyes. *"I run away. I figure it better to be dead."*

Funny, Taylor thought to herself as she drove back toward headquarters. She hadn't doubted the girl's story for a second. Was she so immune to death and destruction, to the very evil living in people's souls, that she was programmed to believe a victim? She knew that wasn't the case, she had a bullshit detector a mile wide. People claim to be victims for myriad reasons. Taylor was pretty good at determining who was lying and who was telling the truth. She'd been duped before, but not often.

Saraya Gonzalez was not a Snow White victim. The reality gave her pause. She'd been so caught up in the Snow White case that many of her other cases had been temporarily shelved. They needed to solve these fucking murders so she could go back to her job. There were people in the city who needed her help. *Give me your poor, your weak, your downtrodden. I'll fight for them.* That's what she was, what she longed to be. That was the very thing her father would never understand.

There it was, that damn scent in her nose. Why couldn't Win Jackson just leave her alone? She tried to shake off the memories, but her primordial olfactory senses defied her and made her doubts rise to the surface as if she was a little girl, vulnerable and weak, unable to win her father's love. She hadn't talked to him for three years, since right before she made lieutenant. They always fought—Taylor had little respect for Win's desire to take shortcuts to the top, and the knowledge that his daughter was a cop rankled him to no end. But the last conversation had been particularly virulent, and Taylor was through. She'd told him to take her trust fund and screw himself.

She knew he wasn't dead. That much she could feel. As divorced as she'd become from her family, from her father, she still had the presence of mind to know that he was out there. She'd be able to feel if he weren't. Wouldn't she?

At least she didn't have to worry about asking him to walk her down the aisle.

She dragged her thoughts away from her past and anchored them firmly in the present. She had another mystery on her hands. At least this one was definitely alive.

Taylor shuddered. Hearing Saraya's story, her tiny, accented voice uttering atrocities so frail, so tortured, Taylor didn't doubt her veracity for an instant. She wondered whether it would have been better to die than be so horribly abused, understood the girl's desperate attempt at flight. She was too weak to make it very far, the massage parlor must be within a day's walk. But Saraya had clammed up, refusing to answer any more questions. Taylor had signaled to Bunch to transport her to the hospital. A warm, safe bed and some nourishment might loosen her tongue. She hoped.

As she neared the CJC, the traffic got heavier. Taylor felt it, palpable in the air. Something was happening. She crawled along, finally turning the corner onto third. News vans lined the street. Satellites were set up, there were people milling about, walking through the street blocking the entrance to the CJC parking lot.

Taylor resisted the urge to take out her weapon and shoot it into the air to clear a path. Instead, she took a flasher from beneath her seat, put down the window of the unmarked and held it out in her hand. She flipped the switch and hit her horn. The noise and the glowing red globe got their attention. The sea parted and she pulled into the parking lot of the CJC, double-parking alongside the Channel 4 news van. She should have them ticketed for blocking the entrance.

Her phone rang and she saw Sam's number. Flipping it open, she walked briskly across the parking lot, shouts ringing in her ears, her hand up in the universal "no comment" posture. Sam was talking loudly enough that Taylor heard her clearly over the din.

"Remy fucking St. Claire is in my lobby, about to hold a press conference," Sam growled.

Taylor threw a glance back over her shoulder. "But all the news trucks are here."

"Oh, trust me, no they aren't. I've got patrol officers trying to keep the entrance to Gass Street clear. I assume she's heading your way after she finishes here. If you hurry, you can get your TV on, see her in all her bony glory. She looks like hell."

"Well, her daughter just died."

"Aren't you the gracious one. Call me later, okay? I need to get this under control. And stay off camera. Man, this hacks me off. Why that anemic bitch decided to have her press conference at my office is beyond me."

Sam was gone, and Taylor shut her phone. To say

Sam and Remy had never gotten along would be an understatement.

As she neared the door, the shouts of the media began to fade away. Each step up the back stairs dumped a load on her heart. This ruckus wasn't for the poor, innocent girl they'd just pulled out of the bushes in Edwin Warner, nor for Giselle St. Claire or Jane Macias. It wasn't about any of the victims.

No, this was for something much worse. A false prophet.

Inside the door, Taylor could hear the commotion before she saw it. The homicide team was crowded around the television set, watching. Taylor took up a position with them.

Remy St. Claire had been pretty when she left Nashville to strike it big in Hollywood. An elfin face, pale blond hair, long legs, a breathy, little-girl voice reminiscent of a packaged young Norma Jean. Hollywood made her gorgeous. They took her under their wing, brought her into the fold, and made Remy St. Claire a star. A shooting star.

The lip injections, cheekbone implants, breast implants, ear tuck, liposuction, rib removal, all of that was de rigueur. Standard operating procedure. Her voice coach had annihilated all traces of Tennessee from her vocal cords, eliciting a low, smoky Mae West tone from deep within Remy's artificial chest. Her long, blond locks were color-treated now, four individual shades of honey blond, highlights so subtle, so perfectly uniform that it took four hours once a week to keep them maintained.

Her figure was emaciated to the point of starvation under a veneer of muscle obtained through stringent daily meetings with trainers—strength, Pilates and yoga. Only her breasts stood out tall; the rest of her body seemed to shrink in on itself, as if the internal organs were so starved that they took the skin for nutrition.

She was linked to a new, younger partner on the cover of the gossip rags at least once a month. For an actress who'd been the toast of Hollywood fourteen years ago, that was pretty damn good. The scandalmongers and cable shows would feast on this news item for days. Remy's precious daughter, dead at the hands of a serial killer. Oh, the horror, the horror.

Somewhere along the way, Remy's poor, murdered daughter would become an icon, a mythical creature, forgotten in life yet revered in death. For Giselle, being the violently murdered daughter of a celebrity didn't mean she would be missed, it meant her mother would get into the news cycle. Movies would be made. Stories told. As it was, the news media had already pounced.

All of this ran through Taylor's head as she watched Remy call on the FBI and the Nashville police to solve the murder. She offered a reward, guaranteeing that they would be inundated with tons of false leads and bogus phone calls. Great.

Taylor looked away from the TV and went into her office. The three-ring circus had officially begun.

When her phone rang, she snatched it up and identified herself without looking at the ID.

"Why, Taylor Jackson, who'd've known?" Fuck. Now Remy was calling her.

The accent was so overdone it was nearly unbearable. Someone somewhere had told Remy that if she were back in her home state, it would bode well for her to

adopt her Southern while she was around the Nashvillians. A less-forgiving group of people would have
called her for the phony she was. But in Nashville, they
smile and nod and graciously pretend not to notice. If
there was one thing a true Nashvillian couldn't stand, it
was a fake. The bitchiness could wait for the back rooms
and dark salons, after the guilty miscreant was gone.
Tongues would wag tonight after Remy St. Claire left
town, that was for sure.

"Remy. I'm so sorry for your loss."

"I just can't believe it. I've just identified the body
of my daughter. What in the world is happening, Taylor?
Why was my baby killed?"

Remy's voice wavered. Taylor imagined the china-
blue saucer eyes filling with tears, a white handkerchief
conveniently clutched at Remy's throat.

"We're doing everything we can to find that answer,
Remy."

"Is there anything I can do?" The accent was gone,
leaving Remy with a hollowed-out voice devoid of any
character or real emotion. She sounded for a brief
instant like Kitty, but Taylor pushed the thought away.

"To start with, when's the last time you talked to
Giselle?"

"Well, I think it was sometime last week. She lives with
her grandparents. You remember my parents, don't you?"

"Of course." The St. Claires were warm, loving
people, and Taylor had always been stymied by how
they'd produced such a selfish, wanting child.

"They're supposed to be watching her. The last I
heard, they were planning a ski trip to that godforsaken
Gatlinburg. I'm guessing Giselle was bored to tears

after being away from home, wanted to do something a little fun. She probably snuck out of the house, went downtown with a friend. You know how teenagers are, Taylor. They like to get into trouble."

That caught Taylor's attention. She made a mental note to talk to Baldwin. They hadn't ascertained where the killer was getting his victims. The elevated blood-alcohol levels coupled with the Rohypnol pointed to a bar setting. But in a town the size of Nashville, with bars every third building, narrowing which establishment had been close to impossible. They'd been unable to determine an exact kidnapping spot up until now. But if Giselle had been picked up by a friend and taken some-place specific, they may have something to go on. Almost too much to hope for.

"Hey there, Remy. Don't go assuming anything. We've talked to your parents extensively, and they've given us nothing to lead us to believe that she was sneaking out at night."

The vision of the tiny gold ring in Giselle's clitoris told the story instead. And with Remy as a mama, the odds of Giselle being a good little girl were slim to none.

"I know my girl, Taylor, despite what you may think. She was a wild child, always in trouble. She's been drinking and smoking, doing drugs and God knows what else since she was twelve. Completely and utterly out of control. That's why she's here in Nashville, away from the Hollywood scene. There's nothing anyone can tell her, either. She needs to experience things for herself. She's always been like that, attracted to the very things that will hurt her. If you stood her in front of a stove and told her the top was hot and would burn her, she'd stick her tongue out at you and touch it, just to make sure you weren't lying to her."

Taylor was struck by the present tense. Giselle's death hadn't truly sunk into her mother's mind yet. She heard the sound of a lighter being struck, then Remy breathed out heavily. She'd just lit a cigarette.

"That's the other thing. She may have been young but she wasn't at all gullible. She had a radar for people, not that it mattered. She could find the best in a grunged-out junkie and the worst in Miss America. That's just the way she was."

"If you're still at the M.E.'s office, you'd best put that cigarette out. Sam will have your head."

Taylor heard a shuffling noise. Remy coughed once, deep. "Taylor, remember that time when we were kids, we snuck Mrs. Mize's cigarettes out of the pack, went up into the woods behind your parents' house and smoked? What were we, ten, eleven, then?"

Taylor laughed despite herself. Mrs. Mize was her parents' housekeeper, a mother, nanny, cleaner, polisher and all-around straight arrow. She'd spent more time raising Taylor than her own parents.

"Eleven. She beat me blue when she found out. You lifted the Crest from her bath so we could wash our mouths out, but you forgot to put it back. She knew she'd just bought a new tube, got suspicious, started counting her smokes. Jeez, she was pissed off."

"She told my parents. They were furious."

Taylor thought about that for a moment. Her own parents had been informed of the incident. Taylor had been grounded, of course, told not to play with the St. Claire girl anymore, but it was Mrs. Mize who'd beat her silly, then loved and hugged her because she hated that she was the one doing the disciplining instead of Kitty and Win. She clucked, and brought hot chocolate and nuzzled Taylor, telling her an old Norwegian folktale that evening.

"Where is Mrs. Mize these days?"

"She passed on last year. Sweet old thing, she went in her sleep. A true martyr, putting up with my family all those years, I'll tell you that." Taylor laughed softly, mind fuzzed with the memory of something good and happy. Then she shook her head and brought her focus back to the woman on the other end of the phone.

"Remy, I'd love to keep on reminiscing, but I have work to do. Is there anything else you can tell me about Giselle, about who she's friends with, people outside the family that might have known her well?"

There was silence, and Taylor realized that no, Remy wouldn't know these intimate details about her daughter. That would be about as likely as Kitty having any clue why Taylor was sneaking smokes with the St. Claire girl. Taylor's heart broke, just a little bit, in a place she wasn't aware had any more room for jagged tears.

"Okay, Remy. Thanks for calling. I'm so sorry about this, I really am. Sam will have everything else you might need. We'll let you know what we find out."

"I trust you to find out who killed my baby, Taylor. I'm glad you're the one who's going to catch her killer. I know that son of a bitch doesn't stand a chance against you."

She hung up, leaving Taylor with a strange, crazy sense of pride coupled with sorrow and longing for what they all used to be. For who they all used to be.

* * *

Taylor sat with her head in her hands for a long moment after the phone call. She felt like the wind was gone from her lungs. What had her life become? Investigating the rapes and murders of her childhood friends' kids? Something was dreadfully wrong with that, she knew it deep in her soul.

Soft knocks on the door made her raise her head.

"Hi, babe. Everything okay?"

Taylor stared at her handsome fiancé. The clear, sea-green eyes, the laconic smile, the black hair peppered with gray. The broad shoulders, the way he towered above her. Safety. That's what she felt every time she gazed upon him. And that was terribly dangerous. She knew it. Vulnerability wasn't her strong suit; hell, she slept with a gun by her pillow. And a night-light. And dreamed of strong arms that pushed away the monsters and the nightmares. She'd found him, this savior of hers.

"Yeah. Just a little tired. What are you up to?"

"I came for a glimpse of the great Remy St. Claire." He grinned and she smiled back.

"You want her autograph? I'm sure I could wrangle that one up for you. She's over at Sam's. We can catch her if you want."

He laughed. "No, thanks."

"What, you don't have the hots for a shallow, plastic bimbo?"

"With you sitting here, wearing my ring, ready to marry me? Hardly. I'm just passing along a message."

"Mmm-hmm. What's the message?"

"The girl found in the park wants to leave. She's fighting with the hospital, trying to sign out against medical advice. They called over, told Marcus. I told him I'd tell you."

"Saraya?" Taylor rubbed a thumb against her right temple. A gnawing pain had started earlier and was growing. She ran her hand through her hair, opened her desk drawer, took out her Advil, popped three, then stood up.

"All right. Where's the drama queen this morning?"

"Charlotte? She's at the field office, getting slaughtered by the media for missing the DNA connection between the national cases. They're dancing on her head, trying to get her to admit that she made a mistake. Maybe she did. I don't know. She's going to be tied up with them for a while, which would be why I'm here. I figure while she's being jerked around by the press, we could go solve this case."

"Aren't you sweet. She is such a lovely girl. I hope the wolves enjoy her." Taylor smiled at him. "But before we go Snow Whiting, I need to hear what my beating victim is so frantic about."

The ride to Baptist Hospital was quiet. Baldwin drove, Taylor rested her head against the cool window and wished for summer. Truth be told, she didn't really want winter to end. She loved the cool, crisp weather, the gray skies, the warm fires and soft clothes. But if it were summer, this would all go away. She'd be done with this case, the wedding would be over, they could go to the beach and lie in the sun, baking brown as bunnies and reading trashy novels. Make love after a few too many rum drinks; lie in a hammock under the stars, the sultry sea air lulling them into a false sense of hope.

That was her one issue with winter. Not the cold, but the bleak despondence of the short days and long nights.

They parked and entered the hospital through the emergency room. Taylor shuddered briefly as a woman on a gurney was rushed past. She'd been there once, and didn't want to go back. She fingered her neck, a habit she'd broken along with her cigarettes. The scar was there, still in sharp relief across her throat. A suspect's last gasp. She'd wear his desperation forever. She'd just gotten used to it. There was something about nearly losing your life— you either let it haunt you or you accepted that it had happened and moved on. She'd chosen the latter. She was perfectly content to be the one doing the killing, thank you very much, not being the one who someone had tried to kill. Being that kind of victim just didn't work for her.

As though he read her thoughts, Baldwin slipped a hand into the back pocket of her jeans and gave her right buttock a squeeze. She tried to ignore him, but it tickled, and she laughed.

"You've been lost in thought. Anything you want to share?"

"Naw. You know me, I hate hospitals. Where's our girl?"

"Four. Here, we can take this elevator." The doors were already open, so they slipped inside and hit the button for the fourth floor.

Baldwin leaned against the metal walls, an eyebrow raised. Taylor watched him, chewing lightly on her bottom lip. Outside of work talk, she was being much too quiet these days, knew he could sense something was wrong. She spun her engagement ring around her finger twice, decided to take a chance.

"Okay. Here goes. I'm a little freaked out about the wedding."

Baldwin snickered good-naturedly. "A little? I'd vote for a lot. I'd actually go so far as to throw out the idea that you don't want to marry me after all."

The hurt in his voice was more than she could bear. She reached over, ran a hand along his jaw, brushed back the forelock of hair that hung across his forehead.

"Baby, you couldn't be further from wrong. That's not it at all. God, how do I explain this? It's not the concept of marriage in general that's got me freaked. Especially marriage to you. You know that you're the only person on the face of the earth I would even consider marrying, much less buy a dress for and book a church."

"You booked a church? And you got a dress?"

His mock excitement made her laugh. "Oh, stop it. You aren't funny. I'm trying to be serious."

The shadow had left his face. "By all means, continue."

"Okay. I'm nervous about the wedding part. Having to stand up in front of all those people—I'm just not a fan of being the center of attention. What if we—"

The elevator interrupted her, and the doors slid open before they could go any further. She was going to suggest that they just elope, run off somewhere instead of dealing with the whole church mess. But the look on his face told her that this was the way he wanted to do it. She decided to save the conversation for later. She'd agreed to the hoopla, and had to deal with her fears. But she reserved the right to act squirrelly up until the moment she set foot in that damn church on Saturday.

She winked at him, then strolled out of the elevator

as if she hadn't been talking about the most important moment of her life.

The nurses' station was unmanned, which was odd. Taylor felt her chest tighten. Something was wrong. Stealing glances, she saw the hallways were deserted, the silence pervasive. Her lips thinned as she strained to hear something. She looked at Baldwin, noticed he'd put his hand on his weapon. She realized she'd already instinctively followed suit and they took a few tentative steps forward, getting a sense for what was happening. There was almost complete silence, the absence of sound deafening. Unheard of in a busy downtown hospital.

Taylor motioned to Baldwin to go right, then took two steps closer to the nurses' station. Her primordial senses kicked in; she smelled the blood before she saw it. She stuck her head over the counter and saw the slumped form, a nurse with gray hair and blue scrubs. The woman was on her back, as if she'd slid to the floor and pleaded with her assailant before he shot her in the forehead. The shot was a little off center, a messy wound that came in at an angle and certainly killed the poor woman immediately.

She pulled her head back, sheltered from possible incoming shots behind the station wall. What the hell was going on? She risked another glance, as if she needed to confirm the gunshot.

Baldwin was crouched next to her, pale. His weapon was steady in his hand, pointing down the empty hallway. They needed to proceed carefully.

Taylor realized it wasn't quiet at all. Bells were going off, people were crying out. Bedlam had ensued in the fraction of a second that they had taken to assess the scene.

A door slam made Taylor jump. She exploded, running down the hallway toward the noise, Baldwin on her heels. She passed a group of people shouting and pointing, went straight for the stairwell. She heard Baldwin behind her, yelling, "She's gone, she's gone," and she hit the stairwell door at a run, slamming the door open with the flat of her hand.

She drew down on the figure retreating below her.

"Police, don't move. Stop!" she screamed, and the figure halted for a fraction of a second, but only long enough to catch her eye before he darted through the door on level two and disappeared.

"Fuck!" Taylor yelled, throwing a long leg over the railing and dropping a floor. Her boots hit with a bang and she almost lost her balance, then she was down one more flight and out the same door.

He'd chosen well, the shooter. Level two was the surgery floor, and this particular entrance was to the Radiograph and Endoscopy Center. No one was there—it was dead quiet, the silence real this time. Taylor listened, ears straining for footsteps or door slams, but heard nothing. Either this son of a bitch was a fast motherfucker, or he'd snuck into one of the rooms.

She wasn't stupid; she wasn't going to search without backup. She stepped back against the wall and pulled out her cell phone just as Baldwin appeared on the other side of the door. She could see his wild eyes through the wired glass. She pulled open the door, shaking her head.

"I don't know which way he went. I was just calling you." She spoke quietly. Baldwin leaned in to hear her.

He whispered back. "I called it in. I don't like this. Not one bit. There's a doctor in her room who was cold-cocked. He's unconscious but alive. Fitz and Marcus are on their way with a butt load of uniforms. They'll cover the entrances. Let's take it slow, start down this hallway on the left."

"Think this might have been the man she works for? The way she told it, she's important to her boss. What in the hell is going on?"

He shrugged. "Either she's valuable as a pro, or she knows too much."

"Yeah. You go left, I'll go right. We're covered below. He's gone, I don't think he's still here. Just don't think I was quick enough."

That's when she realized that her ankle was killing her. She must have twisted it when she jumped over the railing. Superwoman, she was not.

"Okay. Go slow, be careful."

They parted, heading down opposite paths. It didn't take long.

Baldwin sent out a long, low whistle. Taylor back-tracked until she found him standing over a body.

On closer inspection, she made out the small, quiet face of Saraya Gonzalez. Her blood pooled beneath her—that sharp bang. It wasn't Taylor's boots hitting the landing, it was the killer shooting this poor girl.

Taylor holstered her weapon and ran her fingers through her hair. This was turning into one of the worst weeks she'd ever known.

The emergency entrance bay to Baptist Hospital was crowded with police cruisers, overflowing into the street. The blue lights flashed up and down Twentieth Avenue; the area hummed with activity.

Taylor stood at the command post, watching. A manhunt was on for the shooter, though it seemed he'd gotten away from the area. A thorough search had revealed a wig, baseball cap and jacket in the municipal trash outside the emergency room exit. The video had been analyzed; the shooter had exited through the emergency room bay with the disguise intact, and hadn't shed his fake identity until he was well out of range of the cameras. They had a height and approximate weight, but nothing else. Roadblocks had been set in a mile perimeter, but without knowing what they were looking for, they wouldn't be much use. It was time to admit defeat on this event, and Taylor was furious—with herself, Baldwin, the shooter and any available person within forty feet.

Another two bodies for Sam: Saraya and the nurse at the head station. Bad timing for her; if she'd just been in another spot on the floor she might have lived. Jesus. Why hadn't he just shot the girl and been done with it? Why had he tried to take her out of the hospital? Kidnap her, then murder her? Saraya mustn't have been kidding when she spoke of her value to her employer. Damn. The only lead Taylor had into that world was gone.

Fitz was standing nearby, talking quietly into his cell phone. He hung up and looked over at Taylor. She knew something was wrong, the set of his chin was a dead giveaway. Someone else was dead.

She caught his eye, raised an eyebrow. He held up a finger in a wait-a-minute gesture, then finished the call. When he shut the phone, he ran a hand over his face, and Taylor saw how tired he was. Fitz wasn't a spring chicken anymore; the stress of the week was showing on his haggard features. He came to her then, shaking his head.

"We've got a murder scene," he said when he reached her. "Need to head over there. Want to join me?"

"Goddamn. How much more can we take today?" Taylor swept a hand at the chaos. "Is it Jane Macias?"

"Doesn't look that way. It's one of the massage parlors off Nolensville Road."

Relief flowed through her chest. She just couldn't stand the idea of failing one more girl.

"Massage parlor mania today. I thought we had all of them shut down?" They started walking to his car.

"Hey, wait up." Baldwin came after them, jogging. "Where you headed?"

"Just got a call in for a murder at one of the supposedly closed massage parlors. This might tie back to Saraya. We need to head over there. This guy got away, there's no question about that. Marcus is handling the search. He doesn't need us."

"Yeah, he's got it under control. You're right, this is all a bit useless. I can come with, if you want?"

"Why not? More the merrier," Fitz grumbled.

They got into Fitz's department-issued Cavalier and left the afternoon's failure behind.

"Anything new on Snow White's copycat?" Fitz asked as he negotiated the phalanx of blue strobe lights. "I figured that chick from Quantico would be all over us today. You know where she is?"

"I haven't seen her today, thankfully. I've been avoiding my office like the plague," Baldwin answered.

"Pity, that." Taylor's sarcasm wasn't met with denial. Charlotte Douglas was going to be a problem, she could feel it in her bones. "We haven't heard anything new on the Snow White case today. Been a little busy. Though

Remy gave me some ideas on how to track Giselle's movements. I'd like to talk to her grandparents, see if they can point us in the direction of any friends she might have who they don't like. Remy insinuated that Giselle might have snuck out."

Fitz had maneuvered them over the bridge, onto 65 South, and off the first ramp so they could travel the back roads to the massage parlor. He was never a fan of the freeway, and it drove Taylor crazy sometimes. But he was a demon on the side streets, and they pulled up in front of a small, well-kept house within minutes.

"This is a massage parlor?"

"Apparently so. They can't get away with a business front anymore, so they've moved into the private homes down here."

The area was largely dominated by Spanish-speaking residents, with a few Kurds and indigent blacks thrown in for good measure. There were plenty of crack houses in the nearby streets, and a couple of Section 8 government housing projects a few blocks away. Homicide was busy enough in this area, and had to employ trained civilian translators to help solve the crimes. Many of the residents were illegals, and didn't trust the police to do anything that could be construed as positive for the neighborhood.

They unloaded from the vehicle, checked in at the command post, signed the call sheet and got their party clothes—booties, gloves, all the protective accoutrements for a get-together with death.

An officer met them on the front lawn. Bob Parks was one of Taylor's favorites, a happy yet serious man who doubled for the SWAT team. He had a luxuriant black mustache that looked like it had been oiled and groomed recently.

"Welcome, welcome," Parks bellowed. "Nice of you to come and join us this afternoon. We have a lovely time planned for you—blood, gore and a few other unmentionables you'll be thrilled to see."

"Hey, Bob." Taylor greeted him with a thump on the back. "How's the kids?"

"Like Dilbert says, 'bout as happy as a bunch of barefoot squirrels in a tire store."

Taylor snorted back a laugh.

"I'm telling you, LT, having teenagers will be the death of me. Hi, Dr. Baldwin."

"Hey, Parks. Sorry to see you under these circumstances."

Fitz bellied up to the younger man. "What am I, chopped liver?"

"Naw, Fitz, you're just a pain in my ass. How come you haven't retired yet? You're too old to be messing with this shit."

"Parks, you're not that far behind me. Shut the hell up already. What do you have here?"

Parks turned back to the little house, shaking his head. "It's not a pretty scene, I'll warn you. Double homicide, two girls. Both look Spanish, which is fitting for this part of town, but they're facedown, the M.E. hasn't gotten here yet. We were waiting for her to declare before we moved them. Took the pics, and video is rolling."

"Spanish. Let's go take a look." Taylor led them across the lawn to the front steps.

On the small porch the four geared up, covering their

shoes with the booties, gloving their hands. Taylor wound her ponytail into a bun to make sure there weren't any loose strands that could fall off and compromise the scene. Fully geared, they made their way into the house, following the thinly taped guide route one of the officers had laid on the floor.

The inside of the house was dressed in a nearly sterile white. To the left of the entry foyer, white leather furniture with glass tables and lamps dominated a small living room, with white walls and white drapes. To the right, a kitchen with white marble floors and a white countertop completed the monochromatic decor. White Berber carpet led down a short hallway to three doors—Taylor could see a pristine bathroom at the end of the hall and assumed the two other doors led to bedrooms. She was right.

"Door number one," Parks said, gesturing to the right. "And door number two." He pointed left. "Take your pick, they're nearly identical."

Taylor chose the right side first. She stood in the doorway and looked into the room, running her Maglite over the dimness. She didn't need the overhead to see the blood. Copious amounts of red, startling against the contiguous white theme, was very defining. From her vantage point at the doorway, she could see blood everywhere, cast off on the unmade bed and headboard, washed across the wall, soaking the carpet. In the middle of the bed, a dark-haired woman lay on her stomach, facedown on the sheets, which were nearly black. Exsanguination, her mind told her. The woman's legs were akimbo, the left twisted under the right as if she'd fallen at an angle onto the mattress. Taylor couldn't see her arms.

She switched places with Baldwin and Fitz, looking into the left-side room. The scene was virtually identical. A knot formed in her stomach. A double homicide, with both scenes indistinguishable at first glance. Fuck.

She heard talking, turned to see Sam striding toward her.

"Heard you had a bad day," she said when she reached Taylor.

"Couldn't be any worse than yours. You had Remy St. Claire fogging up your office. I'm just on my third and fourth bodies today and Baldwin's former lover is in town with some kind of agenda."

"A stellar day for us both. What do we have here?" Sam was dressed for the scene and obviously champing at the bit to get to work.

"Two dead, lots of blood, and a mess. I was hoping you could shed some light. They haven't been turned, I want to see that. This feels a little too familiar, if you know what I mean."

"Okay. Let me work. By the way, you know we're supposed to go to dinner tonight. I might be running a little late."

Taylor groaned. Yes, they were supposed to have dinner tonight, a joint bachelor/bachelorette evening. She'd forgotten.

"Yeah, well, I won't die if we can't do it."

"Oh, come on, T. The boys are all excited. We'll do dinner, then let them go to the VIBE. There's a nice little bar next door, we'll sit in there and drink. Unless you want to go to the strip club."

"Baldwin's excited to go to a strip club?" She looked over her shoulder; he was back out in the foyer of the house, talking on his cell phone. His brow was crinkled and she wondered who he was talking to.

"No, I think it's more Simon is excited. He hasn't gotten a chance to have a lot of male bonding since the babies came. We'll let him and Baldwin, Fitz, Marcus and Lincoln watch the girlies dance and you and I will have a relaxing hour before they come back. I plan on getting ravished after that. So don't spoil my fun, okay?"

"Yeah, yeah, whatever. We'll probably have to skip the dinner portion of our evening. What's the name of the bar? I'll just plan to meet you there later on. Between the shootings at Baptist and this double, I'm going to be up to my ears signing off on a shitload of paperwork tonight."

Sam thought hard. "I think it's called something like…Control, that's it. Control."

"Sounds like a gay bar, one of the ones up on Church Street."

"Yeah, well, I didn't name it. And it's not. Let's get to it." She went into the first room and did a thorough setup, taking her time. It was a good twenty minutes before she declared she was ready to flip the girl. With a little help from one of the crime-scene techs, the woman was rolled onto the sheet that would help them transfer the body into a body bag.

Taylor was chatting with Parks when she heard Sam's sharp intake of breath.

"What, what is it? What's the matter?" she asked.

"You better come look at this," Sam answered.

Taylor came into the room. It only took a glance at the woman before Taylor realized what was happening. The breath left her body in a whoosh.

"Oh my God."

Seventeen

A fire crackled in the hearth. The cozy scene belied the barely contained vicissitude in the room. Snow White paced, in a fury, leaning heavily on his cane.

"Goddamn you, I told you no. You had no right to move ahead without my permission. That wasn't a part of our deal, you brainless son of a bitch. These things need to be treated carefully, cautiously. You've undone all our work. You're going to get us both caught."

"Shut up, old man. I did what needed to be done. You won't let me kill that stupid bitch we took the other night. I needed to get it out of my system. They're just whores."

Snow White turned to the third member of the room.

"Did you sanction this? Did you tell him he could deviate from protocol? I swear to you, if either of you fuck me, I'll see to it you never forget what it's like to be on my bad side."

The woman turned. "I have no more control over him than you do. You knew that when I brought him to you. He's a sociopath."

The younger man adopted a mocking tone. "Thank

you, darling. Coming from you, that's a high compliment indeed."

She frowned at him. "You're welcome, though I have to say I agree. Going outside the parameters at this stage of the game could derail everything. You want me to be happy, don't you?"

Snow White felt a scream building in his blood. "Shut up, both of you. We need to find out what's happening, see if we need to shut all this down. What have you done to the girl?"

"I haven't done anything to her but look. She's safe. For now."

"I didn't ask that. Where is she? I want to see her."

His protégé casually stretched and smiled. "She's safe. I haven't touched her. But I will, mark my words."

"Lay a hand on her and you'll be dead before you can blink. You've broken the pattern. Defied my rules. I say when you kill. And now you've gone and done this? With these...defiled things. We have standards. First you're dumb enough to choose the daughter of a celebrity. Minor as the mother may be, she's drawing too much attention to us. Then you guarantee even more media for yourself by taking a newspaper reporter? We had an agreement! You might as well have spit in my eye. If you deviate from the plan again, I will have your head, mark *my* words. They will be coming for us now, and it's too soon."

"You didn't realize who little Jane was, either, old man. You were right there in the thick of it with me. Don't think I'll forget that."

"You are not to touch her. Am I understood?"

Snow White glared at his apprentice. His threats were

empty; he had no strength to take control of the situation physically, and the boy knew it. The impertinent fool had gotten greedy, couldn't sate his ridiculous hunger for ending life for just a few days. He knew this was a bad idea.

The door to the room opened.

"Father?"

"Oh, look, it's blind-boy grunt. Come to see what your daddy is up to with the real people? I bet he rues the day you spat forth into this world."

Snow White sniggered, but the woman stood angrily. "Hey. That's my brother you're talking to. Don't you dare speak like that to him. Do you understand me?"

"What are you going to do to me, princess?"

She ignored him, went to the deformed creature she called brother. "He didn't mean it, he doesn't know any better. He's a brute, Joshua. Let's get you something to drink, okay?" She marched from the room, and Snow White sighed.

"She's loved that boy silly since he came out of that twat she called a mother. I don't think Charlotte remembers her mother. She died giving birth to Joshua, you know. They laid him on her chest and she just went. Like she couldn't face what she had created."

"It's a disease, old man. Just like the one you have, but it cripples his face, not his soul."

"Well, aren't you the philosopher today? You were insulting him a moment ago. Changed your mind?"

"Of course not. I don't possess compassion, you know that. But I do admire your darling daughter for her loyalty. Enough of this. I'm tired. I've had a long day. I'm going to get some rest."

"Don't touch the girl."

He left the room, and Snow White slumped in his chair. He shouldn't have listened. Shouldn't have allowed it to move so quickly. Not enough planning, a shortsighted monster who could break his leash at any time. As much as he enjoyed hearing about it, loved to participate, to feel the breath leaving their bodies, see the light dimming in their eyes as their souls fled, he knew it was too much. Too fast, too many. The boy would be their undoing.

Eighteen

Frank Richardson pulled off his reading glasses and rubbed his eyes. His brain was numb. He'd been combing the files, rereading all of his stories, making copies of relevant sections. In all, he'd written more than four hundred stories on the Snow White Killer over the years he'd been active.

He remembered those days. It was a heady feeling, communicating the worst imaginable information to the citizens of Nashville. He'd worked closely with the police, gotten more scoop than any reporter had a right to, legally or otherwise. He was proud of this work, proud of his attention to detail, his meticulous analysis. No prejudice, no accusations against the police for dragging their feet, just solid journalism chronicling the Snow White case.

He knew Taylor was interested in any of his work that had speculation about suspects. She'd informed him about the missing signet ring, and her reservations about Burt Mars. He'd taken the liberty of trying to track Mars down; the last known address for the man was Manhattan. It had taken work, but what he found was astounding. That lieutenant was right to be suspicious.

Mars had moved out of Nashville in 1989 on the heels of a financial scandal. He headed north, looking for money and anonymity. He disappeared off the books for several years, only to come back, no longer anonymous. He opened an accounting firm on the Lower East Side of Manhattan. Within six years, he'd developed a reputation and gotten all over the police's radar. Who sets out to become a notorious check kiter and securities fraud? Mars spent some time in Otisville at the federal penitentiary, had gone down on a racketeering and corrupt organization charge under the RICO Act in 1998.

He was out of prison now, had a new business consulting on REITs—Real Estate Investment Trusts. REITs could be easily manipulated, but according to all the published accounts, Mars's company was clean. Yet in the quiet corners, he was widely supposed to still be involved with the Mafia. He'd been connected to several figures well-known to the New York police, though no active investigations were under way linking him directly to organized crime. If he was dirty, Mars was much more careful now. Nothing on the surface of his company appeared illegal, and it wasn't a crime to be friends with criminals.

But Richardson had been a reporter for a very long time, and with his years of finely honed instinct for getting to the bottom of a story, he smelled a rat. Mars was up to no good.

He'd spent the day doing research, on and off the phone and the Internet, calling in a few favors along the way. He connected some very interesting dots. His hunch had paid off, big. This story was huge.

Richardson felt more alive than he had in weeks, months. Back in the chase. He already had plans to write about this tale, to make a tidy little sum selling the rights to the book. These were the kinds of stories that made millions.

He printed out all the information he could find, including addresses and phone numbers. He was thorough. He liked Taylor Jackson, admired her spunk. Admired those long legs, too. Her fiancé was a lucky man, that was for sure. Truth be told, she reminded him a bit of his wife when she was younger.

Feeling chipper, Frank packed up his things. If he hustled, he might catch the lovely lieutenant at her office before she shut down for the day.

Nineteen

Taylor stared at the body before her. Long black hair, ivory skin, a gaping wound in her neck, bright red lips.

Snow White.

She went out in the hall, cursing. "Son of a bitch! Roll body two, right now!"

Sam followed her. "Taylor, I need to make sure—"

She whirled to face her best friend. "Just do it, Sam. I need to know, okay? Then I'll leave you to it and see if I can't find this motherfucker and nail his balls to the wall of my office."

"T, I need—"

"If you won't do it, I'll do it myself."

She strode into the opposite room. She saw Baldwin out of the corner of her eye. He was heading toward her full speed. Sam came right behind, pushing her out of the way.

"No, no, no, no. Let me do it, damn it."

Taylor stopped, let Sam by. The M.E. came to the bedside slowly, trying to make sure she didn't drastically disturb the scene. When she reached the body, she gently slid a hand under the girl's left shoulder and pulled her up partway, so Taylor would have a clear view.

"Goddamn son of a bitch."

"The same?" Sam asked. "I can't see from this angle."

"Exactly the same. A fucking double. It's too soon. Baldwin?"

"Yeah, I see. Same exact scene as across the hall. The symmetry is beautiful, don't you think?"

Taylor gave him a sharp glance. He'd taken on the dreamy expression he got when faced with the most hideous of crimes. Profilers.

He was murmuring to himself. She strained to hear him. "You notice the mirror presentation? That took some time to get just right. He's meticulous, our fellow. Wanted this to be perfect. Snow White did a double, didn't he?"

"Yes, he did. Danielle Seraphin and Vivienne White. The exchange students. They were mirrored, too."

"Hmm. Clever boy."

"Sick fuck is what I'd call him." Fitz had joined them.

"I agree with Fitz." Taylor nodded.

Sam was still holding the dead girl by the shoulder. "Excuse me. If y'all are done psychoanalyzing, would you mind if I got back to work? I have a lot to do here, and I know you want the posts quickly."

The posts. There were artifacts to recover.

"Yes, Sam, sure. Sorry. Go ahead. We'll get out of your way."

"Thank you." She laid the body down, then bent closer, looked at the girl's face. "Hey, Taylor?"

"Yeah?"

"There's no visible emulsion on the temples."

"Seriously?"

"Nothing remotely like it. Looks like you're right about him shifting the pattern. I won't know for sure until I get them back and do the posts, but I'm not seeing it."

"Will you call me when you know for sure?" Taylor asked, but Sam was already lost, back in M.E. land. Taylor started to say something about canceling the party, but Sam was crossing the hall into the other bloody bedroom. Taylor watched her roll the body gently, look closely at the second girl's face.

"Nope, none here, either."

She set the girl's body back upon the bed. When she swiped a hand, albeit faintly, across the girl's hair, Taylor knew it was time to leave. Sam's communion with the dead had just begun.

The three trooped from the house, waved to Parks and stood by Fitz's vehicle.

Taylor chewed on the cuticle of her left thumb. "Either Jane Macias is still alive or he's broken the pattern. He's moved the double up in the count. Jane should have been number five. But he's mimicked the Snow White's sixth and seventh murders, and Jane's still out there."

Fitz nodded. "Might be we just haven't found her yet."

"Might be. Baldwin, knowing what we know, how likely is it that he'd change the pattern at this point?"

"Considering he didn't do it in the past eighteen copycats, highly unlikely. He may be decompensating. The lack of the frankincense and myrrh oil is interesting. Escalation, distraction, interruption, all are reasonable explanations. And if that's the case…well, suffice it to say that if he has Jane Macias, she could be suffering more than the other girls thus far."

Taylor sighed, stared back at the little house. "Like getting raped and having your throat cut isn't bad enough. I need to go back to headquarters and sort this out. Fitz, you mind sticking around, running the scene for me?"

"Of course. I'll meet you back there as soon as we're wrapped up. Crime Scene will take this place apart. We'll find something, LT."

"Okay if we steal your car?"

"Yeah. I'll get a ride with Parks. You go on now." He tossed her the keys and went back across the lawn, snapping his fingers at a crime-scene tech, who straightened and came to him as if he'd been ordered to march by a general. Taylor smiled. Fitz knew what he was doing. If there was anything to find, he'd be the one to find it.

"Get in. I'll drive."

Baldwin just nodded and slid in the passenger side of the car.

Marcus and Lincoln were in the office when they returned.

Taylor came through the door and went straight to her desk. She picked up the phone and called Mitchell Price.

He answered on the first ring. "I heard."

"Good. We're in a shit of a mess now. Two more apparent Snow White victims, one girl still missing, a dead witness after a shoot-out at the hospital. How much more can this day bring?"

"Don't ever ask that, Lieutenant. It will only bring you misery."

"Yeah. Well, I'm going to slough through some of this paperwork. Fitz is holding down the fort at the massage-parlor crime scene. Is Remy St. Claire still in town?"

"I don't know. She hightailed it out of the M.E.'s office after that damn press conference. Have you heard any more from the FBI today?"

"No, Charlotte Douglas never checked in with us, as far as I know. Baldwin said she's deep into her own investigation about the previous murders. I'll ask the boys about it. Anything else I need to be aware of?"

"No. That should do it. Keep me apprised of the situation, okay?"

"Righto. Are you coming tonight?"

"Miss your bachelorette party? Never."

"I think we're skipping dinner."

Price sighed loudly. "Okay. I'll see you guys there."

They hung up and Taylor went back into the bullpen. Baldwin was finishing a rundown of the scene they'd just come from. Taylor pulled up a chair, turned it backward and straddled the seat.

"That's it from me. I'm going to go check on Charlotte, see what's happening with her, okay? I'll see you later." Baldwin nodded at the boys and gave her a small kiss. She smiled at him.

"Don't get yourself too riled up. You need to go watch naked women dance tonight."

He rolled his eyes at her and waved as he went into the hall. Taylor turned back to Lincoln and Marcus, leaning her chin on her hands on top of the chair back.

"So. How are you guys this lovely afternoon?"

"Fine. Did you see Frank Richardson leaving?" Lincoln gestured toward the door. "He just split, right before you came in."

"No. What did he have to say?"

"Just that he had some information you might find

interesting. He spent the day going through all of his old stories. Too bad you missed him."

"I'll call him later. Where are we with the Baptist shooting?"

Marcus stood up and paced the room. "We're nowhere. Guy disappeared into thin air."

Lincoln scratched his head. "Why would he shoot the place up and run away with the girl, only to end up shooting her, anyway? Why didn't he just kill her in the hospital room?"

"Baldwin and I talked about that. She told me one helluva story. She was an asset, a trained asset. I have to assume that the shooter went in with instructions to take her back alive. We happened upon him at the exact wrong time, and we got her killed. I'm not happy about that."

"Can't say I blame you. Listen, we talked to Remy's grandparents again. They weren't aware that she might be sneaking out, don't know who she could have gone with. According to them, she was a sweet, obedient little girl. We're waiting to hear back from the school about who she hung out with. The canvass of the bars is getting us nowhere. We've got a couple of patrols passing out the pictures of all four girls, but no one re-members seeing them. I think we'd be wise to go to the media with it."

"Damn. I think you're right. Without help, it's needle-in-a-haystack time. Thanks for handling that for me. And let me know what the school says. If they give you any guff, let me know. I've still got friends in the administration. They'll talk if we need them to. What about Jane Macias? What's happening there?"

Lincoln reached over his shoulder and neatly

snagged a laptop off his desk. "Got her computer. I haven't found anything yet. Most of her work is password-protected, and she used rotating binary generator accounts to give random pass codes. Based on the Bernoulli equation."

Taylor shook her head. "Huh?"

"Bernoulli's principle? Increases in velocity, decreases in pressure create lift. Commonly taught as why airplanes fly, though it would have to be a perfect world for that particular equation to work. It's just easy to explain. The binary generator uses the velocity equation from Bernoulli to—"

Taylor started laughing. Despite the urbane exterior, Lincoln was a computer genius, a regular geek at heart. "What you're saying is this is pretty sophisticated stuff for a reporter?"

"For anyone, actually. There's something in here she doesn't want anyone to read, that's for sure."

"Nothing on her family? I'm absolutely shocked we haven't had a frantic call from someone who knows her."

"Not that I've found. Once I have the pass codes cracked, I'll be able to get into her address book. Waiting on a call back from Google about the warrant to get the password to her e-mail."

"If Snow White got to her, why haven't we found her body?" Marcus asked.

Taylor raised an eyebrow. "I've been wondering the same thing. Maybe he didn't take her. Maybe she was working on something that got her into trouble. Or we just haven't found her body. What about the boyfriend? Think he might have anything to do with it?"

Marcus snorted. "Skip. Kid couldn't find his ass with a lamp and a map. He's so moonstruck by her, I ended up wishing *I* had her phone number. No, I'm betting he had nothing to do with this. You just can't fake that kind of distraught."

"So where is she?"

No one answered her. She straightened, redid her ponytail and gave the men a half smile. "Great. That's just great. No signs, no paths, no clues. Clean trails, but the physical evidence should lead us somewhere. Either we're missing something or this guy is brilliantly calculating. Though, the massage girls seem to be a step down for him. There wasn't any of the anointing oils on these new bodies, at least none that Sam could visibly identify. Baldwin thinks he might have been interrupted. Or maybe he's finally screwed up."

She stood, turned for her office. "I'm going to nail some of the shit that's piled up today. Linc, tell me when you get into her laptop, okay?"

Lincoln whistled Lohengrin's "Here Comes the Bride" after her, and she shot him a bird. That broke the tension; they all started laughing.

A loud cough jerked them from their revelries. Captain Price stood in the doorway. Lincoln's whistle switched to a low-pitched version of the theme song to *Dragnet.* Price just shook his head, a smile tugging at the corners of his mouth. His luxurious Yosemite Sam mustache moved vertically, more than making up for the lack of hair on his head.

"Boss, you need to give these boys a raise." Taylor tipped her head toward Lincoln and Marcus. "They've almost got this case cracked."

Price glanced at his watch. "I've got time now, if you want to brief me."

Lincoln stood. "Sure thing. Taylor, you go on, get caught up. Little man and I got this covered."

She flashed him a grateful smile, saluted Price and ducked into her office. She wished she felt like things were coming together. They were running out of time.

Twenty

Baldwin watched Charlotte Douglas pace as she talked on her cell phone. She was wearing a slim, cream-colored sheath of some silky material that swished every time she took a step. He glanced at his watch—nearly 8:00 p.m. It was time to get out of this hotel room, get on with his life. Taylor and the rest of the crew would be at VIBE, waiting for him. He needed to get this done and get out of Dodge.

She'd called him here, to her suite, refusing to meet him at the field office. He knew exactly what she was about, wasn't going to fall for it. He wanted her gone, the sooner the better. He had his whole life in front of him, and Charlotte damn Douglas wasn't a part of any scenario he could imagine.

Charlotte was stalking in front of the plate-glass window, obviously upset. "You really need to work with me here. There's nothing else I can do at the moment. That's right. Yes, sir. Yes. I'll be back this evening. Good. I'll talk to you later."

Charlotte hung up the cell phone and stopped dead

in the middle of the room. She looked at Baldwin and smiled, cocking a hip forward, her legs tensed so the calf muscles stood out and her arms folded behind her back. He knew this pose. She'd used it too many times in the past for him to fall for it. It made her look like a predator, not a sex kitten.

"Baldwin," she began, her voice husky. He knew that trick, too.

He held up a hand. "Charlotte, why are you still here? You've delivered your presentation. There's nothing we have at the field office that you don't have back in Quantico. I don't see you putting forth any resolutions to this case." He nodded at the cell phone, still clutched in her hand. "Obviously Quantico is calling you home. Why aren't you gone already?"

She glanced at the phone, then smiled. "That wasn't who you think, and I'll get on a plane when I'm good and ready, Baldwin. I have some business to conclude here with the field office, if you don't mind."

"Who do you need to conclude your business with, Charlotte? The field office or me?"

"Ooh, Dr. Baldwin. Always the insightful man. Conceited, too. What in the world makes you think any of this has to do with you?"

"It's your MO, Charlotte. I've been there with you, remember? I know what you're up to, and it won't work. You need to leave, now. I don't want to have anything more to do with you."

She turned and looked out the window, the lights flickering across her face. "There was a time, John Baldwin, you wanted everything to do with me. Have you told your darling bride that?"

"Do *not* call me that. And yes, Charlotte, Taylor is fully aware that we've been intimate. And she couldn't care less. You don't threaten her, not in the least."

"I don't?" She turned slowly, edging her way toward Baldwin. He stood in the middle of the room, shaking his head as he watched her approach. An overgrown feral cat caught in a housecat's body, that was Charlotte on the prowl. She'd just as soon tear out your throat as curl up in your lap.

"Leave it alone. You mean nothing to me. Now, tell me what I can do to get you out of my hair? Permanently, preferably."

She threw her head back and laughed. "Oh, you are the poor, put-upon man, aren't you? Can't take a little bit of teasing. I thought you'd at least be civil, for old times' sake."

She was within two feet now, stalking him with her eyes, her arms loose at her side. He stood his ground, damned if he was going to back down from her.

"Listen, I need to go. What is it you so desperately needed to see me about?"

The faint scent of gardenias wheeled into his senses, and he cursed his body as it responded, albeit briefly, to the aroma. There was a time when things were good between them, and those were the moments the flowery scent reminded him of. She was there, against him now, her hips brushing his gently, her face tipped up, those lips full and inviting. He leaned in for half a second, then stepped back.

"No. Stop right now. I know what you're trying to do, and it's not going to happen."

"Ah, shucks, Mr. Profiler. You're just so big and

hard." She started to reach for his crotch, but he caught her hand, twisted her arm hard so she was forced to turn away from him to keep it in the socket. He shoved once, and she sprawled away, stumbling into the chair.

"Bastard," she hissed.

There, that was more like it. Seductress though she may be, the operative word with Charlotte was always *evil.*

"You ever come near me or Taylor again, you *will* regret it, Charlotte. Mark my words." The tone of his voice surprised even him, and Charlotte flinched back as if she'd been hit when he spoke.

He left the room, left her behind, her eyes round with disbelief. The threat was real, and they both knew it. He didn't care.

The door slammed and Charlotte took a moment to recover. A shadow came from the bathroom.

"Don't worry, dear. I'll murder him for the way he just treated you. Though I must admit, I'm a bit disappointed. I would have enjoyed watching you fuck him. He's quite a…large man. He'd be hard to take down without a fight." He flexed his hands, opening the palms wide, then curling his fingers in slowly, one by one.

"Shut the fuck up." She whirled away, went to the window again and stared into the night.

Twenty-One

Nashville, Tennessee
Thursday, December 18
9:30 p.m.

Taylor finished up her paperwork, showered and changed at the station. Knowing she could put it off no more, she took the 4Runner up Church Street, ignoring a call on the scanner about a drug shooting down in the Lischey Avenue projects. Not her problem, not tonight. B-shift homicide could grab that one. But she pulled into the parking lot of VIBE with murder on her mind.

Lots and lots of murder, coupled with a few she'd like to commit herself. She watched an upscale pro dip around the corner of the building with a john on her heels. Ten bucks he didn't know he would be rolled by the girl's pimp for a couple hundred once they'd done the deed. She debated going after them, then decided to skip it. For tonight, she wouldn't be a cop. She'd just be a girl who was about to get married, out on the town for a fun night with her friends.

How in the world had she been talked into this?

The music spilled from the doors. She recognized one of her favorite bands, Garbage. Shirley Manson wanted to know "Why do you love me?" and Taylor laughed to herself. How apropos for a bachelor/bachelorette party.

She crossed the parking lot and ducked inside the club, the music pounding and thumping, the lights flashing. A scent tickled her nose, sweet, with an overlay of patchouli, like a sex-drenched head shop. Girls dressed in see-through negligees with paste-on nipples and G-strings wandered past her, looking her up and down appreciatively. The black-floored stage was covered with a trio of girls, a threesome act—one blonde, one brunette, one redhead. They writhed and twisted around each other, and Taylor couldn't help but stop and watch for a moment. The obvious choreography that had gone into the dance was impressive. Not being entranced like the men sitting in a semicircle in front of the stage, Taylor was able to see past the nudity, see the work the girls put into their performance. They were all young, probably thought that this road was temporary.

Taylor had seen it too many times before—the girls who worked the clubs were favorites among the rank and file at Metro. They were safe, protected to an extent, until they crossed swords with the wrong guy. Then they'd end up like those Spanish girls from the massage parlor this afternoon, or like Saraya Gonzalez, murdered in cold blood.

Taylor didn't see Sam, so she took a table in the back. She reveled in the few minutes of alone time, the first she'd had all day. She ordered a beer from the scantily clad waitress, demurred the invitation to be escorted to a private room in the back for a special lap dance and sat back, tuning out, not really seeing anything happening in front of her.

Nagging at the back of her mind was the story of sexual slavery the Spanish girl had told her. Saraya Gonzalez. The name was pretty, but that face, while delicate and attractive, had been so vacant. Taylor mentally plugged into that conversation, determined to figure out the link between the girl shot at the hospital and the obvious Snow White victims this afternoon. She had one thin, tenuous thread to go by. The massage parlors. Saraya Gonzalez had been trapped in a life of servitude at a massage parlor. The girls killed this afternoon worked in a massage parlor. Taylor had a hunch that if she could tie the two together, she might get a solution. Though the chasm was deep between the two cases, Taylor had been a cop long enough to know you never dismiss a coincidence.

"What is his name?" Taylor had asked Saraya.

"Oh, no. I no tell. I no want to get dead." Poor girl's eyes were dead already, it wouldn't take much to finish her off. The bullets at the hospital had been overkill.

"Taylor!"

She jumped, looked up to see Sam and her husband, Simon, standing over her.

"You were so far gone, girl, where were you?"

"Sorry, Sam. Hey, Simon. How's it going?" Taylor scooted her chair around to make room.

Simon mumbled a reply. A good Catholic boy, he was desperately uncomfortable to be in the strip club with Sam. He'd settle down once she left, Taylor was sure of that. They'd gone to high school and college together; Taylor knew his reticence was simply respect for his wife.

Sam took a seat, ordered two more beers, glanced appreciatively around at the nakedness, the girls writhing on the stage pole and nodded. "Yep, this should do the trick. Get the man so fired up I'll be getting lucky all night."

Simon went a deep burgundy. "God, Sam, could you just leave now?"

Sam nuzzled up to Simon and chucked him under the chin. "Just you wait, sexy man. You'll get rewarded, trust me." She kissed him; he turned a deeper shade of beet-red. Sam turned back to Taylor with a grin a mile wide.

"Jesus, Sam. You're a sick puppy, you know that?"

"Speaking of puppies…"

She pointed at the door, where Marcus, Fitz and Lincoln were standing. It seemed the basic premise of the club. A person came through the door, stood, took it all in, then decided what they wanted—a seat up close, a drink at the bar, a lap dance or a private room. The three men were swarmed in an instant. Captain Price followed them through the door a moment later. Extricating themselves, they spotted Taylor and Sam and wound their way to the table, pulling up chairs and getting settled.

"LT, where's Baldwin?" Fitz asked, leaning in close so he could be heard—the music had bumped up a notch. The bar was filling, the evening getting into full swing.

Taylor looked at the door, and Baldwin walked through it. Her heart filled at the sight of him, at the way he found her eyes, didn't look at the other women, just made his way across the room to her, planted a kiss on her lips, then took the proffered chair next to her.

"Long night?" she asked. Her look asked something entirely different—*did you get rid of her?*

"You could say that." He squeezed her hand, an unmistakable *I hope so.*

She gave him a smile, then stood. "Sam, let's leave these boys alone so they can misbehave." She dropped forty dollars in Baldwin's lap. "Have a lap dance on me, sugar." She blew him a kiss to the hoots and hollers from her coworkers, then walked to the door with her back ramrod straight.

"That's some woman you've got there, Baldwin. Don't fuck it up." Sam gave Simon a quick peck on the forehead, then left them, as well.

Fitz stood, signaling to a group of women in various states of dishabille nearby. "Okay, Mr. FBI man. It's time for you to experience a last night of bachelorhood, Nashville-style."

Taylor was already stomping her feet from the cold when Sam joined her in the street in front of the club.

"About damn time," she grumbled, blowing warm air into her cupped hands. "What were you doing, giving him the lap dance?"

"More like some motherly advice. Got waylaid at the door by some chick. C'mon, let's go in here, it'll be warmer. And quieter. Am I getting old, or was it loud in there?"

"It's loud. They design them to be so loud and flashy your conscience turns off—sensory overload. Makes men do things they normally wouldn't."

"Amen to that."

Taylor glanced at her sharply but followed her into the

small bar next door. Control was nearly empty, the music muted, the lights dim. Taylor felt her shoulders relax.

They ordered beers and took a table in the corner. Taylor took off her jacket, realized she'd forgotten to remove her weapon and holster. Her Glock was still tucked snugly against her right hip.

It wasn't unheard of. She was much more comfortable with the weapon than without, though she usually went with a small revolver in an ankle holster when she was off duty and out on the town.

She saw the bartender making a beeline toward her, his face contorted in anger. He pulled up short when he saw her shield.

"Sorry, Officer." He held up both hands, as if she were trying to rob him on the street and had yelled "Put 'em up!"

"Lieutenant. That's okay. And put your hands down. I'm not arresting you." She shrugged back into the jacket. No sense advertising.

"Yeah, yeah. Sorry about that. How about the next round on me?"

"No problem…." She left it open, and the man supplied his name.

"Jerry. I'm the bartender here."

"I caught that. Thanks for understanding, Jerry. No need to buy a round."

"No, I insist." He disappeared, and Taylor looked at Sam, exasperated. All she wanted to do was drink a couple of beers, get the next two days over with, wrap up the cases and go to Europe. She was running out of patience with the whole scenario.

Sam just smiled and excused herself to go to the Ladies'.

Jerry returned with two beers and a sly look on his face. Taylor took a bottle of Miller Lite from him, then sat back, eyebrows raised. He obviously had something to get off his mind.

She was right.

Jerry leaned close while he handed Taylor her beer. "See that guy that just came in? Don't look, but I think he was here the other night."

"Really? My goodness, a repeat customer. In this neck of the woods. Imagine the odds."

"No, you don't get it. I mean he was here the night that little girl went missing."

Taylor nearly dropped her bottle.

"What are you talking about? Which girl?"

"The little black-haired reporter. Jane. I think the paper said her last name was Macias. I don't remember if the guy was in then, but I absolutely remember that he was here the night Jane disappeared."

"What about the last victim, Giselle St. Claire? Was she in here, too?"

"Couldn't say. I don't remember what she looks like. Jane, I remember. She was a sweet kid. That's not good, is it?" His face fell.

"Uh, Jerry? Did you tell anyone this?"

"Well, no. But I'm telling you now. Isn't that enough? I just put it all together. I didn't see him again, so I didn't really think too much about it. And I don't know if I want to get too involved, you know what I mean?"

He rolled up a sleeve and Taylor saw the ink, the homemade prison tattoos that covered his forearm. Yes, she understood entirely.

"Okay, Jerry. This is great. Thanks so much. Go back

behind the bar now. My friend is coming back. We'll take it from here."

"She a cop, your friend? 'Cause I got a…bat, behind the counter."

"The medical examiner, actually. But there's a gaggle of good police next door, and we're going to get their attention and have a chat with this guy. Okay? Now, go on back to the bar, you're starting to look suspicious. And don't worry."

He went, and she sat back in her chair, looking at the man Jerry had pointed out.

He was at least six foot four, with brushed blond hair cut high and tight, as if he were military. She couldn't see his face full on, just in profile. He sat comfortably, hands loose between his knees, not quite leaning on his forearms. He was strung tight, but not ready to snap. The door to the bar opened and a woman walked through. Taylor watched his body language, saw him open himself. It was almost imperceptible. The woman ignored him, walked right past and went to the bar. She plopped onto a stool, ordered a drink, lit up a cigarette.

The man glanced over his shoulder at the bar, and Taylor felt the waves of anger roll off him. The intensity of the emotion nearly took her breath away; it was overtly negative. Taylor was certain if Baldwin had been in the room, he would have felt it, too.

She felt her breath begin to quicken. The palpable animosity, the powerful frame, the casual yet hip sprung attitude… She glanced at Jerry, who was talking to the woman at the bar and stealing looks at the man.

Sam entered Taylor's pinpoint field of vision. She was walking right at the man, a casual, hip-swaying,

"I'm having a good time" motion to her gait. The man reached out a hand and grabbed her wrist as she walked by. Taylor was up out of her seat before Sam's mouth fell open in surprise.

Three good strides would get her there, and she'd taken two when she heard Sam giggle, roll her eyes, then pull away from the man and head toward her.

"Going potty?" she asked. Taylor just nodded and kept moving. She needed to see this guy head-on.

She made it to the bathroom door, ducked inside, counted to five, then came out, wiping her hands as if she'd just gone in to wash them. He was gone. She took in the entire bar, realized he was nowhere to be seen. His beer bottle wasn't on the table, either. She walked to Jerry, whispered to him, "Where?"

Jerry shook his head. "I didn't see him get up."

Taylor went to Sam. "The guy who grabbed your wrist. Did you see him leave?"

"Yeah. He winked at me as he went out the door. He got up the second you walked past. Why?"

The scent of cigar smoke wafted to her nose. She looked around, didn't see anyone smoking a cigar. The bar was empty. Taylor had her cell phone out, speed-dialed Baldwin's number. She gave Sam a wry smile.

"Whatever you do, don't wash your hands. Something was very wrong with that man. You may have just touched our killer."

Twenty-Two

Charlotte Douglas schemed as the Lear jet left the terminal building. As far as John Baldwin knew, it was flying her away from Nashville.

The sheer audacity of Baldwin, to push her away with so little regard for her feelings. Who was he to say what she was to do with her life? He'd decided she should leave Nashville. He'd decided she would no longer be of use in capturing the Snow White Killer. He'd pushed her away like she was a whore. Well, she wouldn't be treated like that, not by him, not by anyone.

He'd had a field agent escort her to the plane. Five minutes after her friend had left, an earnest young man with jutting ears and a solemn smile knocked on her door. After identifying himself as an agent with the Nashville field office, he'd taken her suitcases and practically thrown her out of the hotel room.

She wouldn't stand for this kind of treatment. Who did these people think they were? They had no idea who they were dealing with.

She left the terminal in a cab and made her way back

downtown. Checking back into the same hotel, she dropped her bags in the room and placed a phone call. She was lonely. She decided to go to the house for the evening instead of hanging at the hotel. A night in her old room, a meal with her father, a thrill with her lover— all would serve to get her back on track. She would come back to the hotel tomorrow, maintain the slim veneer of legitimacy she'd worked hard to conceive.

They weren't finished. She would have her vengeance.

Twenty-Three

Taylor and Baldwin sat close together, re-creating the past half hour. It was entirely possible that the man who'd been in Control this night, as well as the other nights, wasn't their killer at all. But Taylor had felt something so malevolent, so horrid, emanating from him in that one brief moment that she couldn't stop thinking about him.

A crime-scene tech had arrived quietly. If this was the haunt of their killer, they didn't want to draw too much attention to the fact that they were closing in. The tech had gone over Sam's arm carefully but got nothing. The man had paid for his beer with three one-dollar bills, all of which were confiscated for processing, but the odds of them actually finding some kind of DNA or prints that would be both usable and admissible in court were slim to none.

Jerry the bartender had proved worth his weight in gold. He'd positively identified each of the four women killed by the Snow White copycat. All four of them had been in the bar at one time or another. Finally, they had their staging area. Taylor hoped like hell she'd just caught a glimpse of their killer.

A police artist had been working with Sam and Jerry to create a composite, but the end result was too generic. It could be anyone. Their mystery man had nothing exceptional about him except a bad haircut, at least that either Jerry or Sam could recall.

Taylor was furious with herself. She had felt it, the malice that radiated off the man. She'd played the situation wrong. Maybe he'd seen her badge and gun and it scared him away. Maybe she was just imaging the whole thing, and the man she'd seen was just another patron. She was wound so tight, it wasn't so far-fetched.

She was standing by the bar, aggravated as all get out, tempted to topple a pile of Amstel Lights, when the crime-scene tech shouted for her.

"Lieutenant? I've got something here."

She went to the woman, a short, overweight brunette named Ricki with a sweet smile and an even sweeter disposition.

"Hey, Ricki, what do you have?"

She held up a mass of plastic. "Straws. All tied in knots."

Taylor slipped on a latex glove and took the mass from Ricki. She flashed back to an image of the man, his hands loose between his knees. He might have been tying the straws then.

"This is perfect. Perfect. Thanks, Ricki. Bag this for me, okay? That's going to be an important piece, so be careful with it, okay?"

"Gotcha, boss."

"Hold up. What do you have there?" Baldwin came up to her, put an arm around her shoulders. Taylor smiled.

"Show him, Ricki."

Baldwin looked closely at the clear plastic bag, now closed with red evidence tape. "Intricate."

"You could say that. If they match up to the knots in the ropes we have in the lab, we might have something. Ricki, can you test them for trace, too? We're looking for some more of that creamy substance found on the previous victims.

She turned to Baldwin, excitement making her heart pound. "Maybe. Maybe, maybe, maybe. Those knots are so different, so unique."

"That they are. I can imagine a killer this precise using the knots as a tool, a pastime. Something so intricate takes practice."

"Well, he was pissed when that chick came in and blew right past him. The guy that sat here is used to being admired, used to being fussed over. If it was the copycat, I'd bet we're going to have another murder, and soon. How much lead time do you think he needs now?"

Baldwin looked at her, eyebrow raised. "We might make a profiler out of you yet. If he's running on a certain timetable, we won't know until we catch him. But if he's just on a spree, he could take another, kill the one he's got, whatever. He's not thinking clearly, he's upset. This doesn't match up to the original profile of this killer being a meticulous planner. He's already killed two today, three this week. If he's not sated now, he never will be. He's completely broken Snow White's pattern. He's working on his own now. He won't just stop. We're going to have to catch him or kill him."

Taylor remembered the man's silhouette, the tense way he took up space, and shuddered. "I'll be happy to make that happen."

They stayed at the bar for another hour, trying to act normal as the CS techs surreptitiously combed through the place. It was late, and Taylor was tired. When Baldwin offered to drive her home, she didn't resist.

She let him tuck her into bed, accepted a kiss on the forehead, like a child just finished with a bedtime story.

As he was leaving the room, his hand on the light switch, she called to him, "I'm supposed to do some things tomorrow. Girl things. Sam things."

"Wedding things?"

The quick bloom of panic in her chest when the word *wedding* was spoken made her feel stupid. This was silly. She could go toe to toe with killers, yet she was afraid to stand up in front of a crowd? Decision made, game, set, match.

"Yes. Wedding things."

"So we're on?"

"Come here." He did as she asked, came back to the bed. She sat up, slid the covers down to her waist, and pulled him to her, hugging him hard.

"We're on."

Twenty-Four

Nashville, Tennessee
Friday, December 19
8:00 a.m.

Taylor got up early, grabbed a latte and fought the melting snow and ice down to the spa where she was supposed to meet Sam. Even after three days, the roads were anything but clear, but they were passable if you knew what you were doing. Taylor did, and apparently so did the Vietnamese woman who owned the salon. Taylor parked in the lot, one of four cars. The snow was due to start again later in the morning, the temperature was going to drop, making the roads treacherous.

All of this just felt so wrong—she should be at work, should be combing through files, doing everything in her power to stop two killers, one old, one new. Yet here she was, sitting in front of a spa, looking forward to getting a massage, to spending some time away from the cases. The guilt of wanting to be disengaged from it all was bitter in the back of her mouth.

She looked at herself in the rearview mirror. What was she supposed to do? Last night she'd committed not to cancel the wedding, then sealed that promise. Baldwin was right. She wasn't the only cop on the force. They could, would catch the killer. If she were around when it happened, fantastic. If not, the crew would have her never-ending thanks.

Cases don't resolve themselves in a week. She kept that mantra running through her head as she redid her ponytail, turned off the truck and went into the spa.

It was 8:00 a.m., and she yawned. She could have slept in, skipped the whole spa day. But Sam would have killed her. "You haven't had your nails done in months, Taylor," she'd say. "Lighten up and enjoy yourself for once." She took a sip of her latte, hoping the caffeine would kick in soon and help her wake up. She was exhausted. Maybe Sam was right, a day of pampering couldn't be all bad.

She checked in with a young Vietnamese girl, then took a seat, fiddled with a brochure on micro dermabrasion. It looked like it hurt.

Thirty hours from now, she would be a married woman. Looking at the sheet of paper in front of her, she laughed. She'd been doodling while she waited for her appointment to start, and she felt like a teenager when she saw the initials intertwined within a heart that she'd unconsciously drawn. TEJ + JWB = TLA. True Love Always. Oh, God.

She wondered how long this was going to take, then mentally chastised herself. Day off, day off, day off. She kept repeating the words until Sam blew in the door. Wearing sweats and flip-flops, dragging a large Birkin bag that was stuffed with God knew what, she barked a brief hello in Vietnamese to the shop owner, then enfolded Taylor in a rib-cracking hug. Her nose was cold against Taylor's cheek.

"Morning, sugar! I am so frickin' excited. Are you not just about to die? It's tomorrow, finally. Seriously, T, you're getting married tomorrow! I feel like we've been planning this for months."

"That would be because you've been planning this for months. My God, woman, aren't you freezing? Flip-flops in a blizzard?" Taylor looked down at her own practically covered feet, ensconced in her worn pair of calf-high Uggs.

"Taylor," Sam admonished, ignoring the gibe. "C'mon, sweetie. This is going to be a simple, elegant wedding. Nothing fancy, no doves or horse-drawn carriages. It's going to be exactly what you've always wanted. It's very you."

Taylor rolled her eyes at her best friend. When they were growing up, back when they still had some semblance of innocence to them, they'd planned their weddings. They'd picked their fantasy grooms out of magazines, assembled frilly, doily-packed scrapbooks with all the appropriate wedding accoutrements. They giggled and dreamed and grew starry-eyed at the thought of true love.

As she grew older, those fantasies left her. The whole idea of a fairy-tale wedding seemed a bit absurd, so frivolous. But she was committed now. No turning back. No white-sand beach at sunset or Elvis impersonator in Vegas. No, she'd agreed to the whole church thing. Full circle for her. She'd started out wanting that, decided it wasn't for her, and was now reaping what she'd sown all those years ago.

At least after last night, her cold feet were strictly from the weather.

Sam was eyeing her patiently, waiting for some sign that all was well in Taylorville. With a wry smile, Taylor winked at her. Ah, who was she trying to kid? She was excited. Scared witless, but excited nonetheless.

"Okay. You're right. I can't wait. I'm nervous as hell, too, so I hope you made my massage an extralong one. With hot stones and shit. I haven't been relaxed in the two months since the Snow White started. Hey, did you—"

Sam shook her head, interrupting. "Hell. No. We are not, I repeat, are not going to talk about work today. This is your day to relax and get beautiful. You got me?"

Taylor waved her hands in submission. "Fine. You don't have to be so touchy. I was just wondering—"

"Zip it. No wondering." Sam eyed her for a moment, then shook her head. "You just have the bug, don't you? Can't stop thinking about this case for two seconds. To answer your question, no, I didn't find the frankincense and myrrh on the massage-parlor victims. Now, you listen to me. That's it. Moratorium on death and destruction for one day. Deal?"

Taylor smiled at her best friend. "Fine. Deal. What did you do with the twins?"

They were interrupted by a soft-spoken woman with arched cheekbones and blue-black straight hair. "Oh, Miss Sam, Miss Taylor. Pedicure first, ladies."

"Thank you, Mai." The lady led them to a side room where soft music played.

Taylor settled into a massage chair, dunking her feet

in the warm water. Sam was seated to her right, happy to talk about her babies instead of dead bodies. Madeline and Matthew had come into the world only two months earlier, and were already the focus of everyone's attention.

"Simon has them. Bless his heart, he was thrilled at the thought of keeping them today. He's so tickled by everything they do. Me, I love them to death, but I could use a nap. Twenty naps. I'm going to sleep through most of today as it is."

They passed the morning comfortably, chatting, doing the girlie things that would signal to the world that Taylor was getting married. French manicures, pedicures, facials. A lovely massage, a quick eyebrow and bikini wax, then they were ready to go. Five hours of pure, unadulterated primping. As they walked out into the freezing air, Taylor was amazed at how relaxed she felt.

Taylor gave Sam a quick hug goodbye, then turned to her 4Runner. In the window's reflection, a flash of black hair caught her eye. Raven hair, pale face, crimson lips. Just another customer entering the spa. But the image of Giselle St. Claire's broken body popped into her mind, followed by the massage-parlor victims.

The likeness of the pretty young woman to the murdered girls instantly killed all the hours of relaxation she'd just experienced. Snow White was haunting her.

Despite Sam's wishes, she had to swing by the office, wrap up one or two little things, make sure the paperwork was up-to-date for all of her other cases. Maybe get one last glimpse into the Snow White war room before she left. Everything was being handled. The FBI were involved, and that Charlotte Douglas bitch. The case would be well covered by her team. Once she was satisfied all the appropriate wheels were in motion, she could put thoughts of everything else out of her head. Focus on Baldwin, on their life together. The idea of leaving the case open and active made her stomach hurt.

The CJC looked forlorn in the winter landscape. The cold stone appeared colder, the windows seemed to have empty rooms behind them. Since there was more snow predicted, she assumed people had taken off early. Taylor stared at the entrance, the back door she'd come through hundreds of times, realizing that this would be the last time she'd see it from this perspective. Swallowing the misgivings, she bounded up the stairs, swiped her card and took the hallway to her office. She didn't run into a soul, confirming her earlier feeling. The building was practically empty. Except for the homicide offices.

She turned the corner and was greeted with a hail of shouts and cheers.

"Taylor, what the hell are you doing here?" Marcus scrambled out of a chair, making a place by the space heater for his boss to sit. Taylor took the chair gratefully, slipping off her gloves and rubbing her hands together in front of the heater, luxuriating in the billowing heat it dispensed. She noticed Marcus sidling across the room casually. He reached behind him, pulled the door to her office closed. Fitz tried to distract her.

"Yeah, LT, aren't you supposed to be getting all beautified for the wedding?" Fitz was informal today, his hair an exceptional steely-gray, hunter's plaid shirt untucked, his increasingly smaller paunch spilling over the tops of his jeans. He was unapologetic about his garb, just leaned further back in his chair, crossing his arms behind his head. "And what time's the rehearsal again?"

He winked at Lincoln Ross, who had glanced up from his industrious work digging a rock out of the tread of his Timberland boots. Lincoln gave Taylor a smile, the small gap between his two front teeth the only mar on his otherwise handsome face. She smiled back at him, comforted by his tranquility.

"You guys are a regular riot. Why are you all dressed like you're going camping?"

"Because you weren't supposed to be in today and we were all planning on cutting out and going camping," Fitz grinned at her.

"Really? Camping? In a snowstorm?"

"Is it snowing again?" Lincoln went to the window, frowning at the street below.

"It was starting up when I came in." Taylor started to go into her office, but all three men moved toward her, saying no simultaneously. Fitz guided her to his desk and held out the chair for her.

"Any reason in particular I'm not allowed to go into my own office, boys?"

"Nope, no reason. As a matter of fact, you really should bundle up and head on home." Marcus smiled at her, Lincoln nodded his agreement.

"But I need to wrap a few things up."

Fitz shook his head. "No, you don't. Just stop thinking about it, LT. You're going to be gone for three weeks. The Fibbies are all over this like a fried june bug. You get married, go to Italy and have a wonderful start to your new life. We'll get it covered. I promise."

"Has anyone heard from the esteemed Charlotte

Douglas since she returned to Quantico? And is there any word on Jane Macias? There's a serial killer out there, in case y'all have forgotten. I want to help. I think I should postpone—"

Lincoln cut her off. "Oh, hell no, sister. Not a chance. You're getting married tomorrow whether you like it or not. End of story. How d'you like my head?"

Taylor looked him over. She couldn't believe she hadn't noticed it immediately, chastised herself for being so self-absorbed. Lincoln had shaved his head bare, removing the curly dreadlocks he'd been sporting for the past few months. His skin was a shiny café au lait, glistening with conditioner. She got out of the warm chair, circled him a few times, contemplating. He'd looked like a sexy Rasta singer à la Lenny Kravitz with the dreads, but Taylor couldn't place who he reminded her of shaved.

"Very slick, my friend. That tux is going to be stunning on you. You'll be the most handsome bridesmaid in the whole world." She bumped his shoulder lightly with her hip, opened her mouth to speak. He cut her off.

"Naw, don't you go making any speeches now. We're all good with the setup. Fitz walks you down the aisle, Marcus and I have equal standing as bridesmen, even though we'll be on Baldwin's side, and Sam's the maid of honor."

"Matron of honor," Marcus chimed in. "A maid of honor is for someone who isn't married yet." He grinned, happy to have a chance to poke fun at his friend.

"Whatever, butthead. All that matters is our favorite lieutenant's getting married." Lincoln jumped out of the chair. He and Marcus started a chorus. The baritone and tenor filled the room.

"Here comes the bride, short, fat and wide…." They dissolved into giggles before they reached the third line.

Fitz and Taylor watched the two goof off, shaking their heads and laughing at their antics. Despite the specter of a serial killer in their midst, the homicide team was in understandably high spirits.

Taylor looked at Fitz. "Is there really a reason why I'm not allowed in my office?"

"There really is. Wouldn't want to spoil the surprise. Just a little something for your wedding night."

She gave him a dirty look.

"Oh, stop it. We're just wrapping presents. So why don't you go home?"

She looked at him, deep in the eyes, and he sighed. "Okay. Okay. You can stay. But you still can't go in your office."

Moments like this, she wondered who was really in charge of the unit.

Lincoln's phone rang, and he and Marcus stopped horsing around so he could answer it. He rolled his eyes and nodded, hanging up without a word.

"Body. Who wants to go?"

"Me," Taylor stood. When they all started in griping at her, she shot them a look. "Lincoln's primary. I'm just going along for the ride. It will be like I'm not even there. Let's go."

As they packed it up and left, Taylor's emotions were mixed. Every time they got called out now, she expected to find the mutilated body of Jane Macias. Damn, she wanted to catch this guy before they blew the country.

Twenty-Five

Nashville, Tennessee
Friday, December 19
3:00 p.m.

To Taylor's frustration, Lincoln talked about everything but the Snow White murders as they drove to West
Nashville, looking for the address they'd been given. He
refused to be engaged in speculation, insisted that she
stop worrying about the case. Taylor sensed Fitz's in-
fluence in Lincoln's adamant state.

A follow-up call with more details had them on their
way to an apartment complex on West End, to a shooting
that looked like a possible suicide. It did not sound like
a Snow White case, which meant Jane was still out
there, somewhere. Dead or alive, Taylor didn't know.

The address wasn't matching up with the streets they
were seeing. Taylor called in, got confirmation that the
call had been off the mark. Instead, they took West End
to West Meade, continued on Highway 70 over Nine
Mile Hill and pulled into the parking lot of the Iroquois

Apartments. They were well past West End and into Bellevue. Whoever made the dispatch call must have been new and from the east side of town—people often confused the areas west of Interstate 65. Nashvillians called it Old Hickory disease. The road appeared on all four quadrants of town. Though logic dictated you could get from one side of town to the other on the street, that was a fallacy. A confusing fallacy.

They were met by the somber white van belonging to the medical examiner's office, a crime-scene tech and Bob Parks, who escorted them into a dingy apartment that smelled of latent fire damage, bacon grease and Clorox, an altogether terrible olfactory combination.

A bespectacled young man was standing over the body, a puddle of blood at his feet. He looked up, gave them a blank smile.

"Hi. Glad you're here."

"Hey, Dr. Fox." Taylor nodded at the M.E., then stood back quietly and let Lincoln talk.

"Heard this was a possible suicide?" Lincoln walked around the pool of blood, taking it in from every angle.

The young M.E. shook his head. "No suicide on this one. Execution style. He was on his knees. Shooter put the gun to his head, pulled the trigger. See the stippling? It was right up against his temple, flat on the surface. The bullet tore through his brain, went into the wall over there. Crime Scene recovered it. It's flattened, but there's enough to make a match if the gun is in the system. One shot to the temple, he falls face-first and to the right, landing here."

"A temple through and through. Need a big gun for that."

"Yeah, it'll narrow it down."

Fox wasn't much known for his chatty attitude. That was more than Taylor had heard him speak in one sitting since she'd met him, three years prior. He pointed to the body, an older gentleman by the looks of his gray hair.

"Can we move him now?"

Taylor focused on the back of the man's head. The slight edge of comb track was still visible in the steely hair. "Was there no—" A throat cleared, and she looked up just in time to receive a ferocious stare from Lincoln, and stopped. He smiled politely.

"There's no identification on the body?" he asked, knowing full well that's exactly what his boss was about to say.

"No. Nothing. Pockets were emptied. It's probably just a robbery gone wrong."

Lincoln was looking around the room. "This place looks deserted. Who belongs to the apartment?"

Parks handed him a paper, the classified ad circled in red felt-tip pen. "It's vacant. A furnished rental. Checked with the landlord, he gave me the paper."

"It's just a robbery," Fox interjected. "Shooter probably lives in another building, came down to score some crack."

"Brilliantly deduced, Fox. How many robbers do you know who execute their victims like this?" Taylor was tired of this rubbish. "Roll him."

"As you wish, Lieutenant." He wasn't endearing himself to Taylor this afternoon, there was no question of that. Lincoln shot her another warning look that said, *Hey, you aren't supposed to be here, go run off and get married.* She glared back at him.

The body was rolled, and Fox moved out of the way. Taylor looked down. Her breath caught in her throat. She turned and screamed at the wall. "Son of a bitch. Son of a *bitch!*"

Lincoln stood over the body for a long moment. "That's Frank Richardson, isn't it?"

Taylor's head was pounding. The dry air of Captain Price's office coupled with the stress of finding Frank Richardson executed was going to drive her mad. She dug into her pocket, dry swallowed three Advil covered in lint. Being debriefed by her boss was not the way she'd planned to spend the afternoon before her wedding. She was sick to her stomach, the desiccated pills stuck in her throat.

"Give me the rundown, Lieutenant." Shit. Price didn't use her title as a proper name unless he was pissed off.

"Richardson and I met for breakfast yesterday morning. Well, before that, he called me at home on Tuesday night. He'd just gotten back from France, was in New York. We talked for a while—he had pretty sound judgment when it came to Snow White. He pointed out there was plenty of information that didn't make it into his actual print pieces. We agreed to meet for breakfast and planned to go back through all of his old stories, see if something jumped out.

"After we ate we went to the paper. I got called away with the Jane Macias MP report. Frank was going to stick around, go through the files, make some notes. He came to the office last night, trying to get something to me. Lincoln and Marcus saw him, said he didn't leave a message or a note, just said he had some information for me and would drop it by later."

"Do you know specifically what he was looking for?" Price fondled his mustache and twisted the handlebars. Taylor knew they kept their shape because of liberal coatings in wax, but she was still positive that the daily, ruminative stroking was more to blame.

"Not exactly. When I left him at the paper yesterday, he'd just started pulling all the stories he'd run on the first ten Snow White cases. This is on me, Cap. I lost track of him. I was with Daphne, Jane Macias's roommate, then we had the Spanish girl's shooting, the two murders at the massage parlor, all that paperwork, then we went to the strip club. It was a full day. I never followed up with him."

Taylor rested her forehead in the palm of her hand.

"This is all my fault," she muttered.

"It's not. There's someone out there with an agenda. You're not to blame."

"Of course I am. If I hadn't pulled him into the case, he wouldn't be dead. There's just no two ways about that."

"You don't know that. This may be a completely unrelated incident. He may have been a target all along. What's your gut say?"

Taylor stood and paced her boss's office. It was much roomier than her little box downstairs. The box that had belonged to Price before he was moved up the ranks.

Price was a good man. He'd always been an ally for Taylor, as well as a friend. A lesser man may have thrown her to the wolves on any number of occasions. Instead, he always had her back. She had nothing to lose by telling him what was on her mind.

"My gut says he bought it because of something he found yesterday. He came to me, to the office, said he had information for me. We find what that was, we find out who killed him."

"Start with the time of death. Figure out when he was killed, and you'll be able to nail his movements after he left this office."

"Actually, I checked. The M.E. on the scene said he'd been dead at least ten hours. So he would have to have been killed sometime between five last night, when he came to the office, and three in the morning. The call came in at two-thirty today, so it's entirely possible that he's been dead this whole time. We need to see if he ever made it home last night, go trace his phone calls. God, I am sick about this one."

"Okay then. Pass along everything you have to Lincoln. This is his case, let him run the show."

"But—"

"Taylor, there's no but about it. You're getting married tomorrow, in case you've forgotten. You need to go do the things you need to do to be ready for that. Because trust me, I won't let you screw that up. Get out of here. Go home. Get ready for the rehearsal dinner. Let us handle this."

Taylor allowed herself to be shooed out of his office. She talked to Lincoln, asked him to track Frank Richardson's timeline, told him what she was doing. She wasn't going home, not just yet. She needed to make a stop first.

The *Tennessean* offices were still ablaze. Taylor knew they didn't usually put the paper to bed until well after midnight. There would be people around for her to ask for help.

She showed her badge at the front desk and asked for the managing editor. The receptionist pointed to her left, the open stairwell. Taylor climbed up one floor. Greenleaf met her at the door to the newsroom.

"I have bad news," she opened with as they shook hands. Greenleaf had been around the block before, didn't need it sugarcoated.

"Let's go in here." He ushered her into a small conference room off the newsroom, where they could have a little privacy.

"Did you find Jane?"

"No. Not yet. Frank Richardson is dead. He was murdered sometime late last night or early this morning in an empty apartment in Bellevue. I'm sorry to have to drop it on you like this, Steve, but I need to know. Did Frank tell you anything about what he was working on yesterday?"

Greenleaf was dumbstruck. He stood at the door to the conference room, mouth agape. His administrative assistant came with a paper for him to sign. He told her the news and Taylor only cringed a little when his assistant burst into tears. Taylor felt the knot take hold in her neck. She didn't have time to assuage grief right now. She needed to find out what, why and who had killed Frank Richardson.

"Steve," she tried again gently. "I'm sorry. I know you were friends. And I hate to be callous, but I need your help. I need to get on the computer Frank was using yesterday. Please, Steve. This is important. Did Frank tell you what he'd found?"

Greenleaf finally found his voice. He held tightly to his assistant's arm. "No, Lieutenant, he didn't. Oh, my. Oh, poor Frank. He didn't deserve to go like that, in violence. He always wanted to die in his sleep when he was one hundred and eight. That was the age he'd picked. Felt like he'd have lived a full life if he could make it. Oh, no. His wife?"

"The chaplain is over there, I'm sure. Steve, I'm sorry. I need to get on that computer."

She could tell they were terribly upset by her insensitivity, but they rolled with her, getting her into the room Frank had been using. Greenleaf finally excused himself, face still white with shock. He said he needed to go prepare an obituary worthy of Frank's contribution to the paper, and society in general.

She sat down at the computer, wishing she had Lincoln with her. He was the brilliant computer mind; she'd always relied on him. But she wasn't a slouch herself.

She'd been working for an hour and coming up dry when a small noise made her look up. Daphne Beauchamp stood in the doorway.

"I heard what happened. You look frustrated."

Taylor glanced at her watch. Rehearsal was in less than two hours. Still, it was awfully late for the young archivist to be at work. She greeted her, gestured to a chair.

"Why are you here so late?"

"No offense, Lieutenant, but that's kind of a stupid question."

Taylor looked at her closely; there were deep black circles under her eyes. The girl wasn't sleeping.

"Afraid to go home?"

Daphne nodded. "Hell, yes. I'd be an idiot not to be, don't you think?"

"I think it's completely understandable. This is a safe place. If you're happier here, stay here."

Taylor continued scrolling through the computer screen. Daphne stood and looked over her shoulder.

"Can I help you?"

"I don't know. I'm trying to find the information Frank Richardson was looking at. He came to my office, said he had something for me to see but didn't leave anything for me. There was nothing found with his body, and so far, we haven't recovered anything from his house or his car. Which tells me if Frank had his notes on his person, the shooter took the information with him."

Daphne flinched at the word *shooter,* but straightened her glasses and nodded. "So you need to find what he thought was so important."

"Right. I've been going through the files, and I haven't hit on anything that stands out to me. Would you like to give it a try?"

"Why not? Here, shove over." Daphne took a chair and set it next to Taylor's. "Show me where you've been."

Taylor started running through the memory cache of the computer, showing Daphne the steps she'd taken.

They worked comfortably for ten minutes before Daphne spoke again.

"You think she's dead?"

It took Taylor a moment to process. "Who, Jane?"

"Yes."

"I don't know. I honestly don't know. I wish I could tell you no, but she might be."

"Thank you for being honest with me, at least. Skip came over last night all in a dither. He's crazy about her, but he made a move on me. Men are idiots."

"Sometimes they are, Daphne. Sometimes they are."

The girl was staring at the computer. She pushed her

glasses up her nose and smiled. "Oh, and so am I. Hold up a second. Move. Move move move."

Taylor stood and took a few steps away.

"Why did I not think of this earlier?" Daphne scooted her chair closer. She mumbled and grumbled to herself for a second, then a list of files filled the page. "Got it!"

"What do you have?"

"I should have thought of it sooner. This computer has a dedicated printer. I've just resent every document that was printed off of this for the past two days. Somewhere in there, we might find an answer."

The rehearsal dinner was complete, and Baldwin and Taylor were back at the house, looking over the files Daphne had pulled. She'd hit the mother lode. Frank had apparently printed out more than one hundred pages of information, everything from property records to crime statistics. When Taylor left, a stack of papers in her hands, Daphne had looked so forlorn that Taylor had invited her to the rehearsal dinner. The girl had been chatting with Marcus when they cut out. From the look on both their faces, the Titans' football player might just be a thing of the past. Taylor felt like a damn cupid.

The rehearsal had gone as well as could be expected. Their priest, Father Francis, was a kind, white-haired man who'd come out of retirement to see Taylor married off. He'd christened her, given her first communion, counseled her when her father went to jail—it was only fitting that he see her into the arms of marriage, as well. He and Baldwin got along, Taylor knew they'd been meeting for golf dates earlier in the fall when the weather was holding up. At the time she'd found it amusing—her fiancé and the priest playing golf. Now it just freaked her out. Father Francis had played golf with her father for years. He was part of a regular foursome with Win Jackson, Burt Mars and another member who'd passed away years before. Taylor resisted the urge to cross-examine him as he instructed her and Baldwin in their vows.

They hadn't planned a formal dinner for after, just called in to an Italian restaurant nearby the church called Finezza, told them they'd be bringing in nine people. Ten, if you included their newest member, Daphne. They ordered pizza and drank wine out of water tumblers, enjoying themselves, nice and low-key.

There were many toasts to the couple's happiness. Taylor lifted her glass again and again, wondering what the phrase meant. Happiness was a state of mind, sometimes elusive, oftentimes immeasurable. She was happy tonight, in her way. Content, even. But was she the right gauge for the implications of the emotion? She imagined there were people, women getting married, who were simply happy to have a house, a nice ring and a long train to their dress.

Taylor wasn't about that. She wanted to see a week without a dead body, for starters. That would make her happy. She'd like to have Frank Richardson's killer in her sights. Yeah, that would make her happy. She'd like to have the Snow White Killer and his accomplice on their knees in front of her, hands cuffed, a fresh clip loaded into her Glock…panic swarmed her chest. These weren't the right thoughts for a soon-to-be-married bride to be having. She should be dreaming of sugar and spice and everything nice.

Maybe she was a little drunk.

Baldwin saw the way the night was headed, took charge of getting his bride home. She drank a Diet Coke in the truck and felt better. The snow had stopped; the white layers looked like wedding cake. She giggled at the image, and Baldwin laughed with her.

They got home, changed, and tried to find something to do outside of their bedroom. Taylor was too keyed-up to sleep, so she challenged Baldwin to several games of eight ball, then collapsed, wired but exhausted, on their living-room couch.

"What's wrong?"

"I want to figure out why Frank Richardson was killed. And I had to bite my tongue so I didn't interrogate Father Francis."

"Was that why you were acting so weird? I was starting to think you were getting cold feet again."

"You're assuming I ever warmed them up."

"Taylor—"

"I'm kidding. Stop already. No, I'm thinking about Frank, and Burt Mars, and I can't help myself, honey, I need to go over these files."

Baldwin sighed good-naturedly. "What can I do to help?"

Two hours later, Taylor felt confident she knew what was going on.

"Burt Mars was a very bad boy."

Baldwin was stretched out on the couch in the living room. Taylor sat on the floor, the printed papers from the *Tennessean* spread across the coffee table. It was nearing midnight. She needed to get this wrapped up and get out of the house. They'd agreed that she would spend her last night as an unmarried woman at the Hermitage Hotel, a suite they had for the weekend. She'd stay there alone tonight; he'd join her there tomorrow, for their wedding night, then they'd check out and go to Italy Sunday morning. A great plan that hadn't anticipated a late night combing files.

Baldwin played with her hair, then rubbed her shoulders. "Will it wait?"

She sat back, out of his reach. "I think you might want to hear this. Mars is a bad dude. He left Nashville in the late eighties, right about the time Daddy got sent to Brushy Mountain for that stint for trying to bribe Judge Galloway. He was an accountant here, moved to Manhattan, put out a shingle and started to take clients. A few years later he'd gone down on a racketeering charge. A year after that, they got him on a separate RICO charge, convicted him of racketeering since it was the second charge within a ten-year period. This time they sent him to the federal penitentiary. He served six years of a fifteen-year sentence, got out early for testifying against a man named Horace Macon. Macon was a low-level crime boss working for a guy named Tony Tartulo. The trial was the first step in the fall of the Tartulo syndicate. So now Mr. Mars has himself wrapped up in the Mafia. He gets out of prison, and within six months he's running a highly lucrative real-estate firm, and holds a controlling position in a hedge fund that focuses on REITs."

"Real estate investment trusts. Seems like a conflict of interest."

"You think? Here's what so damn interesting. Horace Macon was just a soldier in Tartulo's organization. But Tartulo was sworn enemies with another boss, Edward

Delglisi. Delglisi is in charge of a huge crime syndicate. My bet is he brought Mars in. Testifying against Macon must have been a setup to take down Tartulo. Mars does the dirty work for Delglisi."

"Let me get this straight. Mars used to be your dad's accountant. He's moved to New York and gotten involved with the Mafia, specifically Edward Delglisi. He was planted in a rival organization and ultimately testified against Horace Macon, effectively ending the Tartulo crime syndicate. Edward Delglisi steps into Tartulo's place and becomes a very powerful crime boss."

"That's the nutshell version, yes."

"What kind of hold does Delglisi have on Mars?"

"Good question. And the other question is does Mars know Snow White? Martin Kimball said Snow White's note came from Mars's printer."

Baldwin fingered the notes. "I'd like to know the answer to that."

"Me, too. There's more. It's unbelievable all the information Frank discovered. Mars's business is a real estate investment trust, right? The REIT manages to reduce the taxes that the individual corporations have to pay on these properties, lets them buy under the corporate name, and their holdings are vast. Frank dug up some of the property listings in the REIT. They own everything from apartment building to houses to corporate strip malls. And guess where they have material assets and properties?"

"Nashville."

"Give that man a prize. To be even more specific, that place where the Snow White copycat hit yesterday afternoon? One of fifteen small, low-income houses that are listed on the rolls. If we were to raid all those properties, I'll bet you fifty bucks that more than one operates as a massage parlor.

"This is definitely why Frank Richardson was killed, Baldwin. I don't think this is directly related to the Snow White murders. I think he uncovered the sideline for Burt Mars's little company. Oh, why didn't he just call me? I could have taken care of him."

"You have all the addresses of the properties they hold in the REIT?"

"It's right here." She waved a sheath of papers at him. "I think we need to find Burt Mars."

The phone rang in the kitchen. They both looked at their watches. It was past midnight, late for a call that didn't mean someone was dead. Taylor got up and went to the handset, saw the number was Lincoln's cell phone. She answered it, voice grave.

Lincoln was nearly jovial. "Great, you're up. I have some good news for you. Want to hear it?"

"You know I do. You found Jane Macias alive and kicking?"

"Okay, not quite that good. Ballistics came back on the bullets that were used in the hospital shooting. Octagonal polygonal rifling characteristics, fragments of what looks like a .41 caliber bullet. Forensics says the gun was a Desert Eagle Jericho."

"A Jericho, not the Baby Eagle? They're kind of rare around these parts."

"Yeah. Only made them for a year before they were replaced by the Baby. Here's the good news. Frank Richardson was definitely killed with the same gun."

Her gut was right. The tension came flooding back. "Someone was trying to shut him up."

"Looks that way."

"I think I may know who's responsible, peripherally at least."

"Who?"

"Burt Mars."

"Wait a minute. Isn't he the accountant whose printer was used in the original Snow White case?"

"Good memory. Yep, he's the one." She ran through the information with him, then got off the phone, turned back to Baldwin.

"I cry uncle. This is going to take more work than you or I can handle tonight. I think it's time to pack it in."

She went to the couch and sat, patting the seat next to her, encouraging him to sit down. He obliged, took her hand in his, fiddled with her engagement ring.

"I love this stone," he said, smiling.

"I love it, too. And I can't wait to add that band of platinum to it tomorrow. But I don't know how much more I can take, Baldwin. I feel like I'm abandoning everyone, right in the middle of the biggest case we've had in years. How can I do that?"

She stood abruptly, unable to sit still. She paced the living room, watching Baldwin watch her steps.

"Honey, there's only so much you can do."

"But this one is personal, Baldwin. There's just something here, I can feel it in my bones." She stopped in front of the fireplace, fiddled with a piece of pine garland they'd put up in a meager attempt to dress the house for Christmas. There was no sense getting a tree since they would spend the holiday in Italy. At least, that had been the plan until her world blew up.

"Baldwin, I'm afraid of what we're going to find.

I'm afraid all of these incidents track back to something bigger. I've got a very bad feeling about all of this. My memories, Burt Mars, Frank being shot, everything is pointing in a direction I don't want to go. My instincts are on fire. I'm afraid that this involves my father."

It was Baldwin's turn to pace. "So what do you suggest?"

Taylor bit her lip. "I think, maybe, we should wait about the honeymoon. Postpone Italy just until we get this resolved."

"But go through with the wedding?"

"Yes. Tomorrow goes off as planned. Sunday, we pick up on the case, work it until we get some kind of resolution. At least not leave with so much up in the air. There's obviously something major at stake here. They're killing witnesses. Frank, Saraya. Who knows who else. Couple that with the Snow White copycat, and I just don't feel right about leaving at all."

Baldwin rose and crossed the room to her, put a hand under her chin and forced her to look into his eyes. "You know there's a good chance it won't resolve itself soon."

Taylor shook her head. "No. It will. I can feel it about to break. I just know it will."

He leaned over and kissed her, and she nearly melted with their joining. The man could lay one on, that was for sure. When they came up for air, she put a hand on his chest.

"Do that again and I won't be leaving."

"I don't mind if you stay." He leaned into her again, but she pushed him back with a smile.

"Seriously."

"We can postpone the honeymoon if you want. That won't be a big deal."

"You're sure?"

"No. I want to get the hell out of Dodge, but I can't leave this behind any easier than you. So yeah, let me make some calls. Put everything on a temporary hold."

"You're the greatest man in the world, you know that?"

He just turned and raised an eyebrow at her, a blatant invitation. She shook her head, laughing. "I'm going to head out. I'll see you tomorrow, okay?"

She kissed Baldwin hard on the lips, then drove downtown, checked into the Hermitage Hotel, got her room and climbed into the bed. Relief flooded her system. There was no way she would have been able to leave the city behind with all of the issues they were having. She needed to catch the Snow White and his copycat, find Jane Macias and figure out who killed Frank Richardson. Then her conscience would be clear enough to allow her to leave it all behind.

Feeling more settled than she had in a week, Taylor snuggled into the luxurious sheets. Sleep overtook her.

She dreamed of the New Year's Eve party, the details sharper, more immediate.

She was tucked in her little spot at the top of the stairs. She could see the ball going on below her. There seemed to be hundreds of people, all dressed in the most elaborate of costumes. The music was loud, and the people twirled around like marionettes, flutes of champagne disappearing at an alarming rate—tuxedo-clad waiters circling the foyer and ballroom, keeping the guests well supplied.

Taylor felt herself waiting, impatient, while the scene played out.

The heavy woman in the Marie Antoinette wig, powdered face, the black triangle patch meant to be stuck to the corner of her mouth askew and half-unglued, sat down hard on the bottom step—a full forty-seven steps away from Taylor in her little hiding place. Taylor felt the concussion of the woman's sudden not-quite fall, smelled the alcohol waft up the stairs mixed with another scent, a powdery musky smell. The woman giggled and shooed her would-be rescuers away. After three waiters had helped her up, she waddled off, dress swinging precariously. Her hair had come undone and was sticking out from under the wig, long and dark against the cream-colored corset.

Then there was quiet for a few moments before her father and mother came into view, several people at their heels.

Her mother was complaining about the woman who was dressed so similarly to her. The women were simpering back and forth to one another, commiserating. How rude to neglect to check with the hostess about her costume.

The men talked loudly, expansive with drink.

"Win Jackson, you've obviously made a deal with the devil," a dark-haired man brayed.

"Yeah, Win, your own little Manderley, is it? What did you do in a past life to get so goddamned lucky in this one? The judge should have thrown you in jail, not dismissed the charges." A sandy-haired man with thick black glasses smacked her father on the shoulder. Win laughed.

"Manderley? Shit, let's just hope the place doesn't burn to the ground. Kitty would have my head."

Then one of the men coughed, put his hand up to his mouth....

Taylor fast-forwarded the dream. She remembered the light.

Despite being tucked back in by Mrs. Mize, the music was so loud that she hadn't been able to sleep. She'd crawled out of bed again, wandered unseen to the top of the stairs and secreted herself in the little space she called her own.

In the foyer of the big house, there was a sparkling lamp, which was built out of a multitude of pretty little chunks of crystal. It sat on a Louis XIII desk, against the damask wallpaper. It was nearly white, there were so many shiny pieces, and it caught the light of the chandelier above it.

Taylor focused on the lamp. She could see the reflections of the people passing by in the ballroom to the left, twirling, waltzing, drinking and sitting.

She could smell the champagne, smell the sweaty reek that wafted up the stairs. It was late, they were deep into the party now. Someone had vomited, she could remember the slight stench coming from the hallway bath.

Her mother had given up—the Marie Antoinette wig was sitting on a ladder-backed chair. She'd taken it off at some point, still miffed at her guest's gauche behavior. Taylor imagined her mother was still muttering about the fat old cow ruining her look.

Manderley, Manderley, Manderley. There was something…

The room phone woke her. Sunlight was streaming in the windows. She rolled and answered the phone, vaguely aware that something wasn't quite right. A cheerful voice told her this was the 8:00 a.m. wake-up call she'd asked for. She thanked them and hung up.

What was it? Something from her dream, the party, her parents.

Manderley.

Her heart beat a little harder.

That was the name of Burt Mars's new company. The Manderley REIT.

Twenty-Six

"Has anyone seen my freakin' veil?"

Taylor was turning in circles, shaking her head in frustration. She scattered a stack of boxes, lifted magazines, opened drawers. No veil. There was so much white around, her dress, her train, the flowers, the chairs—she thought for a moment that a snowstorm had come indoors and piled up in her hotel room.

There was no answer to her question. Where in the hell could it be? She could hear the twins, Maddy and Matt, crying and Sam's low voice trying to soothe them. Simon spoke, as well, but Taylor couldn't make out the words. She looked at the clock on the mantel. She was due at the church to walk down the aisle in less than forty-five minutes.

She gave up the search and plopped to the floor, her dress bloating out around her like a mushroom cloud.

She could only imagine what she must look like, sprawled on the carpet, but at this point, she couldn't give a moment to care. She was bloody tired, and all the fuss was making her teeth clench.

The wail of one of the babies was getting louder, and Taylor looked up to see Sam come into the room, a single infant in her arms. Her floor-length white taffeta gown rustled as she moved. A large terry-cloth towel draped toga-style over her shoulder, shielding the dress from any extraneous waste that might appear from either end of her daughter at any inopportune moment. She gave Taylor a weak grin.

"Colic. Perfect timing, huh? God, I'm sorry, T. What are you doing on the floor? You're going to mess up your dress."

"I don't care. I don't want to go."

Sam ignored her. "Get up and let's get you finished."

"No. I'm tired of the commotion. I don't want to get married in front of all these people. My hair is five miles high. That hairdresser was an idiot. I look like a meringue. I'd rather elope. And I can't find my veil."

Sam bit her lip, trying not to laugh. She didn't succeed. After a moment of baleful glaring, Taylor joined in her mirth. Petulance was her first sign of stress.

Sam glided across the room and whipped the veil out of the plastic casing. "It's right here, on the hanger that your dress was on. It was just in the back. Your hair has to have something for the combs to anchor in, and it looks lovely. Do you want to get the veil on now or at the church?"

Taylor rolled her eyes and got up off the floor. "I should wait until the church. I don't want to mess it up in the limo. I just didn't want to forget it." She examined the folded tulle; it looked like a mile of fabric. "Damn, Sam, how long is this sucker?"

Maddy wailed, but Sam didn't miss a beat. "Cathedral. Like your dress, but a little longer, so it will stretch out behind you and look glorious. Now, quit it, would you? I need to get this girl settled down."

Another scream came, this one slightly lower pitched, and Sam's face crumpled. Taylor patted her on the arm. "Go on and deal with them, Sam, I'll be fine. I'm just nervous. You go do what you need to." Sam nodded and disappeared.

So this was it. The moment she'd always dreaded and never thought she'd have. Her emotions were a bit more mixed than she'd expected. Giving herself, the most precious gift she could bestow, to Baldwin was undoubtedly a smart, sound move. But she couldn't help but wonder why she'd agreed to this, why she hadn't insisted on a quiet beach somewhere, which was what she preferred. It was too damn late to worry about that now. A big church wedding wasn't exactly how she'd wanted to do the deed, but here she was. The twin cores of her psyche were both churning—one with nerves, the other with bliss.

Anxiousness wasn't the only problem weighing on her mind, though.

She drew the folded piece of paper out of her bra. Despite it all, she'd wanted at least some part of her father there with her that day. She couldn't put her finger on why—but instead of overanalyzing her feelings, she'd decided to accept that she had them and move on. The newspaper clipping was nearly two months old, worn and creased.

Missing Nashville Capitalist Feared Dead
St. Barthélemy, French West Indies (AP)
The search for a Nashville man who disappeared
while sailing off St. Jean turned into a recovery
mission after rescue teams found his empty yacht,
THE SHIVER.

Search crews on Monday continued to seek
Winthrop Jackson IV, 56, industrialist, entrepre-
neur, banker and convicted felon. Rescuers said it
was unlikely that he was alive after two days missing. His abandoned yacht ran aground just south
of Les îlets de la plage Hotel in St. Jean, the two
motor diesel engines still running.

The article went on, the dry, impersonal tones of an
anonymous young reporter doing his job. Taylor folded
the square and slipped it back into her bra. Win would
be with her, whether he was alive or dead. Two months
of no word, his body never found…it was easy to
believe he was gone. That he'd simply imbibed a few
too many Boodles and tonic and fallen overboard. The
French authorities made it clear that they felt that was
exactly what happened. With a Gallic flair all their own,
they had patted her shoulder and left her to wonder. She
didn't buy it. He was much too experienced a sailor to
get drunk and fall off his boat. But if he'd had a few and
been pushed over…

She glanced at the clock again. Shit. They had to go.

"Sam?" she yelled. "We've got to get out of here. Are
you ready to hit the limo?" As she spoke, Taylor made
her way into the connecting room of the suite. Babies
were crying; Sam was changing a diaper while Simon

tried to get a pacifier into Matt's mouth. The scene was mayhem. Sam looked up and Taylor saw the flash of panic in her eyes. The twins' attack couldn't have come at a worse time.

Simon was stunned into uncharacteristic silence at the sight of Taylor in her wedding dress. Matt screamed louder while his father held the pacifier just a fraction away from his eager mouth. Taylor raised an eyebrow at him, and he blushed, realizing the teasing he was giving his cranky son. One entreating screech discharged, he nodded at Taylor.

"Nice dress, babe. You're going to be a hit."

"Thank you, kind sir. But we've got to get out of here. I don't want Baldwin to be waiting on me. Let's go do this."

They gathered everything they could, tucked crying babies into car seats and left the suite. They made their way down the hall to the elevator, Simon lagging a few steps behind. Taylor looked over her shoulder at him and smiled. He needed help. She put a hand on Sam's arm.

"I tell you what. Do you want to ride over with Simon? Help calm the babies down? I'll be perfectly fine by myself in the limo."

Sam shook her head. "No, I couldn't let you do that."

Taylor could feel the wave of relief the suggestion offered. "Yes, you could. It would probably do me good to have a few minutes to myself, anyway. Gear up for all this. Get my head in the game. Choose whichever sports analogy suits you. A little alone time would be good. And it's only a ten-minute ride. Seriously, Sam, you go on with Simon."

They hit the ground floor and spilled out of the

elevator—white satin and silk flowed into the vast openness of the hotel lobby like a river of ice. Several heads turned, faces filled with delight. Who wouldn't smile at the sight of a bride on her wedding day?

By the time they hit the doors, it was settled. Sam gave Taylor a grateful hug and tucked her into the limousine waiting at the front door. As the door slammed behind her, Taylor drew in what she thought had to be the first full breath she'd had all day. The back of the limo was creamy soft and dead quiet. Bliss. She sank back into the seat and shut her eyes, barely noticing the car leave the curb and start toward the church.

Alone at last.

Taylor felt the adrenaline coursing through her veins. This was it, then, the point of no return. She just hoped she wouldn't pass out at the altar. Good grief, her hands were shaking. Tough girl, falling apart at the mere idea of standing in front of all those people. The beginnings of a stream of panic made her heart start to beat a little harder. *Stop!* she told herself as sternly as she could muster. *He'll be standing there with you.* A few deep breaths, and the trepidation was momentarily quelled.

She opened her eyes and took in the sights as the limo cruised through downtown Nashville.

They were on Sixth Avenue, and the driver turned west on Church Street. They came to a stop at the light in front of the downtown library. To her right, a group of homeless people caroused the park nestled between the buildings, seeking shelter from the chill day. A jogger passed across the street, glancing fearfully over his shoulder, as if the homeless would take him down like a pack of rabid dogs.

They were past Morton's now. Down to her left on Eighth was the Nashville Sporting Goods store, the scene of her first armed robbery. The owner had been shot, but lived, thanks to her quick efforts to save his life. The suspect had never been arrested; the case was still open after twelve years. The owner was dead now, of natural causes. New victims manned the counters.

The YMCA appeared on her right, and she was struck by just how much crime occurred on this strip of road, how much of her history as a police officer could be traced to this route. She'd chased a man right there, up McLemore Street, dodging bullets as he shot at her in an attempt to get away. That one she'd caught, and seen him convicted for stabbing a twelve-year-old boy at the entrance to the Y.

The industrial grit of the city spilled before her, naked in the winter air.

As they passed the NES building, the scene improved. The old and the new sections of the city kissed and made up, working into the medical district, dominated by Baptist Hospital. They flew up Church onto Elliston Place before the limo turned onto West End Avenue and started out of town, toward the church. Taylor was tempted to thank the driver for the tour through her past life, but balked, instead thinking ahead to the moments to come.

Taylor could only imagine the bedlam that was ensuing at St. George's. She was in the midst of an idyllic vision of Baldwin rushing to greet her at the door, telling her he'd decided they should just skip this part and head directly to Italy, when she noticed the limo turn off West End. The idiot driver had taken the exit for 440, the short beltway surrounding the west and south sides of the city. They were headed north; this road led most decidedly away from St. George's. While Nashville had the quaint ability of allowing a driver to get anywhere quickly with fifteen equally amenable routes, this detour was going to make her late.

Scooting forward, she tapped on the divider, signaling for the driver to drop the opaque glass. He ignored her. Laughing now, she realized that this was a fun little trick that was being played on her. Oh, funny, funny. Now she understood why they wouldn't let her in her office. Wrapping presents, my ass. They were planning this little escapade with the limo driver. Imagining each member of her team's gloating faces, she vowed to get them back. The limo was exiting 440 onto I-40 West. Good timing. She knocked on the glass again.

"Okay, very funny. I'm sure they told you to make me sweat. You can tell them mission accomplished. I'm going to kill the bastards, but they got me. So how's about you take this exit for Forty-sixth Avenue and cut across Charlotte through Sylvan Park to West End?"

Nothing. She banged harder.

"Hey! Hey, I'm talking to you. Put this divider down right now. The joke's a good one, but it's over. Either put the divider down or pull over."

At last, the driver complied. He pulled to the side of the road, safely off on the shoulder. Traffic whizzed by on their left. The glass partition didn't budge, and Taylor felt a wave of fury pass through her. The game was amusing, but enough was enough.

She was a cop, for God's sake. She would force the damn driver to put the partition down. She reached for the door handle. The door was locked. She pulled on the handle again and again, with no result. Sliding across the capacious seat, she tried the other door. Also locked.

What the fuck was happening? A vanload of children passed them by, all their happy faces stuck to the windows on the right side of the van, contemplating and waving to the solitary limo on the side of the road. Taylor had a moment of sickening clarity, realized that this wasn't a joke. Calmly, she slid back to the right and knocked on the glass again. There was no response.

She cursed, loudly and extensively. The string of oaths was impressive even to her, and made her feel a little bit better. There wasn't a lot she could do locked in the backseat of a limousine. There was a wet bar packed with champagne, but a drink didn't seem like the best idea. But to the left of the bar was a small green light. A speaker.

"I'll be damned," she muttered. He must have heard everything she'd said. Scooting forward in the seat, she pushed the talk button, trying hard for a more reasonable tone.

"Would you mind telling me what's going on?"

There was still no answer. Fine. If he wanted to play it that way, she was more than willing. She knew the divider wouldn't be bulletproof.

She reached into her satin handbag, a brief moment of thankfulness overwhelming her as she remembered the argument she'd had with Sam over carrying the stupid thing. Purses just weren't Taylor's style. Sam had assured her that she'd need somewhere to stash a few items. Taylor had relented, deciding that she didn't want to strap a gun to her leg for her walk down the aisle. A diminutive pearl-handled .22 that she'd bought at a collectors' gun show a few years back fit perfectly into the tiny bag. Thanking whatever unseen force that influenced her decision to carry on her wedding day, she snapped open the bag and palmed the gun. She drew her fingers out, trying not to draw attention to the fact that she was now armed. It didn't matter. The panel between them dropped.

The driver turned and smiled, and Taylor had a brief moment when she thought, no, I've been wrong, this *is* all a joke.

A flash of black caught her eye and she focused on the object in the driver's hand. Her heart skipped a beat and she sucked in her breath involuntarily. Her brain registered the situation. It took only a fragment of a second, but when the smile widened, she knew absolutely that she had to get her weapon up, now.

The motion was smooth, graceful, lightning quick. Such close quarters, there was no need to aim, just cock the hammer and pull. A full squeeze, the roaring boom. But her body convulsed. Pain shot through her. She dropped her weapon, dropped the bag, her eyes rolled back in her head. Her last thought tore through her like an electrical impulse—Baldwin is going to kill me. Then all was dark.

The driver grinned at his handiwork. Everything was going according to plan. All he had to do now was make the body disappear. He turned back in his seat, turned the key with his gloved right hand and glided back onto the highway. He went a short way, then exited onto the huge flying overpass that led to Briley Parkway. A few miles ahead was an airport and a plane. All he needed to do was reach it, and he would be home free. All the missions accomplished. His boss would be very happy.

Twenty-Seven

Nashville, Tennessee
Saturday, December 20
3:40 p.m.

Baldwin paced outside the grand edifice of St. George's, seeing everything and nothing. He was vaguely aware of being cold; he had no overcoat on, just a formal morning suit—traditional tailcoat in dark gray, a barely discernible stripe in his trousers, waistcoat in a subtle dove-gray check and a slate ascot replete with a mother-of-pearl stickpin that had belonged to his great-great-grandfather. Taylor might laugh at him for being such a dandy, but he only intended to do this once, and he wanted to do it right. Besides, the various shades of gray reminded him of her eyes.

Yet there was no bride.

He checked his watch again. She was forty minutes late. And he was dying inside, shriveling up second by second. Each heartbeat hurt a little more than the last.

In all the fantasies he'd had about this day, Taylor not showing wasn't among them.

St. George's Episcopal Church was situated in Belle Meade, barely fifteen minutes from the Hermitage Hotel in downtown Nashville. Ten minutes if the lights were all green and there was no traffic. There was no reason for the limo to be taking this long to get to the church. If it had broken down, or there'd been an accident, either the limo company or the responding officer would have called to let them know. The wedding party was all law enforcement, either Metro or medical examiner, and most of the guests had their hand in the mix in one way or another. Nashville was small enough that very few members of Metro Police Department didn't know the LT was getting hitched today.

Calls to Taylor's cell phone were useless; Sam had it stashed in her diaper bag because Taylor didn't have room for it.

Baldwin fought the urge to strip off his jacket and run howling into the parking lot. Damn it, where the hell was that woman? How could she do this to him?

A gust of warm air enveloped Baldwin midstride and the strains of Handel's *Water Music* drifted to his ears. Fitz came out of the large wooden doors that led to the nave of the church. An avuncular smile filled his broad features. Baldwin stopped pacing for a moment, happy to have the short-lived heat and the company.

"Son," Fitz began, but Baldwin shook his head and held up a hand.

"I don't want to hear it."

"Son—"

"I know what you're going to say, Fitz." He adopted

a deep baritone with a long Southern drawl. "You haven't known her for that long. Y'all rushed into this. She's a wild one, Baldwin, and I mean that in a good way." He went back to his regular voice.

"I know you were shocked as hell to see her fall so hard for me. What you're saying is that maybe this is for the best. Right? You haven't approved from the beginning." He glared at the older man. "And quit calling me son."

"Hey, Junior. You just don't get it, do you?"

Baldwin rocked back on his heels, staring at Fitz with his mouth open. The indignation grew in his chest and he couldn't help but lash out.

"You son of a bitch. You talked her into running, didn't you? You gave her a way out. I know she's been a little freaked about this big wedding thing, but...I can't fucking believe this." He stomped away, then whirled back, shoulders bunched, hands balled at his side. "And you stand there grinning like a fool, thinking this is funny?"

Fitz coughed into his hand. "Funny? Naw, I wouldn't call it funny. Your reaction is amusing, yes, but I don't think this situation is at all humorous. How well do you really know her, son? Do you honestly believe she'd stand you up at the altar?"

"I..." Baldwin swallowed hard. His hands un-clenched, his shoulders slumped. He gritted his teeth, a small muscle in his jaw leaping to life. Did he? Did he really think that the love of his life would be so merci-less and fearful as to not show up for their wedding? The lump in his chest started to dissolve, only to be replaced by a larger, much more painful knot.

"Finally figuring it out, aren't you, *son?*"

Yes, he was. Fitz was pissed at him because he'd lost faith in Taylor. That he'd believed even for a fraction of a second that this strong, astounding, beautiful woman wouldn't have the guts to tell him to his face that she didn't want to be with him. The dread washed over him like a bucket of water. He looked at Fitz, seeing him for the first time. The smile wasn't pleasant, it was tight and worried, small lines shooting between the older man's brows.

"Jesus, Fitz, what do you think happened to her?"

"I don't know, but I think it's time to go inside and ask for help."

Twenty-Eight

Nashville, Tennessee
Sunday, December 21
11:00 a.m.

The banks of the Cumberland River were rocky and icy. Leftover snow had been tromped through by the search-and-rescue teams, turning it a smoky gray. A helicopter hovered overhead, the whapping drone desultory. Search and Rescue had been revised to Recovery. Slumped-shouldered men and women wandered the bank, looking at each other blankly. It didn't seem possible. Taylor Jackson, drowned in the river that fed vibrant life to her city.

John Baldwin stood on the VIP platform overlooking the River Stages facility. In happier times, the concrete pad would be filled with A-list partygoers reveling in the music of the most famous and popular bands. Now the platform was a staging area for the search. For the recovery.

After ninety minutes, it wasn't technically a "search"

anymore. The Nashville Fire Department, faces ashen and drawn, had called in the Office of Emergency Management Rescue unit. Cadaver dogs were on the bank of the river, two black Labs shivered in the boats floating on the icy surface. OEM had launched a craft loaded with the FISH, the side-view sonar that would be able to distinguish between a lumpy log and a body in the murky, fast-flowing water.

No one needed to say it aloud. In water this cold, Taylor wouldn't have lasted more than five minutes. Logic told them there was a body out there somewhere. The only thing to do was drop the sonar and see what they could see. Which was absolutely nothing. After several hours, the call came to put the drag bar in the water. OEM's Search and Rescue volunteers were doing everything possible to find her body before the river swept her away, the massive currents flowing north toward Kentucky.

Baldwin's face was hard, worn. The lines around his eyes were etched deep, like a vein of quartz running through a Paleolithic stone. Taylor's murder, if he could bring himself to call it that, had frozen his heart in time. He only breathed when he realized he wasn't. He didn't know if the pain would ever cease. He stood, hands gripping the railing, the December winds blowing his hair about, and held himself back from jumping into the river below. He'd asked to be on the dive team. His request had wisely been denied.

Murder. That was the only word for it. She sure as hell hadn't gone into the river in the middle of winter by accident.

The guests had been sent home from the church. The

wedding party, stiff with worry, made their way to the homicide offices. Calls were made, people traced. The limousine service was practically raided; the limousine that had been dispatched and carried the bride into the netherworld found on-site. There were two major problems. There was no trace of Taylor in the car. Video surveillance from the Hermitage Hotel showed the license plate did not match the manifest. It was a decoy. Lincoln was running down the lists of other limousines in the area, trying to match the plates.

The arranged driver of the real limousine was long gone, disappeared into the night. A check of his bank accounts showed a five thousand dollar deposit and a Visa charge for a plane ticket to Mazatlán. The plane had left at four in the afternoon, the same time the wedding was supposed to be under way. A man matching the driver's description had boarded the plane on time. Video from the airport came in and confirmed. A theory was formed. He had been paid to leave town.

After hours of fruitless searching, with no sign whatsoever of Taylor, their leads were diminished to nothing. The dreaded call had come right before 10:00 p.m. A white satin mule had been found on the west bank of the Cumberland River. Photographs confirmed that it matched the pair Taylor had been wearing, the brand and size an exact match to the empty box found in her hotel suite. Time stopped for them all.

Baldwin took a gulp from a coffee cup with Tigermart on the label. Some kind soul was refueling the troops from a local convenience store, he had no idea who. He'd been a part of rescue teams before. With no remains, at some point they would have to stop actively dragging the river. Rescue would continue searching until the body was found. And they always found the body. It might not be immediate, but time and flowing water had a way of spitting out what didn't belong.

Inevitability at the hands of nature wasn't a comfort to Baldwin. Scenarios drifted through his mind, visions of Taylor's adipocere-covered corpse emerging twenty miles downriver in a month. So often, that's how it happened. He choked back a sob at the thought, tossed the rest of the now-bitter coffee over the railing. Fuck. He wasn't helping things by standing there making himself sick to his stomach. He needed to do something. He wouldn't accept that she was gone, not like this.

Thoughts crowded his mind. He knew there was a lockbox high on the shelf of a closet in the bonus room of the new house that held all of her papers, her will, her wishes. He'd never looked at any of that information. She'd told him she wanted to be an organ donor and didn't want to be kept alive if she was brain-dead, but that's as far as they'd gotten. Would she want to be buried in Tennessee? Cremated? If they didn't find a body, what would he do for her? Did her will cover provisions for—

"Stop!" he said aloud. "Stop it," he said again, softer this time. He was getting way ahead of himself. *She wouldn't give up on you so easily.*

Bolstered, he made his way to the command table. Mitchell Price was still on scene, waiting for some news. Baldwin approached him, taking the older man's arm. Price turned to Baldwin, eyes red-rimmed from lack of sleep. His mustache drooped, his bald pate glistened with frosted sweat.

"Captain, anything new?"

Price shook his head. "They aren't getting any hits on anything down there, Baldwin. The river temperature is too cold to sustain her if she went in. The divers are having a hard time themselves. It's not looking good, son."

Why has everyone started calling me son? Baldwin wondered. First Fitz, now Price. He dismissed the welling anger, knew Price didn't mean anything by it. It was meant to be a comforting term. It wasn't their fault that it made his heart shrivel up even more. His dad had called him son, his mom, too. But they'd been gone so long, he could barely remember how their voices sounded. The sweet timber of his mother's Southern belle diction floated through his mind but was gone the moment he recognized it. Damn it.

Price had turned and was guiding Baldwin back toward his vehicle. "Listen, let's get back to headquarters. There's nothing we can do here now. If she went in last night, Baldwin, chances are she's gone. Let's go see if we can confirm that she went in at all. Okay?"

Baldwin looked over his shoulder, stared out over the murky water. Price was right.

They buckled in for the short drive back to the CJC. It was time to start fresh.

Twenty-Nine

This was turning into a very good day.

Charlotte had rejoiced last night, privately. Word spread like wildfire through the subterranean rooms that housed the Behavioral Science Unit, and her friends had seen fit to call and include her in the news. John Baldwin's wedding had not taken place. His bride stood him up at the altar. To celebrate, Charlotte had opened a bottle of Piper Heidsieck, drawn a bath and masturbated furiously in the warm water.

It wasn't that she wished him ill. Well, maybe she did. Maybe she was just so damn happy that he was still a free man that she'd drop by his place, console him properly.

The whisper campaign had started instantaneously. Taylor Jackson had quite literally disappeared. The limousine she'd been riding in was found in the parking lot of the driving service, right where it should be. The driver was nowhere to be found. There was a vague report about a search at the airport. Later, after sundown, a shoe had been found on the bank of the Cumberland River, one that matched the description of the shoes Jackson had been wearing. Divers were in the river until well after midnight. She had not heard the results when she decided to call it a night.

As Charlotte had drifted off to sleep, she had a deep, satisfying knowledge that she was wanted. They needed her, her men. Both of them. All of them. Call it instinct, premonition, whatever. Maybe she would be able to save them.

Now was the time. She left the hotel room with a bounce in her step, understanding innately that the old man and the young one, would need her more now than ever.

Thirty

Snow White was in the midst of a coughing fit when he saw the news on the television. The Jackson bitch was missing. He caught his breath, watched the story unfold. Rubbed his hands together painfully, massaging and massaging and massaging.

He knew what had happened, of course. He couldn't blame the boy. Jackson needed to be silenced. Things were going to come to a head now. It was just a matter of time before his apprentice's impudence and recklessness flashed back on them all. A systemic cleansing was the only way to assure their safety.

Damn that Charlotte. It was all her fault. If she hadn't brought the young pup, hadn't dangled the glory of his past in front of him. She was brilliant, he gave her that. And sentimental. Finagling his ring out of police evidence and back to its rightful place on his right hand was the single nicest thing she'd ever done for him.

His crooked finger traced the outline of the magnificent ring, the crest, the ornate, raised *F.* It used to mean something. It was a badge of honor, of courage. It was his legacy. It gave him immutable strength, an insatiable desire to feel the life bleed from a body. He wondered about his predecessors, whether when they placed the ring upon their hand, they felt the lifeblood flowing from the metal, felt the nubile bodies calling for release.

All he knew was that when the ring was lost, so went his desire for blood. Of course, the ring was lost because he'd begun losing weight, losing strength. The disease was upon him, and he was racked with desire and no ability.

The ring was back on his finger, no danger of slipping off because of the impossible, unnatural angle of the fourth digit. He had a surrogate to stroke the feeble flesh into action once again, to slip the blade through that flesh, two hands working as one. There were moments that he was his old self.

And everything was in jeopardy now. He'd chosen poorly, allowed Charlotte to muddle his brain. His apprentice would be the death of him. He no longer cared.

He shuffled his way from the room, the cane clunking in front of him, and climbed, higher and higher into his house. There was a girl, he could smell her, taste her, and he wanted her. Nothing would stop him now. He must fulfill this destiny.

Thirty-One

The homicide office was bustling with activity. Fitz poured out the dregs of yet another pot of coffee and made a fresh one. They'd gone through four pots in the past two hours. Everyone was wired and cranky, and despite all the artificial stimuli, tired. Marcus, forehead resting on his palm, scrolled through page after page of computer screens. Baldwin was on the phone with the airlines. No one had slept, everyone was fixated on their main lead—the limousine driver who'd pulled an international disappearing act.

Lincoln was on the phone with a contact he had in the Mazatlán area—a man he knew only as Juan. He'd met him at a forensic computing conference four or five years back. His gut feeling told him Juan wasn't the man's real name, but that didn't matter now. He'd sent him an e-mail earlier in the day, asking for help. They were doing the obligatory catch-up dance before they got down to business.

"*¿Hola? ¿Este Juan? Es Lincoln... Sí, hombre, ha sido mucho demasiado largo... No, mi español no es mejor. No tenemos las mujeres aquí digno de practicar encendido.*"

A bawdy laugh pulsed through the phone. "And I thought Nashville had a vibrant Latino community." Juan's voice was deep and cultured. Lincoln didn't know his whole story, but thought that perhaps he'd been some sort of Argentinean or Bolivian spy. He was just too plugged in to be regular law enforcement, though he was currently serving as a chief in Mexico's fractured police department. No, a spy would be a more romantic notion.

Lincoln answered in English, relieved to switch back to his native tongue. "We do have a lot of very fine Latinos, but they smell me out from twenty paces. No one wants to get involved with a cop, you know?"

"Ah, yes, my friend, I do. On to more important things. I have found your suspect."

Lincoln gesticulated to the rest of the homicide office. "Juan, I'm putting you on speakerphone." He hit the speaker button and the disembodied voice raked through the air.

"Your suspect was found on the beach. Specifically, by a cabana on the beach in front of the Pueblo Bonito Hotel. It is a very nice hotel. They did not take kindly to the intrusion, I tell you that. From a distance, it seemed he was passed out drunk on a chaise longue. Upon closer inspection, the flies gave him away."

"He's dead?"

"I am sorry to tell you this. His throat was cut. Very nasty. The hotel people were quite upset. They had to close their beach to their guests. He's not been moved. Do you want him back?"

Baldwin spoke up. "This is John Baldwin. I can have an FBI forensics team on-site shortly to retrieve his body."

"Yes, removing the body, this would be a very good idea. I believe I'd rather not know why you have a team positioned to operate so quickly so close. My government is not happy with this imposition. This is about your woman, Lincoln tells me?"

Baldwin took a step closer to the phone, his voice cracking. "Yes. This man was our only lead."

"There will be other leads, *amigo.* Do not lose hope."

Baldwin sat heavily in the chair by Lincoln's desk. Lincoln shot him a look, then picked up the handset, ending the speaker connection. "Thank you for your help, Juan. I appreciate it."

"I'm sure there will be an opportunity to repay the kindness. *Adiós, mi amigo. Espero que encuentres las conchas dulces y calientes.*"

It took Lincoln a moment; he repeated a few words aloud. Baldwin looked at Lincoln and for the first time in hours, cracked a smile. Juan had very crudely wished Lincoln warm and wet sexual encounters.

Lincoln finally got the gist of what Juan had said, laughed and hung up the phone. He looked at Baldwin, who had gone back to his original position, his head in his hands.

"I didn't know you spoke Spanish."

"I dabble in several languages. Just so you know, your friend isn't Mexican." His tone didn't brook an invitation to find out more. Lincoln took the hint, tried another tack.

"I've suspected that for a while. Is there someone in particular you'd like me to get in touch with to get this taken care of?"

Baldwin raised his head, a slight glisten in his green eyes. "No, that's okay. Let me make the call. I know the team leader down there, he's working the Juarez case. He's vacationing in Puerto Vallarta for Christmas, he can get everything squared away for us quietly." He stood, then gestured apologetically toward Taylor's office door. No one said anything. What was there to say? Baldwin nodded slowly, a man condemned. He went into her office and closed the door behind him.

He refused to crack. She would be so pissed at him if he fell apart now. He sat on the guest side of her desk; couldn't bring himself to take her chair. The office smelled of her, lemongrass and gun oil. He shook it off, dialed the number. Garrett Woods answered his cell on the first ring.

"Baldwin, is there news?"

"Nothing good. We've tracked down the limo driver. He's dead on a beach in Mazatlán. Throat cut. Think you can finesse it for me? Burke Webb is down in Puerto Vallarta, he can manage it, I'm sure. The Pueblo Bonito Hotel."

"Of course. I'll get on it immediately." There was the sound of a pen scratching on paper and a few snaps of his fingers. His voice dropped an octave. "How are you? Seriously. Are you holding up?"

There was no bullshitting Garrett. "As best I can. I can't imagine that she's really gone. I have to keep hoping that she's out there, somewhere. I can handle the thought of her being hurt, wounded, but not dead. I just won't go there."

"Good. Don't. Something is up here, and I'm not sure what it is. There's been a rash of strange—"

There was a loud whooping and the door to Taylor's office flew open. Marcus stood in the entry, a grin lighting up his face. "We've got something."

"Garrett, I've gotta go. I'll call you back." He hung up to Garrett's protests, ignored the cell when it started ringing immediately after he closed the lid.

"What is it?"

"John C. Tune Airport. One of the mechanics just came forward. He didn't know anything about Taylor being missing, just saw the news reports. Says that yesterday evening, a man and a woman got on a Cessna. Normally, it wouldn't be a big deal, but he noticed that the woman was out. Completely. The man was carrying her over his shoulder, told one of the other mechanics that she'd gotten drunk. Get this, Baldwin. He says he remembers her wearing something white."

"Let's go. I want to talk to him. Now."

Thirty-Two

Unknown
Monday, December 22
3:00 a.m.

The noise was deafening. It sounded like the buzz from a bumblebee—one three-times normal size. It flitted close to her ear and she swatted at it. She couldn't lift her arm. Her hand didn't leave her side. What the hell?

She opened her eyes a crack. Well, she didn't think she was dead. Not unless heaven or hell or whatever afterlife place she was going to looked like a warehouse. Maybe she was in purgatory? Naw, she didn't believe in that. It was either up or down. Lord knows she'd spilled enough blood to be heading south. The thought made her grimace, and a sharp pain shot through her head. She tried opening her eyes again, slowly this time, first the right, letting it focus, then the left. Her head buzzed; it wasn't a bumblebee but her brain, sending off sound waves at a thousand decibels a pop. Her eyes focused on what looked like a concrete pillar, then slowly, she moved her gaze across the room. Her head pounded but the impression stood. Empty warehouse.

She tried to stand, barely registering when she couldn't. Her head began to swim, and darkness enveloped her.

He sensed the movement, got up and went to the window, looked into the room. She was awake. Good. It was nearly time. He wanted to talk to her, to hear that smoky voice again. But it was taking her so long to get over the stun gun. Maybe the chloroform was a little much, too. He didn't know how strong she was, how much she was going to fight. She'd actually come to for a moment as she'd been carried toward the plane. He'd felt her muscles tense and slapped a soaked handkerchief across her nose and mouth.

He'd hoped she'd be awake hours ago. Instead she sat, strapped into the chair, and slept. He thought she might even have dreamed—her eyes moved back and forth under the lids and she moaned softly. Those lips. That moan had done more to him in two seconds than any woman had in two years. She was absolutely delicious. He wanted her. On so many levels.

As he watched, she moved slightly, then drifted away again. Maybe it wasn't time, after all. Too bad.

He made a phone call, let L'Uomo know that she was starting to come to. L'Uomo had warned him to keep his hands off, but he longed to touch her skin again, so warm, so tight.

There was motion again in the room. Yes, she was fully awake now.

Standing at the window, he watched her, amazed at her beauty. She tried to shake her head and groaned, to his everlasting delight. Maybe he couldn't touch, but nothing said he had to be a monk about it. His hand went to the fly on his pants and he reached inside, grasping himself. A woman, incapacitated, tied to a chair...a normal man would feel chivalrous, not wholly aroused and harder than a rock. A few quick strokes was all it took. He closed his eyes in bliss as he came.

"Atlas, you revolting creature."

L'Uomo's voice boomed and Atlas opened his eyes in shock, his hand still wrapped around his rapidly shrinking penis. Oh, God, he'd been caught. He stumbled back against the wall, fumbling his dick back into his pants, all six foot eight inches of him crowding the space where a neat, gray-haired gentleman stood, lips curled in disgust.

"I'm sorry, I'm sorry, I couldn't help myself." Atlas bowed his head.

"Obviously you aren't capable of handling this situation, Atlas. You are dismissed. Send Dusty in to replace you. Tell him no books, this needs his utmost attention. You may leave now."

Atlas turned to the window, giving the woman one last glance. "Beautiful," he muttered, then left the small observation room.

L'Uomo stood in the window and watched as Taylor Jackson struggled against her bonds. Beautiful, indeed. But he didn't need his men distracted by a helpless succubus. Dusty would manage her; he seemed to feel nothing for the opposite sex. Of course, the court-mandated Depo-Provera shots the man took neutered him quite effectively.

The girl was fighting it now, fully conscious and

trying to get untied. He watched, feeling a twitch in his own groin as she struggled. She'd fight the bonds for hours if he let her. Tough girl. He was going to have to talk to her, prevent her from hurting herself. She would have to relieve herself soon, and then they needed to get her fed and watered.

He admired her spirit. High praise from a man who admired nothing.

Thirty-Three

Nashville, Tennessee
Monday, December 22
8:00 a.m.

They'd spent the night working the airport staff for clues. The limo had been found. A bullet hole had shattered the windshield. Taylor's veil, tucked into the soft leather, was the only material evidence that she'd been in the car. Physical confirmation was under way—fingerprints being lifted, the car gleaned for blood. Anything that might tell the story of what happened before it arrived at the airport. The only concrete information they had was the bullet had come from the interior of the vehicle, not shot in from the outside. It confirmed that there was a struggle.

They were also looking for the phantom plane. Tracking an aircraft should be easy, especially in the post-9/11 era. But the Cessna seemed to have gone off course, not landing at its destination airport. The pilot had called in less than midway through the flight, telling the Fort Lauderdale private airstrip that he had a sick passenger on board and was turning back to Nashville. Nashville never heard from the plane after he left. There were no reports of planes going down along the Eastern seaboard. It would take hours to trace where the aircraft had landed—the tail number would have to be hand-matched to all incoming flights at all the airports. It would take some time for the FAA controllers to sort through the information.

It was a smoothly planned operation, designed to let the plane literally fall off the radar.

Baldwin felt sick to his stomach. He left the small terminal building and stood on the tarmac, staring north. There was a chance that Taylor was alive, hurt, needing him, and the thought made him want to tear out his hair and wrap his hands around the throat of whoever had stolen her from him.

Fitz sidled up to him, put a hand on his shoulder. Baldwin felt a rush of gratitude, coupled with a nagging sense that while he'd been very busy with his own personal demons at the thought of Taylor's predicament, he'd conveniently ignored the four people who'd known her and loved her the longest, her team. The realization hit him like a punch to the gut and he turned to Fitz.

"God, man, I'm sorry. I've only been thinking about me, about how horrible this situation is for me. I know you love her, too. I'm sorry for being such an asshole."

Fitz waved a hand in front of him. "Naw, don't you go worrying about that. We're all strung a little too tight right now, but no one's pissed that you aren't there mollycoddling us. We're grown-up. At least, some of us are." He grinned and nodded his head toward Marcus

Wade, standing in plain view right inside the door to the terminal. Marcus was riding the staff at the airport, threatened to arrest them all if they didn't cooperate with the investigation. He was leaning in, arguing, and the male agent behind the counter was visibly trembling.

Baldwin gave a tight smile and looked past Marcus. Lincoln was sitting in an orange plastic chair with his laptop perched on his knees, flying through cyberspace, looking for the plane. Baldwin felt certain that if anyone could find the tail number, it would be Lincoln.

Fitz gripped Baldwin's shoulder once more, then smiled. "I'm calling Price, giving him an update. Anything you'd like to relay?"

"Just tell him to be prepared for an all-out onslaught the moment we find anything. I know the purse strings are tight at Metro. I'll be putting some of my own capital into this investigation if need be. I don't expect him to cover my parts. Let him know that."

"Price won't hear of that, Baldwin, you know that. He feels like you're part of this team, even if you are FBI." He flipped open his phone and left Baldwin on the freezing tarmac.

He'd almost left the Bureau, and was more than thankful that his boss, Garrett Woods, hadn't let him go. It would have been difficult to manage the response to this incident with Taylor, the dead chauffeur, everything, if he didn't have the Bureau as backup.

He still wanted to go out on his own, have a consulting firm that was free from the constraints of the government. Hire a couple of private investigators, do the work he wanted to do....

The thought shook him. A private investigator. He

and Taylor had obviously been stalked. Someone knew every detail of the wedding plans, right down to the limousine company. He wondered if there was an unscrupulous member of the P.I. community who might have been on their tail. No sane P.I. would stalk a cop and an FBI agent. That was something that needed to be looked into.

His phone had four new messages, all from Garrett Woods, all wanting Baldwin's attention for a matter outside the scope of the search for Taylor. Baldwin exercised a tiny bit of filial rebellion and chose not to address the phone calls just yet. Woods would tell him if it was vital that they speak immediately. In the meantime, he needed to stay completely focused on Taylor.

Thirty-Four

Two men sat at a table in a corner of a quiet neighborhood restaurant. One had come in through the front, the other through the back. They hadn't met in person in many years.

One was known in many circles. His employees called him L'Uomo, quite simply, the Man. Gray-haired, cultivated, dapper, he gave all the appearances of being a successful businessman.

The other gentleman had a face that was easily recognizable everywhere he went, which is why he rarely went anywhere anymore. But L'Uomo had summoned him. Threatened, actually, with a widely disseminated contract hit if he didn't show his face. After the debacle earlier this year, he'd had no choice. It was either surface or be hunted and killed.

And he'd already died once.

They sat facing one another, the dapper man politely dabbing his mouth with a starched linen napkin between bites. His lips were moist from sipping a vintage red, his everyday wine, a 1985 Châteauneuf-du-Pape. He ate with gusto but delicately, carefully relishing each morsel of food.

His guest didn't drink or eat. Fear coiled in his stomach, making digestion impossible. So he watched, picking at his plate of salade niçoise, wondering why he'd bothered to order anything. French wasn't his preferred choice of fare, but he hadn't had a say in which restaurant they dined in. It was foolish enough for them to be seen together.

L'Uomo enjoyed his meal thoroughly, wading through the three courses and finishing with a cheese plate. Wiping his mouth carefully, he politely belched in gastronomic appreciation and finally looked his dining companion in the eye.

"So. Lazarus returns from the dead at last. I was wondering when you were going to surface. You're like a bad penny. Never know where you might turn up."

"That's not entirely fair," he protested. "You were the reason I needed to disappear. And putting out a hit on me was rather impolite, don't you think?"

L'Uomo flicked a hand in annoyance. "Yes, yes, I'm the source of all your ills. The contract was necessary. You're sitting here with me now, aren't you? Just business. You know that. There has been a development. We need you to have a heart-to-heart with someone. Resolve this situation for me and I'll consider the debt even. You can disappear again, with my assurances that you won't be hunted by my people any longer."

A nice offer, one worth careful consideration. Of course, nothing about L'Uomo was ever that simple. "Who?"

"You'll see soon enough. Are you finished?" L'Uomo looked with derision at the pathetically full plate. He had no tolerance for weakness. "No appetite?"

"No, I guess I don't. Shall we go, then? I'm not comfortable being here. I'd like to get this over with."

"Fine. I have a little present to show you. Perhaps then you'll understand the seriousness of the situation. The limo will pick you up in thirty minutes. Do try to eat."

L'Uomo stood and quitted the room, smiling benevolently at each patron as he walked out.

His companion uttered a single word at his old friend's back.

"Bastard."

Thirty-Five

Taylor shifted in the wooden chair. Her arms were tied tightly at the wrist to the back legs, arching her back and straining her shoulders. She could bend her wrists up toward the ceiling, a mistake on her captor's part. She used her long, dexterous fingers to work on the knots.

She was wishing for a blanket—the room was freezing and they'd stripped her down to her panties and bra—when she realized she wasn't alone anymore. Her fingers stopped; she closed her eyes, feigning sleep. A scent drifted to her nose—cedar, lime, a touch of mint. A man's scent.

"I know you're awake. I've been watching you. Industrious little thing, aren't you?"

Taylor opened her eyes. A middle-height gentleman stood before her. His gray worsted wool suit was a chalk pinstripe Saville Row, the knot in his burgundy tie just so, a crisp white shirt with platinum cuff links in the French cuffs. *Dad had a suit like that once.* The thought nearly undid her. He was wearing a ski mask. Incongruous, the terrorist chic and the British finery.

"Fuck. You."

The man laughed. "Oh, aren't you the little lady? I should wash that filthy mouth out with soap."

"What do you want?"

"There, a much more important statement. Say please, and I'll tell you."

Taylor stared coolly. *Never.*

The man stared back at her, blue eyes burning behind the mask, then arranged his lips in an unpleasant grin. "Good. You're a strong one. That's what I've heard. I have a business proposition for you."

"Untie me first."

"So you can escape? Not a chance. Not yet. I'll let you go when the time is right. When I know you're going to cooperate. And cooperate you will, Lieutenant. Trust me on that."

"I seriously doubt it."

The man traced a finger along Taylor's jawline, slowly working his way to her collarbone. "There are ways."

Taylor jerked her head away and the man laughed. "I love how feisty you are. You will cooperate, and I will make sure you get out of here unscathed. Fight, put up a fuss, and I'll have you killed. That's all. Now. You have a situation back home that I can help with."

"This is about the Snow White case?"

The man turned and raised an eyebrow. "That peon of a killer? Hardly. You're closer to him than you think, Lieutenant. But no, this has nothing to do with him. This is about family. And honor. Things you pretend to respect."

He took a few steps backward, toward the door, as if a bit of distance would give him better perspective on his prisoner. He crossed his arms across his chest and stared her down.

"I don't pretend to respect my family. I have no feelings for them at all. You've obviously misunderstood the situation," she said.

"Hmm." The man put his arms behind his back and cocked his head like a spaniel puppy trying to identify a new noise. "No feelings for your family? Maybe not your parents—that bitch of a mother of yours, that traitorous father—no. I can see you having a bit too much *integrity* to care for them." He bit out the word *integrity,* making it sound sordid and misplaced. Taylor shifted uncomfortably.

"No, I mean your chosen family. Your compadres. Your comrades in arms, so to speak. Those men who hold you in such high esteem. Loyalty is a precious commodity, Lieutenant. But it should never be taken for granted. No, I think you have a great deal of feeling for those people, the ones you choose to share your life with. I'd hate to see something happen to any one of them."

Taylor rocked back in the chair, nearly tipping over in her vehemence. "You bastard! You steal me away and threaten my life, threaten my friends. Who the hell do you think you are?"

He crossed to Taylor in a flash, grabbed a handful of her dirty hair and yanked her head back, exposing her delicate throat. A small knife flashed in her peripheral vision and pressed hard against her carotid, a cold and rigid reminder of how precarious the situation really was. It took every ounce of her being not to flail and struggle. That's what he wanted. To put her in this vulnerable position. He caressed her scar with the point of the knife, and she felt nauseous.

"I'm the one who has you tied to a chair, and don't you ever forget it. Now, stop reacting, or we'll never get anything accomplished. You have a situation that needs to be handled. We can talk about the specifics once you understand the stakes. And if I'm not being clear enough, let me throw this in to sweeten the pot. If something happens to jeopardize my interests in your fair city, I'll start taking your friends' heads off, one by one. Now, you sit tight. Dusty will attend to you, get you some food. Then I have someone who wants to meet you. He'll be here shortly."

He turned the knob and strode from the room, the door slamming behind him with a brutal metal clang.

Well. That was interesting.

The second the door shut, Taylor went to work on her bonds. A little more and she'd have them undone. Then he'd see just how much she was willing to cooperate.

As she dug at the knots, she mulled the voice over and over in her head. Who is that man? What is so familiar about him? There was something, just out of reach, but the connection defied her tries to retrieve it. *The voice. Something about that voice.*

In her mind, a kidnapper had two purposes, extort money or get revenge. There had to be another agenda here. Family. This wouldn't have anything to do with her biological family. The threats against Baldwin and Fitz, Lincoln and Marcus were clear. But why? What in the world had she done to cross this madman's path? Had she wronged him in some way? An old case? He said he had interests in Nashville. What kind of interests would a man like that have?

Perhaps he was talking about his own family. Powerful men were often betrayed.

She heard the New York in his accent. Long Island, maybe. Certainly a long way from Tennessee. She knew her share of New Yorkers, but she didn't recognize that voice. Did she? No, that wasn't it. Perhaps it was a ploy to draw out Baldwin?

She pushed the thought of Baldwin out of her mind like it burned. He was looking for her, there was no doubt of that. Imagining him worried about her, all of the team frightened, wondering where she could have gotten off to, gave her a new spurt of energy. Her fingers cramped, got tired, but she pulled and manipulated the rope religiously. She had to get out of this situation, one way or another.

Just as she decided to take a break, she felt some play on her right wrist. Tiredness forgotten, she picked, picked, picked, and suddenly, the rope loosened. Blood rushed to her fingers, making her hand go numb for a moment, then fire back to life as if shot with electricity. The rope fell away and she pulled her arm to her chest. Breathing hard, she smiled in triumph. She pushed her hair out of her face, took in the large room with exposed pipes, looked for avenues of escape. Being this close to freedom gave the room a whole new perspective. Definitely some sort of warehouse, she suspected. Where, she still had no idea.

She reached around to the other wrist, tugged the

knot open. Both hands free, she sat them in her lap, rubbing them to bring the circulation back.

When her fingers felt like they could work again, she reached down and untied her feet. Standing, she moved the chair out from behind her and stretched luxuriously, like a cat kept in a kennel too long. Taylor took a deep breath, calming and centering. She waited. If they were watching, they'd be in here immediately. Nothing happened, so she went to the door.

She made her way quietly, not wanting to draw the attention of the guard if he stood outside the entryway. She risked a quick glance through the window, realized that it was an inverted glass, meant to magnify the interior of the space. It distorted her view; she couldn't see anything outside properly. She pressed her ear up against the steel but heard nothing. She put a hand on the knob and pushed, hoping against hope. She'd heard the set of locks thrown when the dapper man left. It was worth a try, though.

Locked. Figured.

She walked the length of the room, the ache in her back and legs subsiding with each step. There was a bank of grimy windows on the opposite side of the cavernous space. She went to them, tried to look out, but realized they were so dirty she could only make out the semblance of a river. She jogged in place in her underwear, unsuccessfully trying to get warm, speculating.

This certainly didn't feel like Nashville.

She didn't know how long she'd been unconscious, but the lingering effects of the chloroform from earlier, or yesterday, made her realize it could have been much longer than she thought. She was still a little woozy, and definitely sick to her stomach. The movement was helping to sharpen her reflexes and settle her gorge.

She decided to scout for a weapon, something she could use against the guard the next time he came in the room. And maybe, just maybe, she could use it to break the window. She jogged around the space, her feet growing brown and dusty. This room was obviously rarely used. There was nothing in it, either, nothing she could use against them, or to break free. There was the chair, but she felt certain they would come running at the sound of splintering wood.

She felt warmer and went to the door again, listening. There was a sound—a man's voice. He was singing, and the tuneless chant was growing closer.

She'd only have one shot at breaking away, she was certain of that.

She ran to the chair, set it upright and sat in it. She put her arms behind her, mimicking the angle that would make the guard think she was still tied up. The locks clicked and the door opened. A new man came through the door, this one much smaller than the earlier guard. She'd have a chance at this one.

He had a stupid smile on his face, as if he knew a secret she didn't. He had a tray with him; Taylor could smell the tantalizing fare. The aroma wafted to her nose—fajitas—she could smell grilled onions and green peppers. Out of place in the dirty space, it made her think of good times, drinking margaritas on the deck of her favorite little hole-in-the-wall in Nashville. The home-sickness was overwhelming. She put it aside. At least they'd deigned to feed her, which meant they weren't planning on killing her immediately.

She wouldn't stick around long enough to make a difference.

"I need to use the bathroom." Taylor tried for haughty but scared; the grin on the man's face widened. She'd succeeded in tricking him so far.

"My name's Dusty," he said.

"Great. Hi. Seriously, I need to use the bathroom." Taylor spit the words at him, but he took it as teasing and smiled wider. Idiot.

"Do you like to read?"

Oh, wow. This guy wasn't all there. He was smiling, arranging the plate of food, seemingly oblivious to Taylor's request. She let him get closer.

"Yes, I like to read."

"Do you like to touch?"

Jesus, what kind of freaks were these guys? The big one had stared at her like she was a juicy steak, but this one, with his dispassionate voice that belied his bravado—Taylor doubted he would do anything to her.

"Touch what?"

"You know." He blushed, and Taylor took a deep breath as he drew closer.

He'd have to feed her or untie her hands so she could feed herself. Either way would give her the opportunity she needed. With any luck—yes.

He set the tray on the floor. "I'm going to untie you so you can eat. We can talk. Don't do anything stupid, okay?"

She nodded. He came closer, closer. A fug surrounded him; he hadn't bathed recently, and she tried not to gag. Easy now. Let him reach behind…

Taylor jumped to her feet, knocking the chair out behind her. Dusty's shock lasted long enough for her surprise attack. Whipping her hand around his head, Taylor got a good hold on his left ear with her right hand, got his jaw in her left and twisted away from her body with all her might. She was taller than him, had more leverage than he'd expect. Before he could fight back, his head spun to the side hard and his neck snapped with a sickening, audible crunch.

Taylor let out her breath and released Dusty's head. He crumpled to the floor in a heap at her feet.

She took three steps back and stared down at him. She'd never killed a man with her bare hands before, never had to. She'd always had a weapon at her side to do the dirty work for her. More blood on her hands.

She shook the thought off. She didn't have time to worry about this now. She needed to get out of here. Without a glance behind, she darted from the room. There was a long hallway that ended in a doorway, a window above it letting light gleam in. She headed for it, thrilled when it opened into the bitter winter air.

She took deep gulps of air, cleaning the confinement out of her lungs. Her breath created gusting clouds of vapor, like a dragon snorting out smoke. The street in front of her was abandoned. To her right and left were buildings covered in graffiti, sprawling tags by ghetto artists and gangbangers, making the setting almost feel like home.

A dirty brown river sprawled in front of her, and the lights in the skyscrapers on the other side beckoned like millions of friendly fireflies. There was only one place in the world that looked like that. Even without the familiar landmarks shooting into the sky, it was unmistakable. Now she had her bearings.

The freezing river breeze blew her hair, raising goose

bumps up and down her arms and legs. Without another moment's hesitation, she went down the five steps to the street, jogged south, then took the first street that allowed her to go east, away from the river. She'd hit civilization soon enough.

Thirty-Six

He'd been picked up in the alley behind the restaurant by the giant goon known as Atlas, blindfolded and driven around for what felt like hours before L'Uomo met him at the door to the riverfront warehouse. L'Uomo dismissed his driver, and held the dirty steel door for the visitor. L'Uomo was polite on the surface, if nothing else.

They made their way through a brief warren that ended in a door. To the right was a second door, and L'Uomo went to it, turned the knob and gestured to his guest.

"Please."

This had better be worth it, the younger man thought. He walked through the door and down a long hallway toward a steel door with an inset window. He got closer. L'Uomo was behind him, gestured for him to look. As much as he didn't like turning his back in the man's presence, he didn't have much of a choice. Magnifying glass, his mind registered.

It took his eyes a moment to adjust. On the floor was a body. A man's body. *What the hell?*

He turned to L'Uomo.

"You brought me all the way back from the dead to show me a body? What kind of sick joke are you playing now? Is this just another threat? Because I don't care anymore."

L'Uomo looked confused for a moment, then rushed to the glass.

"Goddamn it! Where is she?"

He rushed out of the observation space and into the room. The man called Dusty was crumpled in a heap on the floor, his back to the ceiling. His head was turned three-quarters of the way around, obviously not in its proper place.

L'Uomo screamed in frustration. He wasn't a man prone to losing control, but this obvious alteration of his Machiavellian plans was the last straw. "She broke his neck. I can't believe it. And managed to get out of here. This is not good. This is not good at all."

The man's eyes were full of fury, and he turned on his guest.

"Son of a bitch, Win. Your fucking daughter killed my man. This will not go unpunished." He swept out of the room, leaving Win Jackson to stare into the milky-white eyes of the dead stranger.

Taylor? Taylor was here? Taylor had done this? Jesus, she must have been pissed off. A state she was perpetually in when it came to Win, anyway.

Son of a bitch was right. If Anthony Malik had

decided to bring Taylor into the scheme, he was going to have bigger problems than he knew.

L'Uomo returned, calmer, his blue eyes troubled. "Your precious little girl made it to the 108th. We need to clear out of here immediately. Do you still have the boat I arranged for you? Yes? Let's go."

He clicked open a cell phone, hit a single digit, spoke tersely to whoever answered. "I need a cleaner at the warehouse. Now."

Thirty-Seven

Long Island City, New York
Monday, December 22
8:00 p.m.

Detective 3rd Grade Emily Callahan handed Taylor a pair of gray sweatpants and a blue NYPD sweatshirt.

"Here, these should fit. The pants won't be long enough, though. What are you, six foot?"

Taylor huffed a smile. "Five-eleven and three-quarters." She slipped the rough white towel off her shoulders and stood, pulling the sweats on. Callahan was right—they were too short by about three inches, but they were warm and better than nothing. She pulled the sweatshirt over her head, stole a rubber band from Callahan's desk, tied her wet hair up in a knot, then sat back down. Just showering had left her exhausted.

Taylor had found the 108th Precinct quickly. Long Island City. The bastards had transported her to New York, of all places. Once out the warehouse door, she'd recognized the signature Manhattan skyline immediately.

As she moved away from the river, she'd actually been on Fiftieth, and the precinct was on her right after a block. Fortuitous. Though jogging up to the doors of a police station in her skivvies was relatively embarrassing, getting safe was much more important than her modesty.

The watch captain had laughed when she ran in, tried to shoo her away, thinking she was some kind of freak. She stood her ground, announced herself with authority, gave her badge number and made a request that they call her captain. Immediately.

The watch captain realized she was the real deal and grabbed her a blanket. Calls were made, concerned glances given. It was Emily Callahan who had come to her rescue, pulling Taylor into her office, giving her food, then arranging a shower and getting her some warm clothes.

Callahan handed over socks, then a steaming cup of coffee. "Vanilla. The boys here are gourmets." She rolled her eyes and Taylor laughed.

"I have a few of those myself. Starbucks has ruined us all."

"You ready to talk to the LT? He's waiting for you. Whenever you're ready, no rush."

Taylor gulped some of the coffee, happy just to have the warmth. It was sweet, almost too sweet, but she recognized that the sugar would be good for her. Callahan had been incredibly kind, fixed her up with some chicken soup, gave her a place to shower, gave her some space to sort through the jumbled-up emotions of the afternoon. The image of that man's head in her hands flooded in, the sound...she shook it off. Flashbacks weren't going to help things now.

Taylor's stomach rumbled, not happy with her choice of beverage. Stress, she thought. She tried to distract herself.

"You been here long?" she asked.

Callahan looked happy that Taylor had chosen to talk. "The 108th? Long enough. I've been in the detective bureau for a year now. I'm hoping to move up a grade soon, but you know how it is."

"Yeah, I do."

"How'd you make LT so young? If you don't mind me asking, that is."

"Worked my ass off, just like you're doing. What are you, twenty-seven, twenty-eight?"

Callahan blushed. "Thirty-three. Thanks for the compliment."

"I never was any good with ages. Just keep busting ass. It'll come. We're a smaller department, and we have lots of turnover in the higher ranks. The opportunities come around more often." She sipped her coffee again, gained as much courage from the sugary bitterness as she would ever get.

"Let's go do this."

"Follow me. We're going to be in the conference room, and it's already pretty crowded."

Callahan led Taylor down a hallway covered in flyer-filled corkboards. There was a sameness here that made Taylor comfortable. Cop shops were alike, no matter the locale.

She opened the door to a long room with a conference table. The room was packed.

Callahan made the introductions, going counterclockwise around the table.

"Lieutenant Tony Eldridge, Sergeant Robert Johnson, Davis Welton, D-1, Zach Brooks, D-2. This is Lieutenant Taylor Jackson, Metro Nashville Homicide."

Lieutenant Eldridge unfolded like a brunette crane, all long legs and skinny frame. He shook her hand. "LT, so sorry you had to come here under these circumstances. Clothes fit okay? Do you need some more coffee?"

"No, thanks. I'd rather get this over with first. Have you been to the warehouse?"

Eldridge was looking at her with a sense of incredulity. "We went there. It was empty."

"Fast," Taylor murmured.

"What do you mean?"

"I mean these were professionals. I killed one of their men and they got the scene cleared away that quickly? Surely you found something?"

Eldridge cleared his throat. "I have a team combing the place now, looking for anything we can get. So far, there's a few partials and some urine on the floor, but not much else."

"I counted at least three different people. One a six-foot-eight or -nine giant, the other about my height, slight build. Called himself Dusty. Creepy, nasty things, both of them. There was one more, definitely the head of the operation. He was well dressed, much more composed and collected than his underlings. He was well-spoken, with a Long Island accent. He wore a ski mask, so I didn't see his features, other than the fact that he has blue eyes and cruel, thin lips. He spoke to me, threatened my crew in Nashville. He said he had interests in Nashville. But he isn't on our radar, as far as I know. His voice was soft pitched, almost…soothing. Or at least it was meant to be. I pissed him off a couple of times. He doesn't like to be challenged, especially by a woman."

Eldridge glanced around the room. Four faces stared at her, all a bit disbelieving.

"What, y'all think I'm out of my mind? Listen, I was kidnapped. At a very inopportune time, mind you. I don't even know what day it is. So if you'd like to dispense with the bullshit, I'd appreciate it."

She sat back in her chair, crossed her arms and glared at them.

Callahan spoke first. "It's December 22. Three days until Christmas."

Taylor felt the news deep in the pit of her stomach. "Jesus. I was gone for three days? They must have been so worried…."

Her voice trailed off. A shadow darkened the doorstep to the conference room. Taylor felt the electricity in the room, knew who was standing behind her without turning around. The room grew silent, and she risked a glance.

Baldwin stood just inside the door, a terrible visage of both joy and pain etched on his haggard features. Their eyes met and they shared a look; it could have been a second, it could have lasted an hour. All Taylor knew was she was safe. She was in his arms before she recalled getting out of the chair. There was no kiss, no words, just arms around each other and a heavy heartbeat. She didn't know if it was hers or his, but it centered her, grounded her, and she squeezed hard, once. Turning around, she saw the looks on her fellow officers' faces and realized they were stunned.

"This is Dr. John Baldwin. FBI. He's…" She looked over her shoulder at Baldwin.

"I'm here for Taylor." He took two strides into the room, held Taylor's chair, waited for her to sit and get settled, then sat next to her. He reached for her hand and held it with both of his in his lap. He indicated to Eldridge with a jerk of his head.

"Please, continue. You were saying?"

Eldridge started to reach across Taylor to shake Baldwin's hand, then stopped, realizing Baldwin wasn't going to comply. Instead, he put his finger to his upper lip and tapped.

"It wasn't that we didn't believe you, Lieutenant. You came up against some major muscle and walked away from it. That doesn't happen. Not with the man we're dealing with."

"You know who's behind this?"

"I've got a pretty good idea."

Taylor was exhausted and famished. She just wanted to collapse and sleep for a week, but she couldn't. Not yet. There was work to be done. They decided to move across the street, get her some food and continue the discussion. Baldwin had brought a bag for her. She took out a sweater and jeans, her favorite boots and some toiletries. She changed into the clothes before they left, brushed her teeth and hair, thankful for the familiar hominess. The actions gave her new energy.

The bar across the street from the 108th was nestled in a row house, identical to the buildings on either side except for a red-and-blue-striped awning and small neon sign that read "Dog Pound."

Baldwin opened the door for Taylor, and they entered to the strains of Frank Sinatra. Frank was warbling about the way she looked tonight. Taylor was just happy to be in the warm environment and was cheered by the prospect of solid food. Despite the universals of the precinct, this felt more like home.

The bar was long and mahogany, varnished to within an inch of its life. High café tables stretched the length of the opposite wall. There were a few men, bundled and white-headed, sitting at the far end. They paid them no mind, continued their discussion without turning.

Baldwin indicated a table by the wall. They sat, and the bartender came around the bar to them with a tired smile.

They ordered Guinness, sat back and reveled in each other. Baldwin stared at her hungrily, as if he'd gobble her up in one bite if she so much as moved. She felt pinned by his stare and didn't know what to say. The waitress returned with their beer and left them to their silence.

"Baldwin," Taylor began, but the group from the precinct wafted through the door, cutting off her statement. They joined them, settling in, good-natured, spirits high.

Callahan sat next to Taylor. As Frank started in anew, this time with "Luck Be a Lady," Callahan leaned in conspiratorially.

"Just a heads-up, the owner's obsessed. Sinatra's the only thing you'll hear in here tonight. Or any night. It's the law."

"Are you serious?"

"As a heart attack. You can go look at the jukebox, it's only got selections from Old Blue Eyes. After a while you won't even notice."

Taylor took a gulp of her beer, rolled her eyes good-naturedly at Baldwin.

They ordered crisp steak sandwiches, which came

smothered in peppers and onions and mozzarella cheese. The smell reminded her too much of the afternoon's escapades; Taylor had to send hers back and have a new one made. Her roaring appetite was gone, the food tasted liked dust, but she managed to get it in her stomach.

Despite the fact that there wasn't a body, the 108th detectives were jubilant when she described the scene, the killing. They recognized her description of the man who called himself Dusty. The knowledge of his past transgressions didn't make his death any easier.

Apparently Dusty, known to the police as Dustin Mosko, had been a regular with the sex-crimes unit. Rape, abuse, torture. How a man with his record could possibly be out of jail was astounding, but that was the system for you. Have him serve his time, let him back out onto the street, and pump him full of drugs that would ostensibly satiate his cravings. It was nuts, and apparently no one would be missing Mr. Dusty.

The other goon Taylor had come in contact with was assumed to be a man called Atlas. A natural-born killer with the size to see his threats to fruition, he was a prolific assassin.

Both men worked for a shadowy man the Long Island City police knew as L'Uomo; killed in his name. The Man. Of course, they had another name for him. Edward Delglisi. A first-class underworld kingpin. The same name Frank Richardson had dug out of Burt Mars's records before he ended up dead.

Running through all the Nashville–New York connections had cemented the clue. Burt Mars was a known commodity to the New York police. The word on their radar was Mars worked for Delglisi, which helped confirm the trail of information Richardson had started before his murder. When Taylor relayed that news, Eldridge had gotten on the phone, ordered Burt Mars brought in for a chat.

No one had ever seen Delglisi. That in and of itself made Taylor's events of the past few days of high interest to the New York cops. Though she hadn't seen his face, she'd become intimately acquainted with his voice. The long, hard tones would stick in her mind for many years to come, she was sure of that, as would that piercing blue stare.

Something about the whole setup still didn't feel right to Taylor. She didn't know anyone named Edward Delglisi. Didn't remember that name in connection to her family, to Nashville, or anything else she could think of. But he certainly knew her.

The answers were there; Taylor could feel them lurking in the deepest recesses of her mind. She was just too exhausted to think things through clearly.

She decided to put it aside for now. To enjoy her freedom. There was plenty of time to figure everything else out. She didn't even want to start thinking about what she'd missed back in Nashville. Weddings were meant to be rescheduled, right?

It was a sign, she was sure of that. Though there was no way she was going to bring that one up with Baldwin anytime soon.

Thirty-Eight

New York, New York
Monday, December 22
10:58 p.m.

Checking into a hotel in the city was a no-brainer. Neither Taylor nor Baldwin wanted to accept the kindness of the detectives from the 108th, who would have been happy to let them bunk overnight at their homes. Once the debrief was finished, Eldridge had personally driven them across the Queensboro Bridge into Manhattan. Baldwin had called ahead to the W Hotel on Lexington for a single overnight reservation. It was Christmas season, the hotel was booked, but the concierge somehow found a room for them. Eldridge had looked at him strangely for a moment, as if he wanted to ask how Baldwin had that much pull, but changed his mind.

To be honest, Baldwin would have much rather tossed Taylor on the FBI plane and gotten her home as quickly as possible, but there were too many loose ends to wrap up.

He glanced at Taylor; she sat in the back of the un-marked car silently, staring off into the night as they crossed the bridge over the East River.

Baldwin was pleased the W could accommodate him. There was no sense in doing anything less. It wasn't every day that he got to spend a romantic evening in New York with his bride-to-be. And he enjoyed that he could pull off something to comfort her. He hoped it would comfort her. Jesus, now that he had her back, he didn't ever want to let her out of his sight again.

The city was dressed and lit in its Christmas finery, but the weather had turned. Snow was coming, flakes were beginning to compete for space, drifting down carelessly. The sky was dark between the skyscrapers, deep and dirty. Off-white clouds drifted through the murk. Fog crept between the buildings; it felt alive, evil and oppressive. Gotham City, living up to its reputation.

Despite the gloomy night, the line into Whiskey Blue was down the block. Patrons of the Waldorf-Astoria across the street shook their heads at the trendy grouping of nightlife fashionistas. Heads turned when Taylor and Baldwin got out of the unmarked car, but as soon as it was established that they weren't anyone famous, the group quickly went back to their own worlds.

They shook hands with Eldridge, thanked him for the hospitality and made plans to meet for breakfast in the morning. The marbled lobby was warm, the discreet fountain separating the space from the restaurant trickled serenely, and Taylor left Baldwin's side to stand in front of it, head cocked as she watched the water flow.

The desk clerk was icily polite, fingers snapping on the keyboard, a room key generated. He asked if there were any special requests, Baldwin declined. No sense advertising who they were to the clerk. They were just another couple who'd had too much to drink in the city and didn't want to make the long drive back to suburbia.

He was worried about Taylor. He'd seen the look in her eyes before, a certain detachment, a faraway gaze that indicated she was looking inside herself for answers.

He'd listened to her talk about the kidnapping ordeal back at the precinct. He cringed when she described the man who had isolated her, threatened her with ultimatums. He felt the anger and fever that consumed her when she explained about breaking the guard's neck and making her getaway. He knew how she felt about it— that she wasn't so upset about taking a life as she was at being forced into that corner. Taylor was a tough woman; she knew the risks of her profession well. Murder, mayhem, all were within her reach. She would have been a good operative—able to compartmentalize her emotions, do what was necessary to get the job done and move forward without regret.

But the hand-to-hand combat, mortal combat, was another beast entirely.

The key was in his hand now, and he led her to the elevators, distinctly aware that she was restraining herself. He figured the minute that door was shut, a scream would erupt, some sort of loosening of the emotions that tightened her face.

She stayed silent, watchful, guarded.

The elevator's muted ding alerted him that they'd reached their floor. He beckoned to Taylor, motioning her out of the elevator and into the hallway. He counted down the numbered doors—1515, 1509, 1507, this was their room. He inserted the key into the locking mechanism, the light flickered green and the door popped open slightly. He pushed the door, held it for Taylor and entered the suite behind her, letting the door swing shut behind him.

A short hallway led to the living room, but they didn't make it that far.

Taylor was on him before the door lock clicked to let them know they were safely ensconced in the womblike area.

Her ferocity astounded him. She took his collar in her hands and forced him back against the wall, her mouth hot on his, her hands traveling the length of his body. He was ready in an instant and it seemed to take forever to get her out of her clothes, though he knew that wasn't the case—he heard something tear just before her smooth skin melted against his.

His clothes joined hers in a pile on the floor and they were wrapped around each other, fusing, sucking, touching. Baldwin lifted her by the buttocks and swung her around, forcing her back against the wall.

Taylor was like a wild woman, an animal, starved for attention, starved for food. Wrapping her long legs around his body, she demanded more. She bit into his neck and he thrust against her, her hips melding into his, her back scraping the expensive paper. A painting fell off a foot away, their hurried coupling shaking the very walls. A scream, deep and guttural, emanated from Taylor's throat as she climaxed, then she was in tears. Baldwin followed suit, lost in her, lost in himself. He came back, realized he had Taylor pinned to the wall so tightly that every breath she took moved his own ribs.

He smiled at her then, desperate longing coupled with relief. She reflected his look, into his eyes, his soul, naked, hungry again. Lost. So very lost.

He lifted her, never taking his eyes off hers, navigating the steps through the sitting room, into the bedroom. Still joined, he laid her gently on the bed and moved slightly, the exquisite oneness of them nearly overwhelming him.

She took, and took, and he gave all he could, sensing somehow that it wouldn't be enough to exorcise the demons from her soul. They moved in ways they never had, connected deeper than before. He tensed and Taylor urged him forward, deeper, faster, her hands grasping his hips and forcing them to drive harder. He cried out this time, but she was silent, taking. When he caught his breath, he rolled off of her, gathered her in his arms, and held her while she fought the tears.

The knock on the door started her awake. She was deep in the bed, covers pulled high on her neck, an arm lodged under Baldwin. He slept deeply, untroubled. She thought back to their frantic sex and smiled. That was a whole new level for them, the desperate clawing passion. She enjoyed it, felt a little guilty that a death had caused such furious excitement within her. *Comfort,* she thought. *That's what I wanted.*

The discreet knocking came again. Baldwin didn't stir. She slid her arm out from under his neck and stepped into the marble-tiled bathroom, pulling a thick terry-cloth robe off the hook behind the door and shrugging it on. She glanced at the clock—3:48 a.m. Who the hell was knocking on their door at this ungodly hour?

Picking up Baldwin's .40, she went to the door, gun pointed down the length of her naked thigh.

"Yes?"

"Ma'am, I have a package for you."

"It's nearly four in the morning. Can't it wait?"

"No, ma'am. The concierge told me to deliver it personally. I'm looking for Lieutenant Taylor Jackson. That you?"

She didn't answer. A communiqué in the middle of the night. She had a brief thought of her mother's middle-of-the-night phone call, two months ago.

"Leave the package by the door."

"I can't do that, ma'am. I promised—"

"Leave it," she barked. She heard a whispered thump, then footsteps retreating down the hall.

Opening the door, weapon up, she glanced right, then left. The hallway was appropriately deserted. She reached her left hand out, taking the package by the corner. It was an envelope, padded, one you'd find in any office supply store in the country. Only about the size of a CD. There was a bulky lump in the middle.

Against her better judgment, she pulled the package inside. With a last look into the hallway, she secured the door, flipping the bolt and slamming the safety lock home.

"What's that?"

She jumped, the deep rumbling of Baldwin's sleep-strewn voice startling her. It was the first words he'd spoken to her since they'd entered the hotel room several hours earlier. She remembered how it was between them and felt herself blush, then pushed it all away.

"A package, hand-delivered. Get the concierge on the phone."

She looked at the manila envelope. It had her name and the name of the hotel. Obviously, someone knew they were here.

Baldwin came back to the hallway. "Concierge said it was delivered by a man about half an hour ago. They ran it through their security checks and an X-ray, said it looked like a cell phone. He didn't seem concerned, said he felt the source was of pure motive, whatever the hell that means. I'd feel more comfortable if we got the local bureau involved, let them send it through the bomb sniffer."

But Taylor had already slit the top of the package, looking inside. There was a cell phone.

"No way, no how, Taylor. This is definitely going to the lab. You don't have any idea what they can do with a phone these days…."

Briiiinnng.

The phone buzzed in Taylor's hand. She looked at Baldwin, then back at the phone. Four rings, five, six, seven. Eight. She took a deep breath.

"If they wanted me dead, they would have done it back at the warehouse."

She flipped the phone open and held it to her ear. There was a bit of static, then she heard a voice. "Taylor?"

"Oh my God. Daddy?"

The voice rocked Taylor to the core. It had been a long time—three years, since she'd seen him in person. He was dead. Missing. Gone. This tortured, broken man couldn't possibly be her father. But there was no mistaking the voice. It was his.

And he was scared.

"Taylor? Are you there?"

"Daddy, where are you?"

"Taylor, I want you to listen to me. You need to do what he says. Just go along with him, sweetheart, and you'll be fine. I'll be fine."

"But, Daddy—"

"Taylor? Are you there?"

"I'm here, Daddy."

"Taylor, I want you to listen to me. You need to do what he says. Just go along with him, sweetheart, and you'll be fine. I'll be fine."

She looked sharply at Baldwin. Exact words. She stopped speaking. The voice came again.

"Taylor? Are you there?"

She didn't respond.

"Taylor, I want you to listen to me. You need to do what he says. Just go along with him, sweetheart, and you'll be fine. I'll be fine."

A recording. Her heart sank. Jesus, still being manipulated by this freak. She handed the phone to Baldwin, let him listen to the loop.

With a shake of his head, he handed it back to her. Not her father. Just a voice recording. It could have been made anytime. There was nothing about it that said he was actually alive.

The fury bubbled up in her chest and she turned the cell phone so it faced her, then screamed, long and loud, into the mouthpiece. She went to hit the end button, but heard a laugh coming from the speaker. She held it to her ear.

That voice she did recognize. The same jeering tones that had spoken to her in the warehouse. He was laughing at her.

Thirty-Nine

Nashville, Tennessee
Monday, December 22
11:58 p.m.

"Father?"

Snow White was asleep in the chair in his expansive library. Charlotte looked at him, his body bent, the misshapen hands, and felt nothing. No pity, no sorrow for the pain he obviously suffered. It was fitting, actually, that a man who had been the source of such agony and misery, who had tortured the life out of ten young women, should be afflicted with a disease that crippled his tools of destruction.

She had that feeling again, fleeting as it may be. She'd always wondered what it would feel like to empty the soul from a body. When it came down to it, she didn't have the power, wasn't able to consummate the burning desire she felt. So she fed on others who could.

Which was the course that led her to her father's apprentice. Where better to satisfy her lust than in the behavioral unit of the FBI? She was fed a steady diet of murder, of psychologically misfortunate beings who felt that same pull. She could study them, get to know them, and in some special cases, work with them on a more literal level.

She'd never done that with her dad. After her mother died giving birth to Joshua, she'd been in charge of the house. When she'd walked in on him murdering Ava D'Angelo, the second of his victims, she'd calmly shut the door and gone to the kitchen to oversee the dinner preparations.

He sought her out, later. He talked to her, discussed the murder with her. It was an experiment, he said. "Like the experiment I did on Joshua's guinea pig?" she had asked. He'd seen it then, that he'd passed along the emptiness of soul that accompanies the desire to take life. Funny, she remembered the very moment when he kissed her forehead and entreated her to keep his secret. He was proud of her. As she was of him.

That was the last they discussed his extracurricular activities. She'd gone away to school, then went on to college, got her Ph.D., and joined the FBI. He was forced to stop killing by the advancement of the arthritis. They were both complete, yet empty.

Then Troy had come into their lives.

It had taken her weeks to write the special program, to upload it into the CODIS database. It was a brilliant deception, a Trojan horse that took the information inputted by the various law enforcement officials across the country and filtered the results. She'd built the program to warn her of possible anomalies in DNA matches before they made it into the official system.

This gave her the freedom to examine the kills, then pass them along unscathed to the official database, keeping back the murders she was most interested in. To be honest, she was astonished the program had failed. The IT support at Quantico must have rolled out an update that kicked her Trojan out of the system. That's why the DNA matches suddenly poured in. Her system wasn't flawless, after all. That could, would be fixed.

She'd found Troy through a Web site designed for killers to talk freely about their escapades, had alerted her perverted CODIS program to his particulars. The sites were filled with poseurs and fakes, like wannabe vampires who had their teeth filed into fangs and drank the blood of their friends but weren't really ever going to be burned to ash by sunlight. That was the kind of miscreant that usually populated these sites, the fantasy seekers. Fallacious seers and the unintended Apocrypha, murderous sycophants. After a few false alarms, she'd learned to spot the real ones.

Once she'd found Troy, she couldn't help herself. She'd known it was a bad idea from the beginning, but was compelled. Obsessed. She wanted to lay eyes on the man who was already such an accomplished, sophisticated killer. She knew he was the one she'd been waiting for.

Troy was difficult at the start. He made no excuses, played no tricks. Except his name, of course. He refused to share his real name with her. It was nearly a deal breaker, but he was just so talented, she decided to let it slide. Feeling a bit like she'd been conquered, she christened him Troy.

Charlotte started to gather the remnants of her father's tea and medications when the phone rang, surprising her. The tea tray clattered to the floor; her father jerked awake with a groan.

She answered the phone, then gave it wordlessly to Snow White. The caller spoke loudly; it wasn't hard to overhear. Picking up the tubes and jars, the teapot and sugar, she listened.

The call was brief. Her father didn't bother to say a word. When he handed the phone back to her, he almost look ashamed. That's when she realized he was scared.

"Who was that?"

"An old friend. Where is Troy?"

"I believe he is teasing the girl."

Teasing, that's what Troy liked to call it. Unlike his mentor, he enjoyed conversing with his victims before-hand, getting to know them a bit. Instilling a tiny fragment of hope into their beings that they might, *might,* get away with their lives.

"Get him out of there, Charlotte. We must release her."

"Are you kidding? That's like taking a gazelle out of a lion's jaws. He's already sunk his teeth into her juicy little neck. I can't just let her go. He's decided on her."

Snow White struggled up from his chair, stiff and slow. He shuffled to the wet bar, poured a measure of whiskey into a lead crystal highball. His hands shook now; he spilled as much as he got in the glass.

"That was Malik. He is convinced the police are on to us."

"Us? You and Joshua?"

"You and Troy, too. I told you he was more trouble than he was worth."

Charlotte tossed her hair over her shoulder in disdain. "Please. You've loved him like a son."

"And now he must go. Malik is furious at the transgression. Troy is out of my control, Charlotte. He is out of your control. He must be excised."

"Who is out of control?" a voice boomed from the doorway. Troy came into the room and poured himself a drink. Charlotte and Snow White froze. What had he overheard?

"You are." Charlotte advanced on him, purring. She could distract him, that was certain. Her father's commands were buzzing through her mind. She wasn't ready to give this up. She was having fun.

"I'm not out of control at all. I'm just getting started. What do you think, old man? We've waited long enough. I need her. Let us climb the stairs together, now, and I will hold my hand over yours on the knife, and fuck her with my dick while you stroke her face and watch the light leave her eyes."

"No!" Snow White slammed his drink down on the table. "You must let her go. We've been over this already. We will find you another. We can go right now, we can take two, three. Whatever you wish. But the girl must go home. The police are too close. I've received a warning from an old friend who would know. Release her."

Troy started pacing through the library. "You can't dictate to me, old man. Maybe I've already killed her. Maybe I've been lying to you all along."

"You haven't. I would smell her blood on your hands." He softened his harsh tone, tried to make the boy see reason. "You must understand, sometimes this is what has to happen. Not every hunter gets his buck each time out in the woods. We will find more. That is all."

Snow White collapsed in his chair, his energy exhausted.

"You can't stop me." Troy turned to Charlotte, his fury palpable, barely contained. "I'm going to take her now. She is mine."

She grabbed his arm. "Troy. You need to see reason here. You've gotten us in a lot of trouble. Maybe it's time for you to listen instead of act. Aren't you having fun? Aren't we giving you everything you ever desired? Aren't we a family? I brought you into our lives because I knew you wanted a chance to grow, to learn. We've given you that, and more. We've given you love."

Troy wasn't going to take that. Charlotte could see the slow burn flame into a raging inferno. He was dangerous when that fuse was lit, and she consciously took three steps back. He noticed her retreat, and that infuriated him all the more.

"What, now you're leaving me, too? What is this, Charlotte, some kind of game? Get me involved only to pull the rug out from under me?"

"No, Troy, that's not it."

"Liar!" he screamed, and slapped her. Her head rang with the blow. This was getting out of hand. Her service weapon was in her purse, but it was on the other side of the room.

"How dare you hit me? When all I've done is help you. You bastard!"

"Stop it now, both of you."

The commanding tone was enough to startle them both. They continued circling each other, warily testing for weaknesses, but the tension came down a notch.

Snow White slowly, painfully lit a cigar. "Let's all

just sit down and talk this through. I'm sure we can find an equitable solution."

"No, old man. That isn't how this works. I will not be directed. I don't want to star in your sad little play. I don't need you. I don't need either one of you." He stormed from the room, leaving Snow White to gaze at his daughter, his face etched in a combination of love and abhorrence for her.

"Your plan will fail, Charlotte." He rubbed his hands together, trying to ease the aching joints. "You can't control a man who doesn't know his own desires."

The shurring noise coming from her father's hands was grating on her nerves. "He knows what he wants."

"Oh, come now, daughter. Surely you aren't that stupid. Why do you think he copies? Why do you think you were able to bring him here, to emulate me? He doesn't know what he is, and is still testing the waters to find out what he's truly capable of. You should be wary, Charlotte. Your mother thought she could control me. Look where it got her."

They were arguing again; he could hear them through the walls into the conservatory. There was a way to settle their dispute. The man she called Troy would be angered, but Father would be pleased. Yes, it was a good plan. He only hoped his father and his sister were powerful enough to keep the bad man away from him.

Forty

"Oh, yes. Yes. *Yes!*"

Charlotte's head thrashed against the pillow as she orgasmed. Her mind was utterly blank for a blessed moment, then the world came back into focus. It was dark in the room, the curtains drawn, the lights from the street muted in the dark velvet folds. She'd been through the ringer tonight, that was for sure.

After the nasty argument with her father, she felt sick. The fight had taken so much out of him. It pained her to see him this…old. Broken. Mentally and physically, he was no longer the robust killer she'd always admired.

She stormed out of the house, drove aimlessly. Took some time to think through what her father had told her. He was right, the bastard. Troy didn't know his own mind. But treating him as an uninformed acolyte was much more dangerous.

Calmed, she went back to Belle Meade. She found Troy sitting on the steps at the base of the entrance to Cheekwood. She spent nearly an hour talking him off the ledge. She felt derision toward his limitation, his inability to put the plan before his own needs. She just needed to get away. The excitement, the danger, it was intoxicating at the beginning. Now it was obvious that he was just another sick guy. She'd chosen her playmate poorly.

The plan had gone awry, and it was time to cut bait and start over. The evening news showed the noose growing ever tighter. Something was happening at work; she could feel things slipping away. She couldn't jeopardize her position. As much fun as this had been, the FBI provided all she needed. She wasn't willing to give that up.

As she drove back to the hotel, she vowed that would be the last she ever saw of the man her father called Apprentice. He was out of her control. She'd returned to the hotel, intent on formulating a new plan. One with her as the hero.

The answer became readily apparent. Arresting Troy wasn't a real possibility; he would have to be killed. Alive, he would implicate her in his schemes. But death, now that would make all the difference. She took a couple of pills and plotted for an hour, lost in her alternate world.

It would be easy enough to kill them both. Stopping the apprentice would make her famous. The fact that she was Snow White's daughter, well, that would make her a legend.

She took another hit of X, stared out at the Christmas lights lining the buildings by the hotel. She had it all plotted out. The headlines, the interviews. How she'd decided to stop home to wish her old, sick father Merry Christmas and found him up to his neck in blood and gore. Oh, she'd have to kill that little girl in the attic, as well. The thought excited her. Tremendously.

The checkmark in her win column would catapult her into the position she so longed for, the head of the BSU.

A knock on the door had startled her. Troy had come to the hotel room, shaken like a little boy who has been exposed to a scary movie. Promised that it would never happen again. Begged her to stay with him, to help him. The sight of him, so handsome, so remorseful—she decided one last little fling couldn't be all that bad. No sense wasting the X.

They'd had frenzied sex, him plunging into her over and over so hard she felt the bruises form. He promised to take care of her forever. He told her he would do anything she wanted as long as she let him stay. He loved her. He'd never felt anything like this before.

He'd made love to her then, taking his time, doing all the things that he knew she loved, until she'd screamed his name, and God's, at the top of her lungs.

Her breath was starting to return to normal. Maybe there was a way to make this work after all. He was still in her, had her pinned against the mattress like a butter-fly on a piece of cork.

"Let me up. I need to wash."

"No, Charlotte. But I do."

The blade was so sharp she didn't feel the cut. Didn't feel the knife sweep through the tender skin on her neck like it was butter. It took a moment to register what was happening, that he'd just done what he'd done. The lying bastard. Her eyes teared, and she tried to scream. There was the pain, finally, as she realized he'd cut her so deep, her vocal cords were severed. In a moment of disgust, she felt him harden in her and realized he was pumping away, coming again, crying out her name as she went away.

Forty-One

Lieutenant Tony Eldridge and Detective Emily Callahan sat across the breakfast table from Taylor and Baldwin, industriously sucking down cappuccinos. They were in the Heartbeat restaurant of the W Hotel, ostensibly coming up with a game plan, a breakfast strategy session.

Ordering the food had taken nearly five minutes with all the specifics the New York cops asked for. Emily had requested organic granola, fruit cut with a fresh knife, local farm yogurt, wheat grass juice and an immunity-boosting smoothie, smiling unapologetically at Taylor. Eldridge opted for the steel-cut oatmeal with brown sugar, cranberries, raisins, toasted almonds and warm milk. Even Baldwin got caught up in the health frenzy, taking pastel eggs with fruitwood bacon and roasted potato veggie hash. Taylor tried to play along but felt like a child, ordering peanut-butter-and-jelly crepes. It was as close to normal as she could find on the menu. Even the food added to her sense of dislocation. The one thing of comfort was the orange gerbera daisy in the stainless-steel vase. Hard beauty for such a gentle flower, but fitting, somehow.

After the waitress left, Taylor fiddled with a ripe pear and took in the multicolored reflective glass column to her right. She wanted out of New York, wanted to get back home and…and…she didn't know. She didn't know what she wanted. Home seemed like a haven now, a place to escape to, to be rid of this city and its implied threats.

Baldwin turned over the cell phone. Eldridge promised to do everything he could to trace its origins, see if they could find some answers.

They talked of the things that gave them common ground until the meal was finished. Eldridge slurped the last of his espresso, setting the cup in the saucer delicately.

"Okay, Lieutenant, let's run through this again. Tell me everything you remember about Delglisi, everything he said. We must be missing something."

Taylor set the pear on her plate. She focused her thoughts, went back to that dank room. Smelled his cologne, heard his voice. Chills ran down her arms.

"A few things stood out. He said he had a business proposition for me. I asked if this had anything to do with the Snow White case, and he said I was closer to him than I thought. He said there was a situation that needed to be handled, and that if something happened to screw with his interests in Nashville he'd take the heads of my team. He talked about family."

If something happens to jeopardize my interests in

your fair city, I'll start taking your friends' heads off, one by one. She swallowed hard at the fury that rose in her gut. Just talking about the threat pissed her off.

"Did you get the sense he was referring to Snow White, or something else?" Baldwin leaned back in his chair, his coffee cup held loosely in his hand.

"Something else. He didn't feel Snow White was a danger, that's for sure. He called him a peon of a killer. Didn't seem to think he was worth his time. I think there's more to it, too. Lieutenant Eldridge, why don't you fill us in a little more on Edward Delglisi? Maybe if I know more about him I'll have an easier time making sense of his threats."

Eldridge looked at Callahan, nodding as he took a sip of water. Her show to run. Callahan cleared her throat and launched.

"Okay. L'Uomo has been around for about twenty years now. We don't know much about him, only get a string of murders that crop up with his signature every once in a while. Businesses fail, storefronts close, and three or four bodies show up. People who cross him don't get to hang around for long. He runs an import/export business, but he's quiet and quick. He floats people around, has a lot of money, and has never been caught. He's got deep pockets and a lot of people on the payroll."

"How does Burt Mars fit in?" Taylor asked.

Callahan handed a file across to Taylor. "Mars. He's a stool. But smart. He was the single biggest reason the Tartulo family went down. He's L'Uomo's bank. Here's some reports you may find interesting. Mars has been shuffling L'Uomo's money around for quite a while.

Uses that Manderley REIT hedge fund. Only we can't
find it. Every time we get close to the source of the
funding, it literally disappears. One of the better money-
laundering schemes we've come across. The feds are
working it, too. Dr. Baldwin, you could probably find
some more information from your end."

Taylor handed the file to Baldwin. He flipped it open,
glanced through it, then said, "I'll do that. Thanks for
the heads-up."

"But there's one little problem. We found Burt Mars
dead in his apartment last night. Shot at close range.
Looked like a typical home invasion." Callahan shook
her head. "Right down to the computers being stolen."

Taylor met her eye. "Let me guess. All of his business
information was on those computers."

"That's what we suspect. He had a huge office—the
master suite of the apartment had been converted. There
was enough wiring to send up the space shuttle. Just
nothing left to plug in."

Taylor felt disappointment roll off Callahan in waves.
"You're sure it was Mars?"

Callahan pushed another file across the table. Taylor
opened it without picking it up. There was a photograph
of a small man with blond hair and Buddy Holly glasses,
a hole where his chest should have been. She recognized
him at once. Her dream flooded in, vivid and raw. A
sandy-haired man clapping her dad on the shoulder.
"Your own little Manderley."

Eldridge brought her back. "One lead gone. But
there's still Delglisi. Like we said yesterday, no one has
ever seen him before—he's like a mythical legend
around these parts. We're not even certain Delglisi is his

real name. It's one of many that he's assumed over the years, but the one that's been the most consistent, the deepest in the files."

Taylor sat back in her chair. "What does he import? Drugs?"

Callahan shook her head. "No. Something much more valuable. People."

"From where?" Taylor asked.

"Everywhere. It's been mostly Hispanic lately, from what we're hearing. He did a stint of Chinese, and some other Asians, but it seems he's switched solely to Mexican and South American immigrants lately. As you can imagine, he's really popular with Homeland Security."

"What happens when they get here?"

"They go to work. In the shops, in the sex trade, wherever they're needed. They need to work off their passage."

Baldwin looked at Taylor. "He's just a plain old slave trader." Taylor snorted through her nose.

"Some plain old slave trader. Things are making a little more sense now."

"How's that?" Eldridge stopped everything.

"We had a case in Nashville last week. A Guatemalan girl by the name of Saraya Gonzalez was found in the woods, injured, in pretty bad shape. She'd run away from a 'massage parlor' where she was being forced to have sex with men on camera. They were making sex tapes. There's just one problem. The same day we found her, Saraya was murdered in the hospital. She was shot by a man who fled the scene. He actually took her from her room, but we caught up to him and he killed her. We recovered bullets and shell casings for ballistics, put them in the system, but we had no leads when I…when I…"

"Was kidnapped," Baldwin filled in.

"Right. Seems a little strange to refer to myself in those terms. Anyway, there was nothing that we had outside of the crime scene that would lead us to the shooter.

"Then a reporter friend who was helping with the Snow White case, Frank Richardson, was killed. He had just found out some information on Burt Mars. You say Mars works for L'Uomo? Well, Frank was killed by the same gun as Saraya Gonzalez. It seems to me that L'Uomo's 'interests' in Nashville are as sordid and simple as that."

Eldridge sat back in his chair. "We're talking about *the* Frank Richardson, right? Guy who won the Pulitzer? You say he was a friend?"

"Briefly. But yeah, he was a good guy."

Callahan was taking notes. "Killed with what kind of gun?"

"Both Frank and Saraya were hit with a Desert Eagle Jericho .41 caliber. Israeli made, they don't make—"

"Them anymore." Eldridge smiled, and Callahan got a look of pure joy on her face. She tapped her fingers on the table. "I may have something for you, Taylor. We have ballistics from several scenes that involved L'Uomo's big assassin, the one we call Atlas. He uses a Desert Eagle. That could be the tie-in you're looking for. If Atlas was dispatched to Nashville to take care of a few loose ends, then we have the answer to your question. And that hole in Mars was made with a big gun. Ballistics will tell us for sure, but I'll take odds that Atlas killed Mars, too. Delglisi is tying up loose ends."

I wonder what that makes Win. Taylor pushed the thought away.

"I'm a little foggy on the particulars. I saw his face, know he was a huge guy, but don't really remember it. You think it was Atlas who snatched me?"

"Yes. Especially if he was already in town on errands. He was most likely instructed to bring you to New York unharmed."

"So Delglisi could try to bargain with me, threaten me? Why wouldn't they just deliver the message in Nashville?"

"That wouldn't show you how much power he has. It was much more dramatic to snatch you from your wedding. Bigger impact."

Taylor looked at Baldwin. "I'm sorry," she said softly. He just nodded and smiled back. They'd had a wedding night of sorts fifteen floors up the night before. There was more to them now than words or paper could provide.

With some effort, Taylor broke eye contact with Baldwin and turned to Eldridge. "So we tie this all up, neat and tidy, with a little bow. Except for one thing."

"Win Jackson," Baldwin interjected.

Taylor gave him a look of gratitude. "Exactly. What does my father have to do with Edward Delglisi?" She turned to Eldridge and Callahan. "Have you come across any information that would explain his presence in all of this?"

They both shook their heads. "No, we haven't."

Shit, Win. As much as she hated it, she was actually worried for him.

She excused herself to use the restroom, giving Baldwin an "I'm fine" look as she left. She crossed the parquet floors, the heels of her boots thudding dully. She stopped at the glass-fronted fireplace for a moment, warming her hands and watching a thoroughly New York woman who was lingering briefly at the entrance to the restaurant so she could be admired. Glossy black hair, dark jeans tucked into chocolate suede boots, a white cashmere scarf wound around her neck—Taylor blinked and the chic girl was in motion, whipping the scarf off, coat and sunglasses gone, and she was across the room and being greeted by her party. Effortless. Not a word Taylor often used to describe herself.

The hotel's asymmetrical floor-to-ceiling windows, frosted glass with leaves pressed between the panes and the occasional cobalt square, looked out onto Lexington Avenue, which was teeming with people getting ready for the holidays. Even the cars and buses and police cruisers radiated good will. The hustle and bustle of the city was depressing Taylor. There was something sinister about this place now. Just knowing that Edward Delglisi, L'Uomo, was involved with her father in any infinitesimal way horrified her. She wondered if Win was still alive, wondered if he was in hiding from something bigger than them all. If Mars had been a target, it stood to reason Win was, too.

She used the restroom and returned to her seat. They'd been talking about her; the conversation ended abruptly as she sat down. To cover her discomfort, she took a bite of the pear, amazed at its sweetness, the grainy texture welcome in her now-tart mouth.

Callahan looked at Taylor strangely, obviously trying to imagine what it must be like for an upstanding cop to have a father who was associating with the lowest of lowlifes. Her brows knitted as if she couldn't quite make the leap. Taylor decided to save her the trouble.

"Win Jackson has been a crook since day one, Emily. Don't worry yourself over it. This is all gelling for me. Now, if we could just wrap up the Snow White case. Baldwin, was there any more news about the Macias girl?"

Eldridge nearly jumped out of his chair. "What Macias girl? What are you talking about?"

Taylor raised an eyebrow. "We had a girl go missing last week, during the height of all the Snow White killings. Fit the vic profile for the Snow White. Her name is Jane Macias."

"Holy shit!" Callahan and Eldridge exchanged looks. Taylor held her hands up.

"What, what is it? Do you know where she is?"

Eldridge had gotten pale. "No, but I know *who* she is. She's a reporter, was a reporter, at least. Did some articles last year about Delglisi's operation. Her dad owned a restaurant up here, in Little Italy. It's the same old story—Delglisi's goons hit the place up, offering protection. Macias said no way in hell. They made it clear that if he wanted to stay open, he'd comply. He must have gone along with it eventually. They usually do. About a year ago, Macias had an accident. Slipped and fell in the kitchen of the restaurant, managed to get the knife he was carrying buried to the hilt in his stomach. His daughter found him.

"Word on the street was he tried to get out, and Delglisi ordered his murder. Jane Macias was working for the *New York Times,* a junior cub reporter. She bylined a story about the corruption in the restaurant business, how the foreign mobs are taking over the city."

"Where's the mother?"

"The Maciases were divorced. She's remarried, name is Ayn Christani. I don't think she lives in the city, though I remember something about her moving to Boston a few years back. So Jane has gone missing in Nashville? What's she doing there?"

"She's working for the *Tennessean,* our daily. She disappeared last week and she fits the profile. We've been assuming all along that she's a casualty, that we just haven't found her yet. But with this new information, it seems like we're off base. Delglisi's cleaning house."

Taylor thought about Frank Richardson, and the photos of Jane Macias. Her father. That silky voice who promised to hurt her if she didn't look the other way. Anger built in her chest.

She looked at Baldwin. It was time to go home.

Forty-Two

Baldwin made a quick series of calls. One to the FBI offices in New York that handled money laundering and RICO matters, one to the pilot of the FBI plane sitting at the ready at Teterboro Airport in New Jersey, the closest private airport to Manhattan. He arranged for a car service to pick them up, then they checked out of the hotel.

Standing on the sidewalk waiting for the car to arrive, Taylor mentally replayed the taped message from the cell phone. Her father's voice. God, she hadn't heard it in so long. It had been so easy to go along with everyone's assumptions that he was dead. To ignore the sense of wrongness in her gut. But the voice on the tape certainly seemed to dispel that theory.

What in the world could her father have to do with Edward Delglisi? Was Burt Mars the key?

She must have made some sort of noise, because Baldwin quickly hung up his cell phone and took her hand in his.

"Want to talk about it?"

She smiled.

"I don't even know where to begin. There've been a few revelations this morning, haven't there? I'm just trying to understand Jane Macias's role in this. I can't imagine it's a coincidence. Can you?"

"I've been thinking about that. What if Snow White took her purposefully to calm things down between him and Delglisi? Jane may be a tool to broker peace. If someone is killing in Snow White's name, under his sanction, but went against the plan and hit the massage parlor, Jane could have been taken to appease Delglisi. Deliver the girl who caused him trouble, get on his good side. Trade one for the other?"

"That's…who knows. Might be what's going on. But how does my father play into all of this? Do you think he's working with Delglisi?"

Baldwin ran a hand through his hair. "Yes. I think you need to prepare yourself that he may be involved with Delglisi."

A black Lincoln slid to the curb, and the driver came around to greet them. He got them settled and pulled away. He spoke over his shoulder as he tapped the horn and jerked the wheel, a perfect imitation of a taxi driver, just wearing a black suit and driving a nicer vehicle.

"Sorry, boss, but we've got to take the tunnel. There's some sort of protest going on at the GW bridge, traffic's all backed up. Won't take but half an hour, boss, promise."

Taylor looked out the window, watching as they passed by all the familiar landmarks, Rockefeller Center, Times Square, on to the West Side before they hit the Lincoln Tunnel exit. She was astounded, as always, by the sheer number of people moving through the city at any given time. Gone was the oppressive night. She wondered how long that was going to last. She put her head back against the soft leather and closed her eyes, finally answering.

"You may be right, Baldwin, but I hope to God you're not."

Baldwin's phone rang as they boarded the Gulf-stream. He answered, then turned to Taylor, who was already seated with a cup of tea in her hand.

"It's Lincoln."

She took the phone, a smile actually reaching her eyes. "Hey, Linc. How's it going?"

"Taylor, we've been missing you, girl. Are you on your way home?"

"We just closed the doors on the jet and the plane is moving. We'll be there in a couple of hours. What's happening back there?"

"Well, I've been doing some snooping around. Found a connection you might be interested in. It's about our missing girl, Jane Macias."

"Funny, we just spent some time at breakfast with the cops from the 108th who told us some very interesting things about her. And her father. He was killed last year by the man who had me taken."

"Edward Delglisi."

"Right. Where'd you get that name?"

"Jane Macias's laptop. I finally cracked the code, found what she had so well hidden. She's got a massive exposé in here, all about Delglisi. His crimes, his setup, the whole shebang. This is big stuff. Front-page-news kind of stuff."

"Great work, Lincoln."

"There's more. Interesting things. There's a name in here that Jane has traced back to Delglisi. One you might recognize. Anthony Malik."

"Anthony Malik? *Why* is that name so familiar?"

The memory hit her like a ton of bricks. The men at the New Year's Eve party. The four who were joking and laughing with her father. Burt Mars was one, Anthony Malik another. And the fourth man, the one she couldn't name, was wearing a signet ring. His wife was the woman who'd so offended her mother by wearing the same Marie Antoinette costume. She was big because she was pregnant. Damn it, *what* were their names?

"Lincoln, what information is in the files about Malik?" The note in her voice made Baldwin look up from his files.

"Not a lot. She hadn't drawn any conclusions about it, just has the name Malik next to all the Delglisis. There is some stuff in here about forged birth certificates, but it's unfinished."

"Okay, Linc. Thanks. I'm going to give you a phone number. I want you to call Detective Emily Callahan and tell her everything you found out in those files. Maybe she can help you trace Anthony Malik to Edward Delglisi."

"Will do. I'll see you soon?"

"Very." She clicked off the phone. Shook her head, met Baldwin's eye.

"And the hits just keep on coming. Lincoln found the name of one of my father's old friends in Jane Macias's computer. She was trying to prove links between him and Delglisi. The name is Anthony Malik. Baldwin, he's one of the men in my memory."

Forty-Three

Nashville, Tennessee
Tuesday, December 23
1:00 p.m.

They arrived in Nashville in clear, freezing, blue skies. They deplaned on the tarmac, a stiff breeze accosting them. Baldwin tossed Taylor his cashmere blazer to keep warm. Though he'd brought her all the necessities, he'd forgotten to pack a coat. She had balked at buying one in New York. She had plenty at home, and didn't see the need to wear one while she traveled by cab to the airport. It wasn't terribly cold in New York. That wasn't the case in Nashville. In one of those strange atmospheric inversions, it was much cooler than its northern neighbor, below twenty degrees. She shrugged into Baldwin's blazer, thankful for its warmth.

They climbed a short metal staircase that led to the terminal building. As they exited the door into the warm interior of the terminal, a small grouping of media started yelling, trying to get their attention. The closer they got to the group, the more the reporters sounded like a hive of bees.

"Lieutenant, can you tell us where you've been?"

"Is it true you were kidnapped by the Mob?"

Taylor spied Fitz and Sam standing a few feet away and went to them, ignoring the throng of gathered reporters. Fitz grabbed her in a bear hug, the snap of cameras and the whir of video making background noise almost loud enough to dance to.

"It's damn good to see you, girl. You had me a little worried there."

She just hugged him back, then turned to Sam. There were tears in her best friend's eyes. They'd talked the day before, and it wasn't words they needed now. Sam embraced Taylor, and they both held on for dear life. She had a moment of sickening clarity. If Sam had ridden to the church in the limo with Taylor as planned, it was quite likely that she would be dead now. Taylor squeezed a little harder and offered up a silent prayer of thanks to whoever was watching over both of them that day.

Baldwin moved toward the media group. Taylor heard him talking, telling them they would have a statement later on. She and Sam broke their hug, and each took one of Fitz's arms. They made their escape down the hallway that led to the outer terminal. Fitz started teasing her immediately.

"I can't believe you ruined all our plans. We were going to put a goat in your honeymoon suite."

"Oh, shut up, you were not."

Fitz nodded, and Sam giggled. "Seriously, we were. You remember Alfred Turner, Taylor? Retired a couple of years back, opened that farm and petting zoo down in Williamson County? He was going to loan us one of his babies."

"So do I want to know what we were supposed to with it, or am I just better off not knowing?"

Fitz shook his head, caught Sam's eye for a moment. His eyes twinkled with merriment. "Naw, you don't wanna know."

"I'll see what I can do to rearrange things so you can play your jokes." Taylor cuffed him lightly on the shoulder.

They reached the doors and stepped out into the frigid air. There were four news vans lined up at the curb. Fitz gestured toward them.

"You're gonna have to talk to the news at some point."

"I'll talk later, once I have a handle on what's been happening here."

Sam squeezed her arm. "I've got to head back to the office. I just wanted to make sure you were okay."

"I'm fine. You go on."

Sam nodded at her, then scooted across the walkway and disappeared into the parking lot.

They got into the unmarked Caprice and Fitz turned the heat on high. Taylor shrugged out of Baldwin's jacket. Within moments, Baldwin clambered into the backseat and they headed toward downtown.

They went directly to the Criminal Justice Center, Fitz talking more of nothing than anything of consequence. Ballistics on Richardson and Gonzalez, Jane Macias, there was nothing new on any of those fronts. When pressed, he told her of the intensity of the rescue and recovery efforts on her behalf, and Taylor vowed to get the names of each and every person who'd spent the night and day on the freezing bank of the river, searching for her. She would have to thank them personally for their efforts. The thought floored her. Baldwin hadn't gone into much detail other than pointing out that he couldn't believe that she was gone and refused to give up looking for her. Fitz, on the other hand, gave her all the specifics, and she felt tears prick the corners of her eyes at the pain she'd caused them.

Baldwin had been quiet on the last half of the flight, distracted when they landed, and Taylor had left him to his devices. She'd been racking her brain trying to put a name to the face of the man with the signet ring. It just wouldn't come. She needed the library, the society pages from her childhood. She knew there had been photographers at the party—the Nashville media were always in attendance at her parents' soirees. The library would have thirty-year-old society nonsense, she was sure of it. She hated to lose the time looking, but she had no choice.

There was a regular welcoming committee when they got to the CJC. Lincoln and Marcus stood on the landing without their coats, both young men jumping up and down in an attempt to keep warm. Captain Price was standing just inside the door, waiting to buss her on the cheek.

She was greeted with hugs and Baldwin with handshakes and back slaps. They didn't linger long over the festivities. They had a killer to catch.

Baldwin took Lincoln aside, speaking to him out of earshot of the rest of the crew. "I have a favor to ask."

"Name it."

"I'd like to have a conversation with your South American friend. Juan. Could that be arranged?"

"Of course. I'll go make the call right now. Would you like him to call you back here or on your cell?"

"My cell would be great. Thanks, Lincoln."

"No problem. Do you…never mind. I'll just go call him right now."

Baldwin went back to Taylor's office, shut the door behind himself and took a seat.

"I have a theory," he started, but her phone rang. She held up a hand in a wait-a-minute gesture, and answered the phone.

"Taylor? Honey, is that you?"

That voice again. This time deeper, richer. Not a tape. Taylor tried not to respond, but the word slipped out. "Daddy?"

"Yes, Taylor, it's me. Dad. Win." He was whispering. "You've been making life a little difficult here lately, sugar."

"Don't call me that. I'm not your sugar."

"Taylor, listen to me. You need to follow Mr. Delglisi's—"

She slipped a finger to the keypad and silently pushed the speaker button. Baldwin leaned forward to listen.

"—instructions. Just make the massage parlors go away. Taylor, I'm sorry for all this. I'm trying to make it all right. I know I've botched everything, but I—"

Her blood started to boil, that familiar sensation of disbelief streaking back into her mind. Her father wasn't dead. He was alive, working for a fucking mobster, and wanted her to turn the other cheek to something illegal he was involved in. Abso-fucking-lutely not.

"Stop. Just stop. What do think I am, Dad? You seem to forget that I'm a sworn officer of the law. I work for the good guys, Win. Not the bad guys. Not the ones like you."

"Taylor, knock it off. You have no idea what kind of situation we're in. You need to cooperate with him, Taylor. If you don't—"

"What, Win? What kind of threat can you throw my way this time? Kidnapping isn't enough for you? Now you're going to have me taken care of?"

A rush of noise spilled from the speaker, what sounded like banging and yelling. Then another voice came on the line.

L'Uomo laughed, a sneering, belittling noise. "Oh, Win. I should have known I couldn't trust you. Leave you alone for a second and you try to warn your sweet girl. Hello, Lieutenant. Lovely to speak with you again. Just wish it were under better circumstances."

"What have you done with my father?"

"Nothing, yet. But I'll kill him if you don't cooperate. Slowly."

Taylor felt herself pale. The mixed emotions—she hated her father, but she loved him, too. Damn it. They were both bastards. She gritted her teeth, snapping off the ends of each word as if they tasted bitter in her mouth.

"Like you did to Burt Mars? I swear, you son of a bitch, if you do anything to him, I will personally take you down."

"No, you won't. You don't have that kind of power. Your fiancé doesn't, either, so don't think about running to him. Mars was collateral damage. I do what needs to be done, Lieutenant. Just remember that. Now, it's time to stop this game. You need to listen to me, once and for all. I'm willing to make a deal with you."

"A deal? With a criminal? I don't think so."

"Oh, I think you'll play along when I tell you what the offer is. Something to sweeten the proverbial pot. You turn your pretty little head away from my business interests in Nashville, and not only will I let your father live, I'll give you Snow White."

Taylor didn't reply, just looked at Baldwin. He wrote her a note, slid it across the desk. She read the message—*calm down.*

Taylor nodded. Tried to sound more reasonable.

"Delglisi, I can't do that. I can't turn my head on illegal activities."

"Yes, you can. And you will. You hold your father's life in your hands. Snow White's head on a platter, Lieutenant. I think that's a generous gift."

She raised an eyebrow at Baldwin, decided to take a chance, con the con.

"Yes, I agree. Very generous. There's just one problem with your offer. I know who the Snow White is. So your little deal isn't going to work. You need to let my father go."

The laughter emanating from the speaker chilled Taylor's spine. "You don't know who he is, or you would have arrested him by now. Last chance, Lieutenant. I'll give you a few hours to think it over."

He was gone. Taylor slumped her head in her hands. Baldwin stroked her arm until she raised her head.

"Now what?" she asked.

"I have a call coming in. If my theory is right, I think we can take him down. There's someone who might know a little more about his activities, know if he's bluffing. And we need to get Snow White. That's our only bargaining chip."

"Bargaining? Surely you can't be thinking of making a deal with that scumbag."

Baldwin rocked back in his chair. "I figured you'd want me to do everything I could to stop him from hurting your father."

"He won't hurt him. They're in this together. I can tell. I have a sneaking suspicion about Delglisi. Lincoln said Jane Macias's notes had the name Malik next to Delglisi's, right? What if Anthony Malik *is* Edward Delglisi? It would explain everything. Eldridge said they know Delglisi isn't L'Uomo's real name."

Baldwin was nodding. "This makes sense."

"And they've been friends for years. That's what I keep remembering—Mars, my dad, the guy who I think must be Snow White, all chummy on New Year's Eve. If I could get deeper into the memory and put a voice to the fourth man, I'll bet you anything it's Malik. Snow White's name isn't coming to me, but I'm sure if I go through the society pages real quick, I can find a picture of him and that damnable signet ring. If there's a shot of Malik, too, maybe I can tie everything together, recognize Delglisi as Malik. We'll have actual proof.

"But I'll be damned if I'll listen to directives from a bunch of old criminals, trying to one-up each other. Sick bastards. My father will have to fend for himself. I'm not bailing him out of this mess."

A knock sounded on her door. "Come in," she yelled.

Marcus opened the door, pale in the glare of the fluorescent bulbs. He stood, seemingly frozen in the door frame, and his voice shook just a bit when he told them.

"We have another victim."

Forty-Four

Nashville, Tennessee
Tuesday, December 23
3:00 p.m.

The procession to the Marriott Renaissance Hotel on Commerce Street downtown was four cars deep. Baldwin and Taylor were in one, Lincoln and Marcus followed, Fitz trailed the medical examiner's van, who had pulled in front of them as they left the CJC. A funeral cortege. They might as well all have their lights on and traffic stopped to show respect for their passage.

Taylor was quiet. She knew who this victim must be, had heard the brief details of the crime scene. A woman, dark hair, throat slashed, overwearing red lipstick. If she had just put it all together sooner. She had failed Jane Macias. In failing her, she had failed everything—her father, her coworkers, Baldwin. The guilt was more than she could bear.

They pulled into the valet section, mindful of the doors to the lobby of the hotel. No sense in advertising too much. There were already four patrol cars in the drive-through. No one would question that something was happening, but if they could keep the Snow White aspects from the case for a bit, perhaps the media wouldn't seize upon it and start the vicious cycle all over again. Wishful thinking.

The manager greeted them in the foyer, a wild-eyed young woman with short, spiky blond hair and a considerable waistline. Taylor eyed her, unable to ascertain whether she was pregnant or just heavy. As a hotel general manager, she was as professional as could be expected, considering a serial killer had struck in one of her guest suites. The woman spied Sam coming in with her gear and snapped her fingers at a bellman, who intercepted the M.E. and guided her away. The service elevator would accommodate the stretcher.

She spoke over her shoulder as they trooped toward the elevators.

"I'm Deborah Haver. We're heading to the seventeenth floor. The maid found her. There's been a Privacy Requested sign on the door for two days, but the couple that checked into the room next door called down and insisted they smelled something. They called the concierge, we came up and agreed. When we got the room open…well. You'll see."

They were in the elevator now, jetting upward into the Nashville sky.

"Who is the room registered to, Ms. Haver?" Taylor asked.

They reached the seventeenth floor and the doors slid open. She bustled out into the hallway and they followed.

"Oh, I have that information…right here…damn it."

The woman was flipping through a notepad, and pulled up short in front of a room whose door stood open. Taylor continued into the room, looking over her shoulder at the manager, who exclaimed "Got it!" just as Taylor saw the body.

They said the name at the same time, one in a normal tone of voice, the other hushed.

"Charlotte Douglas."

"What?" Baldwin had been lagging back, talking on his cell, but he slammed it shut and stepped into the room. Taylor felt the invisible blow as it hit his body. He didn't move, his facial expression didn't alter, but it was there nonetheless.

"Oh, no" was all he managed before he went to her.

The smell of decomposition was strong. Taylor just didn't want to look closely, not yet. She crossed the room, mindful of her steps, and went to the window. The view faced west, and the sun was setting. The clouds were stacked one upon the other like swirls of icing, piling up in the sky, reflected by the setting sun. They looked drenched in blood, stained crimson like the froth from a lung wound. Taylor knew it was simple refraction, the cold, clear nights often caused this unusual sight. Red skies at night, sailor's delight. It should have been a red morning instead, so Charlotte could have been warned.

Jesus, she wouldn't wish this on her worst enemy.

Bolstered at last, she turned and took in the gruesome scene. The back light from the setting sun tinged the room in pink, giving Charlotte's body an almost lifelike glow. The grinning wound across her neck was black with oozed blood, her red-tipped lips were painted into a gruesome smile. Blood had run into her hair, turning the coppery red mass into a tangled claret river, with tendrils spreading across the white pillows, tributaries of fatal essence running away from her heart.

Her limbs were spread-eagle on the sheets, her legs spread wide, open in reception.

Taylor stopped looking at Charlotte and took in Baldwin, who was still standing over her. He hadn't said a word, but he turned to her now, face grim, lips thinner than she'd ever seen them. He looked like a different man entirely. As soon as he spoke, the spell was broken and they became a law enforcement team again rather than two people touched by a tragedy.

"You know what this means?" he asked her.

Taylor nodded. "Yes."

"He's broken the pattern again. This was personal. She wasn't a random victim."

"You're probably right. But we need to check for the article. And the frankincense and myrrh. We need to make sure it's him, Baldwin."

He turned back to the body. "Oh, it's him. I don't think the message could be any clearer, do you?"

"No, but we have to follow procedure. Let's let Sam in here, let her get the body, Charlotte's body, back to the morgue."

They stood together quietly for a moment, then stepped away. They had borne witness.

Taylor watched Sam work on Charlotte Douglas, touched again by how reverent her friend became when she communed with the dead. Just the thought made her realize how close she'd come to being in that position, that she could have died at the hands of L'Uomo. The thought was more than she could take. It was time for action. It was time to finish this.

She left the room and sought out Baldwin, who was in the hallway talking with Fitz. She watched them for a moment, knew that she would die inside if anything ever happened to him. Yes, their wedding had been a disaster. But she didn't need the formality to assure that he was hers, and she was his.

She needed to find the answers, to help him lay this case to rest.

They greeted her, Baldwin giving her a tight smile.

"You okay?" she asked.

"Yeah."

"Good. There's nothing more I can do here. I have to get to the library, find the name of this man from my memory. I know he's Snow White. If I can find his identity, we can stop him. We can stop his copycat. It's time to end this."

She reached up and kissed him softly on the cheek. The stubble scratched at her lips, but she didn't care.

"You want help, little girl?" Fitz asked.

"No. Stay here, make sure Sam doesn't need anything. I need to do this myself."

Baldwin's phone rang as he watched Taylor's retreating figure. She tossed a wave at him as she entered the elevator. He saw the international area code and decided he needed the break. There was a window at the end of the row of rooms. He went there, gazed out on the city he loved and answered the phone.

"Hello?"

"John Baldwin? It is Juan."

He answered in Spanish. *"Hola, Juan. ¿Cómo estás? Gracias por responder a mi llamada tan pronto."*

"Sin problema. Lincoln dijo que era importante. ¿Por qué no cambiemos al inglés? Tú no necesitas prácticar el español como yo la necesito en inglés."

"Okay. English it is. I have a question about a man who may be running people out of some South American countries. His name is—"

"Edward Delglisi."

"How did you know that?"

"Oh, my friend, I was looking into the murder of your poor chauffeur over the weekend. His name came up."

"Would you be willing to give me the context?"

"If you tell me what you are looking for, I would be happy to confirm or deny based on my discoveries at this point. Perhaps you will enlighten me, and I will enlighten you in return. *¿Bien?*"

"Sí." Baldwin scratched his head, trying to decide where to start. "Are you seeing a great number of cases of forced immigration? Illegals being imported into America for illicit activities?"

"Sex trade? Yes. Quite a bit. Human trafficking. The Border Patrol is corrupt in certain pockets, as are a few of the Immigration and Naturalization officers. There were many cases last year of both organizations' employees exchanging immigration status for sex or money. Foreign governments are participating in this scheme, as well. It has become highly lucrative, yet it seems your government is looking the other way. Illegals smuggle illegals, bad men import little girls to sell. It is a very appalling state of affairs."

"Do you have Edward Delglisi on your radar?"

"Yes. He has been under investigation by the Venezuelans, the Brazilians and the Argentinians, yet no one can touch him. He has a system that insulates him. False names, constant moves, safe houses, sophisticated accounting. We cannot get our hands on the cash."

"We just had a run-in with him in New York. Does he keep the cash hidden there?"

"Oh, no, he is much too smart for that. He ships the money out of the country. He is an old-school criminal, does not use electronics to help hide his money. No, he physically moves cash from New York. We have not had any success catching him until recently. We seized a boat in the Caribbean. You may have heard of this situation."

Baldwin stopped taking notes and leaned back in the chair. "A boat in the Caribbean. Was it called *THE SHIVER?*"

"*Sí.*"

Oh, Taylor was going to hit the roof.

"What does the Mexican government have to do with this?"

"Ah, *mi amigo,* you know how these things work. You sometimes need to look one way, while you are moving in another."

"The boat you speak of. Am I safe to assume the connection is sound and has been corroborated?"

"You are safe to assume that. We took nearly four million dollars off that boat. We did not capture the man sailing it, he was able to get away."

"And you have this man's name."

"We do. Winthrop Jackson. The fourth, I believe. That is your woman's—"

"Father. Yes. She doesn't know."

"Well, I wish you the best of luck breaking the news."

"Thank you. Let's talk about the chauffeur. What have you found out about his killer?"

"Only that we have a very dead American who was shipped back to the authorities in your country. It seems to be a case of mistaken identity."

"You don't believe that, do you?"

"I do not. But that is the most convenient theory for the moment. He is not important to the bigger picture, if you understand my meaning."

A dead American national not of concern to the security services in Mexico meant they simply didn't care to investigate.

"There was one piece of information that was relevant. An American flew into Mazatlán on the same flight as our dead friend and caught the evening plane to New York City. His name was unfamiliar to us. Dustin Mosko."

Dustin Mosko. That was the name of the man Taylor had killed in New York.

"His name is not unfamiliar to me. And for the record, he's no longer with us. But he worked for Delglisi."

"Ah. Then your puzzle is complete, yes?"

They talked for a few minutes more, then Baldwin wrapped up the conversation. This was news he'd suspected, but didn't particularly want to deliver.

His next call was to Garrett Woods.

After getting reamed for not phoning in about Charlotte's demise sooner, Baldwin went over the details of his call with the mysterious Juan. Woods would take it from here. They had an opportunity, a chance to right so many wrongs. They discussed ways to apply pressure, to stop at least one bad guy from hurting the innocent anymore. But it would cost, and cost dearly. Baldwin didn't know what Taylor would think, how she would react.

When they finished, Woods relayed the information he'd been trying to give Baldwin over the past few days. Charlotte Douglas's legacy wasn't looking bright. Woods was infuriated as he gave the details.

"We've been through all of her files. It looks like she wrote a sophisticated program that filtered both obscenely violent crimes and the accompanying DNA to a private site for her perusal. When she found something she liked, she'd assign herself the case."

"That's how she found the copycat?"

"Yes. The DNA should have matched with the California files when the Denver cops put it into the system. Instead, the information was sent directly to Charlotte. She'd been watching this maniac's spree across the country. We don't know the extent of her relationship with him, only that she was obviously in contact. Whether she was just another one of his victims or was a part of his plan, I guess we won't know until we catch him."

"Why did she choose to reveal the information about the multiple murders when she did?"

"She had no choice. She was playing a very dangerous game. The IT department confirmed that she called last week to see if they had accidentally discovered her Trojan horse. They hadn't. They had rolled out an upgrade, rekeyed the entire system. The new database didn't have Charlotte's special codes, so the real information made it through to the proper channels. If she didn't come forward, people would have gotten suspicious. This could have gone on indefinitely."

Baldwin felt sick. "How could she do that? And how in the hell did she pass the psych profiles and get into the Bureau in the first place? She was always very enthusiastic about deviant behavior, but I never saw any signs that she could have gone this far over the edge."

"I can't tell you that, Baldwin. Believe me, we're looking for the answers here. We've launched a major internal investigation. Oversight of the department has been in Stuart Evanson's hands. I hate to say it, but he may have to go. He's the one that brought her to her current position as deputy chief. As I recall, you pointed out that she wasn't fit for that position when you transferred. You and I are fine. Evanson probably isn't."

"That will be a loss." They shared a moment of sarcastic happiness. "As long as you're insulated, that's what's important to me. Evanson's a prick."

The industrial-grade clock on Taylor's wall clicked loudly, announcing it was nearly five o'clock. He rang off with Woods, promising to answer his phone if he called again.

Charlotte Douglas. He'd known the woman was poison.

Shaking his head, pushing away his own feelings of betrayal, he gathered his coat. It was time to seek Taylor out, run through the afternoon's bombshells with her.

Forty-Five

The library was a bust. Taylor combed through the records, but didn't find the face of the man she remembered from her parents' party. Frustrated, she took a drive in the cold, hard winter air, trying to clear her head. Before she knew what she was doing, she found herself at the apartment buildings where Frank Richardson was killed.

Oh, who was she kidding? She knew exactly what she was doing. Paying penance to the dead. Would anyone feel that for Charlotte? Was there a soul who would watch for her, pray for her, remember her fondly?

She climbed the stairs to the apartment and saw the door was cracked. She drew her weapon and slipped to the wall, left shoulder flat against the doorjamb. She listened hard, then put the gun away. The cleaners were here.

A horrific job they had, too. Following behind crime and avarice, cleaning up the messes made when a life ends, a heart ceases to beat, by choice or by violence. They were the lost ones, the unnoticed and unknown, the creatures who stealthily eradicated the signs of death.

Taylor looked into the apartment. She recognized the cleaner, a stout lady name Stella, who smoked like a chimney. She claimed the constant cloud of cigarette smoke kept the stench of death from her nostrils. Taylor smelled it on her, the unmistakable scent of burnt tobacco, and was hit with a mouth-salivating craving for a smoke. Shaking her head to literally make it go away, she stepped into the room and greeted Stella.

"Hey, LT." Stella sounded like a truck driver on a bender, but Taylor knew she was a sweet, God-fearing woman who sacrificed her own happiness to help families maintain some sense of closure after their loved one's death. She stopped scrubbing.

"What are you doing out here? I thought this scene was cleared for me."

"Oh, it is, Stella, don't worry. I was just here to say, well, I guess I wanted to say goodbye."

"Knew the vic, eh?" Stella leaned back from the blood pool she was removing from the apartment's carpet. "I could use a smoke, anyway. Want to join me?"

"I wish. No, I think I'll just stay here for a minute."

"Suit yourself." She stood, knees popping, and sauntered past Taylor, a sour look on her face. But she squeezed Taylor's arm in passing, and Taylor knew it was a show of support.

Alone now, she took in the scene. Frank Richardson's blood was black and shiny, several days old and forever interred into the grain of this room. All the scrubbing and cleaning, the replacement carpet and linoleum floors, the fresh paint, none of that would truly erase the imprint of the man's soul, brutally taken from this space. A certain dislocation of the very air would stay in this room forever.

Taylor said a prayer for the man, and apologized out loud. Knowing there was nothing left to do, she turned to leave. As she walked to the door, she spied a file folder, sitting apart from Stella's cleaning supplies.

"Stella, is this yours?"

Stella was on the landing and shouted back to her. "Is what mine?"

"The manila folder. Is that yours?"

"Naw, I found it when I cleaned out the air intake for the air conditioner. There was some blood on the screen and it was inside when I took it off." She appeared in the doorway. "You wanna take a look? I haven't gotten to it yet."

Taylor was already standing over the folder. She bent down and used a pen to open the file. She knew before she started reading what she had. Frank Richardson's notes. The file he was trying to get to her the day he died. Slipping on a pair of latex gloves, Taylor picked up the file.

"Why are you grinning ear to ear, Lieutenant?"

"Because, Miss Stella, this is the missing piece of the puzzle. Thank you so much for finding it." Taylor nearly gave the woman a hug, but Stella held up her hands.

"Yeah, I know. You don't want to be touching me, child, I smell bad. I'm getting back to work."

Taylor went directly to the car and called in to the office. Marcus answered the phone.

"Hey, tell me something. Did you guys ever track down Frank Richardson's last movements?"

"Sort of. We found his car in the parking lot of the apartment building. His cell phone was in the center console, had a voice mail from someone who didn't identify himself but requested Frank meet him at the apartment. So he went there of his own accord."

"Well, that makes sense, then. I just found the file he was trying to get to us. He must have gone to the apartment before the meet, stashed the information for safety's sake. Smart guy. He must have known there was something big in these files. Thanks, Marcus. I'll see you in a bit."

It was all coming together. Now, if she could just find Snow White's identity. It was curled in the corner of her mind like a snake waiting to strike.

Forty Six

Jane Macias started awake. She was cold. A crack in the wall next to where she laid her head was letting in frigid air from outdoors. Her father would never stand for such slovenliness. A man's home was his castle, especially when that was an unembellished statement. There was a responsibility that came with stature, he always said. Show the world how much you care, and in turn, they will care for you.

Her father. God, she missed him. She'd never be able to erase the image of him, pale and shaking on the hard, cold floor. He was nearly dead, the light leaving his eyes when she found him. She'd held him and rocked him, blood soaking through her shirt. He'd mouthed the name just before he died, just as the EMTs arrived to try saving his life. It was too late, but she had the ammunition she needed. Proving it was another story. She was almost there. And now she was being held captive. She was going to fail her father yet again.

This man, this creature who was holding her, was going to kill her soon, she could tell. The cat-and-mouse game was coming to an end. He was too entranced by the blood and flesh of her young body to worry about the decrepit stones in the attic, letting cold air seep into the tiny garret room where she was being held prisoner. It was better than the hole she'd been in before, a room that smelled of sex and blood. She'd been relieved when she was moved.

That beastly thing who'd been salivating over her body, who ran his lips across her neck and promised to take her life, was gone.

She tried to turn over, finding the bonds that held her hands and legs in a frontal vise strong as ever. The young one bound her, night after night. The past two nights, the young one would come, untie her, carry her downstairs because her legs were numb from lack of movement, and sit her in a chair in the creature's library. From behind, he'd strip off the blindfold, so she never saw his face. He would leave the room and the crippled one would talk. Tell her horrific stories, detailing the death of the man's soul. Touching her, but unable to fulfill himself. He made her touch him. That didn't work, either.

She knew who he was, of course. This bent, mis-shapen thing was Snow White.

He'd come to her once, alone and sweating. She heard his labored progress up the stairs, listened with every nerve taut when he reached her door, panting heavily. He'd been too winded to hurt her, though the gleam in his eyes told her that was his intention. He'd taken off her blindfold. She saw the insane desire light up his face from within, like a flashlight was being held just below the surface of his papery skin. He'd stared, then licked his lips. Traced the line of her cheekbone with a bent finger. Her imagination ran wild, as if the touch of his finger had left some sort of filth on her face that she'd never get off. Then as abruptly as he'd appeared, he was gone. She wept for the first time that night.

A sound brought her back, and she heard steps, creeping toward her. This wasn't the young one, she was certain of that. His tread was unmistakable, heavy and purposeful. No, this was someone lighter, who was coming slowly. She had a half-hysterical moment imagining a giant spider crawling across the room to wrap her in its silken web and drain her of life slowly, but shook the thought off. These were human footsteps. Despite the blindfold whispering against her skin, she squeezed her eyes shut, afraid.

A hand touched her face. She couldn't help herself, she cringed. But she didn't cry out.

The hand was joined by another and ten fingers roamed across her face languorously. She felt no malice in the touch, just a gentle curiosity. Just as slowly, the hands were withdrawn.

"You are beautiful," a soft voice whispered in her ear.

"Who are you?" she asked.

He was working on her bonds now. The owner of the voice shrugged slightly, a movement so eloquent that Jane felt it, a dismissive gesture born of repetition. "Nobody. I am no one."

Jane's hands were free now, and he'd moved on to her feet. She stretched her arms hard above her head, rejoicing in the movement. Pulling her arms down, she started to pull off the blindfold.

"Don't. Pleassse."

The longing in the voice caught her, and she stopped. She realized that this man was no threat; the whisper of a lisp made her feel both comforted and a little creeped out. Didn't movie psychopaths have lisps? She started inching away and sensed the man stiffen. She quit moving, let him work on the knots around her ankles. After many interminable minutes, she felt the rope free, and her legs were no longer glued together. He took her hand and helped her stand, massaging the blood back into her legs.

"Can you ssstand?"

Jane tested each leg. Pins and needles, but functioning. "Yes."

"Keep your hand on my ssshoulder. I'm going to get you to the door. Then you can take off the blindfold."

"Who are you?" Jane repeated. "Do you have a name, at least?"

"I have many, but none will mean anything to you."

Jane heard a snick, then tapping. He's blind, she realized with astonishment. The thought made her giggle. The blind leading the blind. This was crazy. Her hands went to the blindfold again, but he stopped.

"Please. It will be quick. I promise. There are many passages through the house."

The tone of his voice made her stop, and she said, "Okay." And meant it.

After a few long minutes of shuffling along, they went down two flights of stairs. Jane could smell bread. A kitchen? Before she could think, her hand was on a doorknob.

"Thiss will take you through the gardensss. Walk sssouth for one hundred paces, then turn to your right.

You'll be in the garden of the house next door. Please, just get a ride from someone, and don't look back." The door started to close, and Jane whipped off the blindfold and looked over her shoulder. All she saw as the door closed quietly behind her was a face that looked like an old candle, melted from continual use. She was glad she hadn't gotten a full look.

"Thank you," she whispered.

Forty-Seven

Nashville, Tennessee
Tuesday, December 23
7:30 p.m.

The apprentice stormed through the hallways of the manse, looking in every room in the upstairs corridor. The girl was gone.

He entered Snow White's library in a fury, not noticing that they weren't alone. Joshua sat in the corner by the fireplace, the flute in his lap, sightlessly serene.

"Where is she? Where is the girl?" he screamed.

Snow White sat in his chair, a fire lit, warming his crippled legs. He rubbed the cream into his hands, massaging the pain away as best he could. He hated the scent of the balm; it crept into his wasted flesh, wouldn't ever wash away. But the pain subsided fractionally when he used enough of it.

"She's in her room."

"No, she isn't. She's gone."

Snow White struggled to his feet. "She was there when you left with Charlotte."

"Well, she's gone now, old man. Kind of fitting, really. So's your bitch of a daughter. I had no choice, really I didn't. But it was so much fun. She died screaming, like a child."

"Noooo!" Joshua's strangled cry sounded from the far side of the room. "You didn't kill her. Tell me you didn't kill her. I let Jane go. Ssshe was sssweet and kind and didn't deserve thisss. You didn't hurt Charlotte. Tell me you didn't hurt Charlotte."

Troy turned and snarled. "She died slowly, little brother. Know that."

Joshua sobbed and ran from the room. Snow White looked at Troy with pain in his eyes. "What have you done?"

The apprentice shrugged. "She was in the way. She was going to turn us in. I had to silence her."

"Did you? Did you really? Or were you just taking matters into your own hands again? So help me God…" Snow White lurched at the man he'd trained, but the younger man was too nimble. He danced away easily.

"What did you expect, old man? That I'd let her live? That I'd let any of you continue on? You were wrong. You were so very wrong."

Grabbing a poker from the fire, he advanced on Snow White. Before he could take four steps, his body jerked. His mouth opened, but the roar of the gun drowned out his scream.

Joshua reentered the room, a pistol wavering in his hand. He squeezed the trigger again, but Troy saw it coming and ducked, rolling away from the fireplace, away from Snow White. He made it to the door before Joshua's empty eyes found him again, disappearing into the darkness of the hallway.

Joshua went to the door and bolted it, locking him and his father in the library. He went to Snow White, who had crumpled, stricken, in his chair. He was keening, a low mourning for his daughter. His son joined him, held him while he cried, and they wept for Charlotte's soul.

Taylor went back to the CJC and found the offices nearly empty. Most people had taken the entire week off for their Christmas vacation. She had a moment's displacement, knowing all that had transpired that prevented her from leaving on her own Christmas vacation, but pushed it away. There would be time for that later.

She'd called Captain Price on her way into the office and told him about the recovered file folder. She hadn't gone through it in detail, but at first glance it contained all the information they'd been speculating about regarding Burt Mars and Edward Delglisi. Her next call was to Baldwin, a request to meet her and go through the information. With any luck, the key to sinking Delglisi's ship would be in these papers. Whatever Richardson had discovered had gotten him killed. She was ready to see what that might be, regardless of her own involvement. Baldwin had extracted a promise from her to wait until he got there to go through the file. The suspense was killing her.

She was toying with the edge of the folder when Baldwin came into her office with two cups. The steaming latte was a welcome treat; she didn't realize how chilled she was until she wrapped her hands around the warm cardboard. She thanked him and sipped gingerly.

"So, can we look now?"

"I want to talk to you about a couple of things first."

"What?"

"I had a conversation with a friend of Lincoln's, an...official with the South American and Mexican governments."

"The spy. Lincoln told me he helped with the chauffeur."

"I wouldn't necessarily say that he's a spy. I think he's more of a facilitator."

"Okay. I won't even ask how he came to be friends with our Lincoln, then."

"There's nothing sordid. Lincoln doesn't know the extent of this man's reach. Anyway, he's had Delglisi on his radar for a while."

"The South American connection."

"Right. Well, they want him. And they're willing to do just about anything to get him. There's just one little problem."

"Win."

Baldwin looked at her. "You peeked into the file, didn't you?"

"No, I didn't. I can only imagine that's what it must be, because you're treating me like a five-year-old. My father is a criminal, Baldwin. I can take it. So spill."

"Okay. Mars was the bank, but your dad is Delglisi's bagman. He's the one moving the money. The authorities were closing in on him two months ago. He went overboard from *THE SHIVER,* but left a cool four million on board when he bailed. So not only are the

South Americans and the Mexicans looking for him, he cost Delglisi a lot of money."

"That's why Delglisi thinks he can trade on Win's life. Win's a dead man regardless. There's no way we can keep this quiet."

"Taylor, there is a way."

She set her latte on the desk and looked Baldwin straight in the eye. "Are you kidding me?"

"No. I've been talking to Garrett this afternoon. He can arrange for the Marshall Service to take him into protective custody. Your dad will have to testify against Delglisi, but they can keep him safe."

Taylor leaned back in her chair, staring up at the watermarked ceiling tile that she'd inherited with the office. Official requests to replace the moldy brown splotch had been effectively ignored. She focused on the mark while her mind whirled. Was she willing to allow her father that kind of judicial forgiveness? She had never been able to muster her own absolution for him. Now the law would do something her heart would never allow, and her mind would fight. She didn't think she could stand by and watch him glide yet again. But at the same time, the greater good *would* be served. Shit. Typical Win, ruining her thought process by simply existing.

"You're right. But here's a question for you. If Win is as big a part of this as we think, what now? He gets to go scot-free?"

"No, that's not really how the witness protection system works. At this level, they'll give him immunity to testify against Delglisi and his cronies. They'll relocate him, probably out of the country, give him a new face, a new name, anything he needs to effectively disappear. It's a lot more dangerous than romantic, I'll give you that."

"I can't help it, Baldwin. It's just not right. Besides, it's all a moot point. He won't do it. He won't. He'll go to jail before he rats Delglisi out. You don't know my dad, Baldwin. He had a chance, way back at the beginning, to get off on the bribery charges. All he had to do was testify against Galloway. But he wouldn't do it. He's too stubborn. He's got just enough of the gentleman in him that he feels obligated to stand by his criminal associates. He won't testify."

"We'll make him, Taylor. The trick is to get Win here. We need to make the deal with him and take down Delglisi."

"I'll tell you what. Let's look at these files first, see what Richardson came up with."

"Okay. Time out on mystery and intrigue for a few moments. You read, I'll look over your shoulder."

"I hate it when you lurk."

"Fine. You read, I'll just sit here and take in your beauty."

She rolled her eyes at him. "I'll pass you the pages." She opened the file. "Okay, Frank. Show me what was so important that it cost you your life."

Black and white. Frank Richardson was a journalist. He had deep contacts, many people he could turn to if he needed a confirmation. He was old-school—two sources or he wouldn't go to print. His diligence had won him the Pulitzer. And a seasoned journalist like Frank Richardson would have hit upon this immediately. The paperwork didn't lie.

Anthony Malik was indeed Edward Delglisi.

There was more. Buried seven pages into the printouts, which were covered in scribbles, block capital letters and speculations, most of which they'd already figured out, there were three words. Two words, really, and a phone number.

Sex. Video. 212-555-3457.

She went back to the page and read it again, and again. She handed it to Baldwin. His eyes lit up.

"Call the number. Put it on speaker."

She dialed, and they sat back. A prerecorded voice cut through the air. "You've reached the offices of New York State Attorney General Conrad Hawley. Our offices are now closed."

Taylor clicked the phone off. That was all they needed to hear. She and Baldwin shared a long look. The shit was about to hit the fan.

She stood and stretched. "I've got to get out of here. Let's walk."

He followed her out and they left the building, trudging up to Second Avenue until they came to the Hooters on the corner.

"This'll work," she said, and they went in. "I'm hungry, anyway. Let's get a couple of beers and burgers and talk this out."

They ordered and Taylor waited until she had a beer in her hand to talk again.

"Are you thinking what I'm thinking?"

"Frank wasn't killed because he discovered Edward Delglisi is Anthony Malik. He was killed because he tracked the whole sordid business to a significant person, someone who could hurt and be hurt. Saraya Gonzalez told me she was filmed having sex with very important men. If all of this is true, if Frank's theory is right, there might actually be a highly inflammatory videotape showing the attorney general of New York State having nonconsensual sex with an illegal immigrant named Saraya Gonzalez. That might be enough to kill a few people to get hold of. If Delglisi, sorry, Malik had that tape, and was holding it over the A.G.'s head—"

"And someone else got their hands on it—"

"Yes, that's exactly what I'm thinking."

"One problem. Where would this mythical tape be?"

"That's the last piece of the puzzle. I think I might know. The massage parlor that the Snow White copycat hit. We seized a ton of pictures and video. I'm assuming that there's going to be more than a few compromising shots among the evidence. If one of them was Conrad Hawley, I'd say we've discovered Malik's ace in the hole."

"And now we know why he wanted you to turn your head. This is big, Taylor. Bigger than us. I've got to let Garrett know. He can work with the team of agents who have been tracking Malik, get them involved in this."

Their food arrived and she took a big bite of her burger instead of answering. Win Jackson's voice ran through her head. Then Malik's joined the fray. Before she could stop herself, she was back in the memory of the party. The image of the four men flashed in her mind. Some fog had cleared; she saw the light, the reflection, the men, gathered at the foot of the stairs, laughing, and the man coughing….

Their names came to her in turn. Anthony Malik, Burt Mars, Win Jackson and the man with the signet ring… Fortnight.

"That's it!" she screamed. Eric Fortnight. How had

it not come to her before now? No matter, that was Snow White's real identity.

"What, what?" Baldwin nearly upset his pint glass.

"Eric Fortnight. That's Snow White's real name, Baldwin, I'm sure of it. Oh my God, it was right there in front of me all the time. The memory I keep having, of the New Year's Eve party. Eric Fortnight was the man wearing the signet ring. His wife's name was Carlotta. She was German or something, foreign. Very dramatic. I think she was actually some kind of countess or something. She was wearing my mother's costume."

Taylor shut her eyes to better access her recall. "Carlotta Fortnight. She died. She died giving birth, I remember that now. My mother was horrified, that's why I don't have any siblings. Dad always wanted another kid. Kitty was having nothing of it. There were all kinds of rumors at the time. The child was sick, I think. I don't know if it lived or not. I think they might have had another kid, too. But Carlotta definitely died. And Baldwin? She had long black hair and always, always wore bright red lipstick."

"Are you sure?" Baldwin asked, but Taylor was already out of her seat and tossing money onto the table.

"Yes, I'm sure. Baldwin, I know where he lives."

They ran the three blocks back to the homicide offices, both on their respective cell phones. Taylor was talking to Price, asking him to assemble the SWAT team, and Baldwin was talking to Garrett, apprising him of the new information Frank Richardson had uncovered. If they knew who Snow White was, it negated a large part of the role Win Jackson would need to play in their game to take down Anthony Malik. They needed to reset the strategy, make sure they could still trade the name for Win Jackson.

The homicide offices were buzzing with life when they burst through the doors, out of breath and chilled. Price was there, Fitz had returned from the Renaissance, Lincoln and Marcus were standing by her office door. All four men were smiling.

"We have a surprise for you." Lincoln beamed.

"Okay." Taylor stopped. "Surprise me."

Marcus threw open the door, and Taylor looked in. There was a girl inside, dressed in blue police-issue sweats, her black hair pulled into an unruly ponytail.

"Taylor, meet Jane Macias."

Forty-Eight

They had the house surrounded. Taylor was right behind the SWAT detail, ready to make entry with them. She hoped for an easy arrest but was prepared for the worst. Who knew what kind of fortification Snow White had put in place? And if L'Uomo had warned him of an imminent betrayal…no, that wouldn't have happened. If her theory was correct, Malik was furious with Fortnight for letting his apprentice hit the massage parlor, killing two of Malik's girls and allowing the videotapes to fall into the hands of the police. Fortnight no longer mattered to Malik. They had nothing to lose.

Taylor gave the go sign and the black-clad human weapons flooded the estate.

The apprentice had secreted himself in the bushes toward the back of the estate while he staunched the flow of blood from his side. It was an easy wound to treat, not terribly deep. The bullet had grazed him, startling him with the intensity of the pain. That fucking blind imbecile had shot him and ruined his plans. He knew he was well hidden; no one could see him behind the dead log in these woods, despite there being no leaf cover. The bleeding had nearly stopped when he heard the fury start, the cars, the silent footsteps, the hushed commands. They knew. They'd found them. He must move now if he had any hope of escape.

The girl, Jane, must have led them here. He knew it was a horrific mistake to leave her alive after that first night. He had begged to be allowed to kill her. It was more than the release; she was a liability. Snow White had refused. He wanted to play with this one, to reclaim some of his former glory. But he wasn't strong enough to hold a knife, much less his own dick.

Once Snow White realized who she was, well, the whole plan fell apart. The shit hit the fan with that New York faggot…. He thought that perhaps Snow White was going to make a present of the girl. A peace offering. What a waste. She would have looked lovely with a blade in her throat.

No more beautiful imitations, no more gaping black smiles and bloody lips. When Charlotte had sided with her father, she had to go.

He watched the rear entry team creep along the back of the house. It was well and truly over now. It was time to move along, find another masterpiece to re-create. He'd learned enough.

Taylor followed the team into the entry hall. They were met with no resistance. The place seemed deserted, the dual staircase vaulting toward the second and third stories devoid of movement. The foyer was clear. She started to hear the clear signs coming through her earpiece, but didn't relax. He was here, she could feel it.

Her feeling was confirmed a moment later.

The team crowded the hallway that housed the locked door. With a silent one, two, three, entry was made.

The den, or library, Taylor corrected herself, seemed empty at first, but she realized there were two men in the room. Neither of them moved when the group drew down on them. One was blind, that was blatantly obvious. The other, an older man, bent at the shoulders and crippled, sat in a large cordovan leather chair, his twisted hands folded awkwardly on top of a bone-handled cane.

Time froze for a moment as Taylor realized she must have been wrong, that this creature would never be able to kill.

And then she saw the ring, glowing from its home on his bent finger.

"Eric Fortnight, you are under arrest." She didn't lower her weapon, but came closer, trying to look into the eyes of a killer.

It was bound to happen. Things had gone so well, so quietly, until now. When Taylor met his eyes, she saw the coldness, the emptiness. He smiled at her, made her skin crawl. Ten women had died at his hands. An additional six under his tutelage.

When he lunged at her, she didn't think, just squeezed the trigger.

His body jerked, recoiled against her bullets. He was on the floor in a heartbeat, and the pandemonium began.

* * *

Taylor stood in the driveway of Eric Fortnight's house, blankly looking toward the windows. It was a clean shoot, but Price had arrived and taken her weapon. Standard administrative details. She would be on leave until the shooting was ruled justifiable, and she'd seen the shrink. Maybe that wouldn't be such a bad thing, considering.

It was over. The Snow White Killer was dead. But there was no sign of his apprentice. The ruined thing that was Eric Fortnight's son Joshua wasn't the man Taylor had seen at Control. He was in the wind.

The evidence was mounting. At least two mysteries had been solved. The emulsion of frankincense and myrrh that was on all the dead girls' faces had been matched back to the house. A small jar of Boswellin cream, a pain reliever used for rheumatoid arthritis, sat on the table next to Snow White's chair. He had the cream all over his hands. The image of how that had gotten on the dead girls' temples, of Snow White holding their heads, transferring the benign material to their faces, made her want to throw up. Despite his infirmities, he'd helped kill these girls, held them, stroked them. And there was a room on the third floor that contained knives, rope and dried blood. Taylor was confident there would be three DNA matches—to Elizabeth Shaw, Candace Brooks and Glenna Wells. She prayed there weren't more.

The drive was cluttered with police cars. A small crowd had formed on the street, a row of neighbors who were straining to see the show. Taylor turned from the house and watched them watching her.

She saw Baldwin's car make its way into the driveway, and was thankful he was here.

He was forced to park and walk up the long drive. His shoulders were slumped; he was the bearer of bad news, she could tell. She'd learned all his signs now.

When he reached her, he grabbed her and held her tight. The warmth was welcome, but Taylor didn't feel anything, not just yet. She'd just taken her second life in as many days, and she wouldn't turn back on for a while yet.

"I have some bad news."

She nodded, looked deep into his green eyes.

"Is it Win?"

He looked startled for a moment, then shook his head.

"It's about Charlotte. I spent some time with Jane Macias, then had to do some checking. Charlotte was his daughter. She was Snow White's daughter."

"What?" she said.

"I know. I have an entire deposition from Jane. She claims that Charlotte is Fortnight's daughter. That Snow White came to her and talked, gave her details of his crimes, like she was his confessor. He told her Charlotte was his child, that her mother, Carlotta, had died giving birth to Joshua Fortnight, her brother. He hated Carlotta, but loved her, too. When she died, leaving him with a deformed child and an uncontrollable daughter, it was the ultimate betrayal. The murders were his way of bringing her back."

"Tell me this again, it's too fantastic for words. Charlotte was Eric and Carlotta Fortnight's daughter?"

"Jane swears she saw Charlotte at the house on two occasions, talking with Snow White and the apprentice. She gave us a description of him, it matches the man you saw at Control. He wasn't here?" Baldwin swung a hand toward the house.

"No, there's been no sign of him. The house was empty except for Snow White, I mean, Fortnight, and his son. Holy crap. Charlotte was his daughter. God, that explains a lot. I knew she was batshit crazy."

Baldwin had an unreadable mask in his eyes. "I talked with Garrett earlier. He's been able to confirm Jane's claims. The FBI is going through all of Charlotte's personal effects now, combing through her computer. They were checking on the abnormalities in her protocols, but when they cracked her firewall, it seems she had a trap set on all the information. Her system wiped itself clean when they tried to access her data files. They have their work cut out for them."

Taylor's head was spinning with all this new information. Charlotte Douglas, the child of Snow White. That meant she was from Nashville. Taylor had never met her before. Which was strange, since her parents and Charlotte's were friends. She must have gone away to school after her mother died. Or something like that. A moment of pity wormed its way into Taylor's conscious. She pushed it away. The thought would take unraveling, and Taylor didn't have the time to deal with it now.

"So do we. The copycat is still free. And we need to get to Malik. As soon as he knows that Fortnight is dead, then my father is of no use to him anymore. We have to talk to him now."

"Let's go."

They ran to Baldwin's car, and he tore out of the driveway, forcing the onlookers to scatter before him.

Forty-Nine

Anthony Malik was torn between laughing and crying when he saw the videotape for the first time. Saraya was such a good girl. And Conrad Hawley was such a bad boy. How they had gotten so lucky was beyond him. Now he had his ticket, a piece of ingenious editing that would guarantee him safe passage forever.

The attorney general for the State of New York had paled when the news was shared of his frolics being recorded. He had begged. It was a satisfactory feeling. Malik had dangled the key to the safety deposit box in front of Hawley, guaranteed him it was the only copy, and laughed when the man got tears in his eyes.

He was just that powerful.

Malik never thought he'd actually have to use the tape. Just knowing it was out there should have been enough.

And he had a backup stashed at the house in Nashville, just in case Hawley got crazy and went after him.

But now, with Win Jackson the turncoat looking for a way out of this mess, Mars dead and one of his trusted men gone, Malik needed a new plan. The time had come to start cashing in some of his insurance policies. He called Atlas, asked him to come by the apartment, and began to pack. New York was getting a bit too warm for his tastes. A trip down south would serve two purposes, getting him away until things shook out, and allowing him a personal cruise through the orphanages for some new blood.

When the doorbell to Malik's apartment rang twenty minutes later, he didn't think twice about answering. This was his safe house, one where he couldn't be surprised. He had several, scattered across several countries. In Manhattan, only Atlas and the poor deceased Dusty knew the address.

It was a fatal mistake. Men in black balaclavas, armed with automatic weapons, poured through his door. They stormed the room, slapping handcuffs around his wrists and a rough sack that stank of blood and vomit over his head. He was silenced easily, forced out the door and shoved into the back of a car before he could catch his breath.

He had bigger problems now. His captors weren't speaking English.

Baldwin answered the phone on the first ring.
"*Hola,* Juan."
"*Hola, amigo.* We've got him."
"Fantastic. Who will be extraditing him?"
"I'm not sure who is going to lay claim to him first.

Several South American governments what to talk to him. But if it weren't for your help, we would have never caught him. I want to thank you personally. I have a gift for your woman."

"What's that?"

"We will not press charges against her father."

Fifty

Taylor was searching the house for Hershey's Kisses. She knew there'd been a bagful in the dining room, in the Italian pewter basin on the sideboard, but the bowl was empty now. She foraged through the kitchen cabinets, found three packs of Smarties left over from Halloween and transported from the cabin, but that wouldn't work. She needed chocolate. Something inside her was craving the sweetest thing she could find, as if that sweetness could fill the chill in her soul.

After the usual rigmarole—the meeting with the department shrink, the placement on administrative duty, Baldwin had taken her home. They'd gotten to bed much too late, and she'd woken abruptly at three, her hands tight around L'Uomo's neck. She'd strangled him in her dream. Unable to get back to sleep, she'd played a round of pool, then sat and stared blankly at the television, watching reruns of the day's news until she drifted off again.

She woke in desperate need of something. She knew she was subconsciously craving a cigarette. Damn Stella.

Finding nothing on the first floor of the house, she made her way upstairs, ostensibly to wake Baldwin and demand he tell her where her Kisses had gotten off to. She went into their bedroom. Baldwin had fallen asleep fully clothed the night before, on top of the bedding. His head was at a funny angle, and Taylor immediately went and placed a pillow under his cheek. He smiled and mumbled something unintelligible. The television was still on—a documentary about the Sex Pistols. She watched it vaguely for a few moments, then turned it off and shut off the light, leaving Baldwin to his dreams.

Chocolate, chocolate, chocolate. Where could she find some? She didn't feel like going out. She really hadn't wanted to leave the house at all. Purely a psychological reaction to having her life taken out of her hands, she knew that. She puttered around in the kitchen, opening cabinets, until Baldwin's voice made her jump.

"Look in the freezer."

She turned and saw him smiling at her. It wasn't a happy, good-to-see-you smile, it was more of a grim reminder of what they'd both been through over the past couple of days.

She gave him a look. "How do you know what I'm looking for?"

"You're looking for chocolate."

"How do you know that? How in the world could you possibly be that in tune that you know what I'm thinking, what I'm looking for? I hate it when you do that." She went to the freezer, started scavenging. Behind two Tupperwares of soup, there was a bag of chocolate chips, left over from some cookie-making venture.

She saw the hurt in his eyes, and started to apologize, but something held her tongue.

She pulled the bag out and crossed to the counter, hauling herself up onto a corner. Legs dangling, she dove in, filling her mouth with the sweet goodness. They were hard and crunchy, but delicious.

Baldwin went to the refrigerator and grabbed the milk, then set about making her a cup of tea. She watched him, then accepted the steaming cup. Somewhat mollified, she sipped and said, "Thank you."

"Wanna talk about it?"

She looked up from the yellow bag. Baldwin was staring at her intently.

"Not really, no."

"You need to get it out of your system. I can't imagine all the feelings you must be having now, knowing what's happening. You did everything right, did what you were supposed to do. And you're safe, for which I am forever grateful. But you still need to talk about what happened. The kidnapping. Snow White. About your Dad and Malik. About the cases. Us. Anything, Taylor."

She sipped her tea, not certain why she was angry at Baldwin. He'd done nothing wrong. "No, I really don't."

"Babe—"

"I said, no, I don't. Don't push me, Baldwin. It was my wedding, too. I'm not in the mood. I've killed two men this week, found out my father is alive but I have to send him to jail, my wedding was ruined…."

He took three strides and invaded her space.

"I don't care what kind of mood you're in. You have to talk about what happened. We have to talk about all of this. It will fester if you don't. You have to tell me what's happening in your head so I can be sure I'm not putting you in a situation—"

"What? What the hell are you talking about? *You* putting *me* in a situation?" Taylor jumped off the counter, threw the empty bag in the trash. "I can handle myself just fine, Agent Baldwin. Don't forget it."

She stomped out of the kitchen through the mudroom and into the garage. How dare he? She was fuming. She knew she was overreacting, but couldn't help herself. She slapped the button and the garage door started its lumbering journey up. She went down the steps and yanked open the door to her 4Runner. Baldwin came to the door of the garage, looking at her with an incredibly hurt, inquisitive look on his face. She ignored him, got in the truck and backed out into the driveway. Damn him!

And God *damn* Win Jackson. This was all his fault. How he had the conscience to put her in this position, to make her choose between the right thing to do and his life. Well, fuck them. Fuck them all.

She drove, not thinking about where she was going. There were fields to her right, a fence and a tree on a hill. One Tree Hill Farm, she knew. Brilliantly original name.

As a rule the bucolic setting calmed her spirit, made her happy. They raised cattle, and normally had two sets of calves a year, one in the spring and again in the fall. She loved to drive by and see the babies trotting after their mothers, lowing for milk. It was one of the reasons they'd bought off of this road, because for a brief moment, Taylor felt like she was in the country driving to and from work.

There were three vultures sitting on the fence posts, leering at a grouping of cattle. Taylor slowed, watching them, so out of place in her mind and her pastoral getaway. Vultures meant death. She glanced at the bulk of black and realized that it was a grouping of cows, each facing outward, protecting something at the center of their circle. She looked closer, trying to figure out what was happening. Her mind filled in the details.

A calf had been born, hopelessly out of season. It was struggling for life. The vultures were there, smelling death, knowing that they would have full bellies this evening. And the cows were protecting the calf from the harpies who would celebrate the end of its life with a feast.

She realized she'd stopped the car only after she was out the door, screaming in fury at the vultures. They hopped away for a moment, glaring at her with all-knowing eyes. Short of hopping the fence and taking the calf in her arms and spiriting it away, there was nothing she could do to stop this.

The anger welled in her, bright and furious. She blamed the farmer for allowing one of his cows to mate out of season, for not watching closer to make sure she gave birth in the barn instead of on a snow-drenched hilltop. She blamed the vultures for being such disgusting beasts. To sit and watch your dinner die in front of your eyes…she imagined the conversation between them. "Oooh, fresh meat, fresh meat." The thought infuriated her even more, and she was punching the fence, kicking at the posts with her boots, tears tearing down her face.

One of the cows caught her gaze. It stood, implacable, watching her tantrum. It met her eyes and lowed, a bovine acknowledgment of her pain. She was feeling helpless, as well, knowing the life of the calf was ebbing behind her. The sound stopped Taylor's fury and she dropped to the ground, all the pain releasing in frustrated tears. The vultures took their place on the fence post again, patiently awaiting their turn.

Taylor had no idea how long she'd sat on the ground, crying over the doomed life of a sickly calf. She got up and returned to her truck. She'd left the door open when she got out. She glanced back over her shoulder and saw the cordon of predators shifting slightly. It was time for them to strike, she could sense it. She looked around and found a large rock, which she hurled at the birds. It struck one in the wing, but the vulture simply shook it off, so focused on its meal it couldn't be bothered.

Taylor wiped the rest of the tears from her eyes. There was nothing more she could do. This was a part of life, this process of the dead feeding the living. The survival of the fittest, the weak providing sustenance for the strong. It didn't have to be this way, not in this instance, but it had happened so many countless times in the past....

Taylor got in the truck and pulled away. She did a U-turn and headed back toward the house. She owed Baldwin an apology. Damn that man for being right all the time.

Fifty-One

Taylor sat at a round café table, the pungent aroma of coffee permeating the room. She took a sip of her latte, not tasting the contents of the cup. She resisted the urge to put her head in her hands. What a position to be in. She adjusted her weapon, settling it into a more comfortable spot under her arm. She rarely carried concealed, and wondered briefly why she had eschewed her normal hip holster in favor of the shoulder harness. Baldwin preferred the harness, wanted the easy access of the gun coupled with the concealment afforded having the weapon tucked away. Not Taylor. She preferred it hanging on to her hip like a barnacle.

The door jangled, and she looked up, breath in her throat. It was time, then. Baldwin had made the arrangements.

She had her role to play.

Win Jackson cast furtive glances around the small café. Taylor recognized him casing the place, looking for exits, assessing the crowd, making sure he could get away. She put her hands on the table in front of her, the diamond on her left hand winking. Just a normal coffee date between a father and his daughter.

Taylor got caught up in the fantasy for a moment. As he drew closer, she fought the urge to stand and throw her arms around him, greet him warmly with a long-overdue hug. Instead, she stayed put, a stone figure. This man, her own flesh and blood, was up to his ears in mobsters and friends with serial killers. Jesus.

Win reached the table and sat heavily. His eyes were bloodshot, his gray hair mussed. The sour stench of day-old beer reached her nostrils. He looked like he'd been on the run for a while.

"Nice ring," Win opened.

Taylor spit out a little laugh. "Yeah. Not so bad. How are you?" *Damn it, Taylor, what are you doing? You don't care about this man. Why are you asking how he is?*

Win looked surprised by the question. "I've been better, actually. Being dead isn't so easy."

"You shouldn't have gotten yourself in that position in the first place."

"Who are you to judge, Taylor? I remember your philosophy when you were a kid. There but for the grace of God go I, and all that? What happened to that little girl, huh?"

"She grew up." Her tone was frosty. Win had just made a tactical mistake. Playing on their old relationship, fragile as it may have been, was not the gambit that was going to work with her. She felt her heart shut down, became all-business.

"Why did you want to meet with me, Win?"

"I don't even warrant Father from you anymore, Taylor? That is what I am, after all. Your father."

She met his eyes. A combination of diffidence and begging lurked behind the gray irises, so very like her own, and he looked away.

"You can't even meet my eye. How am I supposed to call you Daddy when I know what you are?"

"What am I? Huh, Taylor? Answer that. You don't know anything about—"

"Don't push me, Win. It won't work." She leaned back in the chair, lifted her cup to her lips. This charade needed to end.

"Seriously, Win. Why did you want to meet with me? It's a little dangerous to go meeting with the cops when you're on the run from us, isn't it?"

"Because I need your help. And you need mine."

"Really? I need your help? Hardly."

Win leaned forward. "Get me a cup of coffee and I'll explain."

"You'll explain now. I don't have time for cloak-and-dagger shit, nor do I intend to sit here all afternoon while you try to play your little games. Talk."

Win folded his arms across his chest, closing himself off. "You have a hard heart, daughter. I'm sure that fiancé of yours is in for quite a ride."

"Leave him out of it." She pushed the argument away.

"No. I…I need him, too."

The flash of anger came so intensely she had trouble tamping it back down. Now she knew what was happening. Good old Win. He didn't want to see her, like he claimed. Nope, that wasn't it at all.

"Talk," she commanded.

"Only for immunity. I'll give the feds everything they need to take Malik down. And trust me, I know where the bodies are buried."

"I'm so proud," Taylor murmured.

"And I need witness protection. I want to disappear."

"That shouldn't be so hard. You've been a master at that my whole life."

"I'm serious, Taylor. I need protection. Malik is capable of many things, and he has a lot of friends who are just as bloodthirsty. They'll see me dead before they let me talk. I need your word, Taylor."

"No," she said, as calmly and softly as she could muster.

Win Jackson's eyes bulged. "What do you mean, no? You can't say no. You're not authorized. You don't work for them. You can't make a decision like this." The desperation in his voice was so hard to hear. Damn it, he *was* scared. But that wasn't her problem. Her heart was stone.

"I'm sorry, Win. Malik was taken into custody this morning and turned over to the Argentinean government for human trafficking. He's being extradited as we speak. We don't need you. I don't need you."

She stood, swallowing the lump in her throat.

"Goodbye, Dad." She turned and started for the door. Damn Anthony Malik. L'Uomo. The Man had fucked them both. He'd taken a man who might have had a future, and tossed him down the rat hole. He'd taken her father and turned him into just the kind of man Taylor despised.

"Taylor, please?"

She turned and saw Win, standing by the table, his

hands out. "Taylor, you can't do this. He'll kill me. It doesn't matter whether he's in custody. You have to get me out of town. I need money and transportation. You need to save me. For God's sake, I'm your father." He took a step toward her; her hand automatically crossed her body, went to her weapon. She dropped it as soon as she realized, but Win had caught the movement.

"What, were you going to shoot me?"

"No, Win."

"You have to help me. Please," he begged again. Something in her tore.

It was too much to ask. This charade was impossible. She was a cop. That's who she was always meant to be. It was ingrained in her DNA, in her blood. Blood she'd spilled in pursuit of the truth, to be honest, and faithful to the law.

This was the plan, that she'd exit the building, walk away from her father and his crimes forever. Baldwin had told her that the Argentinean authorities weren't going to press charges against him, that he was in essence a free man.

Damn Baldwin, he knew her better than she knew herself. How did she think she was going to live with letting her father, the criminal, walk away? She wasn't. She realized she'd made the decision several minutes before and just hadn't let the conscious thought into her mind.

"Taylor?" Win asked again, sensing the struggle she was having. There was hope in his voice. "You'll help me get away?"

Taylor gave her father a smile. "Yes, Win. I'll help." She crossed to him, three long strides, grabbed his right wrist and spun him around, latching her handcuffs on to his wrist. She got his left arm before he could struggle and whipped it behind his back, slapped the cuff on.

"Win Jackson, you're under arrest. You have the right to remain silent. You—"

"What the hell are you doing? Taylor? Let me go. Taylor, you can't do this. You can't put me into the legal system. He has men everywhere, Taylor. They'll kill me. They'll kill you."

"Yeah, Win, he might. But at least I'll die knowing *I* did the right thing." The faces of the café workers were wide with shock. She finished Mirandizing him and took him outside. Marcus was waiting in the parking lot, a cruiser with a plastic divider waiting with its door open, just like she'd asked. Just in case. She handed the still-protesting Win off to him.

"You may want to Mirandize him again at the station. There may be a conflict of interest."

"Why?"

Taylor caught Win's eye, his face cloudy with a portending storm. There was naked hatred in his gaze, and Taylor's last little bit of love for him melted away. She turned to Marcus, a tight smile on her face.

"I assume there's some crazy technicality that precludes me from Mirandizing him because he's my father. And if there isn't, he'll find a lawyer to drum one up, get this all thrown out on appeal. Just humor me."

She stepped away, trying not to listen as Marcus read Win his rights, then instructed him to get in the back of the car, to watch his head.

She watched Marcus drive out of the parking lot, saw Win look back over his shoulder at her, pleading in his eyes. She hardened her heart. She could no sooner let him walk away than she could stop breathing. It was his own damn fault.

She hit the door open button on her key fob. She saw a reflection in the window, and turned to see Baldwin standing behind her. He didn't say a word, and neither did she. She just went to him and let him comfort her.

Fifty-Two

Nashville, Tennessee
Saturday, December 27
4:00 p.m.

Taylor and Baldwin were finished packing and were waiting on a cab to take them to the airport. The preparations were effortless—their suitcases were ready to go from the previous Saturday and all they needed to do was throw in their overnight bags, catch a cab to the airport and disappear.

Baldwin was pacing around the front of the house, staring out the windows. Taylor was sitting at the dining-room table, sipping a cup of tea. She could not wait to get out of town, away from all the mess.

Her father had been arraigned on several charges, including embezzlement, bribery and RICO statutes. All white-collar crimes. He'd be going to a nice little prison where he could wear chinos and drink coffee out of real cups instead of Styrofoam. Taylor didn't care; she was just happy he was being punished for his role in L'Uomo's businesses.

Conrad Hawley, the A.G. of New York, had quietly resigned when the Nashville police let him know they had a tape of him having sex with an underage illegal who was being forced into prostitution. He was not so quietly being indicted this week, along with a slew of other men who'd been captured on the multitudes of videotapes. Identifications were still being made on many of the participants.

Jane Macias had returned to her home in Long Island, obviously jaded about Nashville. Taylor couldn't blame her. Being that close to a serial predator, knowing you were next, wasn't easy. Her exposé on L'Uomo was being published by the *New York Times*.

Snow White had been buried next to his daughter and wife in a private cemetery in north Nashville. His son, Joshua, kept the house, though a full-time nurse was needed to care for him.

Frank Richardson's family was developing a journalism scholarship in his honor. Daphne Beauchamp had been hired to run the foundation.

The many victims of Snow White and his apprentice were lauded in several articles written by the *Tennessean*. The world looked on as the cases were dissected and ultimately solved. Giselle, Glenna, Elizabeth and Candace had all been in the bar called Control. Their faces would haunt Taylor's dreams.

The apprentice disappeared.

Taylor mulled over all of these developments. The past few days had been crazy, to say the least. But it was time for them to go away now.

Baldwin stopped pacing and came to her in the dining room, putting one hand over hers as she set her tea mug down.

"So, what do we do about getting married?"

Taylor shook her head. "We don't. I think that was all a sign."

"We don't, ever?"

She stood, pointing out the window. The cab had arrived at last. "Let's just go take our honeymoon. We can talk all this out over there."

Baldwin smiled, leaned in for a kiss. "Whatever you say, Taylor."

Fifty-Three

Three weeks later

He sat in a quiet corner of the café, watching rain drizzle down the plate-glass window. He sipped a delicious concoction of chocolate and espresso, topped with fresh whipped cream and flakes of white chocolate. A decadent treat, a reward for all his hard work.

He licked a piece of chocolate off his lip and tapped the keys on the keyboard.

Taylor and Baldwin stumbled through the garage door into their kitchen, laden with suitcases and packages. The house felt empty, unused, and Taylor dropped her bags on the hardwood floor and took in the sight. Home. Their home.

"Let's just leave these in the dining room and have a glass of wine. What do you think about that, *cara?*"

Taylor turned to Baldwin. "I think that sounds like a lovely idea. How about you pour? I want to glance through this stack of mail real quick."

He went to the wine refrigerator and started combing through the bottles. Taylor flicked through the pile of mail idly, not really that interested in what it contained, just trying to acclimate to being home. A white envelope caught her eye. It was addressed to her, under the wrong name. *Mrs. Taylor Baldwin.*

Well, they had certainly jumped the gun on that one. She assumed it was from someone who was attached to their postponed wedding, someone who didn't know that they hadn't gotten married.

She picked up the letter, slit the top with her opener. There was no return address, but it was postmarked three days earlier from Seattle. Seattle? They didn't know anyone in Seattle. A single sheet of paper, folded three ways, was in the envelope. Something set off Taylor's senses. She set the letter on the counter, grabbed two plastic sandwich Baggies from the second drawer and slipped them onto her hands.

She teased the letter out of the envelope, unfolded it and read the short message. Then she read it again, her heart beating just a little faster.

"Baldwin," she called. "You need to see this."

Her voice sounded strange, hollow, unreal. She watched Baldwin come back into the kitchen, saw him register that she was in operational mode, with the Baggies on her hands, and followed suit without asking why. He nodded at her, and she handed him the letter. He read it aloud, twice, to let the words sink in. He looked at Taylor.

"This is a problem."

"You think?" She took the letter back from him, reread the lines and realized they might never have a moment's peace.

Baldwin had retrieved his cell phone from his briefcase and was calling in to Quantico. They'd want to know all the details.

Taylor folded the letter up neatly and put it back in the envelope, the typewritten words burned into her mind.

An apprentice no more.
You may call me the Pretender.

* * * * *

ACKNOWLEDGEMENTS

When you're a writer, it never feels like enough to say thank you to the people surrounding you day to day. We write the books, they make them into novels. I have several magicians I'd like to send my humble thanks:

My extraordinary editor, Linda McFall, and the entire MIRA team, especially Adam Wilson, Heather Foy, Margaret Marbury and Dianne Moggy, and the brilliant artists who create these fabulous covers!

My incredible agent, Scott Miller, of Trident Media Group.

My independent publicist, Tom Robinson, who is such a pleasure to work with and feeds me blueberry pie.

Detective David Achord of the Metro Nashville Homicide Department, a true friend and a great man.

Bob Trice, Response Co-ordinator/CERT program manager/ESU supervisor at the Nashville Office of Emergency Management, for giving me the tools to make the drowning scene work.

Laura McPherson, who taught me good journalism rules, which I in turn gleefully broke.

Vince Tranchida, for the medical expertise.

Pat Picciarelli, for giving me Long Island City and the bar across from the 108th precinct.

Tribe, for the Spanish bits.

The Bodacious Music City Wordsmiths—Janet, Mary, Rai, Cecelia, Peggy, Del Tinsley and my wonderful critique partner, J.B. Thompson, who read, cheer, suggest, support and love.

First reader Joan Huston for making all the difference, as she always does.

My darling Linda Whaley for babysitting on the rainy nights.

My esteemed fellow authors, Tasha Alexander, Brett Battles, Rob Gregory-Browne, Bill Cameron, Toni Causey, Gregg

Olsen, Kristy Kiernan and Dave White, for constantly cheering me on and making me laugh.

My fellow Murderati bloggers, who keep me honest. Lee Child, for the always spot-on advice.

John Connolly, for the music.

My parents, who always tell me I can do anything I put my mind to, and Jay and Jeff, the best brothers a girl could wish for. My parents gave me the spine, my brothers built the ribs. And my amazingly generous husband, who suffered through too many pizza nights and 2:00 a.m. loads of laundry to count. It just wouldn't be any fun without you, baby.

Nashville is a wonderful city to write about. Though I try my best to keep things accurate, poetic licence is sometimes needed. All mistakes, exaggerations, opinions and interpretations are mine alone.

No, please don't

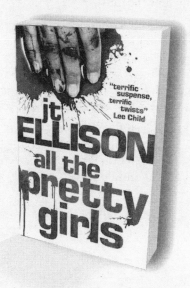

"terrific suspense, terrific twists"
Lee Child

jt ELLISON
all the pretty girls

Nashville homicide lieutenant Taylor Jackson is pursuing a serial killer who leaves the prior victim's severed hand at each crime scene.

TV reporter Whitney Connolly has a scoop that could break the case, but has no idea how close to this story she really is.

As the killer spirals out of control, everyone must face a horrible truth: that the purest evil is born of secrets and lies.

www.mirabooks.co.uk

MIRA